Thrill!

Jackie Collins is one of the world's top-selling writers, with over four hundred million copies of her books sold in more than forty countries. Her twenty-five bestselling novels have never been out of print. She lives in Beverly Hills, California.

Visit her at www.jackiecollins.com

'A generation of women have learnt more about
how to handle their men from Jackie's books than from
any kind of manual . . . She seems to know every Hollywood
player and just where to find their dirty laundry basket.
She is a consummate observer. An outsider with an
insider's knowledge. That's her signature trick. She is,
at once, both intimate and detached . . . Jackie is
very much her own person: a total one off'
Daily Mail

'Jackie, we salute you!'
Cosmopolitan

'Jackie is queen of conspicuously consuming blockbusters
about American high life'
Wendy Holden

'Miss Collins knows how to entertain – and that is
a very precious commodity'
The Times

'She has a very sharp eye for character and situation'
Guardian

Also by Jackie Collins

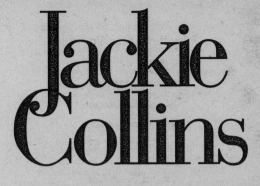

Jackie Collins

Thrill!

PAN BOOKS

First published in hardback 1998 by Macmillan

First published in paperback 1998 by Pan Books

This edition published 2009 by Pan Books
an imprint of Pan Macmillan Ltd
Pan Macmillan, 20 New Wharf Road, London N1 9RR
Basingstoke and Oxford
Associated companies throughout the world
www.panmacmillan.com

ISBN 978-0-330-47826-7

1 3 5 7 9 8 6 4 2

A CIP catalogue record for this book is available from
the British Library.

Typeset by SetSystems Ltd, Saffron Walden, Essex
Printed in the UK by CPI Mackays, Chatham ME5 8TD

*For all my friends and family, who are
always there for me.*

*Also, all my friends at Simon & Schuster
and Macmillan – two great teams, who are
a pleasure to work with.*

*Mort Janklow and Anne Sibbald – who give
great agenting.*

Andrew Nurnberg and the gang.

*And a big thank you to Marvin Davis
for his caring counsel and warm friendship.*

*A special thought for Felipe Santo Domingo,
whose smiling face I shall never forget.*

*For Vida – who patiently deciphers my writing
and gets it on the word processor in time!*

*And Melody and Yvonne and Jacqui – who force me
out there at 5:00 a.m. to do satellite TV,
amongst other tortures!*

And, of course, to Frank – my own very special hero.

PROLOGUE

☆

Here's the truth of it – I can fuck any woman I want any time I want – no problem. Every one of them is ripe and ready, waiting to hear the magic words that'll persuade them to do anything. Married, single, older, younger, desperate, widowed, frigid, horny – point 'em out, and they're mine.

You see, I know what to say, I discovered the key, and believe me it opens the lock every single time.

My mother was a hot-looking natural blond from Memphis who got herself murdered when I was seven. She was beaten up and strangled, then thrown from a moving car. For a while the cops suspected my old man, they even took him into custody for a day or two. But he had an airtight alibi, he was in bed with his mistress at the time – a pie-faced redhead with the biggest tits I'd ever seen.

My dad had the face and attitude of a handsome gangster. He was an extremely snappy dresser – only the best for him. He wore the finest Egyptian cotton shirts, silk ties, hand-tailored suits, gold cuff links and a Rolex watch – all the trimmings. He could have any woman he wanted, and did. I remember when I was growing up I used to watch him operate. He owned a fancy restaurant, and cock-walked the room flirting with all the female customers. Women were his for the taking, and from an early age I got an education observing him in action. He always had plenty of pussy, but after my mom died there were more women than ever. They felt sorry for him – and he ate it up.

He drank, though, and I was smart enough not to want to end up like him. He started off the evening looking like dynamite, halfway through the night he was a wreck, and by the time his restaurant closed he was falling-down drunk.

We lived in an apartment and had a maid come in twice a week. He was screwing the maid, too. He didn't give a toss what the women he bedded looked like, in fact, he used to say, 'Get an ugly one between your legs, an' she'll really show you what it's all about. They're cock-hungry and very grateful.'

My dad didn't have much time for me, so I became a loner. Instead of having other kids over, I joined a gang at school and began getting into trouble. Running the streets stealing cars and knocking off liquor stores was more of a kick than sitting in an empty apartment waiting for my dad to stagger in whenever he felt like it.

I started following in his footsteps. Fuck 'em and leave 'em was his motto. Why shouldn't it be mine, too?

By the time I hit fifteen and he was fifty, the restaurant was long gone and so were his looks. His handsome face was puffy and bloated. He had a big beer gut and rotten teeth – too chicken-shit to visit a dentist, he simply let 'em fall out.

One memorable day I asked him something I'd wanted to for years. I demanded to know if he'd killed my mother.

He whacked me so hard he split my lip, still got the tiny scar to prove it. 'Leave my fucking house,' he screamed, his bloodshot eyes bulging with fury. 'I don't ever wanna see your ugly face again.'

Fine with me. I had two steady girlfriends and plenty of contenders.

I chose to move in with Lulu, a twenty-year-old stripper who was happy to have me. Of course, she had no idea I was only fifteen on account of the fact I looked about nineteen and pretended to be twenty.

The nice thing about Lulu was that she didn't care I had no job, she was happy to indulge me. When she wasn't working we spent all our time at the movies – both getting off on the fantasy. Hollywood – the ultimate dreamland. 'You're so talented,' she was forever telling me. 'You should be a movie star.'

Brilliant idea! As far as I could tell, movie stars didn't have to do much, except stand around looking macho – women worshipped them, and from what I read in Lulu's fan magazines, they made plenty of big bucks.

Lulu found out about an acting class, and even sprung for the bucks for me to go. Nobody could ever accuse her of not being a sport.

After we'd been together a year, I came home early one day, and caught her in bed with another guy. My dad had warned me not to trust women. I figured he was wrong on that score, but then I'd never imagined they'd screw around on me.

Big surprise. There was Lulu with her legs in the air moaning and groaning. Horny little bitch.

I pulled the guy off her and he ran, shaking, from the apartment, because I looked mad enough to beat the crap out of him.

Lulu lay there, thighs spread, naked and scared, begging my forgiveness.

I knew then I had the power. I didn't even slap her, although she deserved it. Instead I packed my things and made a fast exit. No woman was ever going to get one off on me again. Next time I'd make sure I did it first.

An unclothed Lulu chased me down the hallway yelling her guts out. 'It was a mistake! You can't go! Please! Don't leave me!'

Too late. By that time I'd figured out what I wanted, and it wasn't some cheating whore who didn't know how to be faithful.

I wanted to be a movie star and own the whole fucking world.

I was sixteen, what did I know?

1

Lara Ivory stepped carefully towards the camera, managing to appear cool and collected under the crushing weight of a heavy crinoline gown, her slender waist cinched into an impossible seventeen-inch span, lush cleavage spilling forth.

Lara's fellow actor in the shot, Harry Solitaire, a young Englishman with tousled hair and droopy bedroom eyes, walked beside her, delivering his lines with an enthusiasm that belied the fact that this was their seventh take.

It was eighty-four degrees in the South of France garden setting, and the entire crew stood silently on the sidelines, sweating, as they waited impatiently for Richard Barry, the veteran director, to call cut, so they could break for lunch.

Lara Ivory was, at thirty-two, an incandescent beauty with catlike green eyes, a small straight nose, full luscious lips, cut-glass cheekbones and honey-blond hair – right now curled to within an inch of disaster. She had been a movie star at the top of her profession for nine years, and miraculously the fame and glory had never changed her, she was still as likeable and sweet as the devastatingly pretty girl who'd arrived in Hollywood at the age of twenty and been discovered by the director Miles Kieffer, who'd spotted her when she'd come in to audition for a minor role in his new film. Miles had taken one look and decided she was the actress he had to have to play the lead. Gorgeous and fresh, she'd portrayed a naive hooker in a *Pretty Woman* style movie – beguiling everyone from the critics to the public.

From that first film, Lara's star had risen fast. It only took one special movie. Sandra Bullock was a prime example with *Speed*. Michelle Pfeiffer had gotten her break in *Scarface*. Sharon Stone with a spectacular performance – not to mention flashing her pussy – in *Basic Instinct*.

The public never forgot a star entrance. The trick was keeping up there.

Lara Ivory had managed it admirably.

At last Richard Barry called out the words everyone was waiting to hear. 'Cut! Print it! That's the one.' Lara sighed with relief.

Richard had been a successful director for nearly thirty years. He was a tall, well-built man in his late fifties, with even features, a well-trimmed beard, longish brown hair flecked with grey at the temples, and crinkly blue eyes. He also had dry humour and a sardonic smile. Women found him extremely attractive.

'Phew!' Lara repeated her sigh, her smooth cheeks flushed. 'Someone get me out of this dress!'

'I'll do it!' Harry Solitaire volunteered with a lascivious leer, flirting as usual.

'That's OK,' Lara retorted, smiling because she liked Harry, and if he wasn't married he might have been a contender. She considered married men strictly off-limits, and refused to break her rule for anyone – even though she hadn't had a date in six months, ever since she'd broken up with Lee Randolph, a first assistant director, who, after a year of togetherness, had been unable to take the pressure of being with so famous a woman. The sad truth was that what man enjoyed being background material? Relegated to second place? Attacked by crazed stalkers and fans? Referred to as Mr Ivory by waiters and limo drivers?

It took an exceptionally strong man to cope with that kind of deal – a man like Richard Barry, who'd handled it admirably for the four years he and Lara had been married.

She and Richard had gotten divorced three years ago, and along with Richard's new wife, Nikki – a costume designer with whom he'd hooked up while shooting a movie on location in Chicago – they were now good friends.

Nikki was dark-haired, feisty and extremely pretty in a gamine-like way. She also knew how to bring out the best in Richard. Early on in their relationship she discovered that like most men he was a lot of work. Before she entered his life he'd been a smoker, a philanderer and a heavy drinker, plus he expected to get his own way at all times, and when he didn't, he sulked. Nikki had taken stock of his strengths and weaknesses and decided he was worth the effort. Somehow she'd calmed him down, fulfilled all his needs, and now his biggest vice appeared to be work. He was a bankable director, much in demand, whose movies always made money, and in Hollywood that's all that counts.

Lara considered Nikki her closest girlfriend. Right now they were all enjoying working together on *French Summer* – a beautifully scripted period film that Richard was passionate about. The three of them were sharing a rented villa on the six-week location. Lara hadn't wanted to intrude, but Nikki had insisted, which secretly relieved Lara, because the loneliness of being by herself was sometimes hard to cope with.

'That last take was magical,' Richard said, coming to her side and squeezing her hand. *'Definitely* worth waiting for.'

Lara frowned; she was her own sternest critic. 'Do you think so?' she asked, worrying that she could have done better.

'Sweetheart,' Richard assured her, anticipating her concerns because he knew her so well, 'seventh take perfect. Nothing to improve.'

'You're just being kind,' she said, her frown deepening.

'Not kind – truthful,' he replied sincerely.

Her disarmingly honest green eyes met his. 'Really?' she asked.

Richard regarded his exquisite ex-wife and found himself wondering if her painful insecurity had contributed to the demise of their marriage.

Maybe. Although catching the make-up girl giving him head in his trailer had been the final nail in the coffin of his infidelities – that was one he hadn't been able to talk himself out of.

For a year after their somewhat public and acrimonious divorce they hadn't spoken. Then Richard met Nikki, and she'd insisted in her usual no-nonsense way that it was crazy they couldn't all be friends. As usual, she was right. The three of them had gotten together for dinner and never regretted it.

Nikki strode over, looking enviably cool in baggy linen pants and a yellow cotton shirt knotted under her breasts, exposing her well-toned midriff. She was in her early thirties, shorter than Lara, with a lithe, worked-out body, cropped dark hair worn with long bangs, direct hazel eyes and an overly ripe mouth. Nobody would guess that she had a fifteen-year-old daughter.

Richard enjoyed the fact that Nikki was smart and sassy, and most of all that she wasn't an actress. After losing Lara he'd considered never getting involved again, because there'd never be another woman who could live up to her. Nikki and her upbeat ways had changed his mind.

'Get me out of this dress!' Lara implored. 'It's cutting me in half. Worse torture than being married to Richard!'

'*Nothing* can be worse than that!' Nikki joked, rolling her expressive eyes.

'Wasn't Lara great in that last take?' Richard interrupted, putting an arm around his current wife, trailing his fingers up and down her bare skin.

'He's just being kind,' Lara said with one of her trademark deep sighs.

'I know the feeling,' Nikki responded crisply. 'That's exactly what he says when he praises my cooking.'

Lara widened her eyes. 'Don't tell me you cook for him?' she exclaimed. 'I never did.'

Nikki pulled a face. 'He forces me, you know how persuasive he can be.'

'Oh, yes,' Lara agreed. They laughed conspiratorially.

Richard frowned, pretending to be annoyed. 'It's really irritating that you two are such good friends,' he said. 'I hate it!' Truth was he loved having both women in his life.

'No, you don't,' Nikki retorted, looking at him with the kind of expression a woman gets when she's totally secure of her man. 'You get off on it.'

With an amused shake of his head, he walked away. Nikki signalled one of her wardrobe assistants to follow them to Lara's trailer. 'For a grown man, Richard can be such a baby,' she remarked.

'That's why our marriage didn't work,' Lara said lightly. 'Two giant egos fighting for the best camera angle!'

'And one of them screwing around like Charlie Sheen on a bad day.'

'You cured him of *that*.'

'I hope so!' Nikki said forcefully. 'The moment he points his dick in another direction, I'm gone.'

'You'd leave him?'

'Immediately,' Nikki said without hesitation.

'I bet you would,' Lara said, wishing she had the inner strength her friend possessed.

'Hey, listen,' Nikki said, wrinkling her freckled nose. 'I'd expect him to dump me if I screwed around, so why shouldn't the same rule apply?'

Lara nodded. 'You're absolutely right.'

Why didn't I do it? she thought. *Why didn't I tell him to take a hike the first time I suspected he was being unfaithful?*

Because you're a pushover.

No. I simply believe in second chances.

And third ones and fourth ones . . . Richard hadn't known when to quit.

They'd met when he'd directed her in her third movie. Although by that time she was a star, she was still impressed at meeting the great Richard Barry – a man with quite a reputation. He moved in on her like a carnivorous snake. She was twenty-four and by Hollywood standards a total innocent. He was forty-six and difficult. Their wedding at her agent's house in Malibu made headline news, with helicopters hovering overhead and paparazzi lurking in the trees. It was a media circus, which pleased neither of them. The divorce had been even worse.

'We're going to Tetou tonight,' Nikki announced. 'I hear the bouillabaisse is to die for.'

Lara shook her head. 'I can't do it. I have lines to learn and sleep to get, otherwise I'll resemble an old hag in the morning.'

Nikki raised a disbelieving eyebrow. The irritating thing was that Lara acted as if she looked like any other mere mortal, even though she was certainly the most beautiful woman Nikki had ever seen – a woman who never acknowledged her powerful physical beauty. 'You're coming,' Nikki said determinedly. 'I've already checked – you have a late call tomorrow. It's about time you forgot about this damn movie and had some fun.'

'Fun – what's that?' Lara said innocently.

'Exactly how long *is* it since you've gotten laid?' Nikki asked, cocking her head to one side.

'Too long,' Lara muttered.

'It doesn't have to be a big thing, y'know,' Nikki offered. 'How about a one-nighter? There's some hot-looking guys on the crew.'

'Not my style,' Lara said softly.

'You gotta have a man's mentality,' Nikki said, with a knowing wink. 'Fuck and run. I used to – before I married again.'

Richard was Nikki's second husband. Her first was Sheldon Weston, whom she'd wed when she was sixteen and he was thirty-eight. 'I was searching for a father figure,' she often joked. 'And I got stuck with an uptight shrink.' Their daughter, Summer, lived in Chicago with her dad.

'You're different,' Lara said. 'You can do that and get away with it. I can't. It has to be a committed relationship or I'm not interested.'

'Whatever,' Nikki replied vaguely, not understanding at all. 'But you're definitely coming tonight.'

2

Joey Lorenzo burst into Madelaine Francis' Madison Avenue office as if he had every right to be there, even though he didn't have an appointment and hadn't seen her in six years.

A harassed secretary chased after him. She was a round-faced girl with ample hips encased in a too-short mini.

'What the hell is going on—' Madelaine began to say. Then her bleak eyes, hidden beneath tinted prescription glasses, recognized Joey, and she quickly waved her secretary away. 'It's all right, Stella,' she said with a weary sigh. 'I'll handle this.'

'But, Miss Francis,' Stella said, full of piss and outrage, 'he told me to—' she hesitated for a moment, two bright-red blobs colouring her chubby cheeks, 'the F-word off.'

'Thank you, Stella,' Madelaine said, dismissing her. 'You're excused.'

Still glaring at Joey, Stella backed out of the well-appointed office, while he threw himself into a leather chair opposite Madelaine's large antique desk, draping his long jean-clad legs over the side of the expensive chair.

'I'm back,' he said, with an insolent grin.

'So I see,' said Madelaine, shifting uncomfortably, wondering what wrong deed she'd committed to have Joey Lorenzo reappear in her well-ordered life.

Six years ago they'd been living together – the forty-eight-year-old agent and the twenty-four-year-old actor. An unlikely combination, but for eight months it had worked. Then one night she'd arrived home to find Joey gone, along with seven thousand dollars in cash she'd kept in her safe.

Now she was fifty-four and he was thirty and the bastard was back.

'What do you want?' she asked, her voice a tight coil of buried anger.

'You're pissed, aren't you?' Joey said nonchalantly, as if he'd merely popped out for cigarettes and a beer. '*Really* pissed.'

'Yes, Joey, I am,' she said, removing her tortoiseshell-framed glasses and staring at him bitterly. 'Wouldn't *you* be?'

'Guess you musta wondered what happened t'me,' he mumbled.

'Yes, I wondered – about you *and* about my money.'

'Oh yeah, your money,' he said, groping in the pocket of his weathered leather jacket and producing a packet of hundred-dollar bills neatly tied with a rubber band. 'Here's three thou. I'll get the rest to you in a coupla weeks.'

She couldn't believe he was returning her money. Not all of it, but three thousand dollars was a start. She continued staring at him. Six years had done him nothing but favours – he was more handsome than ever. His hair touched the back of his collar, thick and black – too long, but it didn't matter. His body was nicely muscled with a washboard stomach. He had grown into a man, with knowing eyes, full sensual lips and a smile that would melt stronger women than she. She remembered that smile. She also remembered his cock, even though she tried not to. Perfect. Like the rest of him.

Pity he was a thieving sonofabitch.

'What do you want?' she repeated, keeping her voice on the hard side, knowing time had not been as good to her as it had to him. Her reddish hair was flecked with grey. Lines and wrinkles abounded. And she'd put on fifteen pounds of disgusting fat.

'Here's the thing,' Joey said, fixing her with his intense eyes, seeing right through her. 'Before I took off, you'd gotten me two movie roles.'

'That's right,' she said coldly. 'Your career was just about to happen. You ran out on that, too.'

'Somethin' went down that was outta my control,' he said restlessly.

She refused to give him the satisfaction of begging for an explanation. 'I don't care, Joey,' she said, shuffling a stack of papers on her messy desk. 'If you return the rest of my money, we'll leave it at that.' She paused a moment, remembering the first time he'd walked into her office – a cocky kid from the Midwest, with way too much attitude. She'd seen the potential and decided to help him. Eight months of craziness and great sex. Eight months she'd never forget.

'I didn't go to the police,' she said slowly, 'even though it's what I should've done.'

He nodded, face sincere, faint stubble on his chin adding to his look. 'Y'know, Maddy,' he said. 'I wouldn't've taken your cash unless it was an emergency.'

She was silent. How many times could she ask him what he wanted from her now? Obviously it wasn't money.

He broke the silence, placing his hands on her desk. Long artistic fingers, pianist's fingers. She noticed his nails were manicured – which surprised her, considering Joey had always favoured the macho look. 'I need to get back into the business,' he said. 'An' you're the person who can do it for me.'

She raised a disbelieving eyebrow.

'Here's what I'd like,' he continued. 'Another movie. Not TV. I'm not into TV. Fuck that *ER* shit. I gotta be back on the big screen.'

Well, nobody ever said he didn't have nerve. But surely he didn't expect her to resurrect a career he'd run out on?

'Joey,' she said, deliberately pacing her words, watching his face as she spoke, 'you blew your career, such as it was. You had your shot and you ran.'

'No fuckin' way!' he shouted, banging his fists on her desk. 'Don't you get it? If you did it for me once, you can do it again.'

A moment of pure satisfaction. 'I have a reputation to uphold,' Madelaine said. 'And I am not about to ruin it by sending you up for anything.'

'That's bullshit,' he muttered.

'You're unreliable,' she continued, quite enjoying putting him down. 'And worse than that – you're a thief. No, Joey,' she continued, shaking her head, 'I'm afraid I can't recommend you to anyone, so do yourself a big favour and get out.'

She waited for his anger to deepen, remembering his

sometimes violent temper. But this time she wasn't frightened, he wouldn't dare lay a hand on her in her office.

Instead of more anger he went the other way. Little boy lost. So handsome and alone. She'd never been able to resist that stance and he knew it. Joey could turn it on like nobody else.

'OK, I get it,' he said, pushing his hand through his thick hair. 'I'm like yesterday's news. Nobody'll hire me. Guess I may as well go back to drivin' a cab.' He got up and went to the door, pausing with his hand on the knob. 'Can I buy you dinner? Try to explain what happened. I owe you that.' His intense eyes tracked her from across the room. 'Can I, Maddy?'

She was well aware that if she accepted, she'd look like a pathetic old fool . . .

It didn't matter, because there was no way she could resist.

☆

Joey knew exactly what he was doing, every move thought out way ahead. Dinner at a small Italian restaurant; a bottle of house red wine – three-quarters of it drunk by Madelaine, who didn't realize he wasn't keeping up. Intimate conversation – mostly about how much he'd missed her, and how great he thought she looked.

Lies, lies, but what did she care? By the time they took a cab back to her apartment on 66th Street, she was feeling sexy and womanly and very horny. Joey had fed her some story about a sick aunt in Montana and a family business he'd had to single-handedly save. She didn't believe him, but so what? He was paying her more attention than she'd had in six years and she desperately wanted him to make love to her.

Joey didn't disappoint. His lovemaking was even better than she remembered. Prolonged foreplay; leisurely oral sex; and then long, steady penetration until she cried out in a torrent of ecstasy.

She didn't feel over fifty and fifteen pounds overweight. Joey made her feel like a beautiful, desirable woman.

He stayed overnight, making love to her again in the morning, his hard body pressing her flesh in the most incredibly exciting way. She knew she was hooked again. One night of lust made up for six years of anger.

'Why didn't you call me? At least let me know where you were?' she asked plaintively, her fingers trailing up and down his smoothly muscled back.

'I'm here now,' he responded. 'Isn't it enough that I came back?' And his lips pressed down on hers, weakening her crumbling resistance until it ceased to exist.

Two days later he moved back in. A few days after that she asked him to drop by her office.

'I'm sending you up for a small role you could be right for,' she told him. 'If you get it, that'll be a start in the right direction.'

'You're the best, Maddy,' he said, smiling the irresistible Joey smile.

And she knew she was probably being used, but somehow – once again – it didn't matter.

3

Tetou was a famous fish restaurant perched above the sandy beach between Eden Roc and Juan Les Pins. Popular for many years, it was an expensive hang-out for rich locals and affluent tourists – nothing in the South of France was cheap.

Nikki had also invited Harry Solitaire and Pierre Perez to join them. Pierre was a French actor with brooding eyes and a dreamy smile – he'd flown in from Paris that morning and was due to start work on the movie in two days.

'Pierre's not married,' Nikki whispered as they sat down. 'Not even engaged. Use a condom and go for it.'

'Will you stop!' Lara said crossly.

Pierre was as charming as Harry was persistent. Richard glared at them both disapprovingly. He was extremely protective of his ex-wife; she might be a famous movie star, but she was fragile and needed nurturing, only *he* knew how much.

'Why did you invite these two assholes?' he muttered to Nikki, as Lara parried the attention.

'To piss you off,' Nikki muttered back, grabbing his crotch under the long tablecloth.

'Quit that!' he said sternly.

She grinned. 'Why? You know you love it.'

'There's a time and a place.'

'The time is now,' she said, attempting to unzip his fly.

He couldn't help smiling as he shifted her hand. Nikki never gave him time to think about other women, she was always up to something.

When dinner was over and they were lingering over coffee, Harry leaped to his feet. He lived for locations, a legitimate separation from his wife was one of the perks of being an actor. 'Let's go dancing,' he suggested enthusiastically. 'I know a terrific place in Monte Carlo.'

'Count me out,' Lara said quickly.

'Why?' Harry persisted, his eyes saying: *You like me, don't you? You're attracted to me – so come on, let's get down and dirty.*

'I have lines to go over,' she demurred.

'Perhaps five minutes in the Casino?' Pierre suggested.

She glanced at Richard for help. He rallied immediately – now that he wasn't her husband he was for ever her knight in slightly tarnished armour. 'As Lara's director,' he said, sounding a tad pompous, 'we're taking her home.'

'Christ!' Nikki muttered under her breath. '*Why?*'

'What?' Richard said irritably.

'Let her go,' Nikki insisted, glaring at him.

He returned her glare with one of his own. 'Lara's free to do as she likes. She *wants* to come home with us.'

'Don't talk about me as if I'm not here,' Lara interrupted, sensing tension.

'You have an early call,' Richard said possessively. 'You should come home.'

'Maybe, maybe not,' Lara retorted, a glint of annoyance suddenly surfacing.

Harry got the picture and quickly helped her up, gallantly escorting her to the door. 'Your ex still has a hard-on for you,' he said in a half amused, half pissed-off voice.

'Excuse me?' she said coolly.

'It's obvious,' he said as they stood outside the restaurant, the warm Mediterranean air ruffling her honey-coloured hair, now freed from the excruciating curls of earlier.

She shook her head. 'You're wrong.'

'Oh, no, I'm not,' he said, grabbing her hand and running her across the busy coast road to the parking lot.

'I am *not* going dancing, Harry,' she said firmly.

'Don't be foolish, Lara,' he said, still flirting. 'I give you my word as an Englishman that I will not attack you.'

'I'm *so* relieved,' she replied with a sarcastic edge. They held a long steady look, then the others joined them.

'Come along, sweetheart,' Richard said, taking her arm and hustling her towards his car.

Lara didn't like his proprietary attitude, and she noticed Nikki was not thrilled either.

'You know what,' she said, loosening Richard's grip, 'I'm taking Pierre up on the Casino idea. Not that I gamble, but I'd enjoy seeing the inside of a French casino. Is it like Vegas?'

Pierre smiled his dreamy smile. Harry scowled. Richard began to object, but Nikki stopped him. 'Have a good time,' she said with an encouraging wink, giving Lara a little shove toward Pierre's car. 'And don't worry, we won't wait up!'

☆

The casino in Monte Carlo was not like Vegas at all, it was an imposing building located in a busy square close to the sea. Accompanied by Pierre and Harry, who'd insisted on coming too, Lara walked around, watching the avid players intent on losing their money. Old women in beaded evening gowns, bedecked with expensive jewels, played next to obvious rogues busy piling stacks of chips on their lucky numbers as the roulette wheel turned; steely-eyed card-sharps sat next to stone-faced blonds at the blackjack tables; craps, chemin de fer and other games abounded.

'It's so . . . unbelievably grand,' Lara said, groping for the right description. 'Almost from another era.'

'Rather decadent,' Harry said with a jolly laugh. 'I like it!'

An alert floor manager with boot-black hair and a matching dinner jacket swooped down, landing on Lara with an ingratiating smile. 'Mademoiselle Ivory, it is a pleasure to welcome you to our casino,' he said in velvety tones. 'Would you and your friends care for a drink?'

'No, thank you,' she said, introducing Harry and Pierre.

The manager's whiter than white smile was in overdrive. 'Anything at all we can get for you, please do not hesitate to ask.'

She smiled back.

'You are a wonderful actress, Mademoiselle Ivory,' the manager added, his English impeccable.

Lara dazzled him with another smile. 'Thank you.'

He was on a roll. 'And may I say that in person you are even more beautiful.'

Excessive compliments bothered her. Even after all this time she still felt a deep flush of embarrassment when people singled her out. They had no idea who she really was.

Nobody knew the true story – not even Richard, and he'd gotten closer to her than anybody.

'She certainly is,' Harry said, hanging in because only *he* knew the way to her villa, so goodbye Pierre.

'Will you be playing tonight?' the casino manager asked. Finished with her beauty and talent, he now wanted her money.

She smiled sweetly. 'Perhaps another time.' The manager drifted away. She turned to Pierre. 'Shall we go?'

Pierre took her arm. Harry moved protectively in on her other side. Together they escorted her to the door.

Lurking on the steps outside the casino were several paparazzi. They sprung into action, yelling her name, flash-bulbs bursting into light all around her.

Automatically she shielded her eyes, as Harry quickly distanced himself, making it appear that she and Pierre were a couple.

Great, Lara thought, *now I'll be all over the tabloids*. She hated being linked to someone she hardly knew. Last month she'd been in the same restaurant as Kevin Costner, and the supermarket rags had written they were planning marriage!

The paparazzi chased them all the way to their cars. Harry was furious, it meant he couldn't make his move without being photographed – his wife was a jealous woman who wouldn't appreciate late-night photos of him and the delectable Ms Ivory getting into a car together while she sat at home in Fulham with two under-five children and his seventy-six-year-old mother. He had no choice but to allow Lara to go with Pierre.

However, all was not lost – he had a plan. Jumping in his rented Renault, he stuck close behind Pierre's car as they moved off into traffic.

As soon as he was sure they were not being followed, he began honking his horn and flashing his lights, forcing Pierre to pull over.

'What's the matter?' Lara asked, as Harry leaned in the window.

'Richard insisted I drive you home,' he said. 'I promised I would.'

'Why?'

'Because Pierre will never find the house.'

'Of course he will.'

'Do you have the address?'

'No . . .' she said, hesitating for a moment. 'But it's in St-Paul-de-Vence. I'm sure I can direct him.'

'There's a hundred twists and turns up there. You'll have to come with me, otherwise you'll be driving around all night.'

'Harry—'

He shrugged as if he didn't care. 'Listen, luv, whatever you want.'

What she didn't want was to be lost in the hills with a French actor she hardly knew. 'You're right,' she said, reluctantly getting out of Pierre's car and into Harry's.

Pierre was not upset. It was late and he was tired – too tired to try scoring with an exquisite American movie star who would probably reject him. Besides, his real preference was men – a secret he'd managed to keep to himself on account of the fact it would ruin his blossoming career as a leading man.

Lara waved goodbye to Pierre, settling back in the passenger seat of Harry's Renault. She closed her eyes, and decided she must have been crazy leaving the security of Nikki and Richard to run around Monte Carlo with a couple of actors. Why did she always manage to do the wrong thing?

For a moment her mind drifted and she thought about Lee – her former boyfriend. Lee was a genuinely nice guy, admittedly not the most exciting man in the world – but he'd satisfied her needs.

What *were* her needs?

Someone to cuddle up with. A warm body in the middle of the night. Occasional sex. Companionship.

Christ, Lara, you sound as if you're seventy-five!

She frowned.

Harry glanced over at her. 'Don't look so happy,' he chided.

'I was thinking.'

'What about?'

'My ex-lover, if you must know.'

'Did you dump him?'

'He dumped me, actually.'

Harry laughed disbelievingly. 'That's impossible.'

'Told me he couldn't take the heat.'

'You have to be joking.'

A long deep sigh. 'I'm not.'

Harry considered the possibilities of a red-blooded male actually dumping Lara Ivory. It seemed highly unlikely. 'Why would he do a thing like that?' he asked at last. 'Was the fool brain-dead?'

'Too much attention,' Lara said wryly. 'And all directed at me.'

'You need to be with a fellow actor,' Harry said confidently. 'We *know* how to share.'

Sure, Lara thought. *The only thing actors know how to share is a scene, and then they'll kill for the close-ups.*

She'd met enough megalomaniac actors in her time.

The movie star with the polished pecs and the wry humour. He was addicted to steroids and only slept with models.

The macho action hero with the slit eyes and thin smile. He got off beating up on women and sexually abusing them – but only if they were below the line and couldn't fight back.

The popular black star who only considered busty blonds candidates for his extremely large waterbed.

The charismatic king of comedy with the enormous dick who was currently screwing his children's nanny.

And the 'serious' New York actor who could only get it up for transvestites.

Ah yes, movie stars, a charming, well-adjusted bunch.

While she was busy with her thoughts, Harry seized his opportunity. Swerving the car to the side of the road, he leaned over, pressing his warm lips down on hers.

'Harry!' she exclaimed, managing to push him away. 'What *do* you think you're doing?'

Words tumbled from his mouth in a senseless torrent as his hands went for her breasts. 'You're so fucking beautiful, Lara ... so gorgeous ... the first time I saw you ... my wife's a cold fish ... we never sleep together ... maybe a couple of times in the last year ... my cock burns for you ...'

She slapped him hard across the face – a theatrical gesture, but one that seemed to work.

'Good God!' he exclaimed, stopping his extended grope.

'Harry,' she said, sounding more calm than she felt. 'Get control of yourself. I do not get involved with married men, so kindly start the car and take me home.' He slumped away from her like a rejected fool. 'It's not that I don't find you attractive,' she continued, her voice softening. 'But everyone has to stick to their principles.'

Her smooth words soothed him. 'Sorry, Lara,' he muttered, quite abashed. 'It won't happen again.'

You bet it won't, she thought. *'Cause this is the one and only time I'll find myself alone in a car with you.*

'I'll forget if you will,' she said quietly, saving his damaged pride.

'Thanks,' he mumbled, and drove her to the villa where Richard waited at the front gate – standing outside like a protective father.

'Wasn't sure you had your keys,' Richard said, glaring at Harry.

Lara marched into the villa without a word to either of them.

Men! If only she could find one worth keeping, then maybe she'd be happy.

Or would she?

Could anyone make her forget the dark memories of her past?

Could anyone make everything all right?

4

Alison Sewell was never the pretty girl – always the outcast, a loner with no friends. By the time she was fourteen, she already weighed over a hundred and sixty pounds. Hefty and round-faced, the kids at school taunted her, calling her all sorts of names. 'Sewer' was a favourite, 'the Dump' and 'Big Boy' two others. Just because her mother made her cut her hair in a manly crop, it wasn't fair to call her Big Boy – that was downright mean. But Alison didn't care, she knew she was smarter than all of them, even though she managed to flunk out in most subjects.

'You're an idiot,' her father often said to her.

Then one day he fell off a ladder, hitting his head and suffering an untimely death. Who was the idiot now?

Shortly after her father passed away, Alison and her mother, Rita, a small sparrow of a woman who worked as a laundress at a downtown hotel, moved in with Rita's brother, Cyril. He lived in a small ramshackle house a short walk from the seediest part of Hollywood Boulevard. He was divorced and childless, and since he'd recently broken his leg while 'on the job', he needed help.

On the job for Cyril was photographing celebrities – usually when they didn't care to be photographed. He hung around outside popular restaurants and clubs, camera at the ready – grabbing any shots he could. His big claim to fame was catching Madonna and Sean Penn in a steamy embrace before anyone knew they were a couple. Pure luck, really. But he made plenty of money from those particular photos, and garnered a modicum of respect from the other freelancers, who couldn't believe Cyril had finally scored.

Alison was fascinated by Uncle Cyril, to her he was a celebrity himself. As soon as he recovered from his broken leg, she began following him around, watching in awe as he went about his job. Since Cyril had no children of his own, he didn't mind Alison trailing him, especially as she was strong enough to carry his equipment, and big enough to shove other photographers out of his way – a task she seemed to relish.

By the time she reached the age of twenty, Alison was taking pictures too. She knew where to go to catch the famous faces, and she didn't care what she had to do to get the shot. She proved to be more tenacious than Uncle Cyril, chasing her famous subjects aggressively into their cars and limos if they failed to cooperate – taunting them with insults – getting away with it because she was a female. Not an attractive one by any means – overweight, surly, pushy and rude. But because she was a woman they didn't dare fight back.

Uncle Cyril said she was a natural, but the other photographers loathed her. They nicknamed her 'the Hun' and steered clear.

Over the years Alison made some good scores. Whitney Houston screaming at Bobby Brown outside The Peninsula. Charlie Sheen screaming at *her* as she chased him and his sexy date to his limo. A dishevelled Nicholson exiting a club. A drunken Charlie Dollar falling down a flight of stairs. An abashed Hugh Grant outside the police station after being arrested for dallying with a prostitute. And Kim and Alec with their baby – a rare sighting.

And then, one day, into her life came Lara Ivory, and everything changed.

Obsession wasn't the word for it.

5

French Summer was almost finished and Lara felt the usual sadness that another film coming to an end always brought. Making a movie – especially on location – was like becoming part of an extended family – the family she didn't have. The nice thing was that everyone looked out for her – from the hair and make-up people to the teamsters and grips. She was a special favourite with film crews, because even though she was an enormous star, she wasn't a prima donna, and knew how to treat everyone with fairness and respect. Most of the male members of the crew usually fell in love with her. And why not? She was exquisitely beautiful with a gorgeous body, and as if that wasn't enough, she was smart, friendly, *and* a good sport.

Nikki had organized a lavish wrap party to take place at the rented villa. There were huge tables of food set up in the garden, and plenty of beer, wine and spirits to accommodate the mostly English crew. The tennis court had been transformed into a flashy disco complete with a dreadlocked disc jockey who was into sixties soul.

'Everything looks wonderful,' Lara exclaimed, emerging from her room, dressed in a filmy white sleeveless dress and flat sandals, skin glowing, her shoulder-length hair freshly washed.

'Enough with the wonderful shit,' Nikki responded, hands on black leather clad hips. 'I worked my butt off to make damn sure it's the wrap of the year. I want everyone to know that when they work on a Richard Barry movie, they *know* they're appreciated.'

'I hope Richard appreciates *you*,' Lara remarked.

'He'd better,' Nikki said with a grin.

'You've been so good for him,' Lara continued. 'He's a much nicer person.'

'Want him back?' Nikki asked jokingly.

Lara laughed. 'No, thank you.'

'That's good,' Nikki said, with another wide grin. ''Cause he's totally unavailable.'

As if he sensed he was the subject of discussion, Richard appeared, strolling out to the garden wearing beige linen pants and a casual silk shirt.

'Hmm . . .' Lara remarked. 'He even dresses better now.'

'Of course,' Nikki said. 'I drag him to Neiman's twice a year and make him spend all his money!'

'Are you two talking about me again?' he asked, as usual pretending not to enjoy the attention.

'You know, Richard,' Lara said, lightly touching his arm, 'you're incredibly lucky to have found a woman who cares so much about you.'

'Hey—' Richard objected. 'What about her? She got me!'

'Ah . . . the ego gets bigger and bigger,' Lara murmured.

'And that's not all,' Nikki said with a lewd wink, flinging her arms around Richard's waist and hugging him.

'Seriously, though,' Lara said. 'I couldn't be happier for the two of you.'

'Now all we have to do is find the right guy for you,' Nikki said, ever the matchmaker.

'I keep on telling you,' Lara said patiently, 'I'm perfectly content by myself.'

'Bull*shit*!' snorted Nikki. 'Everyone needs somebody.'

'I'm sure Lara is quite capable of finding him on her own,' Richard said, aggravated that Nikki was so intent on setting Lara up.

Lara wished they'd both leave her in peace. She was happy by herself – most of the time. 'I'm going to miss you guys,' she said wistfully. 'It won't be the same without you.'

'You'll be slaving so hard on *The Dreamer* you won't even notice we're missing,' Nikki said, referring to Lara's next movie, which started principal photography in the Hamptons in a week.

'I want to work with you two again,' Lara said. 'This was a memorable experience.'

'Tell your agent,' Nikki said crisply. 'According to him, you're booked for the next three years.'

'Nonsense!'

'Richard,' Nikki nudged her husband, excitement lighting her face, 'shall I tell Lara about the book I took an option on?'

'What book?' Lara asked curiously. 'And why are you mentioning it now when I'm practically out of here?'

'It's called *Revenge*,' Nikki said, her eyes sparkling with enthusiasm. 'A true story about a schoolteacher who gets gang-raped – nearly dies – then recovers and exacts her own form of punishment.'

'Sounds exciting.'

'I'm producing,' Nikki announced proudly. 'My first attempt.'

'That's great!'

'Richard's promised to help – which means he'll be keeping a steely eye on everything I do. I'm going for a hot young director. Unfortunately, it's a depressingly low budget. But the lead's a fantastic role for an actress.'

'I don't get it,' Lara said. 'Why didn't you *tell* me?'

Nikki shot a baleful glare at Richard. '*He* said I shouldn't bug you.'

'Which is exactly what you're doing now,' Richard interrupted, with a *What am I going to do with you?* look. 'I've told you, Nikki, this is not the kind of movie Lara would be interested in.'

'Do you have a script yet?' Lara asked.

'Nothing I'm satisfied with.'

'I'd love to read it.'

'Just for fun?' Nikki asked hopefully.

'I'm curious to see what you're letting yourself in for.'

'She has no idea,' Richard said drily. 'Try stopping her – *I* can't.'

'Isn't that what life's all about,' Lara said gently. 'Helping other people achieve their dreams?'

'Right on!' agreed Nikki, squeezing Richard's arm. 'And when I'm a big fat mega-rich producer with an out-of-control coke habit, a live-in stud and a majorly inflated budget, the *first* person I'll hire will be Richard Barry – who by that time will be an ancient out-of-shape drunk, living in Santa Barbara with nothing but his memories and a couple of senile fart-filled dogs.'

'Thanks, darling,' Richard said ruefully. 'You sure know how to make a person feel good about himself.'

'Only joking.'

'Like I didn't know that?'

'Don't get uptight.'

'Who's uptight?'

'You two,' Lara said, shaking her head and laughing. 'You're acting like a roadshow version of Virginia Woolf!'

'Let's go get a drink,' said Richard. 'We may as well be first.'

☆

Much later in the evening Harry Solitaire grabbed Lara on the dance floor. He was sweating through his red polo shirt, his hands clammy as he placed them clumsily on her shoulders. His wife, a pleasant-looking English girl who'd arrived in time to spend the last weekend with her husband, sat in a corner conversing with the first AD. Lara felt sorry for the poor girl. After Harry's aborted attempt at making it with her, he'd had a series of one-nighters with her stand-in, the continuity woman, and two extras. There was no such thing as a secret fuck on location, everyone knew the moment it happened.

'I want to thank you for not saying anything about the other night,' he said, shooting a furtive glance at his wife, feverishly hoping the first AD was not saying anything he shouldn't.

'Why don't you try being a gentleman and stop cheating on your wife?' Lara suggested. 'What would you do if she carried on the same way?'

'She wouldn't,' Harry said gruffly.

'Maybe she should,' Lara retorted crisply. 'See how you'd like it.'

'My wife's not that kind of woman,' he said, sweat beading his upper lip.

'What makes you so sure?'

'It's different for men,' he said, as if she should understand. 'Everyone knows that.'

'No,' Lara said unwaveringly, 'that's where you're wrong.'

Harry was not about to argue. He had the delectable Lara Ivory in his arms, and this was his last chance to score. He pulled her so close she could feel his erection pressing against her thigh. Before she could move away, he managed a sly – 'I'd give my left ball to make love to you. You know that, don't you?'

'Oh, for God's sake, grow up, Harry,' she said, pushing him away and leaving the dance floor.

Wrap parties. Sometimes they were too much of a good thing.

☆

The next morning Lara departed early for the airport. Nikki and Richard came to the door of the villa to see her off – both clad in terry-cloth bathrobes, bleary-eyed with monster hangovers.

'Can't believe it's over,' Nikki said, stretching her arms high above her head.

'I know what you mean,' Lara agreed. 'I feel the same way.'

'Be sure to look after yourself, sweetheart,' Richard said, squeezing her hand. 'Anything you need – call me. You know I'm always here for you. Day or night.'

'I hate goodbyes,' Lara said, giving them both a quick hug and jumping in the car, her luggage already loaded. She didn't look back as the car left the driveway.

Her loyal assistant, Cassie, met her at Nice airport. Cassie was an overweight woman in her mid-thirties who bore a fleeting resemblance to Elizabeth Taylor in her Larry Fortensky years. She'd worked for Lara for six years and made sure everything went smoothly. Today she was anxious to get Lara on the plane to Paris, where they would make a connection to New York.

'I'm tired,' Lara said, yawning.

'You don't look it.'

A man from the airline fell all over himself to help them aboard. Another airline representative met them in Paris and escorted them to their Air France flight to New York. Lara settled into her first-class window seat. Cassie handed her the script of *The Dreamer*, and a large plastic bottle of Evian water.

'Thanks,' she said, taking an unladylike swig. 'If I fall asleep, don't wake me.'

'Not even for food?'

'No, Cassie, especially not for food!'

A businessman across the aisle was stretching his neck to get a better look at her. Finally he couldn't stand it any longer and came over. 'Lara Ivory,' he said, his middle-aged voice filled with a mixture of awe and admiration.

'That's me,' she said brightly, knowing exactly what he would say next.

She was right. 'You're far more beautiful in the flesh,' he managed.

She smiled, dazzling him – even though it was still morning and she had on casual clothes and hardly any make-up. 'Thank you,' she murmured.

Cassie ran interference, placing her considerable bulk between Lara and her admiring fan.

He took the hint and returned to his seat.

'Civilians!' Cassie muttered.

Lara wondered what it would be like to go out with a civilian. The only men she came in contact with were connected to movies – actors, producers, directors, the crew. She'd met Lee while working on a film – Richard had set up their first date. Lee had been painfully shy – a condition not helped by being thrust into the limelight as her boyfriend. They'd spent most of their year together at her house in LA. She'd known two months before the break-up that it was coming. There was no passion left in their relationship, and Lee wasn't happy living in her shadow. Plus she was being tracked by an obsessed stalker which made him crazy. Eventually they'd agreed to part amicably, and she hadn't heard from him since.

'The steward wondered if he could get your autograph,' Cassie said.

'Sure,' she replied. 'Tell him to come over.'

A few minutes later, the steward – a gay guy with impossibly long eyelashes and gentle eyes – knelt beside her seat. 'I'm *so* sorry to disturb you, Ms Ivory,' he said in reverent tones, 'only my friend would hang and quarter me if I *dared* to come home without your signature. Is it a terrible imposition if I ask you to sign his book?'

'Of course not,' she replied, with a faint smile. 'Do you have a pen?'

'Right here,' he said, fumbling in his pocket.

'What's your friend's name?' she asked, taking the blue leather book from him.

'Put "To Sam, the man of my dreams".'

Graciously she did as he requested. Some stars wouldn't sign autographs at all, others made their fans pay for it. Lara felt privileged that she even got asked. Being a movie star was a big responsibility – people looked up to her. She remembered seeing Demi Moore on *David Letterman* once, stripping off to an almost non-existent bikini. At the time Demi was the highest-paid female star in the world, and it seemed so dumb that she would get up and blow her image in front of millions of viewers – becoming just another babe with a body. Of course, she'd redeemed herself with a stellar performance in *GI Jane,* but was that enough?

Lara slept most of the journey, waking half an hour before their arrival in New York. She'd hoped to spend a few days at her house in LA, but there wasn't time. Three frantic days of costume fittings and interviews in New York, and then she had to leave for the house the studio had rented for her in the Hamptons. Cassie had flown in several weeks earlier to check the place out. 'It's absolutely your style,' Cassie had assured her. 'Very Martha Stewart – comfortable, with a pretty garden and beach access. Oh yes, and you'll love this – extremely private.'

Cassie knew her well, when she wasn't working she loved seclusion. Parties and the night life were not for her.

A limo took her straight to the St Regis Hotel, where she was booked into the Oriental Suite, courtesy of Orpheus Studios, who were in charge of her for the next seven weeks while she shot *The Dreamer* – a light comedy about two divorced people who meet, fall in love, fall out of love, and finally get together for good. It was a contemporary piece – a welcome change from Richard's film, where day after day she'd been locked into excruciatingly uncomfortable period gowns. She'd loved making the movie – hated wearing the clothes.

Her co-star in *The Dreamer* was Kyle Carson – a bankable star who'd recently separated from his wife of seventeen years. Lara had met Kyle briefly at several industry events and he'd seemed attractive and charming – she hoped his recent separation hadn't changed him. The director was Miles Kieffer, an old friend, who'd directed her in her first movie.

The hotel staff greeted her with welcoming smiles, remembering her last visit. She was gracious to everyone, it wasn't in her nature to be otherwise.

The manager personally ushered her upstairs to the sumptuous suite, making sure she had everything she required.

She often reflected on the strangeness of her life. Limos and rented houses, first-class travel, everybody ready to grant her slightest whim. It was understandable that movie stars grew to believe their own publicity and importance. They were so protected and cosseted that reality ceased to exist.

She'd been thinking about Nikki's project, and wanted to read the book. She called out to Cassie, who was in the bedroom, busily unpacking for her. 'Do me a favour, Cass,' she said, wandering into the room. 'Call Barnes & Noble and have them send over a copy of *Revenge*.'

'It's done,' Cassie said, heading for the phone.

The book arrived within the hour. After eating a light room-service dinner, she sat down to read.

She read way into the night, finally falling asleep with the book in her lap. She awoke early, and at nine a.m. New York time called her agent in LA.

'Quinn,' she said, 'is it true I'm booked for the next three years?'

'You're as busy as you want to be, Lara,' Quinn replied, struggling to wake up. 'I could have you working steadily for three, four, five years – take your pick.'

'What if I felt like making a small low-budget movie?'

That *really* woke him. 'Why would you even consider such a thing?' he asked, alarmed.

'*Could* I do it?' she persisted.

'It's possible.' A pause. 'Is there something I should know about?'

'Not right now.'

'Good,' he said, relieved. 'Can I go back to sleep?'

'You certainly can.' Thoughtfully she replaced the receiver. Quinn was an excellent agent, but like most agents his prime interest was making money. She pictured his face if she told him she wished to do Nikki's film.

And if the script turned out to be as powerful as the book, there was a strong possibility.

6

They formed a group in the corner of the room – two casting women, the male director and a female producer. Joey concentrated on the women. One by one he gave them powerful eye contact – penetrating looks that signalled *If this was another time – another place – I'd like to fuck you until you screamed for mercy. Until your hot little pussies couldn't stand it any more. Until you came ten times.* Women read into his silent looks, it worked every time.

The female producer – pretty in an older bimbo kind of way – cleared her throat. Joey knew she must have humped some poor schmuck to get this gig – maybe she was even married to the geezer.

The two casting women were opposites. One young, one old. One fair, one dark. One short, the other tall. They were both unattractive. He gave them the treatment anyway.

The director was a straight white male, married with a shiny gold wedding ring to prove it.

'Are you prepared to read?' the female producer asked.

Joey nodded, glancing briefly at the pages he'd been studying in the waiting room. Then he placed the typed sides on a table, and performed the scene from memory, with the younger casting woman reading the other role. He gave it his best and when he was finished he knew that he'd managed to impress them.

The older casting woman lowered her spectacles, staring directly at him. 'Weren't you in *Solid*?' she asked.

''S right,' he responded, pleased she remembered.

'That was—'

'Six years ago,' he interrupted, saying it first so it didn't seem as if he had anything to hide.

'What have you done since then?' asked the director,

twisting his wedding ring as if he wanted to wrench it off his finger.

'My mother got sick,' Joey said, turning on the sincerity full voltage. 'Hadda go home and look after the family.'

'I'm *so* sorry,' gushed the female producer, playing with a strand of stringy blond hair. 'I do hope she's better now.'

'No,' Joey replied in his best Little Boy Lost voice. 'She, uh ... died. I stayed to see my little sister through school.'

'That's so *caring* you would do that,' exclaimed the younger casting woman, hungry eyes coming on to him.

'Well . . .' he said modestly. 'Now I'm back, an' I gotta get my career goin' again.'

'This is a very small role,' warned the director.

'Can't expect the lead every time,' Joey quipped.

'Nice reading,' said the female producer.

'Thanks for coming in,' said the director.

'We'll be in touch with your agent,' said the older casting woman.

Joey knew dismissal when it was staring him in the face. But that didn't mean he wouldn't get hired. They liked him, he could tell.

He exited the office with a jaunty swagger. Outside, in the waiting room, were a dozen young actors sweating their turn. 'Don't bother,' he informed them, cracking his knuckles. 'I nailed it.'

Nothing like making them feel insecure.

Four days later he got the part.

'It's decent money,' Madelaine informed him. 'Three days' work spread out over two weeks' location in the Hamptons – they'll pay for your hotel and a reasonable per diem. Don't let me down, Joey.'

'Would I do that, Maddy?' he asked innocently.

That night he satisfied her in bed, sending her to sleep with a smile on her face. He'd slipped a Halcion into her decaf cappuccino, causing her to sleep so soundly that she was unaware when he left the apartment.

He roamed the streets restlessly, finally going into a strip club and paying a cheap-looking girl with large silicon-enhanced breasts to perform a private lap dance. She did nothing for him. She was a whore. He hated her. Why did he keep on punishing himself with fast cheap sex that meant nothing?

He took a cab back to Madelaine's apartment and eased into bed beside her. He'd never had a relationship that meant a damn thing. Never. In this life you had to use or get used. Sex was power. That's all.

He lay on his back, eyes wide open, unable to sleep.

Sometimes the screaming in his head was so loud it was impossible to live with.

☆

Madelaine took out insurance and paid for Joey to go to an acting coach. Even though he'd let her down once, she was so pathetically grateful to have him back she convinced herself he would never leave her again. Somehow she managed to ignore the nagging voice of her subconscious that kept assuring her he would.

Patsy Boon, his acting coach, was a big brassy Australian blond, who favoured billowy kaftans and addressed him as 'sweetie'. 'Do it this way, sweetie.' '*Never* slouch, sweetie.' 'Pitch is everything, sweetie.'

Patsy chain-drank tea and spent half her time in the bathroom, but she gave him confidence. He hadn't acted in six years and he needed the reassurance that he could still do it.

Of course he immediately charmed Patsy, and she soon offered extra coaching for free.

By the time he set off on location, he felt pretty secure he was ready to deliver a worthy performance – one that might get him noticed and back on track. Fuck it. He had no time to waste.

As soon as he arrived in the Hamptons, Madelaine called. 'What's the hotel like?' she asked.

'Small, nothin' fancy.'

'I thought I might come down for the weekend – spend a couple of days.'

'That'd be great, Maddy.'

No. It wouldn't. Didn't want the cast and crew knowing he was schtupping the old bag. Even worse – an agent old bag. They'd all think she'd gotten him the part. Truth was she hadn't. His *talent* had gotten him the part. His *presence*.

He was smart enough not to put her off. At the last minute he'd think of something to keep her safely in New York.

He was supposed to go straight to the wardrobe trailer and get fitted for his clothes. Instead he took a stroll around, getting his bearings. Parked behind the hotel were the huge mobile movie trailers, lined up like a long circus procession. Clothes, make-up, camera equipment, props, lighting, the stars' trailers, and a scattering of trucks and cars driven by union men who sat around swapping dirty jokes and playing cards. Joey checked out the names on the stars' trailers. Kyle Carson and Lara Ivory. One of these days maybe his name would be on the side of a trailer. *Joey Lorenzo.* That would be a day to make him proud.

After exploring, he went back to his room and took a shot of vodka from the minibar. It wasn't like he had a drinking problem, he simply wanted to be as relaxed and charming as possible when he hit the set.

The truth was he wanted everyone to love him.

7

'I **want to** read the script before anyone else,' Lara said, holding the phone away from her ear as Roxy, her hair person, attempted to streak her hair, folding thin strands of honey-blond locks into skinny strips of tinfoil.

'You loved the book *that* much?' Nikki exclaimed excitedly.

'Couldn't put it down. I was up all night reading. I look like Quasimodo today.'

'Yeah, sure,' muttered Roxy. 'In a freakin' pig's ear.' Roxy was a Brooklyn girl with razor-cut bright-red hair, a skinny body, and several fierce-looking body piercings. She'd done Lara's hair on three movies and they had a congenial working relationship.

'I should have something I'm happy with soon,' Nikki said. 'Maybe I'll deliver it myself, spend a day or two.'

'Will Richard allow you to do that?'

'*Allow* me!' Nikki said, laughing. 'Are you *serious*? Besides, when we get back to LA he'll be shut in the editing rooms eighteen hours a day – you know what he's like when he's finishing a movie.'

'Yes, I remember,' Lara said, recalling many long and lonely nights.

'I'm completely psyched you like the book!' Nikki said.

'It's very empowering.'

'True story. I met the woman it happened to, she's a real survivor.'

'Get me a script as soon as possible,' Lara said. 'If it's as strong as the book, we're in business.'

'Oh, wow! This is crazy.'

'Why?'

''Cause there's no way we can afford you.'

'How about scale and a piece of the action?'

'Quinn would *never* let you do that.'

'I spoke to him this morning.'

'You *did*?'

'He may *think* he controls my career – the truth is, I'm in charge.'

'Tell me about it,' Nikki said knowingly. 'Everybody imagines you're this delicate little flower, but underneath the sweetness lies a heart of stone, right?'

Lara chuckled. 'Right.'

'And talking of your stony heart, you'd better find someone to date on this movie. You're definitely in need of thawing out.'

'How many times must I tell you?' Lara sighed. 'I'm perfectly happy on my own.'

'In that case I'm buying you a vibrator for your birthday.'

'You're vulgar, you know that?'

'What's vulgar about a vibrator? It's better than a man any day, and vibrators don't give you any shit. They're reliable, always on time, and you don't have to look your best.'

Lara laughed and hung up.

'Did I hear the word vibrator?' Roxy asked, skilfully folding tinfoil.

'My friend Nikki,' Lara replied. 'All she's interested in is fixing me up.'

'Nikki . . . Nikki . . . isn't she the costume designer who *married* your ex-husband?'

'That's her.'

'Jeez – you're understanding,' Roxy said, rolling her eyes. 'I got two exes, an' if I see either of 'em walkin' down the street, I cross over to avoid 'em. They're both bastards. One of 'em was screwin' my sister – an' the other one I caught wearin' *my* best black dress along with *my* gold evening shoes. How's *that* for balls of steel?'

'I'm sure you handled it perfectly.'

'You bet! I raced into Bloomingdale's, charged five thousand bucks' worth of designer clothes on his credit card, then divorced the cross-dressing sonofabitch.' She shrieked with laughter. 'I wasn't around to see his face when he got the bill – gotta hunch he's *still* payin' it off.'

Lara smiled, for as long as she'd known Roxy there were always tales of dastardly men who'd done her wrong. Yoko, her regular make-up person, also had man problems, as did Angie, her stand-in. It was nice that on this movie she'd be surrounded by familiar faces – women she'd worked with before, and enjoyed having around.

'Did you run into Mr Carson yet?' Roxy asked, standing back to admire her work.

'Not yet.'

'Major babe,' Roxy said, sucking in her cheeks.

'What's his reputation?' Lara asked, knowing that Roxy always had the inside story.

Roxy spoke and worked at the same time. 'His wife threw him out on account of the fact she found him playin' you show me yours I'll show you mine with some bimbo TV anchor. *I* should be so lucky. A week later she ran off with her trainer. Word is, Kyle wants wifey-pie back, 'cause she's goin' for half his fortune. An' since he's made like a jillion movies in the last ten years, she could score big.'

'*Very* big.'

'You know what surprises me about guys?' Roxy said, raising her thinly pencilled eyebrows.

'What?' Lara asked, amused.

'They're always ready to give up their pissy little dicks, but when it comes to money, they hang on like we're nailin' their precious balls to the hood of a 1965 Cadillac!'

'You're so eloquent,' Lara said, still smiling.

'Yeah, that's what my date said the other night – right after I told him to screw off on account of the fact he came all over my new Anne Klein skirt.'

'Roxy!'

'Well, he did,' she said indignantly. 'What was I *supposed* to do? Kiss him? I don't think so.'

As Roxy finished twisting the last strip of tinfoil there was a knock on the trailer door.

'Who is it?' Roxy yelled out.

The door opened a few inches and Kyle Carson stuck his head in. He was good-looking in a laid-back way – kind of a latter day Gary Cooper. He had an easygoing smile and fine brown hair that seemed to be thinning in the front, although a cunning hairpiece hid this fact from his adoring fans.

'Hello,' he said. 'Is Lara Ivory around?'

Lara twisted in her chair. 'You've caught me in my tinfoil,' she said, pulling a rueful face.

'Will it embarrass you if I come in?'

'Not at all.'

'Hi,' he said, ambling inside. 'I've heard nothing but good things about working with you. I'm delighted we're finally doing it.'

'So am I,' she said, as he moved over to shake her hand. 'And meet Roxy, she's the hair genius who always makes me look good.'

'Oh, yeah,' Roxy muttered. 'It takes a lot of geniuses to make *you* look good.'

'Thought I should come find you,' Kyle said. 'Since we're starting work tomorrow.' He was staring at her beauty – very evident in spite of her tinfoiled hair. 'Uh . . . if there's anything I can do for you – if you'd like to run lines before we get together in front of the camera, that's fine with me. Maybe dinner at the hotel tonight?'

'I'm not staying at the hotel,' Lara replied. 'The studio's rented me a house.'

'That's what they were going to do for me,' he said. 'Only I figured since I recently separated from my wife, I wouldn't enjoy being stuck alone in a house. Thought a hotel might make things easier.'

'I'm sure you're right,' she agreed.

'You *do* know I'm separated?' he asked, making sure she was aware he was semi-available.

'I heard.'

'About tonight – I could drop by *your* house if that makes it easier for you.'

'You know, Kyle, I just got back from Europe and I'm still jet-lagged. Would you mind if we rehearsed on the set tomorrow?'

'Hey,' he shrugged. 'Simply trying to accommodate you.'

'That's very sweet, I appreciate it.'

He gave her another easygoing smile before exiting the trailer.

'Oh, boy,' Roxy said. 'Has he got a hot nut for you!'

'He's being polite,' Lara said.

'Polite my ass – he was drooling all over you.' Roxy sighed wistfully. 'But then, they all do, don't they? You ever get sick of it?'

'It's the image they drool over,' Lara replied thoughtfully. 'As an actress I create characters on the screen people fall in love with.'

'*You* call it love – *I* call it lust!' Roxy said with a dirty laugh. 'I gotta tell you, there's not a guy I know that doesn't wanna screw you.'

'Thanks, Roxy,' Lara said drily. 'That's exactly what I wanted to hear.'

'Honey, the truth is the truth. Wake up and smell the hard-on.'

A few minutes later, Miles, the director, appeared. He was a tall man in his early fifties with a mane of longish silver hair, steel-rimmed glasses and an animated expression.

'I guess this is my day for getting caught with my hair in a mess,' Lara said as he bent down, kissing her on the cheek.

'You're always exquisite, my dear. I'll never forget the first time you walked into my office.'

'I'll never forget it either, Miles. You started me on this road.'

'And you've travelled it well, my sweet.'

'Thanks,' she said, indicating her hair. 'I thought the lighter blond streaks would work for the character.'

He squinted at her hair. 'You were right.'

'It's Roxy's idea – she's doing a great job.'

'I can see.' He perched on the edge of the counter, facing her. 'So, how was it, working with Richard now that you're divorced?'

'Absolutely a great experience. I love him *and* Nikki.'

'That's a healthy attitude.'

'Being married to him was a nightmare. Having him as a friend is a whole other deal.'

Miles nodded as if he totally understood. 'I hear good things about the movie.'

'Yes?'

'The word is excellent.'

'Richard's a marvellous director. He knows exactly what he's doing.'

'So do you.'

'I'm looking forward to working with *you* again, Miles.'

'We'll have a splendid time.'

'How's Ginny?'

'Still into her charity thing in LA. I'm sure she'll try and visit. Oh, and she sends you her love.'

'Send mine back.'

'How about dinner tonight?'

'Do you mind if I pass? I'm planning on getting a good night's sleep so I'll be bright and camera ready in the morning.'

'Then I'll see you tomorrow.' He blew her a kiss and left the trailer.

'Another one with a crush on you,' Roxy remarked.

'You think everybody has got a crush on me,' Lara said, exasperated. 'Miles is a married man.'

'The worst kind,' Roxy said with a knowing wink. 'Show me a married man and I'll show you a hard-on in full bloom, only it ain't directed in the wife's direction.'

'You're such a cynic.'

Roxy laughed. 'You got that right.'

Later, back at her rented house, Cassie had arranged for the Filipino cook to fix them a light salad. They sat out on the back deck overlooking a stretch of white sand and the sea. There were wooden steps leading down to the beach, edged with a profusion of evergreens and colourful wild flowers.

Lara took a deep breath. 'I know I'm going to love it here,' she said, gazing out at the ocean. 'You picked a winner, Cass.'

'I'll do my best to keep out of your way,' Cassie said. 'All you have to do is yell when you want me around.'

'Hey – I *asked* you to stay here with me, I'd be nervous on my own.'

'Not much crime here,' Cassie remarked.

'It's not crime I'm worried about,' Lara retorted. 'Ever since I was stalked by that crazy woman last year, I feel more comfortable not being by myself.'

'At least *your* stalker's in jail.'

'She'll be out,' Lara said, her beautiful face grim for once.

'That's stardom,' Cassie said with a flippant laugh. 'Your own personal stalker!'

'Something I can *definitely* do without,' Lara said, thinking briefly of the obnoxious and frightening woman who'd followed her everywhere for several scary months, taking photographs, sending numerous letters and gifts – and worst of all – turning up at her front door on countless occasions.

'The good news is,' Cassie said, 'that we've got a guard every night. He'll be sitting in his car at the front of the house – probably asleep on the job, but we can buzz him any time we want.'

'I hate having to live like this,' Lara fretted.

'The studio's paying,' Cassie said, practical as ever. 'What does it matter?'

Cassie didn't get it, but that was OK. Being stalked was a living nightmare. 'I think I'll take a walk along the beach,' she said. 'Care to join me?'

'Much as I fancy the idea,' Cassie said, shifting her comfortable bulk, 'I'd sooner have a piece of chocolate cake and a carton of ice cream.'

Lara raised a disapproving eyebrow. 'What happened to your diet?'

'I left it in LA along with all those hard bodies.'

'Hmm . . .' Lara said. 'When we get back I'm buying you a year's membership at a health club.'

'I'd sooner have a Porsche!'

'Very funny,' Lara said, laughing. 'I'm going to walk before it's dark. Be sure I get a wake-up call at five thirty.'

'It's done,' Cassie said, her favourite expression.

The beach was windswept and deserted. Lara strolled by the seashore, kicking off her sandals and walking barefoot, loving the feel of the damp sand on her feet.

She thought about Nikki's book, and the role of Rebecca – the rape victim who takes her own revenge. She wanted to play the part; it was a challenge, and life *should* be a challenge sometimes.

Of course, it wasn't a star vehicle, but if the script was good, she was definitely interested. She had all the success she could ever possibly want – why not take on something risky? Something that would stretch her as an actress? Something that could maybe help her avenge her past?

Lara Ivory – beautiful movie star. If people knew the real truth . . .

If they only knew . . .

8

After being away from LA for almost three months Nikki had a thousand things to do. Her fifteen-year-old daughter, Summer, was arriving any moment, so her main concern was opening up the Malibu house and getting everything organized. Summer sometimes spent vacation time with Nikki, but mostly she stayed with her father in Chicago.

Nikki often reflected on her former life and wondered how she'd ever been that person. Mrs Sheldon Weston – respectable wife and mother – locked into a loveless marriage simply because she'd gotten herself pregnant at the age of sixteen during an adventurous six-week fling with an older man. Sheldon had done the right thing and married her. Well, he'd had to, he was twenty-two years older than her and a respected psychiatrist – he couldn't risk tarnishing his spotless reputation. Plus her uptight parents had insisted he marry her. If it wasn't for them she might not have been such a wild child, but since sex was never allowed so much as a mention in their house, she'd had to go out and find out for herself. So, even though she'd balked at going through with it, neither Sheldon nor her parents had given her a choice. She'd been sixteen – what did she know?

Apart from being an extremely successful psychiatrist, Sheldon was a very controlling man – similar to her father in a way. Once they were married, Nikki found he expected her to obey his every whim, and while at first she enjoyed playing the obedient little wife, it soon grew to be a burden – especially after Summer was born.

By that time Nikki was seventeen and craved fun.

Sheldon was thirty-nine and expected her to always be at home waiting for him.

After a couple of years she had a hunch he played

around. She knew that many a society woman flopped down on his couch and told him everything, and while they were there, she suspected he did a lot more than listen. It took her years to catch him – and when she did, she had no firm evidence to take to court.

Divorcing Sheldon had not been easy. He hadn't relished letting her go, in fact, he'd threatened that if she left him, she'd never see Summer again.

His threats had not worked. She'd hired a canny female lawyer and fought back, ending up with shared custody.

Summer was eight when they split, and extremely verbal about spending the majority of her time with her father at his rambling house in the suburbs of Chicago where she could ride horses and keep her pet rabbits. She hated her mother's small apartment, so Nikki gave up – allowing her to stay with Sheldon.

It was a mistake. Summer bonded with her father and began treating Nikki like a slightly crazy older sister.

Nikki was hurt, but over the years she'd grown to accept it. Instead of parenting, she'd concentrated on getting together a career, starting as an assistant and eventually becoming a much in demand costume designer on movies – much to Sheldon's chagrin.

When Richard Barry had arrived in town to shoot a film, he'd requested Nikki as clothes designer. She'd been flattered and intrigued.

Their first meeting was classic Richard, he'd shot orders at her as if she was still an assistant, which infuriated her. After a while she'd taken him to one side and set him straight. 'I know you're this big Hollywood director,' she'd told him, 'but I have a reputation of my own, so please don't tell me how to do my job – and I won't tell you how to direct your movie.'

Two nights later they were in bed together, and to her surprise and delight it was pretty sensational sex.

By the time the movie was finished, Richard had asked her to marry him and she'd accepted – even though he was another older man.

Now they had been married two years, and although Richard didn't approve, she'd decided she wanted to become a producer and was trying to get *Revenge* together.

Since she'd married a famous film director and moved to Los Angeles, Summer was a lot warmer toward Nikki. Now she actually seemed to look forward to spending vacation time with them. Of course, the fact that they had a beach house in Malibu helped.

Summer was extremely pretty, tall and coltish, with long white-blond hair – natural of course – and a Lolita-type demeanour. Richard had nicknamed her jailbait, and whenever they were together they giggled a lot. It occurred to Nikki that Summer got along much better with men than women.

Recently Sheldon had married again. Nikki had thought Summer would hate Rachel, Sheldon's new bride, considering she was only three years older than Summer. But quite the contrary, the two girls had become quite close; in fact, Summer had even asked if she could bring Rachel with her for a few days.

'Absolutely not,' Nikki had said, horrified at the thought.

Nikki ran around the house making sure everything was right. She was thrilled Lara had asked to see the script, what a coup if she agreed to make the movie!

Today the writer was delivering his final draft. She hoped it arrived before Summer, because all she really wanted to do was sit quietly in a corner and read.

☆

Summer Weston checked out the young limo driver holding up a white card with her name printed on it in big bold letters. He was cute in a goofy way, with sticking-up carrot-colour hair and a cheeky expression. He stared at her bug-eyed, and couldn't believe his luck when she headed straight for him.

'Hi,' she said, casually. 'You're meeting me.'

'I am?'

'Yup,' she said, thrusting her carry-on bag at him.

He took the bag and said, 'Uh ... shall I bring the car around, or d'you want to come with me to the lot?'

'I've got like luggage.'

'A lot?'

'Six bags.'

'You're here to stay, then?'

'Maybe,' she said, flirting.

'Whyn't I take you to the luggage carousel, then I'll go get the limo.'

'Cool,' she said, excited that Nikki had sent a limo to meet her.

They began the long walk. 'You an actress?' he asked, throwing her a sideways glance.

She giggled, flinging back her long blond hair. 'What do you think?' she responded, pleased that he thought she was.

He squinted at her. 'You look like that girl in *Clueless* – y'know, Alicia something.'

'Well, I'm not.'

''S OK,' he said casually. 'You're prettier.'

'Honestly?'

A laconic— 'Yeah.'

This was an excellent start to her trip. A sure sign LA was the place for her to be. Her father had wanted her to go to the Bahamas with him and his teenage wife, but much to his annoyance, she'd refused. The less time she had to spend with him the better.

They arrived at the luggage carousel and waited for her bags to appear. 'I'm Jed,' her driver said, edging close to her. 'Doing this job to make the rent – in real life I'm an actor.'

'You must meet a lot of cool people.'

'Yeah,' he laughed. 'Like you. Only you can't score me a job.'

'My stepfather's a famous director,' she boasted.

'No shit? What's his name?'

'Richard Barry.'

His eyes bugged. 'I'm impressed.'

Later, sitting in the back of a long silver limo heading for Malibu, she reached in her purse and lit up a joint. She'd been smoking grass for two years, it helped her get through all the things she had to put up with. Without it she didn't know what she would've done.

Jed caught on immediately – sniffing the air – eyeing her in his rear-view mirror. 'You're gonna stink up the car,' he remarked.

'So,' she said haughtily. '*I'm* paying.'

'Right,' he said, snickering. 'You an' your rich daddy.'

'Want a drag?' she offered. 'It's free.'

He hesitated for a moment, then said, 'Why not?'

She moved over to the glass partition, passing him the joint. He dragged deeply. A veteran.

'I could get canned for this,' he said, not sounding too upset at the prospect.

'Yes, but think how amazing you'll feel for the rest of the day,' she said with a giggle.

'You got that right,' he responded, with a crooked smirk.

By the time the limo reached Malibu he'd given her his phone number and the name of a club where he hung out when he wasn't working. 'Come on by,' he said, hot for this girl with the long blond hair and the primo grass.

'Maybe I will,' she said, still flirting.

'Maybe you should,' he replied, thinking that he'd finally found a live one.

☆

Nikki heard the limo pull up and hurried to the door, throwing it open.

'Hi, Mom,' Summer said, emerging from the car, slightly stoned but hiding it well. 'Where's Richard?'

'Editing,' Nikki replied, hurt that the first words out of Summer's mouth were, *Where's Richard?* 'Don't I get a hug and a kiss?'

'Whatever,' Summer said casually, giving her mother a perfunctory hug.

Nikki wasn't sure, but for a moment she thought she smelled the strong aroma of pot.

The young driver was busily unloading suitcases from the trunk. Nikki directed him to Summer's room.

'LA's awesome,' Summer announced, wandering through the house. 'Chicago's like *soo* hot and muggy. Ugh! *Disgusto* weather!'

'It *is* beautiful here,' Nikki agreed, following her. 'I guess I never take the time to appreciate it.'

'Course, I could've gone with Daddy and Rachel to the Bahamas,' Summer continued. 'Thing is I've already been there twice and it's way boring. Besides, I wanted to see Richard – and you, of course.'

'That's terrific,' Nikki said, checking out her daughter's outfit, shades of early Madonna crossed with Courtney Love

– a look that did not suit Summer's fresh prettiness. 'Let's go shopping tomorrow,' she suggested. 'We'll explore Melrose, there's plenty of new stores I'm sure you'll love.'

Summer groaned, as if it was the worst idea she'd ever heard. 'C'mon, Mom, y'know we don't have the same taste.'

'I'm hardly an old fuddy-duddy,' Nikki replied, resenting Summer's comment. 'In fact, I am one of the most successful clothes designers in movies.' *I'm also younger than Madonna,* she thought. *So don't treat me like some decrepit old fart.*

'Yeah, Mom. Thing is – you like *so* don't get me.'

Great! She didn't get her own daughter.

'I'm starving,' Summer said, racing into the kitchen. 'Is there anything to eat?'

There was plenty to eat, but Summer had this infuriating habit of flinging open the fridge and saying, 'Yuck! Nothing edible!' She did it now. Then she threw open every cupboard in the kitchen, failing to close them.

Nikki tried to stay calm, her daughter's messy habits drove her totally insane.

'Bummer!' Summer exclaimed. 'Richard's not home and there's no food.'

'Tell me what you'd like, and I'll send the maid to the market.'

'Forget it, Mom. I'm gonna hit the beach. I plan on getting a way cool tan.'

So much for mother–daughter bonding, Nikki thought ruefully.

☆

The moment the messenger delivered the script, Nikki grabbed it and hurried onto the deck overlooking the beach. Summer was lying down below on the sand, topless. Since she was almost flat-chested it didn't really matter, except that it *was* inappropriate – especially as this was a public beach where you were not supposed to do that kind of thing.

She contemplated calling down and telling her to put on a top, but what was the good? Summer would do so for two minutes, and as soon as Nikki turned around she'd take it off again.

Clutching the script under her arm, she curled up in a comfortable wicker chair and began reading.

For an hour and a half she was completely absorbed. It was a brilliant final draft – the writer she'd hired had done an excellent job incorporating all her notes. Placing the script on a table, she shivered with excitement. Lara had to see it immediately.

It crossed her mind she could deliver it personally. Then she remembered that Summer was staying, and it wouldn't be fair to leave her alone with Richard. Maybe she'd Fed Ex Lara the script, give her a chance to read it, and then get on a plane. Yes, she decided, that was the way to handle it.

She called Richard in the editing rooms. 'The script's here,' she said. 'I just finished reading, it's exactly on target.'

'Don't get too excited,' he warned. 'The money people have to take a look, and they *always* have comments.'

'Who cares?' she said recklessly. 'I think it's good enough to send to the directors I have in mind, get their reactions.'

'Well . . . they're all waiting to see it,' he mused. 'Only remember I'm tied up for the next few weeks, I won't be much help.'

'I can handle it,' she said confidently. 'This is *my* project, and although I appreciate your input, I'm OK on my own.'

'You're sure you want to do this?'

'Absolutely.'

She was about to call Federal Express and package the script off to Lara when she remembered Summer, who'd definitely been out on the beach too long. She went over to the edge of the deck and peered down. Summer was sprawled on the sand – still topless. A muscled boy was crouched down next to her, talking nonstop. *Hmm*, Nikki thought, *it hasn't taken her long to find some local action.*

She realized she shouldn't be so critical, but she didn't want the same fate happening to her daughter that had befallen her. Pregnant at sixteen, married at seventeen, divorced at twenty-five. A little voice murmured in her head, *It's not your problem, it's Sheldon's. He's in charge.*

She called out Summer's name.

Her nearly naked daughter swung her head around, looking up at her as if she was a total stranger. 'Yeah?'

'Shouldn't you come in now? You don't want to get too much sun on your first day.'

Summer whispered something to the boy. They both shrieked with laughter.

Somehow Nikki knew she was the butt of their joke, but she pretended not to mind and hurried back into the house. She called Federal Express and dashed off a short note to Lara. After that she sat down at her desk and began calling the directors she planned on sending the script to, alerting them it was on its way.

☆

Summer knew there was one thing she could do without any effort: attract boys – or men, it didn't matter as long as they were male. Five minutes on the beach and this big burly surfer came along and started chatting to her. She took off her top, told him everyone in Europe sunbathed topless, and while his eyes bugged out of his head, she asked him where she could score some grass. He informed her he could get her anything she wanted, invited her to a party and fell in love.

Men! Summer thought disdainfully. *They're all so easy!*

Later, she wandered into the house barefoot and sandy, a thin shirt barely covering her bikini. 'Gotta go out,' she told her mother. 'Can I borrow a car?'

'You're too young to drive,' Nikki pointed out. 'You have to be sixteen, remember?'

'I drive Daddy's car all the time,' she said, pouting.

'Maybe Daddy's prepared to take the risk,' Nikki answered crisply. 'We can't do that.'

'I'm a way cool driver, Mom.'

'I'm sure you are, but you're not allowed to drive here. It's the law.'

'I won't get caught.'

'I said no.'

'You're such a downer,' Summer mumbled, thinking that her mother was not going to be as easy to manipulate as Daddy Dearest.

'Where are you off to, anyway?' Nikki asked. 'I thought we'd all have dinner tonight.'

'Can't,' Summer said. 'Going to a party.'

'Already?'

'You wouldn't want me sitting home, would you?'

'Does your father give you a curfew?'

'A curfew? *Me*? Huh!'

'Don't get smart, Summer. What time do you have to be home in Chicago?'

'Any time I like,' she replied boldly. *Or*, she thought, *any time he says*. Because Sheldon always liked to know she was there when he wanted her to be.

'The rules are different here,' Nikki said, tapping her watch. 'Back by midnight.'

'Midnight!' Summer squealed. 'Parties don't even get *started* until then!'

'How do you know?'

'I've got friends here.'

'You have? Who?'

'Nobody you know.'

Oh God! Summer had reached the difficult age. Nikki gritted her teeth. She was going to need Richard's help, and at the moment he was totally unavailable. 'I'll give you cab money,' she said at last, not wanting to come down too hard. 'And be home by twelve. Deal?'

'Whatever,' Summer muttered, stomping off to her room, thinking what an uncool drag her mother was.

☆

Richard didn't arrive home until past ten. He was elated. 'The movie's looking incredible,' he said, fixing himself a hefty drink. 'The South of France locations are exquisite, and Lara's performance is luminous. The way she's grown as an actress is quite remarkable.'

'How long before it's all together?' Nikki asked.

'I should have a rough cut in about six weeks.'

'That's exciting. Do the clothes look good?'

'Come over tomorrow and see for yourself. You'll be pleased.'

'I will?' she said, putting her arms around him.

'Yes, my dear, you will.'

'I love you, Richard,' she said, nuzzling her face against his chest.

'Love you too, sweetheart,' he responded, not really concentrating. 'Where's Summer? Wasn't she supposed to be here today?'

'She arrived, caused her usual chaos and went out.'

'Left you here by yourself?'

'She's not exactly my companion, Richard. I said it was OK for her to go out. Told her she had to be home by twelve. We don't have to wait up, I've decided to trust her.'

'Good for you.'

'You've been neglecting me,' Nikki said, wishing he would pay her more attention. 'Who comes first – the film or me?'

'You know it's always the movie,' he said, teasing her.

'You're such a bastard,' she said, standing on tiptoes and kissing him. 'I don't know why I love you.'

He wrapped her in his arms, almost sweeping her off her feet.

'Carry me in the bedroom and ravish me!' she joked. 'Take advantage while I'm in the mood.'

'I'm hungry,' he said. 'All I've had is coffee and doughnuts.'

She put on her best sexy voice. 'I'll give you something to eat you'll *really* like.'

'Yes?'

Now she had his full attention. 'Oh, yes, Mr Barry. You'll like it plenty.'

Laughing, they retired to the bedroom.

So there I was, sixteen years old and out on my own again. I wasn't about to stay with Lulu, the cheating little whore.

I had a couple of options. One of them was Avis Delamore, the old bag who ran the acting class I'd been attending. Avis claimed she was a famous stage actress from England. I wasn't so sure, because every time she got excited, I noticed a touch of the Bronx in her accent.

When I got to know her better I discovered I was right. She'd lived in England for a couple of years with some loser bit-player she'd picked up in a bar. That was the extent of her English heritage.

Avis had a big crush on me, so when I rang her bell and told her I had no place to stay, she immediately said, 'You'd better sleep on my couch.'

Yeah – sure. That night the couch turned into her bed and I was in with a vengeance. Like I said before, if I really concentrate I can get any woman I want.

Unfortunately Avis wasn't Lulu, with her tight stripper's body and perky tits. Avis was a big woman with floppy breasts and heavy thighs.

I soon learned what it was like to fuck a woman who hadn't been getting it in a while. My old man was right. Grateful was good. Grateful meant they'd give you anything you wanted. And she did. All I had to do was ask.

I never thought about my dad or what he was doing. As far as I was concerned, he was yesterday's news. I'd moved on and didn't give a shit.

Of course, like Lulu, Avis had no idea I was only sixteen. Told her I was twenty, an' she bought it.

She got me to do jobs around her crumbling old house – informing everyone I was her assistant. For this I got to screw her *and pocket fifty bucks a week. Trouble was she wanted it every night, and I wasn't inclined to give it up on such a regular basis.*

I compromised by making sure she gave me plenty of head. I like getting head – it means I can lie back and not get involved. Avis on her knees, and me fantasizing about movies and all that Hollywood shit. It doesn't matter what they look like as long as they give a decent blow job.

The one good thing about being with Avis was that I got to study acting every day. And the class was hot – there were always different girls coming and going – so naturally I took full advantage of the situation.

Avis was my bread and butter. The girls were my delectable desserts.

Of course, I made damn sure Avis didn't know – didn't even have a suspicion. I was smart enough to realize she wouldn't take kindly to me putting it about.

Everything went smoothly, until one day Avis's daughter, Betty, returned from California, where she'd been visiting her dad – Avis's estranged husband. By this time I was seventeen and quite settled into my new life, so when Betty appeared I wasn't expecting problems.

Betty was the same age as me, and not at all pleased to find me in residence. I heard her arguing with her mom the first night she was there. 'What the hell is he doing here? It's disgusting – he's young enough to be your son.'

Avis didn't like confrontations, which was one of the reasons her husband had run off in the first place. 'It's my life,' she said, defending her position. 'We're very happy.'

'Well, I'm not happy,' Betty yelled back. 'And I'm not living here with him.'

Betty and I hated each other for three weeks. On the fourth week we had unbelievable sex on her mother's bed, then things got really complicated.

Betty was a bad girl, the kind I'd always been attracted to. She loathed her mother, and couldn't believe I was sleeping with her. 'How can you do it with such an old bag?' she sneered. 'You're really a low life.'

I didn't appreciate her calling me names.

One night she came to me with a plan. 'I know where my mom keeps her jewellery – let's take it an' run. We can stay with my dad and his girlfriend in LA.'

'You mean steal her stuff?' I said, sounding like jerk of the year.

'No, we'll ask her for it,' Betty said with her best sneer. 'What d'you think I mean, dummy?'

Avis had been good to me, but then I'd been good to her, too.

On the other hand Betty offered excitement and adventure. She was young, pretty and totally wild. I had nothing to lose and a shitload of adventure to gain.

So we grabbed all of Avis's jewellery from the safe deposit box she kept under her bed, and took off for California.

I was finally on my way to Hollywood.

9

Joey prowled restlessly around the hotel. He'd explored the town, checked out the beach and now he was bored. Two weeks' location and only three days' work spread out over fourteen days – he'd go crazy if he didn't think of something to keep him occupied.

He considered visiting the set – they were shooting at a beachside restaurant. But hanging around sets when not working was hardly smart. Besides, it was boring.

Yesterday he'd finally gone to the wardrobe trailer – manned by Eric, a gay guy with a muscular body and white crew-cut, and Trinee, a young Hispanic girl with glossy jet hair hanging below her waist. They'd fitted him in a black silk T-shirt, and a white Armani suit. He got off on the look, it was straight out of *GQ*.

Now – since he had nothing else to do – he decided to return to the trailer. He left the hotel and slowly strolled over.

Trinee was the only one there. She was busy organizing racks of clothes, while quietly humming a Gloria Estefan song under her breath.

Joey leaned against the door watching her for a few seconds. 'Where's Eric?' he asked, like he cared.

She barely glanced up. 'On the set with Kyle Carson.'

'How come *you're* not there?'

'I'm in charge of the trailer today,' she replied, a touch pleased with herself.

Joey took a closer look. She was very pretty with bold eyes, a crushed rosebud mouth, and small inviting breasts. Unfortunately she was short, and diminutive girls failed to turn him on.

'Can I try on my stuff again?' he asked.

'Everything fit, didn't it?'

'Putting on the clothes helps me get in character.'

'OK,' she said, reaching along the rack for a hanger with a cardboard tag bearing his name. He noticed she had a small pearl ring on her engagement finger – which probably accounted for the fact she wasn't falling all over him.

'I see you're engaged,' he remarked.

A pleased smile spread across her pretty face. 'Two weeks,' she said proudly, holding up her ring hand and waving it in his face.

'I'm engaged, too,' he lied, deciding that it wasn't a bad idea to pretend he was. Trinee would spread the word and it would give him more substance – plus it would keep the women on the movie at bay. He had a rule he tried to keep – never fuck where you work.

'Really?' Trinee said, cheering up considerably. '*My* fiancé is a boxer. What does yours do?'

Joey considered his reply. He wanted to make himself look good – no models or actresses need apply. 'A lawyer,' he said at last. 'She's the youngest lawyer at her firm.'

'Wow!' Trinee responded. 'Cool!'

'Very,' Joey agreed.

He tried on his outfit again.

'You look hot,' Trinee said admiringly.

He stared at himself in the full-length mirror, wishing that his role in the movie was bigger. He was capable of anything and ready to fly, nothing was going to hold him back – not after where he'd been. 'Do I get to keep the clothes?' he asked.

'That's up to the producer,' Trinee replied. 'It's not usual unless you're the star.'

'One of these days I'll *be* the star,' Joey said confidently. 'You can bet on that.'

'Well . . . you're sure handsome enough,' she agreed with a light laugh. 'Y'know, I'm surprised they hired you.'

'How come?'

'Kyle Carson's gonna shit when he sees you're better looking than him.'

He smoothed back his dark hair, still gazing at his reflection. 'You think I am?'

Now that they were both safely engaged she indulged in a little light flirtation. 'Oh, c'mon, man, you *know* you are.'

'The director liked me,' he mused. 'So did the producer – what's her name?'

'Barbara Westerberg.'

'She liked me a lot.'

'I'm totally in shock you slipped by Kyle.'

'What does *that* mean?'

'I worked on his last movie,' she said with a knowing nod. 'Oh boy! Every actor had to be older and less handsome than him.' She lowered her voice to a confidential whisper. 'He's losing his hair, you know.'

'That's gotta make him real insecure.'

'Not really,' she replied. 'He still tries to jump everything that moves.'

'Yeah?'

'Only females, though,' Trinee said with a giggle. '*You're* safe.'

'Gee, thanks,' he said drily.

'When do you work?'

'Tomorrow. The bar scene.'

'I'm sure you'll be great,' she said. 'You'd better take the clothes off now. Those pants have to be pressed.'

☆

Lara hit the set surrounded by her all-female entourage. There was Roxy, dressed up for the first day's action in a lime green micro-mini and ankle-clinging white go-go boots, her red hair a blaze of glory. There was Yoko, her make-up girl – Japanese and pretty, with flat black cropped hair and a wide face. There was Angie, her stand-in – a poor man's version of Lara, with a tired look about her, due to the fact that she was married to a stuntman who continually gave her a hard time. And then there was Cassie, trailing behind, cellular phone in hand, plus yellow legal pad and poised pen ready to make notes.

Lara recognized several of the crew she'd worked with before. She greeted them by name, adding a warm handshake and sincere enquiries about their families. They all loved her for remembering.

Kyle was already on the set lounging in his canvas director's chair, long legs stretched out before him. He got up as Lara approached. 'Morning, beautiful,' he said in a deep rich voice. 'You get a good night's sleep?'

'I certainly did,' she replied.

Miles came over. 'You look particularly gorgeous,' he said, kissing her on both cheeks. 'That hair thing really works.'

Instinctively her hand reached up, touching her newly streaked hair. 'Thanks,' she said modestly. 'It's all due to Roxy here.'

Miles didn't acknowledge the hairdresser, she wasn't important to him. 'Let's do an immediate walk-through,' he said, ready to set the scene.

Roxy pulled a face behind his back.

Cassie handed Lara her script.

'How come,' Lara said to Miles, 'that the first scene on the first day is always a kissing scene?'

He laughed. 'Can you come up with a better way to get the two of you hot for each other? Raw sex, honey, it works every time.'

She ignored his crassness and quietly stated her case. 'Surely you understand that if you arranged it for later in the schedule, the actors performing the scene would have more chemistry together.'

'Don't worry, hon,' Miles said, in a patronizing tone. 'You and Kyle are set to burn up the screen.' He winked at Kyle, who winked back. All boys together.

Lara remained silent. She'd learned that as a successful woman in the movie industry it wasn't worth getting into an argument over small things. Better to save her power for when it was really needed.

Miles blocked the action, showing them exactly what he wanted them to do. When he was finished, they started to rehearse, running through the page and a half of dialogue several times.

Soon it was time for the kiss. Lara turned to Miles and said, 'Do you mind if we wait until we're actually shooting? It'll be more spontaneous that way.' She wanted to add *no tongue*, but decided to wait and see if Kyle was a gentleman. Fortunately, this was a fully-clothed kiss. Later in the script there was a nude scene. Her contract stated she did not do nude scenes, but she *had* agreed they could hire a body double.

Kyle obviously didn't know this, because when he pulled her close, readying himself for the first kiss, he whispered, 'Don't worry about a thing, Lara, when we shoot the sex scene, I'll be right there to protect you.'

He was talking to her like she was a novice. She'd made nine highly successful movies, she knew exactly what she was doing.

After a few more rehearsals Angie moved in front of the camera while the scene was lit. Lara took a break, sitting in her chair while Roxy fussed with her hair and Yoko touched up her lipstick. Fifteen minutes later they were ready to shoot.

Lara loved the silence that descended after the first assistant yelled, 'Settle down, everybody, we're going for a take.' She enjoyed acting, becoming someone else, creating fantasy. It was her life – the only life that made her feel secure.

They would have gotten the scene in one if Kyle hadn't fumbled his lines. 'Sorry, babe,' he muttered.

She noticed little beads of sweat on his forehead and wondered if he was nervous. His make-up person, a statuesque black girl, strolled over and powdered him down, followed by his hair person, a short gay guy, who squinted at his hairpiece making sure it was securely in place.

'OK, let's go again,' Miles shouted. 'We're ready for another take.'

This time it was second take perfect, right up to the kiss. Lara kept her lips firmly clenched together when Kyle bent to kiss her, but he had other ideas as he pushed against her soft lips, managing to insert his slippery thick tongue.

She immediately jerked back, uncomfortable at this sudden intimacy.

'Cut!' Miles called. 'Is there a problem?'

'I feel like she's shoving me away,' Kyle grumbled. 'We're supposed to be falling in love. Shouldn't she be more into it?'

Lara threw him a look. There was nothing worse than a leading man who tried to insert a little tongue action when shooting a love scene. It wasn't necessary, the camera couldn't see. And why was he talking to Miles as if she didn't exist?

Sensing tension, Miles quickly drew her to one side. 'What's the matter, hon?' he asked in his *I care about actors* voice. 'Something bothering you?'

'He's coming on too strong, Miles,' she complained. 'There's no reason for him to put his tongue down my throat.'

'You want me to talk to him?' Miles asked soothingly.

'Yes, do that,' she said, walking over to her chair.

Roxy approached. 'Hmm . . .' she remarked knowingly, tugging at her too-short skirt, which kept riding up over her skinny thighs. 'The old tongue trick, huh?'

'Right,' Lara agreed.

'You can't blame the guy for trying,' Yoko said.

'It's unprofessional,' Lara said.

'It's a man thing,' Roxy responded. 'They see a mouth – they want in!'

Yoko nodded in agreement as she went to work on Lara's lips, outlining them with a steady hand.

Miles obviously spoke to Kyle, because he came over a few minutes later, and said a contrite, 'Sorry if I offended you, Lara. Only doing what comes naturally.'

'You didn't offend me, Kyle,' she replied coolly. 'It's simply not necessary for you to French kiss me.'

'Most actresses love it,' he boasted, going for the macho swagger.

'Well,' she said, as sweetly as she could manage, 'I'm not most actresses.'

The line was drawn. Kyle was on his side of the fence, she was on hers.

At lunchtime they both sat with their people at different tables. Roxy began carrying on about Yoko's boyfriend back in LA giving her a hard time and how she should dump him. Yoko retaliated by saying that Roxy only dated weirdos and perverts and was obviously jealous. Angie announced that her husband was working with a mega action star who was notorious for beating up his three ex-wives and had gotten more plastic surgery than any woman. And Cassie listened to it all, finally saying, 'Give me food over a guy any day!'

Lara was glad she had none of their problems. She didn't need a man, she was perfectly happy on her own. Or so she kept trying to convince herself.

☆

Later Joey returned to the hotel and lay on top of his bed watching an old Clint Eastwood movie on television. He was relaxed and feeling good. At least he was back in action.

Madelaine called. 'How's it going?' she asked.

'Nothing much happenin' yet,' he said, aiming an imaginary gun at Clint. 'Think I work tomorrow.'

'Well, Joey, do your best,' Madelaine said, sounding like his seventh-grade teacher. 'Don't let me down.'

He wished she'd stop saying that, it was getting on his nerves. He'd baled on her once, but he was back and at least he'd started paying her the money he'd taken. She had no idea what he'd gone through, how tough things had been. 'Hey, listen,' he said, with a slight edge. 'When did I ever let you down?'

'Let's not get into that,' Madelaine said, her voice sharp. 'I'll definitely be there this weekend.'

Fuck! He had to think of a reason for her not to come.

'Great,' he lied. 'I could use the company.'

☆

At the end of the day Lara was tired. Much as she loved it, making movies drained her energy, there was so much down time doing nothing. That's why she liked her group around her – Roxy, Yoko, Angie and Cassie. They amused her with their raunchy dialogue, kept her from getting bored. Besides, they were her family, her only real friends.

After the kissing incident, the atmosphere between her and Kyle had definitely cooled. Between takes they stayed away from each other, although on camera they still generated enough heat for her to know the scenes were working.

Back at the house she studied her script, preparing for the next day. In the upcoming scene, Kyle's character picks a fight with her in a restaurant and walks out. Then a guy at the bar begins flirting with her, comes over, they have a conversation, and just as she's about to dance with him,

Kyle reappears. The scene ends with Kyle punching the guy out.

Hmm, Lara thought, *Kyle's probably into all that macho stuff men get off on.* Most leading actors loved playing the hero. In fact, many of them had it written into their contract that they couldn't play anything else on account of the fact they felt the public had to see them in a shining light at all times.

She checked the call sheet to see who was playing Jeff, the guy at the bar. Joey Lorenzo – an actor she'd never heard of.

Cassie had gone to the movies with Angie, so since she had nothing else to do, she went to bed early and was asleep by nine o'clock.

In the morning she was up long before her wake-up call. Throwing on a tracksuit, she jogged along the deserted beach. She was lucky, she could eat anything and not put on weight, which meant she didn't have to slave away in the gym getting the hard body that was a requisite for most young actresses today. Jogging was different, it cleared her head and gave her energy.

When she got back to the house, Cassie was sitting in the kitchen eating a substantial breakfast. 'You were up early,' Cassie remarked, her mouth full of cereal.

'There's not much to do around here except sleep,' Lara said. 'I'm making the most of it.'

'Miles left a message last night. They're showing dailies at lunch-time, and he wondered if you'd like to forgo lunch and take a look.'

'Absolutely,' Lara said, although seeing herself on screen was always a painful experience.

When she arrived at the location she found Yoko and Roxy indulging in their usual banter. They were sitting at one of the long trestle tables set up by the catering truck, facing each other. Roxy had a plate piled high with scrambled eggs, toast and bacon, while Yoko chewed on a granola bar.

'You're early,' Roxy said, scooping up eggs.

'Who wants me first?'

'I do,' Roxy said, mouth full. 'I'll put your hair in rollers, then you're all Yoko's.'

Lara stood by the table a moment. 'I'll be in my trailer,' she said. 'Send somebody to fetch me when you're ready.'

'I'm ready now,' Roxy said, stuffing a piece of bacon into her mouth.

'There's no rush. Finish your breakfast.'

'I need my strength,' Roxy giggled. 'Had a heavy night.'

'Yeah,' Yoko said, rolling her eyes. 'She dated one of the drivers. The fat charmer that sits around reading porno magazines all day.'

'He's *not* fat,' Roxy objected. 'He's big-boned. Besides, I like something I can hang on to in the middle of the night.'

'Oh, yeah, and I bet you did *plenty* of *that*,' Yoko sneered.

Lara left them to it and went to her trailer. It amazed her that in this day of AIDS both Roxy and Yoko were so casual about sex. Didn't they realize how dangerous it was out there?

She'd never been like that, for her it was always a relationship or nothing.

Maybe she was wrong. Maybe one-night stands were the way to go.

No. It wouldn't work for her. Eventually someone worthwhile would come along. And if he didn't . . . well, she had her career, her house in LA, her dogs and horses and her friends . . .

Deep down she knew it wasn't enough.

10

Joey was having fun on the set. Females were everywhere, and they all wanted to make sure he was a happy camper.

He was happy all right. The cute little Japanese thing who'd done his make-up was sweet as candy. And when her red-headed hairdresser friend came in, she was all over him too. It was some smart move telling Trinee he was engaged. Naturally she'd informed the world. They could look, but not touch.

Trinee had elected to leave the wardrobe trailer today to make sure his clothes were OK. 'I've got to watch out for you in the fight scene,' she'd explained. 'We've got another pair of pants – no more jackets, so try not to get too messed up.'

'I'll do my best,' he said, grinning.

'You do that,' she responded, grinning back.

They both knew why she was there.

☆

Lara leaned back in the make-up chair while Yoko attended to her face – working fast with a light touch.

'Can you believe Roxy?' Yoko said, shaking her head in disgust. 'That girl is one loco woman!'

'What happened now?'

'Well,' Yoko shrugged, 'she picks up this dude on the set yesterday, and last night she's rolling around in bed with him. The guy's gonna tell everyone. Her reputation's shot.'

'I hope she used a condom.'

'Ha!' Yoko said. 'Probably not. Roxy's under the impression she's immortal.'

'Perhaps you should mention it to her,' Lara suggested. 'I mean, using a condom is merely common sense.'

'You tell her,' Yoko said pointedly. 'She never listens to me.'

'Maybe I will.'

Jane, the second AD, entered the trailer. She was a tall, lanky woman with a long horse face. 'Yoko,' she said pleadingly. 'Do me a big one and make up the actor playing Jeff.'

'I'm only supposed to work on Lara,' Yoko said with a stubborn expression.

'I know,' Jane said. 'But there's a problem with one of the other make-up people, and I need this favour. Lara, you don't mind, do you?'

'Doesn't bother me,' Lara said. 'I'm nearly finished.'

'What about Kyle's guy?' Yoko said, standing her ground. 'Can't *he* do it?'

'Kyle takes longer in make-up than Lara,' said Jane. 'It'll hold everyone up.'

'OK.' Yoko said, with a put upon sigh. 'Send him in. What's his name?'

'Joey Lorenzo. And wait till you get a look at him.'

Lara got up from the chair. 'Am I finished?'

'Can't improve on the original,' Yoko said, stepping back and admiring her work in the mirror. 'I merely enhance the rose.'

Lara leaned close to the mirror. 'This lipstick is a good colour,' she said. 'I'll let you know how it comes across in dailies.'

'Maybe I can go with you,' Yoko said hopefully.

Lara shook her head. 'Miles is very particular about who watches.'

'That's dumb. Everyone connected with the movie should be allowed to see 'em.'

'He gets uptight.'

'Directors!' Yoko muttered.

Lara made her way to the hair trailer. Roxy greeted her at the door clad in a tight leopardprint sweater, black leather micro-skirt, and faux tigerskin shoes. 'Shit!' she said excitedly. 'You gotten an eyeful of the actor playing Jeff?'

'No,' Lara said.

'We're talkin' a twenty,' Roxy enthused. 'Trinee says he's engaged. But you know *me* – makes me want him even more!'

'What's he been in before?' Lara asked, more interested in his track record than his looks.

'According to what I heard, he had a promising career going, then he had to go take care of his sick family or something. Sounds like a *real* nice guy.'

'Did you see him this morning?'

'He dropped by my trailer, an' I directed him to the other hairdresser.' She rolled her eyes. 'I must be gettin' soft in the head – the man's a freakin' stud!'

'Really?' Lara said. Actors didn't do anything for her, they were too self-involved and needy, always concerned about themselves first.

'Kyle's gonna shit a brick when he sees him,' Roxy said with a manic giggle. 'Shit a *freakin'* brick!'

'He's *supposed* to be attractive,' Lara explained, sitting down. 'Why would my character let him pick her up if he wasn't?'

'There's attractive, then there's major babe,' Roxy said knowingly, licking her glossy lips. 'This one's m.b. I'm tellin' you, Kyle ain't gonna like it.'

Half an hour later Lara strolled over to the set where Miles greeted her with a kiss on each cheek. 'Gorgeous as ever, my darling.'

She looked around. Kyle was nowhere in sight.

'Our other star is on his way,' Miles said, reading her thoughts. 'He's having a slight hair problem today. As soon as he arrives, we'll rehearse.'

'Where's the actor playing Jeff?'

'Under that swarm of women over there.'

Lara glanced across the set. 'Everyone's talking about him. Who is he?'

'Didn't think he'd cause *this* much of a commotion,' Miles said, clicking his fingers at Jane. 'Bring Joey over. Miss Ivory would like to meet him.'

☆

When Jane tapped him on the shoulder and told him the director wanted to see him, Joey was on his feet in a flash.

Lara watched as he approached. For a second she felt a jolt of pure sexual hunger – the kind of feeling she hadn't experienced in a long time. Roxy was right, this was one good-looking guy.

Cassie, hovering somewhere behind her chair, muttered an awed, 'Oh, my! Time to go on a diet!'

Lara remained cool, checking him out as he drew nearer.

Joey took one look at Lara Ivory and was overcome by her startling beauty. She was exquisite – from her honey-blond hair falling softly around her smooth shoulders, to her beautiful face and incredible body. He was immediately aroused, something that never happened to him unless he wanted it to.

Miles stepped between them. 'Joey, say hello to Lara Ivory. I'm sure you've seen her in many movies.'

Lara stood up and extended her hand. He took it in his. An electric shock went right through him as he stared into her direct green eyes. 'It . . . it's a privilege to be workin' with you today,' he managed.

She smiled, a soft, generous smile capable of driving a man totally crazy. 'Thank you,' she said.

'While we're waiting for Kyle to put in an appearance,' Miles said, oblivious to the sexual tension steaming up the set, 'let's run your dialogue.'

'Good idea,' Lara agreed.

Joey continued to stare, unable to take his eyes off her – she was mesmerizing.

In the scene he was sitting at the bar while she and Kyle were at a table exchanging insults which culminated in Kyle's abrupt exit.

Joey began to read from his script – even though he'd learned his dialogue and was word-perfect.

'I've been watching you,' he said, in character as Jeff. A pause. 'Was that your husband who walked out?'

'He's not my husband,' Lara replied, suitably flippant.

'Then . . . I guess you're free to dance with me.'

A coquettish tilt of her head. 'Why would I do that?'

''Cause I think it's what you want to do.'

At that point in the script she was supposed to get up and head for the dance floor with him. It was a short scene, but their chemistry together was undeniable.

They read the scene through twice, and were about to do

it a third time, when Kyle appeared, striding onto the set like the movie star he was.

Miles said, 'Kyle, meet Joey Lorenzo – he's playing Jeff.'

Kyle nodded curtly, barely acknowledging him. 'Let's go,' he said to Miles, cracking his knuckles. 'I'm ready to rock 'n' roll.'

'Fine with me,' Miles said. 'We'll start with you and Lara at the table. Joey, for the master you'll be at the bar.'

They all moved in front of the camera, Lara and Kyle in the foreground, Joey at the bar.

'OK, everyone,' the first AD shouted, 'we're going for a rehearsal. Let's have some quiet.'

Kyle and Lara rehearsed their scene several times before Miles was satisfied. Then the make-up and hair people ran in, powdering and primping the two stars. Finally they were ready to shoot.

Kyle was not one-take Charlie. They went through nine takes before Miles was satisfied and yelled a terse, 'Cut! OK, print it!'

Joey had nothing to do except sit at the bar watching them. He was hot and pissed off, with a hard-on against Kyle Carson, who'd treated him like he was a lowly extra. Big movie star asshole. Who exactly did he think he was?

Lara Ivory had his attention full-time. Ms Ivory, he decided, was too fucking beautiful for her own good.

At the lunch break Trinee commandeered him. 'Let's go,' she said cheerfully. 'I'm accompanying you to the lunch truck, protectin' you from the women.'

'What're you talkin' about?' he asked, like he hadn't noticed that every female on the set was trying to get close to him.

'I'm with you, man,' Trinee announced, appointing herself best friend. 'We engaged people gotta stick together.'

He grinned and kept watching Lara as Miles took her arm and they left the set together.

Was she sleeping with the director?

No, she had too much class for that.

'Where's Barbara Westerberg?' he asked Trinee, thinking it was about time he put his charm to good use. 'Haven't seen her around.'

'She doesn't get to the set until the afternoon,' Trinee said. 'Stays about an hour – then leaves. That's what producers do, unless they're the line producer – then they're on your ass the whole time.'

'How long you been in this business?'

'Two years,' Trinee answered proudly. 'I'm learning. One of these days I'm gonna be a producer.'

'Can you do that?'

'Why not? It's about time. How many Hispanic female producers you see around? Anyway – my fiancé says I can.' She giggled. '*I'll* be a producer, and *he'll* be world heavyweight champion. What you think?'

'Sounds good to me.'

'We'd better put an old T-shirt on you,' she said. 'Just in case you ruin your clothes over lunch.'

He followed her to the wardrobe trailer where Eric was stretched out on the floor engaging in vigorous push-ups.

'Oh!' Eric exclaimed. 'It's the engaged couple!'

'*Veree* funny,' Trinee said, stepping over him.

'Is there a gym around here?' Joey asked. He needed to work out, keep himself in prime physical shape.

'Yes, and it's Kyle's,' Eric said. 'Mr Carson has his own personal gym trailer. I'm sure he'll let you use it. *Not!*'

'He seems like a nice enough guy,' Joey said carefully.

'Just you wait,' Eric said, pursing his lips. 'Mr Americana is a snake in the ass.'

'What's *that* mean?'

'How many lines do you have?' Eric asked, getting up off the floor.

'Not that many.'

'You'll end up with one line and a knockout punch,' Eric said knowingly. 'That's if you're lucky.'

Joey's stomach knotted up, it was shit being nobody. *He* should be the star. *He* should have everything Kyle Carson had.

'Hey,' he said easily. 'Doesn't bother me.'

Trinee tossed him an old denim shirt. He took off his jacket and shirt and put it on.

She hung his movie clothes on a hanger. 'You coming for lunch, Eric?' she asked.

'Wouldn't miss the maddening crowds,' Eric said, reaching for a pink sweater to throw over his Hawaiian shorts.

☆

They watched the dailies in Barbara Westerberg's trailer. Lara studied her performance, noting every move. The streaks in her hair worked perfectly, she made a mental note to congratulate Roxy.

Kyle had genuine screen magic, and they were definitely a hot couple, which pleased her. This would be an easy shoot, and the result was sure to equal excellent box office. She needed a light frothy comedy to counterbalance the more serious roles she'd been playing lately.

'*I'm* happy,' Miles said, as Barbara clicked off the VCR. 'Everyone else satisfied?'

'No criticism,' Barbara said. 'Nice hair, Lara.'

'How about me?' Kyle said, glaring a little.

'Kyle, you *know* you're the best-looking man on the screen today,' Barbara said, feeding his ferocious ego. 'You put Kevin Costner and Michael Douglas to shame.'

'Michael Douglas!' Kyle exploded. 'He's fifteen years older than me.'

'And *looks* it,' Barbara assured him.

'I'm off to grab a quick bite of lunch,' Lara said, anxious to get out of Kyle's way.

'I'll come with you,' Miles said, taking her arm.

They left the trailer together. 'I know you think Kyle's an asshole,' Miles said. 'But you have to admit the two of you are pretty damn hot together.'

'Ah . . . movie magic,' Lara said, laughing softly. 'Fools 'em every time.'

'*You've* always had movie magic,' Miles said admiringly. 'Even in our first film together. You were so young and innocent and—'

'And playing a hooker,' she interrupted matter-of-factly. 'Every healthy American male's fantasy. The sweet little whore who stops turning tricks for the right man.'

'It worked for you, babe,' Miles said, with a quick laugh. 'Made you a star. Did the same for Julia Roberts in *Pretty Woman*.'

'There's nothing like a good hooker role to jump-start a career,' Lara said drily.

'That or a spread in *Playboy*,' Miles added. 'Which, of course, you never did.'

'No, Miles. Taking off my clothes for a bunch of horny guys to jerk off over is not my idea of a good time.'

Cassie appeared as they approached the catering truck. 'Can I get you anything, Lara?'

'I'm fine,' she replied, noticing Joey Lorenzo sitting at a table surrounded by women.

Miles said, 'I'll have a bite in my trailer. Work calls.'

Lara turned back to Cassie. 'Same for me. Something light, maybe a salad.'

'It's done.'

She took another look at Joey and his female entourage. He glanced up. Their eyes met for a few seconds. She smiled, that cool little smile she used to such good advantage. Then she turned and walked to her trailer.

He was an engaged man. A flirtation was out of the question.

11

Joey caught her looking at him a few times, but that was about as near as he got to the delectable Ms Ivory. He kept his distance, well aware she must be so used to men going apeshit over her that the only way he had a chance was to make her realize he was different.

He sat at the bar playing background all day, waiting for them to reach his scene – which they never did on account of the fact that Kyle Carson was the slowest actor on two legs and seemed incapable of getting anything right.

Trinee kept him company between shots, giving him a running commentary on everyone involved with the film. She'd warmed up considerably since he'd revealed that he too was engaged.

'Tell me about Lara Ivory,' he asked casually. 'What's she really like?'

'Oh, everyone loves Lara,' Trinee replied. 'She's very popular. No big-star trips with that lady.' She shot him a quick glance. 'Gorgeous, isn't she?'

Joey nodded. 'Who's she sleeping with?'

'How would I know?'

'C'mon, Trinee, if she's in bed with someone it must be all over the set.'

'Word is she doesn't do it with just anyone.'

'How come?'

'She's particular.' Trinee yawned, bored with talking about Lara. 'So,' she said. 'Your fiancée gonna visit us?'

'She might,' Joey answered vaguely. 'How about yours?'

'Marek's coming for the weekend,' Trinee said, with a huge grin. 'An', man, this girl can't wait!'

☆

That night Lara had a long phone conversation with Nikki. They spoke about Richard and his satisfaction with her performance and the way the editing was going on *French Summer*. Then they discussed *The Dreamer*, and Lara began telling Kyle Carson tales.

Nikki started to laugh – she couldn't get enough. 'He sounds like the definitive Mr Big Star,' she said. 'A true pain in the ass.'

'You've got that right,' Lara responded. 'And slow. The crew are calling him Ten-take Kyle!' They both giggled. 'How's Summer doing?'

'I can't control her,' Nikki said. 'All she cares about is parties, parties and more parties!'

'It's her age,' Lara assured her. 'She fails to see you as a mother figure. After all, you're only seventeen years older than her, she's probably a little jealous.'

'Nonsense,' Nikki said firmly. 'Why would Summer be jealous of *me*? She's gorgeous.'

'So are you – with personality, a great career, and a well-known and respected husband.'

'No,' Nikki said. 'It's not the jealousy thing. Girls of Summer's age think everyone's a raving idiot, and that they're the smartest person on the planet. I know I was like that, weren't you?'

'I don't remember,' Lara said quickly.

Nikki knew Lara didn't like talking about her childhood, it obviously hadn't been very happy. All she knew was that Lara's parents had been killed in a car crash when she was very young, and that she'd been raised by various relatives. Once she'd asked Richard. 'Lara doesn't get into her past,' he'd said. 'Leave it alone.' So she had.

'Anyway,' Lara continued. 'Don't worry about Summer, she'll come around.'

'I sure hope so,' Nikki said glumly. 'I'm beginning to feel like nag of the year.'

'I'll read the script as soon as it gets here,' Lara promised.

'Then call me at once. Can't wait to get your reaction.'

Lara put the phone down and wandered out onto the back deck, staring out into the darkness. She wanted to walk along the beach, but not by herself, the dark was too scary.

Sometimes everything was too scary . . . Especially when

the memories came back to haunt her. The nightmare memories . . .

☆

'Scaredy cat!' Andy, her older brother, yelled in her face. 'Skinny little scaredy cat!'

'I'm not! I'm not!' Lara Ann responded.

'Yes you are,' said Andy. He was eight and very handsome. When they weren't fighting Lara Ann worshipped him.

'Mommy, Mommy – can I have another piece of chicken?' Lara Ann asked.

'What, honey?' Ellen, her mother, seemed distracted as she moved around the kitchen.

'More chicken, Mommy, it's sooo yummy.'

'Sorry, honey, I have to save some for your daddy.'

'Why must we wait for him?' demanded Andy. 'He's always late.'

''Cause Mama says we have to,' Lara Ann said, primly.

'You shut up,' Andy said, sticking out his tongue behind his mother's back.

'No, you shut up,' Lara Ann retorted, red in the face. 'Mama's always right – aren't you, Mama?'

'Hush, both of you,' Ellen said, brushing back a loose strand of hair. She was an exquisitely pretty woman, with wide-set hazel eyes and natural blond hair that fell in soft waves below her shoulders.

Lara Ann gazed up at her mother and sighed wistfully. 'I wanna be just like you one day, Mommy. You're sooo pretty.'

'Thank you, darling,' Ellen said, removing a carton of chocolate ice cream from the freezer. 'You're pretty too.'

'No, she's not,' taunted Andy. 'She's a stupid dumb girl.'

'Can I be a famous artist when I grow up, Mama?' Lara Ann asked, ignoring him. She'd been thinking about school and all the fun she'd had in painting class. 'Can I?'

'You can be whatever you want, my sweet,' Ellen answered, gently touching her daughter's cheek.

'I know what you can be,' sneered Andy. 'You can be the ugliest girl on the block.'

'I've told you once, Andy,' Ellen said crossly, 'and I'm not telling you again. Do not be mean to your little sister.'

'I'm *not mean*,' Lara Ann said proudly. 'I'm *nice*.'

'You're mean, too,' Andy retorted. 'Mean! Mean! Mean!'

'No I'm not.'

'Yes you are.'

'Will you two behave yourselves,' Ellen exclaimed. 'I'm not in the mood today.'

'Can I watch Charlie's Angels, please, Mama?' Lara Ann asked.

'No, I wanna see Dukes of Hazzard,' Andy interrupted.

'It's Lara Ann's turn to choose,' Ellen said. 'Tonight you'll both watch Charlie's Angels.'

'Piss!' Andy said.

Ellen frowned. 'What did you say?'

'Piss! Piss! Piss!'

'When your father gets home he'll wash your mouth out with soap, young man.'

'Don' care.'

'You will when he hears what you've been saying.'

'Mama,' Lara Ann asked, her pretty little face completely innocent, 'what's a cocksucker?'

'What? What did you say?' Andy began to snigger. 'Where did you hear a word like that?' Ellen asked, her cheeks flushing red.

'Daddy said it one day about Mr Dunn.'

'Your daddy does not use language like that.'

'He does! He does! I heard him.'

'No, he doesn't. And don't ever say that word again. It's a very bad word.'

'What's it mean, Mama?'

'I know what it means,' Andy said, smirking. 'It's when a man puts his dickie in a stupid girl's mouth.'

Ellen turned on him angrily. 'Stop it, Andy. Stop it right now!'

At that moment the door opened and Lara Ann's father, Dan, walked in. He was a big, blustery man – handsome, although heavy around the jowls, with a gut that was growing every day.

'Daddy, Daddy!' Lara Ann squealed, running over to him, throwing herself into his arms. Dan swept up his little daughter, hugging and kissing her. She smelled liquor on his breath, but she was used to it. Her father owned a liquor store, and every Saturday morning he took her there, and sometimes, when it wasn't busy, they'd sit in the back and he'd let her drink as many Coca-Colas as she could manage, while he'd swig Scotch from the bottle and warn her not to tell.

'Can I have half your chicken, Daddy?' she asked, cuddling up to him.

'You're late,' Ellen said, moving over to the stove, sounding grumpy.

'Glad you noticed,' Dan replied, putting Lara Ann down.

'What's that supposed to mean?' Ellen asked.

'You know what it means,' he said, swaying slightly.

'No, I don't.'

Dan pulled out a chair at the kitchen table, sat down, and told the two children to go in the other room and watch TV.

'I wanna stay with you, Daddy,' Lara Ann objected, clinging onto his hand.

'No, pumpkin,' he said, giving her a little shove. 'I'll see you after I've had my dinner.'

'C'mon, scaredy cat,' Andy said, pulling her arm.

Ellen wagged a warning finger at her handsome son. 'Don't forget – Charlie's Angels.'

Lara Ann sat quietly in front of the television staring at Farrah Fawcett and her glorious mane of golden curls. Andy picked up a toy car and began zooming it around the living room floor making loud car noises. 'Be quiet, Andy,' she said.

'No!' he said, sticking out his tongue again. 'You're a stupid girl. Girls gotta shut up.'

'No they don't.'

'Yes they do.'

'No they don't.'

They were so busy arguing that at first they didn't hear the raised voices coming from the kitchen.

Then Andy said, 'They're fighting again – shush!'

'Bitch!' they heard Dan shout. 'Cheating bitch!'

Then Ellen's voice. 'How dare you accuse me.'

'I'll accuse you of what I want. Everybody in town's talking about you and that dentist! It's not just your teeth he's filling, Ellen . . . it's not just your fucking teeth.'

'Elliott Dunn is nothing more than a friend.'

'Yeah, a friend who screws your ass off.'

The raised voices frightened Lara Ann. 'What are they talking about?' she whispered.

'Dunno,' Andy said.

'I refuse to be the laughing stock of this town,' Dan yelled. 'Oh, no – not me. Not Dan Leonard.'

'People like to gossip, there's nothing going on.'

'Says you.'

'It's the truth.' A moment of silence – then— 'Dan . . . Oh my . . . what are you doing? What are you doing?'

'Defending my fucking manhood. Something I should've done a long time ago.'

'Don't be silly, Dan.' Ellen's voice rose in panic. 'This . . . isn't . . . sane. PLEASE DON'T . . . DON'T . . . NOOO!'

There was a terrifically loud explosion. Lara Ann jumped, and covered her ears. She knew something bad had happened.

Andy leaped up.

'Don't go,' Lara Ann whimpered, clinging to his arm. 'I'm frightened, Andy. Stay here with me.'

'I gotta go see,' he said, pulling away and running into the kitchen.

Lara Ann cowered on the couch. She heard her father bellow something, then the sound of a short struggle, and after that another loud explosion.

She stayed exactly where she was, still covering her ears.

Suddenly her father ran into the room with a wild look in his eyes. 'C'mon, pumpkin,' he said, pulling her up.

His eyes were all bloodshot and scary, but she loved her father more than anything in the world, so she didn't argue.

'Where are we going, Daddy?' she asked meekly.

'Away from here,' he muttered, scooping her into his arms and carrying her through the kitchen.

Sprawled on the kitchen floor was her mother, a thin spiral of smoke snaking out of a gaping hole in her chest.

Slumped by the door was her brother, his head blown half away. There was blood everywhere.

'Daddy! Daddy! Daddy!' Lara Ann began to scream. 'Mommy's been hurt. Mommy's bleeding. So's Andy.'

He wasn't listening. He carried her out the door and almost threw her in the back of his car. Then he jumped in the driving seat and roared away from the house.

'Daddy, Daddy,' she whimpered, so frightened she could scarcely breathe. 'What happened? Why's my mommy on the floor? Why's Andy all bloody?'

'Nothing,' he muttered, picking up a bottle of Scotch from the seat next to him and taking a swig. 'They'll be fine.'

She squeezed her eyes tightly shut, bringing her knees up to her chest. 'Daddy, something bad happened! Who did that to Mommy and Andy? Who did it?'

'Your mother got what she deserved,' he muttered. 'Cheating bitch!'

Lara Ann began to cry, big gulping sobs that shook her entire body.

Dan drove to a motel, stopped at the desk and got a key. Next he parked outside a room and carried her inside. She was still crying, a river of silent tears running down her face. She loved her father, and yet she knew in her heart he'd done something terribly bad.

'Sit down and watch the TV,' he ordered gruffly.

'I wanna go home,' she whimpered.

'Do as I say. Switch on the TV, and don' start whining like your mother.'

He slumped into a chair, taking another swig from the bottle of Scotch, which was now almost empty.

Her daddy had never spoken to her so harshly, but she knew his anger had something to do with the bottle in his hand. Andy had told her that when people drank stuff like that they got drunk. And when they were drunk they got sick and talked in a funny way. Her daddy was sick.

As the evening wore on, she grew more and more exhausted. Her father went out to the car and came back with another full bottle of Scotch. She peeked at him as he drank the whole bottle, muttering to himself.

Later that night she heard the sound of police sirens in the distance. Her father heard it, too, because he sat up very straight and stared right at her. 'Y' look jus' like your mother,' he said, slurring his words. 'You're pretty, but inside you're a slut, like your mother. An ... ugly ... little ... slut. Thass' what all women are. Unnerstan' me?'

Her eyes filled with more tears and rolled down her cheeks. Her father had never said such horrible things to her before. She'd always been his favourite, he'd always loved her.

Her world was crumbling and there was nothing she could do. 'I want Andy,' she cried out. 'And I want my mommy.'

Dan took a gun from his pocket.

Thrill!

Lara Ann stared at the harsh glint of metal. He was going to shoot her, just like she'd seen people get shot on Charlie's Angels, *just like he'd shot Mama and Andy. She wouldn't even have a chance to grow up.*

'Daddy—' she started to say, her little face puckering.

'Doncha ever forget,' he mumbled, his mouth twitching. 'Inside you're an ugly slut, jus' like your cheatin' mother.'

Then he put the gun in his mouth and blew his brains out.

Blood and hair and pieces of flesh splattered all over her.

She was five years old.

☆

After a while Lara went back inside, contemplating another long lonely night.

It was OK, she was used to being by herself. She'd manage. She always had.

12

Alison Sewell first spotted Lara Ivory at a film premiere. At the time Alison was trapped behind a pack of stinking sweaty men, all of them blocking her way.

Alison was not popular with her fellow photographers, so any time they could keep her from getting the shot, they did. Truth was they hated her.

Alison didn't care, she had ways to outsmart them – her ways. A swift kick in the shins. A lethal knitting needle thrust into a vulnerable body part. A feigned fainting fit. Oh yes, Alison had tricks that could get her anything she wanted. After all, she was a woman – so the pigs thought twice about fighting back.

One guy tried. He tripped her up, following this move with a vicious punch. She promptly sued him. They came to an arrangement out of court, giving her a six-thousand-dollar settlement. It was a warning to all of them. Don't mess with Alison Sewell or you'll regret it.

She'd been in the business for eight years, taking over from Uncle Cyril when he succumbed to throat cancer. She made a reasonable living catching celebrities and politicians doing things they never wanted to be seen doing. Once a month she flew to New York. Three times a year she covered Washington. Every night she was out on the streets staking the openings, fancy premieres and parties. She had photos of OJ during the famous freeway chase; she was outside the house when he was arrested; she'd caught Johnny Romano with a hooker; Madonna in Miami with a new toy boy; Venus Maria topless by her swimming pool.

Yes, Alison Sewell got the gritty pictures the tabloids craved. And for that, several photo editors paid her handsomely, although none of them particularly liked her.

Alison didn't give a damn; she had no personal life. Men didn't attract her, nor did women. Sex was the cause of all evil, and Alison Sewell simply wasn't interested.

She lived with her mother – now bedridden – in Uncle Cyril's house, which he'd left to them in his will. Most days she slept, hitting the streets at night clad in her uniform of army combat pants, sturdy hiking boots, brown T-shirt and a flak jacket with numerous pockets in which she stored her precious film.

Alison worked alone. She didn't need anyone slowing her down.

In all her travels she'd never actually seen Lara Ivory in the flesh. And the first time she did, it was a striking revelation. Pure innocent beauty. A face so perfect Alison almost cried out.

She automatically raised her camera above her head, popping off as many shots as she could. Then she went home and developed the film in the shed Uncle Cyril had converted into a dark room at the back of the house.

When the finished images came to life, Alison was stunned by Lara's incomparable freshness and staggering beauty. Hers was the most special face she'd ever photographed, and she immediately wanted more.

After that she didn't look back. Lara Ivory became her major obsession.

Like a ravenous lion tracking its prey, Alison set about finding out everything she could concerning the famous star. She changed her working habits to include any event Lara might attend and was always up front, kicking anyone who got in her way.

Soon Lara began to recognize her, favouring her with a smile, a friendly wave. Alison saw this as a sign. She began writing notes and printing up photos for her idol and handing them to her – or trying to. Usually some unwanted publicity flack or bodyguard came between them, blocking her line of communication. This infuriated her, because surely – without interference – they could become friends.

Alison had never had a friend, somebody to talk to and confide in. All she had was her mother, who did nothing but whine and complain as she lay in bed withering away, her frail body riddled with cancer.

'*That'll* teach you to smoke,' Alison scolded almost every day, the same thing she'd said to Uncle Cyril when he was dying.

Alison didn't smoke. Instead she ate chocolate bars – sometimes seven or eight a day. They might make her fat, but she wasn't stupid enough to smoke like her two closest relatives. Look where it had gotten *them*.

One day Alison decided to pay Lara a visit. She'd located her address in a 'map of the stars' book, and kept it beside her bed for two weeks before getting up early on a Saturday morning, and setting off in her beat-up old station wagon for the long drive to Hidden Valley Road – which, according to the star book, was located somewhere off Sunset.

Alison was excited. It was a bold thing to do, but she knew in her heart that Lara would welcome her. She took with her a scrapbook she'd put together – a pictorial record of Lara's comings and goings for the last three months. There were some wonderful photos, but the only one the tabloids had chosen to run was Lara and her current boyfriend, a man called Lee Randolph, having an obvious fight in public.

Alison did not like this Lee Randolph character. He was not good enough for her Lara, she deserved better. Although why Lara needed a man was beyond Alison's comprehension. Men were pigs. They farted and swore and spat and fought. They were liars and cheats and philanderers and Alison hated them all.

When she reached the house she was surprised to find it unprotected. No high hedges or big iron gates. Just a driveway leading up to the simple-looking – although quite large – ranch house.

She rang the doorbell and waited. Just her luck – Lee Randolph came to the door.

'Yes?' he said. 'Can I help you?'

'Uh . . . I've got something for Lara.'

'I'll take it.'

'No! I need to see her personally.'

He gave her a funny look and told her to wait. Then he closed the door in her face, and ten minutes later the police were there asking what she wanted.

That bastard! If Lara only knew what he was doing. He

wasn't protecting her, he was isolating her from her real friends.

She informed the cops she was a loyal friend of Lara Ivory's, but the sonsofbitches didn't believe her, and she was forced to leave, mission unaccomplished.

After that she started writing Lara letters – one or two a day – rambling on about how unworthy Lee Randolph was – what a moron her publicist was – how if only people would get out of their way they could be friends.

And then she started going back to Lara's house – sometimes seeing the housekeeper or Lara's assistant or Lee. Each time she was there someone called the police, until eventually the cops told her that if she came back again they'd arrest her for stalking.

Stalking! Who did they think she was – John Hinckley? What a bunch of dummies. She was Lara's friend, that's all. She didn't mean her any harm.

But Alison didn't want trouble, so she stopped visiting the house and instead continued sending letters and photographing Lara whenever she could.

After a while she started noticing that the people around Lara – her so-called protectors – began instructing their star not to look in her direction or go near her at premieres and big functions.

At first she thought it was her imagination. But no, it was actually happening. Lara no longer smiled and waved. The intimate looks stopped. And Alison began to get furious. Truly furious.

She had to do something to regain Lara's trust and attention.

Something that nobody would forget.

13

Before Joey knew it, Friday arrived, and they still hadn't gotten to his scene. For three days he'd been stuck on a bar stool observing Kyle Mr Big Star Carson blow take after take, while Lara sat there serene and lovely – never once complaining.

Kyle was a major dick – he refused to acknowledge him, acting as if he didn't exist, which pissed Joey off as he wasn't used to being ignored. The women on the set made up for it. In spite of the fact they thought he was engaged, he was getting more invitations than he could handle. Truth was he could've nailed any one of them, including Trinee. But he didn't. There was a time and a place, and this wasn't it. Besides, since setting eyes on Lara, he had no desire to do so. Instead he concentrated on charming them all, weaving tales about his lawyer fiancée and how smart she was.

They ate it up. Women loved a man they thought they couldn't get.

Every day Lara seemed to go out of her way to greet him with a friendly wave and a smile. They'd never had a conversation, but he knew she was aware of his presence. Of course, it would be hard for her not to be, since he was always in the background of her scene, watching her.

He'd made it his business to find out more about her. Trinee was right, she *wasn't* in bed with the director, she *didn't* have a current boyfriend. She was staying in a rented house on the beach with her assistant and a guard, and everyone seemed to love her.

In spite of her friendly demeanour it appeared to Joey she was a loner – exactly like him. His kind of woman. But for once in his life he was too edgy to go for it.

Joey Lorenzo. Stud supreme. There was no way he'd risk a turn-down.

Madelaine had threatened to arrive that evening, so his immediate problem was figuring out a way to stop her. He borrowed a cellphone from one of the crew and called her. 'You're not gonna believe this,' he said in a husky voice.

'What?' Madelaine asked suspiciously.

'I got a bitch of a sore throat. It's so freakin' bad I can barely speak. Only good thing is they'll never get to my scene today. I gotta be OK by Monday, so I'm gonna spend the weekend in bed drinkin' hot tea an' missin' you.'

'Wouldn't hear of it,' Madelaine said briskly. 'I'll come look after you.'

'No, honey, no,' he said. 'I'm serious about this. I have to rest up.'

'But, Joey,' she said, hating herself for sounding needy, 'I was looking forward to seeing you.'

'Jeez, Madelaine,' he snapped. 'Don't make me feel guilty about bein' sick. It's my big scene on Monday – you understand, don't you?'

'Yes,' she said reluctantly. 'I suppose you're right.'

'Doesn't mean I won't miss you,' he said, turning on the charm again.

'Are you sure?'

Now the full seduction voice came into play. 'C'mon, baby, you *know* I will.'

That taken care of, he headed back to the set.

☆

Lara had read through the script of *Revenge* three times, and although it was a tough read on account of the language, honesty and violence, she'd recognized that it was a powerful piece – and with the right director it could be an amazing film.

Placing the script in her purse, she left her trailer and headed for the set, literally bumping into Joey Lorenzo on the way.

'Sorry!' he said, stepping back.

'No, *I'm* sorry it's taking so long to get to our scene,' she said, and for some unknown reason she felt her heart fluttering. 'You must be going nuts watching us flub lines.'

Once again, up close and personal, he marvelled at her dazzling beauty. ''S OK,' he said, managing to sound casual. 'I'm gettin' used to sittin' on a bar stool – takes me back to my juvenile delinquent days.'

'Oh, yes?' she said, with a beauteous smile, thinking that he was quite incredibly handsome and funny too. 'Was that so long ago?'

'A while.'

'Shy about your age,' she teased.

'I'm thirty – how old are you?'

She was not used to being asked such a direct question. 'Actually, I'm thirty-two,' she said, answering him anyway. 'My publicist keeps on urging me to say I'm twenty-nine. But since every magazine knows the truth, I keep on telling him it's somewhat pointless.'

They both laughed.

'It can't be easy being as famous as you,' he said, unable to stop himself from staring.

'It's not,' she replied, meeting his gaze. 'Although it does have compensations.'

'Yeah,' he grinned. 'I bet.'

Jane barged between them. 'Both of you are needed on the set,' she said officiously.

'Thank you, Jane,' Lara said, dismissing her in a nice way. She began walking towards the action. Joey fell into step beside her.

'I hear you're engaged to a lawyer,' she said. 'That must be an interesting profession.'

'Yeah,' he said. 'When the OJ case was goin' on I had my own runnin' commentary. *She* should've been up there instead of Marcia Clark – she'd've done a better job.'

'Have you been engaged long?'

'A year,' he lied. 'It's kinda like a commitment without being the final closed door, y'know what I mean?'

She laughed softly. 'I'm sure your fiancée would love to hear *that*.'

'Hey—' he said quickly, lest she thought less of him. 'I didn't mean it in a bad way. It's just that – well, y'know, marriage is important to me. When I get married, it's gonna last for ever.' He looked at her intently. 'Isn't that how you feel?'

'My track record's somewhat blurred,' she said, thinking that was exactly how she'd felt when she'd married Richard. 'I'm divorced.'

'Didn't know that.'

'Hmm ... I guess you don't read *People* magazine,' she said lightly. 'My divorce was rather public.'

'Who was the lucky guy?'

'Richard Barry, the director,' she replied as they arrived back on the set.

'How long were you married?'

'Long enough to realize it was a mistake. The good news is we're friends now.'

'That's nice.'

'Time to work,' she said crisply. 'And if Kyle stops tripping over his lines, maybe we'll get to your scene this afternoon.'

'That'd be a surprise.'

They held a long, steady look. He was making her nervous, the way his eyes seemed to penetrate right through her. 'Uh ... I'm glad we finally got to talk,' she said.

'Yeah,' he said, still watching her closely.

'Is your fiancée visiting you this weekend?' she asked. *Oh, God, Lara, what a stupid question!*

'No, she's workin' a case. Why?'

'Oh,' she said, groping for a reason. 'I ... uh ... was going to invite the two of you to a party at my house tomorrow night.'

'Yeah?'

She couldn't believe the words coming out of her mouth. Was she insane? She had no party planned. 'It'll be fun,' she continued. 'Yoko and Roxy are coming, and most of the crew.'

His black eyes continued to draw her in. 'OK if I drop by alone?'

'Of course,' she replied, slightly breathless.

'Then I'll be there.'

'Good. Oh, and if your fiancée *should* arrive, please bring her.' She made a quick escape, hurrying over to Miles, who waited impatiently. *I'm having a party*, she thought. *Better get Cassie on the case immediately. She'll be thrilled.*

Joey watched her go. She was certainly something else.

Knockout beautiful, incredibly nice and friendly. Not like any woman *he'd* ever known.

Lara Ivory was the real thing and he desperately wanted her.

Joey Lorenzo had never met the real thing before.

14

Nikki sat on the American Airlines plane on her way to New York. She'd told Richard a couple of days ago that she planned to visit Lara.

'Why?' he'd asked irritably.

'Because it's important. I need to get her reaction to the script.'

'*Revenge* is not a project for Lara to be involved in,' he'd said in his *I know best* voice. 'She's a big movie star, you're making a small film.'

'I know. But she is considering it. Think what a coup it would be if I got her!'

'You can't go asking favours.'

'It'll be entirely her decision.'

'She won't do it, Nikki.'

'Wasn't it you who said that one of the most important things a producer can do is follow their instincts? Well, that's what I'm doing.'

'If you have to – then go.'

'And you'll take care of Summer?'

'She'll be fine with me.'

Later, she'd spoken to Summer, telling her that Richard had promised to watch out for her.

'Excellent!' Summer had said. 'Richard's the greatest.'

'I'll be back in two days. You'll have a nice time together.'

'I'm having a good time anyway,' Summer had said. 'LA's amazing. Wish I could stay here for ever.'

'Do you?' Nikki had said, quite surprised. She could just imagine Sheldon's face if she told him his daughter wanted to live permanently in California. He'd be furious. Summer was his precious prize – there was no way he'd let her go.

'We'll discuss it when I get back,' she'd promised.

Now she was on her way, ready to talk Lara into the role of her life.

She slept most of the flight, trying to avoid conversation with the German businessman sitting beside her whose reading material consisted of *Penthouse, Playboy* and the *Wall Street Journal.* He ignored the *Journal,* and studied the centre-folds at least twenty times, grunting to himself.

'You need to get laid,' she muttered, as they disembarked.

The man frowned, small raisin eyes under monstrous bushy eyebrows. 'Excuse me?'

'I said the stewardess needs to get paid – for the headphones.'

His frown deepened. American women were very strange.

Lara had sent a limo to the airport. Nikki got in and settled back, enjoying the ride to the Hamptons.

By the time she arrived it was past seven and Lara was home from her day's work.

'What a house!' Nikki exclaimed, walking around. 'It's so charming.'

'I'm considering making an offer,' Lara said.

'You're not contemplating moving?'

'No. I'd use it as a retreat, somewhere nobody could find me.'

'That's right – become even more reclusive!'

'I'm not reclusive.'

'Says you.'

Later they had dinner on the back deck.

'Well?' Nikki asked, unable to wait any longer. 'What's your opinion of the script?'

'Truth?' Lara said, teasing her.

'Of *course* the truth.'

Lara smiled. 'I love it!'

Nikki sat up straight. 'You do?'

'It's everything I wanted it to be.'

'Am I pleased to hear that!' A beat. 'Now the really important question – will you do it?'

'Well . . .'

Nikki leaned across the table, her excitement palpable.

'Yes!' Lara said. 'I will!'

'Thank you, God,' Nikki said fervently, clasping her

hands in front of her. 'I promise I'll be good for the rest of the year!'

☆

With Nikki safely out of the way, Summer planned on having an even better time. She called Richard in the editing rooms and begged off dinner – saying she had to attend a friend's birthday party.

Richard was quite agreeable. 'Don't be home too late,' he said. 'And for God's sake don't tell your mother I didn't take you to dinner.'

'Is it OK if I invite a few friends over on Sunday?' she asked, figuring she'd strike while he was in an amiable mood.

'Fine,' he said. 'I'm working all weekend.'

Goodbye, Richard, she thought gleefully. Much as she liked him, she preferred total freedom.

Jumping out of bed, she tried to decide what to do today. If only she could drive. Well, the truth was she *could* drive, but if she got busted behind the wheel of either Richard's or Nikki's car she'd be in deep shit on account of the fact that she wasn't yet sixteen, and she didn't think that either of them would appreciate a visit to the police station to bail her out. Cabs were eating up all her cash, even though she was getting money from Richard, Nikki, *and* her father. She'd sent Daddy Dearest a frantic letter informing him that Nikki hardly gave her anything, and in return he'd mailed her five hundred dollars without so much as questioning what she needed it for.

She'd already made up her mind that the best thing would be to stay in LA, have Daddy Dearest send her money, and eventually move into a place of her own. After all, she'd be sixteen in a couple of months – she'd be able to drive legally. How radical would *that* be!

Of course, she thought sourly, Sheldon wouldn't appreciate her staying in California, he'd hate her being so far away. But if he put up a fight she could always blackmail him. She had stuff on Mr Big Shot Famous Psychiatrist that he wouldn't want anyone knowing – not even his precious Rachel, who in spite of being nice was a bit dense.

Oh, yes, if she wanted, she could blow his happy little

deal in a second. *And* blow everyone's mind in the process. Especially Nikki's.

Hmm . . . if Daddy Dearest *didn't* cooperate, maybe she'd do just that.

She called Jed, who offered to pick her up and take her on a club spree. Jed had turned out to be the perfect contact, he seemed to know everybody – introducing her around as Richard Barry's daughter – which got her plenty of attention. She'd already been out with him a couple of times, and met all kinds of people – including Tina, an amazing-looking girl of eighteen, who, she'd decided, would be her new best friend. At school she always hung out with the older girls – fifteen-year-olds were too immature to bother with.

Jed had tried to make out with her the second night she was in town. She'd shoved him away – having already made her decision. If she was going to do it with anyone, it had to be a movie star. Still . . . Jed was a useful guy to keep hanging.

The club scene was way different from Chicago. There were all sorts of temptations – booze, coke, a variety of pills. Summer didn't go for any of it; an occasional joint was her only vice.

Back home guys were always trying to get her drunk, but she was too smart for them. Besides, her father watched over her with an unhealthy zeal – always waiting when she came home at night, checking to see if she'd been drinking or drugging; asking questions; grilling her to find out what she did with boys.

It was a big drag.

He was a big drag.

She couldn't wait to finally cut loose.

Jed was driving the limo when he arrived at the house. 'Got an airport pick-up later,' he explained.

'When?' she said, frowning.

'One a.m. Which gives us plenty of time,' he said, making a clumsy attempt to grab her.

She eluded his clammy grasp with a light giggle, shooting out the door to the sleek elongated limo.

'You'd better sit in the back,' he said, chasing after her. 'That way – if I run into any of the other drivers, they'll think I'm still on a job.'

'OK,' she said cheekily. 'I'll be your rich client giving you orders.'

'Like hell you will,' he said, leaning into the back seat, trying to grab a quick feel.

Summer had learned at an early age that all members of the male sex were easy, all she had to do was bat her big baby blues, show a little leg, and they were hers. In Chicago the boys came panting after her. In Hollywood it wasn't so different. Although when she looked around the clubs she realized the girls in LA were a lot prettier than the ones back in Chicago – especially Tina, who was so cool and sophisticated with her long brown curls, vampy lips and sparkling cat-eyes. Summer realized she could learn a lot from Tina. And the sooner the better.

'Let's go, driver,' she said imperiously. 'I do not wish to arrive late.'

'You're a tease, you know that?' Jed said, looking perplexed.

When was he going to realize he didn't have a chance?

☆

'Martini?' Richard offered.

'Why not?' Kimberly Trowbridge responded.

Kimberly was a tall, attractive woman in her late twenties, with bobbed strawberry-blond hair and an understated way of dressing. She was Richard's temporary assistant – hired to replace his permanent assistant, who'd left to have a baby.

Kimberly was not only attractive, she anticipated his needs and was extremely efficient. Since she obviously worshipped him, he enjoyed having her around.

Tonight, when he'd finished editing, he'd asked her if she wanted to grab a bite to eat. A perfectly innocent offer, because since marrying Nikki and practically giving up drinking he'd been nothing but faithful. Dinner seemed an innocent way of repaying Kimberly for all her hard work.

He'd taken her to Trader Vic's, where the exotic drinks tasted innocuous – and packed a punch capable of felling a mule! In his drinking days Richard could have downed three Navy Grogs in a row – no problem. Tonight he wasn't sure if he could manage one.

Kimberly was impressed by the restaurant. 'I've never been here before,' she said, gazing around.

'Then you must have one of these.' And he ordered her a Navy Grog, and a selection of appetizers.

She downed the exotic mixture as if it was lemonade, nibbled on a couple of spare ribs and an egg roll, and trotted off to the ladies' room.

When she returned he was already into his second drink, and there was another one waiting for her.

He noticed she'd undone a couple of buttons on her blouse, touched up her make-up, and sprayed herself with a musky scent. Talk about signals!

'You smell good,' he said.

'I thought you'd never notice,' she responded. And after that it was only a matter of time before he invited her back to his house.

☆

The first club Jed took her to was too crowded.

'Drag,' Jed said.

'Major,' Summer agreed.

They moved on to Pot, an outrageous dance club that operated out of different venues every weekend. Tina was there, and so were some of Jed's other friends. They all joined up.

Every time she ran into Tina, she was with a different guy. 'I get easily bored,' Tina confided with a giggle when Summer asked her why. 'Jed's OK, though. You should stick with him for a while – until you get to know your way around.'

'I will,' Summer agreed.

'I see you've been putting in time on your tan,' Tina said. 'Awesome! Maybe *I'll* do the same.'

Summer was flattered Tina wanted to copy her. Tina – who was so cool with her long dark curly hair and radical outfits.

'You can come out to my beach house any time,' Summer said, scrambling to jot down her phone number.

'Maybe I will,' Tina said.

Jed informed her that Tina worked as a model for a clothes manufacturer downtown.

'Wow!' Summer sighed enviously. 'I'd give *anything* to get into that kind of deal.'

'Ask her,' Jed said. 'Maybe there's an opening. And while you're at it, tell your stepfather to star me in one of his movies!'

'As if,' Summer snorted.

They both laughed, and Jed whirled her onto the crowded dance floor.

☆

Richard fixed two Martinis before walking Kimberly out onto the deck.

'This is *fantastic*!' she breathed, sipping her drink. 'A house – right on the beach – it's always been my dream!'

Richard put his Martini glass down on a ledge. He was mad at Nikki; how dare she desert him and go running after Lara, trying to persuade her to appear in her nothing little movie. Especially after he'd told her not to. Yes, he was mad, and now he was drunk, and it was all Nikki's fault. Ambition was a dangerous thing.

He reached for Kimberly and her musky scent. She melted into his arms as if she belonged there.

He put his hands in her hair, pushing it behind her ears. Then he went for the buttons on her blouse – undoing them one by one.

'Aren't you going to kiss me?' she asked.

Oh yes, of course I am.

He put his tongue in her mouth, wondered if he had a condom, hoped that she did because he had no need of them any more. Except now. To consummate this act of adultery.

God! If Nikki finds out she'll leave me.

There's no way she can find out.

He undressed Kimberly slowly. She had on lacy lingerie straight out of a Victoria's Secret catalogue – which really turned him on. First he undid her front-fastening bra – revealing nice tits with chewable nipples. Then he peeled off her thong panties – exposing her shaved bush. Finally he unclipped her garter belt and rolled off her stockings.

When she was naked he laid her across the outdoor glass table and fucked her quickly – pumping away for only a few minutes before coming.

The moment it was over he wanted her gone.

Get rid of her!

Get her out of here before Lara finds out.

Lara . . . he thought mournfully, *I never should've let you go. Why did I allow it to happen?*

Kimberly had other ideas – she was determined to experience the after-glow and nothing was going to stop her. Pulling him down on a lounger, she wrapped her long legs around his, trapping him in a tangle of damp luscious limbs. 'That was delicious,' she murmured, as if she had just consumed a dish of pasta and meatballs.

'Gotta call you a cab,' he mumbled, trying to disentangle himself. 'It's late.'

'I thought your wife was away,' she said accusingly. 'Why can't I stay?'

'My stepdaughter . . . she'll be home any minute.'

Risky business. What if Summer had walked in on them?

He finally managed to extract himself from Kimberly's clinging limbs and staggered to the phone, quickly ordering a cab. Then he gathered her clothes and gave her a little shove in the direction of the guest bathroom.

When she emerged a few minutes later she was dressed, but not happy. 'You didn't satisfy me,' she complained. 'I didn't come.'

What was wrong with women today? Wasn't it enough that she'd put a smile on *his* face? 'Next time,' he promised.

An awkward wait until he heard the cab drawing up. Then he stuffed a hundred bucks in loose bills into her hand and escorted her outside.

'What's this?' she said, staring disdainfully at the crumpled banknotes, almost ready to turn the money down.

'Cab fare,' he said.

'Oh,' she said, and kept the money.

Just as he was about to deposit her safely in the back of the cab, a limo drew up to the house, and out jumped Summer.

'Richard!' she exclaimed in surprise. 'Is Mom back?'

'Uh . . . no,' Richard said, completely thrown. 'My . . . uh . . . assistant and I were just finishing off some work.'

'That's right,' Kimberly said.

Summer chewed on her thumb. It was quite obvious he was up to something. Did he think she was a total dweeb?

Jed jumped out of the limo, determined to get introduced. 'Mr Barry . . . sir. I'm a big admirer of your work. You're one of the stalwarts of the industry.'

'Thank you,' Richard said stiffly. Did stalwart mean old? Who was this jerk anyway? And why was he bringing Summer home in a limo?

'Night,' Summer said, skipping inside the house, relieved she didn't have to fight Jed off.

Richard shoved Kimberly into the cab and followed Summer into the house, slamming the door behind him.

'Sleep tight, Richard,' Summer said, standing at the door of her room, looking cute, rumpled and very, very pretty.

'You, too,' he replied, completely unnerved.

The sooner Nikki came home, the better it would be for all concerned.

15

The party at Lara's house – put together by a frantic Cassie at the last moment – was a raging success. Everyone was letting loose and having a good time.

Lara sat at one of the tables in the garden with Nikki. Seated with them were Miles and his Hollywood wife, Ginny; a solo Barbara Westerberg; and Kyle Carson, who'd flown in a date for the weekend – an anorexic English model who appeared to be no more than fourteen with her waif-like face and concentration camp body.

'If I'd realized you were planning a party,' Nikki said, sipping a Margarita, 'I'd have brought better clothes.'

'You always look great,' Lara said, smiling at her friend – a knockout in a short red Thierry Mugler dress.

'Thanks,' Nikki replied. 'And *you* always know the right thing to say.'

'Yes, like I'll do your movie. Right?'

'Right!' Nikki grinned, thrilled that Lara understood and loved the script.

'Is Richard OK by himself in LA?' Lara asked, remembering that he couldn't stand being left alone when they were married.

'He's got Summer to look after him,' Nikki replied, sipping a frozen Margarita. 'Crazy, isn't it? She loves my husband – hates me. How did I become such a failure as a mother?'

'You're *not* a failure,' Lara said, choosing her words carefully. 'I told you – she's going through a phase.'

'I guess . . .' Nikki answered doubtfully. 'Anyway, I thought the two of them could bond even more. Eventually, if we have kids of our own, it'll be like we're all one big happy family.'

'Are you planning on having a baby?' Lara asked, surprised.

'*No,*' Nikki said quickly. 'Right now I'm *planning* on making a terrific movie, which – if everything falls into place – *you'll* star in. *Then* maybe I'll consider having another child – but only if Richard wants to.'

Ginny Kieffer – Miles's wife – leaned into their conversation. She was a well-preserved blond of indeterminate age, with carefully sculpted features – the pride of her plastic surgeon. 'Kids!' she muttered dourly, having swallowed several glasses of wine too many. 'Hate 'em. Lil' bastards don' appreciate anything you do for 'em. All they're after is your money.'

'That's not true, dear,' Miles interjected, surreptitiously moving her wineglass beyond her reach.

'How would *you* know?' Ginny said, throwing him a hateful glare. '*You're* never home.'

Nikki exchanged glances with Lara. The battling Kieffers were at it again.

'*I* wouldn't mind 'aving a baby,' piped up the anorexic model, who although she looked fourteen was actually twenty-two.

'Not with *me,* darling,' Kyle interrupted, loud enough for everyone to hear.

Two bright-red spots coloured her hollowed cheeks. 'I wasn't asking *you* to make me pregnant,' the girl said in a strong cockney accent. 'Got me a ton of guys in New York who'd *faint* at the privilege.'

Nikki decided the girl resembled a pretty young corpse. Someone should feed her. And soon, before it was too late.

'One cover on *Vogue* and they think they own the world,' Ginny mumbled, groping along the table for her wineglass.

'Lara, I marvel at how quickly you put this party together,' Barbara Westerberg said, twisting a strand of wispy hair around her finger. 'It's darling of you to invite the crew – they're *very* appreciative.'

'It seems silly to always wait for the wrap party at the end of the movie,' Lara said. 'I thought it would be fun to do one at the beginning.' She didn't add that her inspiration was Joey Lorenzo, who so far had not shown up.

Where was he, anyway? And why did it matter?

Hmm . . . wasn't she being foolish, considering he was engaged, and even if he wasn't, every female on the movie had eyes for him.

'*Such* a lovely idea,' Barbara enthused, always especially nice to her stars. 'Wish I'*d* thought of it.'

'Maybe you can pay for it,' Nikki said, *sotto voce.*

Barbara pretended not to hear. 'Oh,' she said, jumping up. 'There's Joey. Poor thing – he looks lost. Shall I invite him to join our table?'

'Who's Joey?' Nikki asked, chewing on a carrot stick.

'An actor,' Lara said vaguely, her heart starting to race, which infuriated her because he meant nothing to her.

'You mean that great-looking guy heading toward us?'

'That's him.'

'*Very* fuckable,' Nikki murmured. 'Why don't *you* lay claim before Barbara wets her panties?'

'Don't be ridiculous,' Lara said crossly. 'He's engaged.'

'Engaged means nothing,' Nikki said flippantly. '*Marriage* is the only condition that counts.'

Lara picked up her glass of non-alcoholic fruit punch. 'Actors don't interest me,' she said firmly, thinking – in spite of herself – that this one did.

'Haven't you ever heard the words "location fuck"?' Nikki said mischievously. 'It's a perk of the business. One great fling with a fantastic-looking guy, and at the end of the movie you both go your separate ways. Everyone does it.'

'Is that what you used to do before you met Richard?'

Nikki nodded enthusiastically. 'You bet your sweet ass.'

Roxy danced by, clad in a tigerprint jumpsuit. She was clinging tightly to her trucker, rubbing up against him as they rocked and rolled their way past.

Hmm . . . Lara thought, trying to get her mind off Joey, *Yoko's right – he* is *a fat one.*

Roxy was followed closely by Yoko with *her* boyfriend, a muscled hunk who looked like he belonged on the cover of *Playgirl.*

Right behind them came Trinee, accompanied by her fiancé – a solid tree-trunk of a man who favoured a kind of crazed Mike Tyson look, and towered over the diminutive Trinee.

Lara waved, happy to see everyone having a good time, forcing her thoughts away from Joey once and for all.

'Oh, boy,' Nikki said, sitting back and observing the passing couples. 'There'll be plenty of fucking on the beach tonight!'

☆

Joey circled the edge of the party, winked at Trinee on the dance floor, and decided not to go over to the above the line table where Lara was sitting. Kyle would probably treat him like shit, and he wasn't into being humiliated in front of Lara.

He noticed Barbara Westerberg heading in his direction with a determined look on her face. 'Hi, Joey,' she said, greeting him warmly.

'Barbara,' he replied, knowing he could have her any time he wanted. 'Knockout dress – *veree* sexy.'

She basked in his compliment. 'Thanks, Joey.'

Trinee had given him the scam on Ms Westerberg. She'd been married to a well-known producer who'd gotten her into the business. After a couple of years he'd run off with his accountant, leaving Barbara to manage his flourishing production company by herself. She'd kept working, divorced husband number one and married husband number two, a writer who never worked unless she got him the job. They both slept around.

Barbara grabbed his hand and squeezed it. 'You look lonely, Joey,' she said, giving him a *you can fuck me if you want* look. 'Couldn't your fiancée make it?'

'Uh . . . she was all set to fly in, then somethin' came up. She's workin' a real important case. We were on the phone – that's why I'm late.'

The truth was he was late because he'd sat in his room waiting for Madelaine's call. Sure enough, she'd phoned at nine o'clock, checking up on him. He'd wheezed and coughed over the phone, and as soon as he'd gotten rid of her, he'd left a message with the switchboard he was not to be disturbed and raced out.

'What a shame,' Barbara said, not sorry at all.

'Yeah,' Joey agreed. 'Hey – gotta let her do her thing, she's busy makin' a name for herself.'

'I insist you come and sit with us,' Barbara said.

'Gonna pass,' he said, shaking his head. 'Kyle doesn't like me.'

'Kyle doesn't like *any* man he considers competition.'

'Me? Competition?' Joey said, laughing derisively. 'Me? Who's got three lousy scenes?'

'I know,' Barbara agreed. 'Try to understand, Kyle's getting older, losing his hair,' she lowered her voice. 'Look what happened to Burt Reynolds. And to add to Kyle's humiliation, he's now dating children.'

'Huh?' Joey said, his eyes straining to watch Lara.

'The girl he's with tonight can't be more than seventeen.'

'What a loser!'

Barbara glanced around, making sure no one was listening. 'Try not to say that anywhere Kyle can hear you. And Joey, if you repeat any of the remarks I've made, I'll deny them.'

'You can trust me,' he said, trailing her to what was obviously the A table.

Lara rose to greet him. 'Hi, Joey,' she said graciously. 'So glad you made it.'

He stared at her incredible face. She was a Madonna for the nineties – breathtakingly pure and beautiful. He wanted to ravish her there and then, and yet he realized she was special – not just another conquest. 'Looks like a happenin' party,' he said easily. 'Thanks for invitin' me.'

She smiled, lighting up the night. 'It is.' Nikki gave her a sharp nudge. 'Uh . . . meet my friend, Nikki Barry,' she said, getting the hint.

Joey nodded at the pretty, dark woman, hardly noticing her – as far as he was concerned everyone paled in comparison to Lara.

'Well, hello,' Nikki said, sitting up straighter.

Barbara took his arm in a possessive fashion. 'Come sit over here, Joey,' she said, pulling him away.

'Excuse me,' he said politely, as Barbara steered him to the other side of the table.

'You're excused,' Lara responded with an amused smile – just to let him know it didn't bother her that he was in demand.

'She's hot for him,' Nikki murmured, watching him go. 'And who can blame her?'

'They're *all* hot for him,' Lara replied calmly. 'I don't think he plays around.'

'*That* makes a nice change,' Nikki said archly. 'A guy who actually *doesn't* walk around with a permanent hard-on! Surely you jest?'

Lara smiled and wished she could stop her heart from pounding uncontrollably. 'His fiancée is a lawyer.'

'Older than him?'

'How should I know?'

'How old's he?'

'I've no idea,' she said coolly, although she did know. 'I told you – I'm not interested.'

'Oh, yes, you are,' Nikki said with a knowing wink.

'Why do you say that?'

'I can tell. As soon as he walked in, you got that itchy-pants look.'

'Bullshit!' Lara said, swearing – something she almost never did.

'Oh, bullshit, huh?' said Nikki, thoroughly amused. 'Now I *know* you're interested.'

Lara jumped up, sometimes Nikki could be the most annoying person in the world. 'You're such a fucking pain in the ass!' she exploded.

'*Two* swear words!' exclaimed Nikki, still laughing. 'I do believe you're in love.'

Lara took off, wandering around the party, furious at Nikki for making such a big deal out of nothing.

And why was Barbara Westerberg coming on to Joey, anyway? Wasn't she aware he was engaged?

Freddie, the focus puller, who'd indulged in one vodka too many, grabbed her hand as she passed. 'Lara, Lara, Lara,' he said pleadingly. 'Dance with me?'

'Love to,' she said, on automatic-pilot response.

Freddie pulled her onto the dance floor, slippery palms gripping her slim waist. 'What a party!' he exclaimed. He had fuzzy ginger hair, out-of-control matching eyebrows, and a cheeky lopsided grin.

'It's fun, isn't it,' she responded.

'Never thought I'd get the courage to ask *you* to dance,' he said, bowled over at his own nerve.

She smiled, having learned over the years how to be friendly but not overly familiar. It worked every time. Nobody dared make a move unless she gave them a green light.

She glanced over at her table as Freddie whirled her past. Miles and Ginny were bickering as usual. Barbara Westerberg was leaning into Joey, speaking intently. Kyle had struck up a conversation with Nikki, while his date stared blankly into space.

She decided it was foolish to be mad at Nikki, who after all was right – she *did* find Joey attractive, although she'd never admit it because that would mean nonstop teasing.

'Thanks,' she said, deftly spinning out of Freddie's grasp. 'You're a delightful dancer.'

'I'll never wash my hands again,' he said, cheeky grin going full force.

Later that night, when the waiters were packing up and everyone had gone home, Nikki said a contrite, 'Sorry if I pissed you off.'

'You didn't,' Lara responded.

'It's just that I hate seeing you by yourself,' Nikki explained. 'I'd like nothing better than for you to be with a guy who'll be as good to you as you'll be to him.'

'Listen, Nik,' Lara said, her beautiful face quite serious. 'I know you mean well, but it's *my* problem, not yours. And you know what? It's not even a problem because I don't *need* a man. I'm very happy by myself. In fact, I'm a lot happier than I was when I was with Richard.'

'Ouch!' Nikki said.

'So do me a favour,' Lara continued. 'Stop pushing. Joey's an attractive guy – which every woman on the set will attest to – but *I* am *not* interested. So quit teasing me about him.'

'I get it, boss,' Nikki said, mock saluting.

'Why are you calling me boss?' Lara snapped.

''Cause you're going to star in my movie. *You'll* be the one with the clout.'

'No, Nik – learn this now – *you're* the producer, which makes *you* the boss. It has to be that way, otherwise everyone will step all over you.'

'Got it,' Nikki said.

Lara surveyed the waiters, still busy clearing up. 'I would say the party was a success.'

'Made *you* Miss Popular,' Nikki said, reaching for a chocolate and popping it in her mouth. 'Oh, did I tell you about Kyle?'

'What about him?'

'He invited me back to his hotel.'

'I thought he was with that skinny model.'

'Hmm ... I think Mr Movie Star had a threesome in mind.' She giggled. 'Do I strike you as a swinger?'

'As a matter of fact—'

'Don't start,' Nikki said, tossing a napkin at her.

'Would you have?' Lara asked curiously. 'In your single days?'

'Let's just put it this way,' Nikki said. 'Why do you think I'm so nervous about Summer? When I was single, I'd have tried anything.'

Lara stood up, stifling a yawn. 'Let's go inside, it's bedtime.'

'Yes, and I've got to catch an early plane.'

'Wish you could stay longer,' Lara said wistfully.

'I have to get back. Can't leave them alone too long. You know Richard – he expects my full attention.'

'Tell me about it,' Lara murmured.

They entered the house where Cassie was busy supervising the caterers as they packed up.

Lara headed for her bedroom. 'Don't forget,' she called over her shoulder, 'when you're selling the movie – use my name, that should get you all the financing you need.'

'God, Lara, I *really* appreciate it,' Nikki said gratefully. 'Can't wait to tell Richard.'

'Oh, you'll return the favour one of these days.'

'Any time,' Nikki replied earnestly. 'You call, I'll be there.'

☆

Joey left the party early, Barbara Westerberg in hot pursuit. There was no point in staying when he couldn't get close to Lara – everyone wanted to be near her and he wasn't about to join the line. Now was not the time to make his move.

In the hotel lobby he extricated himself from Barbara, who was intent on luring him up to her room. 'Look,' he finally said, 'you're a very sexy woman, but I'm engaged. I can't do this and have a clear conscience.'

'Nobody will know,' Barbara assured him, licking her lips suggestively.

'Everyone will know,' he replied. 'Besides, you've got a husband.'

Barbara played her ace card. 'Y'know, Joey,' she said, circling him with words, 'I have three movies in development . . . it's quite possible I can help you with your career.' A meaningful pause. 'We're talking big-time help.'

If Lara Ivory hadn't existed he might have been tempted. Why not? If he could sleep with Madelaine Francis he could certainly sleep with Barbara Westerberg. But things had changed. Since meeting Lara he had no desire to do anything that might jeopardize his relationship with her. 'Sorry,' he said regretfully, trying to let her down easy. 'Can't do it.'

Her expression was flinty. 'Can't or won't?'

'It doesn't matter,' he said, making his escape, and going up to his room, where he lounged on the bed, staring at the television for a while.

There was a bottle of vodka on his dresser. He got up, demolished half of it, fell back on the bed and eventually drifted into a troubled sleep.

In the morning he made up his mind. He wanted Lara Ivory more than he'd ever wanted anyone in his life.

And somehow or other he was going to get her.

Betty was out for adventure. Well, of course, I was not averse to a little adventure myself, so we made the perfect pair. There I was, seventeen, ready to rock 'n' roll, and on my way to California.

I gotta tell you, though – Betty was the biggest pain in the ass a man could ever get stuck with. She nagged the shit out of me. The only time she was quiet was when I was jamming it to her – and that didn't last long.

We hitched most of the way. I lurked in the bushes while Betty stood at the side of the road in the shortest shorts known to man and an almost non-existent tank top – upright little tits on red alert. Every trucker screamed to a stop. As soon as they pulled up, I'd run out from my hiding place and we'd both climb aboard. They weren't happy, but tough shit – there was nothing they could do. A few of them came on to her anyway, and she winked at me and asked what they'd pay for a threesome.

I wasn't into that. To tell the truth, I didn't even know what a threesome was. Years of living in California and it was my speciality – me, two sexy girls, and three thousand bucks a show. Money for pleasure, we all got off.

But I'm getting ahead of my story.

Finally we arrived in LA. I had it in my head we were on our way to a fancy house with a big swimming pool just like I'd seen on the movies. But no, Betty dragged me down to Oxnard, a small seaside town halfway between LA and Santa Barbara where her dad and his girlfriend lived. Thing is, you gotta be where it's all happening. Oxnard was a stopgap. I knew we were going nowhere if we stayed there.

It wasn't a problem, because Betty's dad took one look at us and more or less told us to piss off. He wasn't into his daughter screwing up his life. So we hit the road again, hitching our way back to LA – where we lived on the streets around Hollywood

Boulevard for a couple of months, even though we still had Avis's jewellery stashed in Betty's backpack.

Betty got off on living on the streets, she was into spending time with all the other kids who'd run away from home. It wasn't my scene, sleeping in abandoned houses with a bunch of misfits, scrounging food from the back of restaurants and hanging out on the Boulevard. I was used to comfort and a proper bed.

'We should sell your mom's jewellery and rent an apartment,' I informed her.

'Then we'll havta pay rent every month,' Betty complained. 'How're we gonna make enough bread t'do that?'

She had a point. Truth was I didn't know. I'd never had to make money, there was always a woman to take care of me.

In spite of Betty's objections we sold the jewellery and rented a one-room apartment. When the money ran out, Betty started hooking to pay the rent and buy her coke – a habit she'd gotten into in a big way.

Since Betty was the only one making money she thought I should get a job. We fought all the time. 'Shift your lazy ass and do something,' she'd yell at me.

Who made her ruler of my fucking planet?

I had my eye out for another deal, and one day, while walking down Sunset, I found it. Attractive woman in her late thirties; white convertible broken down; car phone out of action.

'Hey,' I said, zeroing in – 'cause I knew a good thing when it was staring me in the face. 'You look as if you need help.'

'My car died,' the woman said. 'Can you do me a favour and call AAA for me if I give you my card?'

I did better than that. I fixed her car myself, then I asked her to give me a lift to Fairfax. By the time we got there, I'd told her I was an out-of-work actor who'd recently broken up with his girlfriend and was looking for a place to crash.

'What the hell – you can stay in my pool house for a couple of nights,' she said, checking me out and liking what she saw.

That's all it took. Three days later I moved into the main house and into her bed with the fake-fur bedspread and smooth satin sheets.

Although she wasn't in the movie industry, she certainly had money. And after I showed her a good time in bed, she wasn't averse to passing some of it my way.

I didn't tell Betty I was moving on, because I knew she'd make a scene. I simply never went back.

So here I was, two days before my nineteenth birthday, living with a hot babe in a house in the Hollywood Hills, feeling like I'd definitely arrived. Trouble was, I still didn't have any money.

Soon after moving in I discovered my new lady love was a high-class call-girl, which didn't bother me at all.

'You should do what I do,' she told me one day, lounging on satin sheets wearing nothing but stiletto heels and an enigmatic smile. 'The women in this town are desperate. The men too. You can take your pick.'

And so I started a new career. It wasn't the one I'd had in mind, but it would do. For now.

Becoming a movie star would have to wait.

16

When Nikki arrived home from New York the next afternoon, she found Summer entertaining. The house was full of young people lounging around in their shorts and swimsuits acting as if they owned the place.

She stood in the hallway perplexed. What the hell was she supposed to do now?

'Have you seen my daughter?' she asked a long-haired surfer, who gazed at her blankly with glassy eyes and a dazed smile. 'Summer,' she repeated, 'my daughter.'

'Oh, yeah, Summer,' the guy said, scratching his chin. 'She's like on the deck.'

Seething, Nikki made her way out to the deck, where she discovered a dozen other bikini-clad babes and long-haired dudes lolling around. She spotted Summer over in the corner necking with a bare-chested boy in tightly fitting chinos sitting dangerously low on his skinny hips. Marching over she said a sharp, 'Excuse me.'

The boy had his thumbs in the top of Summer's bikini pants. He barely turned his head. 'Get lost,' he mumbled.

'No,' Nikki responded. '*You* get lost. This is *my* house, and that's *my* daughter you're slobbering all over.'

Summer pushed him away and sat up. 'Oh, hi, Mom,' she said, casual as can be. The boy took off.

'I don't remember you asking if you could throw a party,' Nikki said, quietly furious.

'Well, you were away, an' Richard said it was no biggie,' Summer said, little Miss Innocent.

'You're sure about that?'

'Yeah, I mentioned I was like having a couple of friends over, and he said I should go for it.'

'Summer, there are at least fifty people trashing my house. That's not exactly a couple of friends.'

'You know how it is, Mom, word gets on the street, an' it's Sunday and people have nothing to do, so it kinda turned into a crowd. 'S not my fault.'

'Who's fault is it? Mine?' *Oh, God!* Nikki thought. *I'm beginning to sound like my own mother!*

'Hey,' Summer's pretty face clouded over, 'like what do you *expect* me to do – throw them out?'

'Yes,' Nikki said. 'That's exactly what I expect you to do. Get everyone out of my house. And do it now.'

'Gee, Mom,' Summer said, curling her lip in disgust. 'You're sounding so *old*.'

'Five minutes,' Nikki said through clenched teeth. 'Do you hear me, Summer?' She turned and marched back into the house, going straight to her bedroom.

There was a naked couple making out on her bed. The girl couldn't have been more than fifteen, the boy maybe a year or two older. 'Are you aware you're in a private home?' she said angrily. 'And this is my bedroom.'

The girl grabbed her panties, the boy grabbed a joint, smouldering in an ashtray on the floor next to the bed. She couldn't help noticing he was well hung and very muscular. They grew them big these days.

'Listen,' she said wearily, 'I'll look away while you get dressed, then kindly get the hell out of here.'

She turned around and listened to them scrambling for their clothes littered all over the floor. A few moments later they ran past her out of the room.

Locking the door, she picked up the phone and called Richard in the editing rooms. A woman answered.

'Who's this?' Nikki asked.

'Kimberly. Who's *this*?'

An assistant with attitude, just what she needed. '*This* is Mrs Barry. Get me my husband.'

After a few moments Richard came on the line. 'Hi, sweetheart, you're back,' he said.

'Yes, I'm back, and our house is full of sex-crazed teen-agers,' she said sharply. 'Did you tell Summer she could have a party?'

'Excuse me?' he said, sounding completely uninterested.

She knew why. He was sitting in front of the editing machines with his team of editors, completely absorbed. He couldn't care less if Summer was entertaining the Dallas Cowboys.

'Summer said *you* told her it was OK if she had people to the house,' she said accusingly.

'You can't begrudge her that on a Sunday afternoon. The kid had nothing to do, so I told her it was all right to have a few friends over.'

'The few friends turned into fifty people. When I went into our bedroom there was a couple of under-age sex addicts making out on our bed!'

'Aw, Jesus!' he groaned.

'Weren't you supposed to give her some kind of supervision while I was away? Obviously, she's running wild.'

'Then *obviously* you shouldn't have left her with me,' he said sourly, like *she* was the one in the wrong.

Nikki took a deep breath, striving to stay in control. 'I don't want to fight over this.'

'*You're* the one making it into a fight.'

'I am not,' she said indignantly, furious he was taking Summer's side.

'Look,' he said abruptly, 'I'm working. I can't handle this kind of pressure.'

'Thanks a lot!' she said, slamming down the phone. She couldn't believe that with all the good things about to happen in her future, she had to deal with this shit. And Richard was no help, all he thought about was his precious movie.

She waited a good fifteen minutes before emerging from her bedroom. The house was clear.

'Summer,' she called out. No response. She hurried into the guest room – Summer's temporary quarters. It looked like a disaster area. 'Summer,' she yelled again.

Still no answer.

She went back into the living room and out onto the deck. Summer had taken her party down the beach. They were camped in front of somebody else's house like a raggedy band of gypsies – a portable CD player blasting loud rap music.

She went back into the house, it was a shambles. They'd

broken into the liquor cabinet, spilled drinks on the carpet, ashtrays were overflowing, boxes of half-eaten pizza everywhere. They'd even invaded Richard's study, although they hadn't touched his desk. Thank God for that. Or maybe it would have been a good thing if they had – *finally* he'd wake up to what a devious little madam Summer really was.

'*I'm* not clearing up,' she muttered to herself, picking up the phone and trying to reach Sheldon in Chicago.

'Mr Weston, he away,' a heavily accented maid informed her.

'When is he coming back?'

'Don' know. He in Bahamas.'

Trust Sheldon – he'd gotten rid of Summer and gone off on a fabulous vacation. Typical. The kid was with her and he didn't give a damn. At least he could have warned her what a prize pain in the ass their daughter had turned into.

No. That wasn't Sheldon's style. He'd wanted her to find out for herself.

☆

'Rad party!' Tina remarked. 'Shame your mom had to ruin it.'

'I know,' Summer agreed, swigging from a can of beer as they sprawled on the sand watching the party disintegrate around them. 'She's a real downer.'

'Wouldn't've thought it – her being so young and all.'

Summer picked up a handful of sand and let it trickle through her fingers. 'She left me when I was a kid. Took off.'

'Who looked after you?'

'My dad. He's a big-deal shrink.'

Tina nodded, like she understood. 'I bet he spoils the shit outta you.'

No, that's not what he does, Summer thought, wishing she had the courage to confide in Tina. *He comes into my room late at night, slobbers all over me, then shoves his thing inside me. He's been doing it since I was ten. Now that he's married to Rachel it's not so often, but he still does it when he thinks there's nobody around to discover his dirty little secret.*

'My dad's in Chicago,' she said flatly. 'I'm staying here with my mom and her new husband.'

'Oooh, stepfathers!' Tina said, with a fake shudder. 'They creep me out! I've had three, and the pervs all came on to me. That's why I split when I was sixteen – I so couldn't take the hassle. I mean it's *embarrassing* – some old dude with a hard-on chasing you around the room while your mom's out cruising Saks.'

Summer wished *she* could put things into perspective the way Tina did. 'Your mom ever find out?' she asked.

Tina shrugged. 'Who knows? Who cares?' She jumped up. 'I'm getting another beer. Want one?'

Summer shook her head as Tina took off. The party was going on all around her, but she didn't feel like joining in. The mere thought of her father was enough to bring back the old familiar sickness in the pit of her stomach that had been such a part of growing up.

The first time he came to her room was bad enough, but after that he'd visited her once a week, and there was absolutely nothing she could do. She was ten years old and petrified. Besides, he'd sworn her to silence, threatening all kinds of terrible things if she talked.

After a while she'd learned to tolerate his abuse. She was too ashamed to tell, because whoever she confided in would think she'd condoned it. So, as painful as it was, she'd kept the terrifying secret to herself.

Maybe if she told Tina it would make things better.

Maybe.

Maybe not.

☆

'Your wife sounds like a real bitch,' Kimberly whispered in Richard's ear.

He glanced over at his two editors to see if they'd heard. They were too intent on the Avid machine to notice.

Kimberly's hand rested on his crotch. 'She obviously doesn't understand you,' she whispered.

Wasn't that supposed to be *his* line?

'Richard,' Jim, his chief editor said, turning around, 'take a look at this – see if it's what you meant.'

He moved away from Kimberly to view the sequence of film they'd put together at his request. 'We need the close-up on Lara,' he said brusquely. 'My mistake. Put it back in.'

Kimberly was right, ever since Nikki had gotten it into her head she could be a producer, she had turned into a bitch. Treating him like the goddamn babysitter. Phoning up and complaining when she knew he was working. Where the hell was she coming from?

Jim put the close-up of Lara back in. Richard viewed the film and was satisfied. It had been a long week, but they were getting there, the assembled footage looked great.

'Thanks, guys,' he said, standing up and stretching. 'See you early Monday. Go home to your families, they've probably forgotten what you look like!'

Kimberly hung around, waiting until the two men left. Richard was busy entering notes into his laptop.

'Don't you have a boyfriend?' he asked, when he finally realized she was still there.

'I do now,' she said in a sexy voice.

He was just about to say, 'Oh, no you don't!' when she stepped out of her dress, and there were those chewable nipples staring him in the face, and he hadn't eaten all day . . .

Sometimes temptation was just that.

☆

Summer wandered back into the house at sunset. 'Sorry, Mom,' she mumbled, like it was no big deal. 'The party kinda got outta hand.'

'Out of hand!' Nikki exclaimed, to her horror sounding more and more like her mother every minute. 'They've trashed my house. Who's clearing it up?'

'The maid'll do it,' Summer said, slouching into the kitchen and opening the fridge.

'The maid will *not* do it,' Nikki said, flushed with anger as she followed her daughter into the kitchen. '*You*, young lady, will take care of it yourself.'

Summer almost laughed in her face. 'Not me,' she said. ''S not *my* mess.'

For a few seconds Nikki was completely at a loss for words. This damn kid was pissing all over her, and she wasn't going to take it any more. 'Summer,' she said, attempting not to lose it completely, 'get something straight. You might do what you want when you're with your father. However, when you're here, I call the shots, and if you don't like it, you'll be on the next plane back to Chicago. Get it?'

Summer got it. By the time Richard arrived home the house was clean, and Summer – clad in an innocent-girl long paisley dress, her white-blond hair pulled back in a ponytail – greeted him with a kiss and a hug.

'Thanks for looking after me while Mom was gone,' she said, her expression angelic. 'You're the best!'

Richard glanced at Nikki as if to say – *What are you complaining about? This kid is perfect.*

Nikki wanted to say – *It's an act, Richard, get with the programme.*

But she didn't, and the three of them went out to dinner at Granita, and Summer behaved perfectly all night.

During dinner Nikki told Richard that Lara had agreed to be in *Revenge*. He didn't say a word.

'Isn't it great?' she pressed.

'No,' he responded, grim-faced. 'You're in for nothing but trouble.'

She wasn't about to get into it in front of Summer. In fact, she didn't want to get into it at all. He had his opinion, she had hers.

Later, in bed, when she wanted to make love, he demurred. 'I'm tired,' he said. 'I've been working all day.'

'And *I've* been on a plane,' she said. 'But I'm not too tired.'

'Tomorrow,' he said, turning his back and going to sleep.

She realized it was weeks since they'd made love, and decided she'd better do something about it. Maybe a weekend in Carmel or San Francisco, somewhere romantic, where they could be alone with no outside disturbances.

In the morning when she awoke, Richard was gone and so was Summer. He'd left a note on the kitchen table.

Taken Summer to see how it's done. Will call you later.

She felt a small pang of jealousy. Why wasn't he inviting her?

Don't be ridiculous, she told herself. *He's being helpful. Taking Summer off my hands before she drives me totally nuts.*

Besides, he knew she was meeting with one of her potential directors today – and the truth was that right now her movie was more important than anything.

17

It was Monday morning and they were about to begin shooting at the same restaurant location. The make-up and hair trailers were buzzing with talk of Lara's party. 'Some insane blow-out!' Roxy exclaimed. 'You certainly know how to throw a party. Plenty of booze, amazing sounds, wild dancing. I had a blast, so did everybody else.'

'Thanks,' Lara said, smiling. 'I had a pretty good time myself.'

'Yeah, *I* saw you whirling around the dance floor with Freddie. He hasn't stopped creamin' about it ever since.'

'I'm glad everyone enjoyed themselves.'

'Show me someone who didn't, an' I'll show you a party pooper,' Roxy said, checking out her reflection in the mirror as she finished styling Lara's hair. 'Yesterday I had one *bitch* of a hangover – couldn't even function. Today I'm back to my usual wonderful self.'

'That's nice to know.'

'By the way,' Roxy added, in her best confidential *I've got a secret* tone. 'Did you hear about Joey and Barbara Westerberg?'

'What about them?' Lara asked, her stomach sinking.

'She tried to lure Joey up to her room after your party, and he turned her down. Miz Westerberg is not a happy camper.'

Why did she feel so relieved? *He's an engaged man, get over him*, she told herself sternly. Besides, she wasn't some man-hungry desperado like Barbara Westerberg.

'My heart goes out to her,' she murmured, uncharacteristically bitchy.

Yoko was equally enthusiastic about the party, as was Jane when she escorted her to the set.

As soon as Miles saw her, he grabbed her arm, manoeuvring her to one side. 'We have a big problem,' he said, chewing on a wooden toothpick. 'Kyle doesn't like the actor playing Jeff. He wants him out.'

'*Excuse* me?'

'I know, I know, it's crazy. He's been in the background of your scene for the last three days.'

'What will you do?'

'Keep the actor and ignore Kyle's shit. We don't have the time to reshoot three days' work. I'm warning you, 'cause he's bound to get on your case.'

'I can deal with Kyle.'

Miles laughed drily. 'I'm sure you can.'

'I hope you haven't mentioned this to Joey.'

'What do *you* think? We're shooting his scene this morning.'

'That's good,' she said. 'Because you know how sensitive we actors are.'

'Yeah, especially Kyle,' Miles said, with an ironic laugh. 'That guy's about as sensitive as a racoon's ass!'

Angie, her stand-in, was sitting in her place while they lit the scene. Joey was at the bar surrounded by women. Lara noticed that Trinee, the pretty wardrobe girl, was constantly by his side.

'Here's the plan,' Miles said. 'We'll shoot the scene. Once it's in the can there's nothing Kyle can do – except be totally pissed off. If he stirs up too much crap, I'll deal with it in editing.'

'I can't believe he's this insecure,' Lara said, shaking her head.

'Believe it – he's an actor.'

'Thanks a lot, Miles. Didn't I just tell you how sensitive we actors are?'

'Honey, you're not like other actresses I've worked with. You've got your shit together.'

Did having your shit together mean being by yourself? Always lonely? Always wondering why there was nobody there to take care of her, hold her and share her secrets?

'OK,' the first AD yelled out, 'we're going for a rehearsal. Everyone settle down.'

Lara moved to the table. Miles followed her. Joey came over.

'OK,' Miles said. 'Joey, you'll enter the scene from camera left.'

'Finally,' Joey said with a wide grin.

Lara smiled back at him, murmuring a succinct, 'Guess what? Mr Carson will *not* be on the set this morning, so if we're lucky, this'll fly.'

'Now *I'll* probably start blowing lines,' he said ruefully.

'No, you won't.'

'I haven't done this in a while.'

'You'll be fine.'

'With you, anybody would be fine.'

Was it her imagination, or did their eyes lock every time they looked at each other?

Miles blocked the scene, then told them to take a short break while his cinematographer lit it and the second AD placed his extras.

'Wanna get a coffee?' Joey asked.

'I don't drink coffee,' she replied. 'Maybe an Evian?'

'Let's go,' he said. 'Kraft service awaits.'

They walked together to the Kraft service stand set up outside. Joey picked up a bottle of Evian and a plastic glass, handing them to her with a flourish.

Cassie came running over. 'You OK, Lara?' she asked protectively.

'I'm fine, Cass,' Lara replied calmly. 'I'll call you if I need anything.'

'OK,' Cassie said, shooting Joey a suspicious look.

'You've got people watchin' you all the time, huh?' he said.

'Not all the time,' she responded, marvelling at his impossibly long lashes, shadowing his brooding dark eyes.

'I hear Kyle wants me out.'

'Where did you hear that?'

'I got an antenna for trouble. Only they can't do it on account of the fact I'm in all the background shots.'

'Exactly.'

'So what's Miles gonna do?'

She took a sip of Evian from the plastic glass. 'He's certainly not firing you. And if he dared to do so, *I'd* have something to say about it.'

He looked at her quizzically. 'You would?'

'It's not fair.'

'Nobody said leadin' men had to be fair.'

'I'm a leading lady and *I'm* fair.'

He broke into a big smile. 'Well, yeah, everyone knows – you're the fairest of them all.'

Was he coming on to her, or merely being friendly? She was so confused. 'I hear Barbara Westerberg gave you a hard time,' she said, deciding he was being friendly.

'News travels around here.'

'With Roxy and Yoko there are no secrets.'

He paused a moment before answering. 'Barbara's a nice lady,' he finally said. 'Guess she didn't realize I'm taken.'

'You really are an old-fashioned gentleman, aren't you?' she said, regarding him quizzically. 'You refuse to say anything bad about anyone. I like that about you, Joey.'

He fixed her with an intense look. 'You want me to list the things I like about you?'

She was wrong – he was definitely being more than friendly. 'You wouldn't be flirting with me, would you?' she said lightly.

He laughed. 'Wouldn't dare.'

'No?'

'No way.'

'How did your fiancée's case go?' she asked, figuring it was safer to move on.

'She's workin' it.'

'What did you say her name was?'

His mind went completely blank. Shit! He'd invented a fiancée who had no name. 'Uh . . . Phillipa,' he blurted, and wished he hadn't because it sounded like such an uptight name.

Jane appeared behind them, all business. 'Lara, Joey – you're both wanted on the set.'

He took the plastic glass from her, causing their hands to touch for a moment.

His touch weakened her. Abruptly she turned away and hurried to the set. *Admit it, Lara. Nikki's right, you are interested, and there's nothing you can do about it.*

Their scene together went smoothly. First Miles shot his

master, then several close-ups of Lara, and a couple of tight shots on Joey. Nobody blew any lines and they were finished before noon.

'Wow!' Lara said, fanning herself with a newspaper. 'This makes a nice change.'

'Good going,' Miles said. 'For once we're ahead of schedule. We'll shoot the fight scene next.'

'Guess that means I've got the rest of the day off,' Lara said jokingly.

'Not you,' Miles said. 'You're *watching* the fight scene, remember? You're the damsel in distress.'

'Actually,' Roxy said, hovering over Lara's hair with a brush and a can of hairspray, 'she's the bitch who caused all the trouble in the first place!'

They all laughed.

Jane rushed over, urgently whispering in Miles's ear.

'OK, we're taking an early lunch break,' he said, sounding annoyed.

'How come?' Lara asked.

'Kyle's not ready,' Miles said grimly. 'Apparently he's having trouble with his fucking hair.'

Joey realized that if he was going to do something about Lara, he'd better do it soon, before it was too late. Once they shot the fight scene, his work on the movie was over.

He grabbed his opportunity before she vanished into her trailer. 'Dunno about you,' he said quickly, 'but I've had it with the food off the catering truck. Wanna sneak off to this burger place I found down the beach?'

She regarded him for a long silent moment. Cool green eyes and the most beautiful face he'd ever seen. 'Yes,' she said at last, thinking that the sooner she got over this mild crush, the better. 'I'd like that.'

18

Nikki met with three directors, the last of them being Mick Stefan – a rat-faced twenty-nine-year-old, with gap teeth, long, wild-man hair and oversized, heavily magnified glasses. A brown herbal cigarette dangled from the corner of his thin lips and he couldn't seem to keep still.

'I wanna shoot your script,' Mick said, fidgeting uncontrollably. 'I wanna make something fuckin' ferocious.'

'Ferocious?' Nikki responded.

'Yeah – you got the heroine chick-babe in deep shit, and here's the item turns me on – she's a chick-babe with balls. I dig that. The way I'm gonna shoot it, we'll *touch* her rage. We'll make it clear to every motherfuckin' member of the audience that this is one angry pissed off outta her head chick-babe.'

Nikki was delighted he liked the script. Mick Stefan was a comer who'd already directed two small, highly acclaimed films, both of which had won several prestigious awards. Now he was hot and the studios were after him.

'I have good news,' she said.

Mick chewed on the end of his herbal cigarette while peering at her through his alarmingly large glasses. 'Give it up.'

'Lara Ivory has agreed to play Rebecca.'

'Ya *gotta* be shittin' me,' he said, kind of disgusted like.

'Do you have a problem with that?'

'Yeah, I got a problem. Lara Ivory's a fancy fuckin' movie star. I wanna make this movie with no names.'

'I don't understand,' Nikki said, hoping he wasn't going to be difficult. 'How do you expect me to complete financing with no names? You should be jumping up and down that Lara Ivory has agreed to play a role like this.'

'Jesus!' he said, pointed nose twitching. 'She's one of those glamour chick-babes – can't act for shit.'

'Oh, yes, she can,' Nikki said, defending her friend. 'Lara's a very talented actress.'

'Yeah, in all those big fuckin' over-the-top sixty-million-dollar movies.'

'Mick,' Nikki said earnestly, 'surely you understand that with Lara Ivory we'll have a real chance of getting this film off the ground? Without her it could get lost.'

'You think somethin' *I* do is gonna get ignored?' he said sharply.

She was beginning to think that his ego was so big it was going to trip everybody up. Wait until he met Richard – they'd surely butt heads. *You're the producer*, a little voice screamed in her head. *Assert yourself.*

'You know,' she said quietly. 'If I was forced to make a choice – you or Lara Ivory – who do *you* think I'd choose?'

Mick removed his glasses and threw her a gap-toothed grin, brown cigarette sticking to his lower lip. 'Me?' he said, attempting to be cute and lovable. It didn't work.

Nikki shook her head. 'Wrong. Not only is Lara a fine actress, she's also a friend of mine, *and* she's agreed to work for scale. So Mick, if you're *not* interested, let me know now and we'll stop wasting each other's time.'

'Oh, a tough chick-babe, huh?' Mick said, screwing up his eyes. 'I get off on tough chick-babes.'

Ignoring his sexist tone, she spoke seriously. 'This is my first movie as a producer, and I want it to happen on all levels. I'd love to hire you if you can be part of a team. If you can't, say so now.'

'She gonna do the rape scene?' he demanded, small eyes blinking rapidly.

'Yes.'

'None of that body double shit?'

'No,' Nikki said, although the truth was she hadn't discussed with Lara how far she was prepared to go.

''Cause if she's gonna play prima donna – I'm out. But if she's into it all the way – I'm in.'

After Mick left, Nikki paced around the house. Out of all the directors she'd met, he was the one she wanted. He had the passion and the enthusiasm. Plus she loved his work – his movies were edgy with a real nineties style.

She glanced at the clock. It was just before six. Where the hell was Richard? He and Summer had been gone all day and he hadn't even bothered to call. Right now she needed his counsel and advice before making a decision to hire Mick. It was important that she spoke to Lara, too. Nothing could go wrong, and it was up to her to make sure of that.

☆

After sitting around watching Richard edit his movie, Summer got bored and called Jed, who happened to be home. He took her surfing – or at least she got to watch him do it. Jed had settled into a respectful crush, because she'd made it very clear she wasn't interested. 'Platonic,' she'd warned. 'Or nothing.'

He'd settled for platonic.

Later in the afternoon she met up with Tina, who took her to the showroom downtown where she occasionally worked, modelling lingerie and swimsuits for out-of-town buyers. The owner of the place was a round-faced Greek man who followed her around with a lecherous leer – that is until his fat wife appeared, then his smirk was quickly replaced with a sour expression.

'His old lady's swallowed his nuts,' Tina said, with a tough little giggle. 'I'm surprised she lets him employ me. Course,' she added thoughtfully, 'the buyers love to ogle my fine young bod – especially in all the see-through shit.'

'How long have you worked here?' Summer asked, wondering if she too could get a job.

'Long enough,' Tina replied, pulling a face.

'Is it fun?'

'Dunno,' Tina said, not sounding as sure of herself as usual. 'Sometimes, when I see all these old cockers with their eyes bulging like they've never seen a *female* before, *then* it's fun.'

'Oh,' said Summer. And suddenly she was glad it wasn't her up there with a lot of horny old men eyeballing her body.

Tina drove her back to town in her red sports car,

dropping her outside Century City. 'Call you later,' she said. 'Maybe we'll do something.'

Summer nodded. She knew that whatever they got up to, it would certainly be more fun than Chicago.

19

'So, here we are,' Joey said. 'And me feelin' like I've kid-
napped the golden princess.'

Lara regarded him seriously. 'What does that mean?'

'Did you see Cassie's face when you said you were takin'
off for lunch?'

'She's . . . protective.'

'Gotta feelin' everyone's talkin' about us.'

'Why would they? I mean, my God, if two people can't
have lunch together . . .'

'Hey, I'm with *you*.'

'Anyway, you're right,' she said, sipping a glass of water.
She'd changed out of her film clothes into faded jeans and a
baggy white T-shirt. She still looked sensational. 'I couldn't
face another of the caterer's chicken à la king dishes. A
burger is exactly right.'

Joey had a million sure-fire lines he could use, but he
abandoned all of them. She was too good to listen to his
bullshit.

'C'mon, Lara,' he said, fixing her with his penetrating
eyes, 'tell me somethin' about you I'm not gonna read in
a magazine. I've told you about my love life, so it's only
fair.'

She laughed easily. 'I don't *have* a love life.'

'Cut me a break,' he said disbelievingly.

'Well . . . I did. I was with someone for a year . . . we
broke up six months ago.' She sighed deeply. 'It's not easy
being with me.'

'Why's that?'

'Isn't it obvious? Whenever I go to a movie premiere or
an opening, photographers jump all over me. The man I'm
with is merely the escort who'll make the tabloids because

he's new in my life. It does nothing for a man's ego. How would you like it?'

'Hey – my ego's pretty secure.'

She couldn't help smiling. 'So I noticed.'

He grinned back. 'Yeah?'

'I've been watching you on the set – all these women flocking around you. You're not famous yet, but it's definitely in your future. How will you handle it then?'

'Same as I do now.'

'No, you don't understand,' she said, her eyes clouding over for a moment. 'Everything changes when you're famous. You find yourself surrounded by people who'll do anything for you.'

'You're wrong, Lara, people do anything for *you* 'cause you're nice.'

'How can you say that?' she said, staring at him. 'You hardly know me.'

'I've been doing nothin' but watchin' you for the last three days.'

'That's because you had to,' she said lightly. 'Stuck forever in the background of our scene.'

'I do know,' he said, sincerely, 'that you're the most beautiful woman I've ever seen.'

'Genes,' she murmured, laughing uncomfortably. 'It's all on account of my . . . parents.'

'You don't like compliments, do you?'

'They embarrass me.'

'Why?'

'How do I know?' she said, biting into her hamburger and wondering for the twentieth time what she was doing with him. He was taken. She was free. Not a good mix.

'Whaddya do every night?' he asked, watching her eat.

'Oh,' she said flippantly, 'throw wild parties, hang out on the beach. And you?'

'Sit in my hotel room.'

'And speak to your fiancée?'

'She's too busy,' he said, dismissing the fictional Phillipa as quickly as possible. 'Always workin' – never stops.'

'And you accept that?'

'I dunno,' he said. 'As a matter of fact . . .' he hesitated. 'Naw, I'm not burdenin' you with my problems.'

'Go ahead, burden me. I've a few of my own I can discuss.'

He laughed. 'Yeah – sure. Tell me and I'll sell 'em to the tabloids.'

'I bet you would.'

'Anythin' to make a buck.' They grinned at each other. 'It's funny,' he said, suddenly serious. 'How many people do you meet where you get to feel an instant connection? Y'know, a kinda brother–sister thing.'

'I could be your big sister,' she said good-naturedly.

'Hey, don't get carried away – you're only two years older than me.'

'I feel like I'm playing hooky from school,' she confessed. 'I never leave the set when I'm working. This is fun.'

'Like I said, they're probably all talking about us.'

'Little do they know how innocent it is.'

'Maybe we should give them somethin' to talk about,' he said casually.

'Like what?' she asked, equally casual.

'Like how about I take you to dinner tonight?' he said, leaning across the table. 'There's this little fish restaurant I discovered.'

She took a long deep breath. 'Uh . . . Joey, I should warn you, if we're spotted anywhere in public, there's likely to be paparazzi leaping out the bushes. Lunch is one thing – but I've a strong hunch Phillipa wouldn't appreciate photographs of us dining out in all the tabloids.'

'She's not jealous,' he said flatly. *She doesn't even exist.*

'I would be,' she said quietly.

'No,' he said. 'I can't see you being jealous.'

'You'd be surprised. I can be a bitch.'

'Oh no,' he said, shaking his head. 'Not you.'

And then his dark eyes met hers again, and she felt an intense connection that made her very nervous indeed. 'Uh . . . we should be getting back,' she said, glancing at her watch.

'Yeah,' he said. 'I gotta rehearse with Kyle and the stunt coordinator. Should be interesting.'

She stood up. 'I'm sure Kyle will make it *very* interesting. Just remember – everyone's on your side.'

They walked outside to her car and driver.

Joey opened the door and she slid onto the back seat. 'Dinner?' he asked. 'We doin' it or not?'

She felt a flutter in her stomach. This was absolutely ridiculous . . . and yet – why not? 'Yes,' she said breathlessly. 'Let's live dangerously.'

He nodded as if he'd known she'd agree. 'Pick you up at seven.'

☆

Lara sat in the make-up trailer having her lips touched up. For some unknown reason she couldn't stop thinking about Joey – his dark brooding eyes, long hair, sensational smile.

'Hmm . . .' Roxy remarked, busy with a pot of pale lip gloss and a thin brush. 'He's quite a hunk.'

'Who?' Lara asked, snapping back to reality.

'The Pope,' Roxy answered good-humouredly. 'Who do you *think*? Joey Lorenzo, of course.'

'Oh yes, Joey. He seems like a nice enough guy,' Lara said, keeping her tone noncommittal.

'*Ha!*' Roxy exclaimed. 'And how was your lunch?'

'Actually, Roxy,' Lara said sweetly, 'it's none of your business.'

Roxy knew when to keep her mouth shut.

☆

Joey was working with the stunt coordinator when Kyle finally put in an appearance, striding over to the stuntman, once again failing to acknowledge Joey's presence. 'Give me the moves,' Kyle said curtly. 'Let's get this over with.'

Screw you, Joey thought. *You and your phony hairpiece and phony smile. Big fucking movie star. Who gives a shit?*

The stuntman began explaining the way the scene should go – telling Kyle exactly how to throw a punch without actually striking Joey.

'I know, I know,' Kyle said impatiently, cracking his knuckles. 'Done it a thousand times.'

In rehearsals all went well, but as soon as Miles called for a take, Kyle hauled off, hitting Joey for real, landing a crunching blow to his jaw.

It was so unexpected that Joey fell like a stone.

He was professional enough to stay down until Miles yelled, 'Cut!' When he got up he was ready to kill.

Miles stepped between them and said to Kyle, 'What the hell happened here?'

'Guess my hand must've slipped,' Kyle said, a sneer in his voice. 'Better do it again.'

Miles edged Kyle to one side. 'Stop the punch when you're supposed to,' he ordered tersely.

'Yeah, yeah,' Kyle said, as if he gave a shit.

There was silence on the set as they shot the scene again. This time Kyle behaved himself and pulled his punch.

'OK, once more,' Miles shouted, still not satisfied.

Roxy nudged Yoko. 'Watch him cold-cock the poor bastard,' she whispered.

'Settle down, everybody,' yelled the first AD.

Kyle hit Joey so hard he thought the sonofabitch had broken his jaw, and although it dredged up a lot of bad memories, he managed to stay down until Miles shouted, 'Cut! Print it, that's a take!'

As soon as he knew the camera had stopped rolling, he was on his feet, chasing after Kyle, spinning him around, hauling back and punching him on the chin.

For a moment Kyle couldn't believe he was under attack. Then he responded with a left hook of his own, and before anyone could stop them, the two actors were embroiled in a serious fist fight.

'Told you!' Roxy said.

Several of the crew stepped in to separate them, but not before Joey had managed to bloody Kyle's nose.

'You fucking prick!' Kyle screamed, eyes bulging, hairpiece slipping. 'I'll make sure you never work again, you dumb fucking asshole!'

Rubbing his knuckles, Joey walked away.

Lara came after him as he left the set.

'The jerk asked for it,' he muttered.

'You were provoked,' she said. 'Everyone saw what happened.'

'Yeah, but I should've taken it out on him later,' he said, furious at himself for losing control. 'Not here, in front of everyone.'

'Joey, he deserved it.'

'That's what I like about you,' he said ruefully. 'You always support the underdog.'

She placed her hand lightly on his arm. 'I'd hardly call you an underdog.'

He looked at her intently. 'We still havin' dinner tonight?'

'Of course,' she said, clear green eyes gazing into his. 'Wouldn't miss it.'

And he knew that it wasn't long before he'd make her his.

20

The incident had happened on a hot June night. Alison Sewell was not in the best of moods. Her mother was infuriating her with her constant whining and complaining – so much so, that Alison had paid the neighbour's kid – a fourteen-year-old freak who needed money for her heroin habit – to sit with her while she was out. The teenager had green hair and a ring through her nose and God knew where else. This did not sit well with Mother, who told Alison she'd sooner be dead than subjected to this kind of company.

OK with me, Alison thought. *Then perhaps I can get some sleep around here.*

She'd taken off at six to land a good position outside the Directors' Guild for a screening Lara Ivory was due to attend. Alison obtained celebrity attendees lists from an acquaintance. Of course she had to pay him, but nothing in life was free – including the new hiking shoes she'd recently purchased which were squeezing her feet, making her even more bad-tempered.

She stood at the back, wondering who Lara's escort would be tonight. According to *Hard Copy*, Alison's favourite TV show, she'd recently gotten rid of the Lee Randolph creep – he was history. So now Lara was free again. Alison hoped she didn't start dating just anybody. If Lara made bad choices she'd be forced to warn her – 'cause Alison knew plenty about all of them. She knew who cheated on their wives; who was in the closet; who liked transvestites; who was into hookers.

So much for Hollywood's so-called Macho Men. A bunch of perverts with dicks.

The reason Lara had dumped Lee was probably because she'd taken heed of all the warnings Alison had written her.

Sometimes she'd sent her three or four letters a day, just to make sure she knew that Alison Sewell was on her side, rooting for her. She'd been thinking that now Lee Randolph was gone, she might resume her visits to Lara's house. Only today she'd written her a long letter telling her idol they could now spend plenty of time together since the loser was history. The loser being Mr Lee Randolph himself, who, if she had her way, would have gotten a bullet in his brain because it was his fault she wasn't living in Lara's house and hanging out like real girlfriends did.

And when that happened – *Bye bye, Mother. You can whine yourself to death all by yourself, 'cause your little Alison has moved on to bigger and better things.*

'Here comes the Hun,' she heard one of the other photographers say as she elbowed her way to the front. 'Must be our lucky night.'

'Fuck your mother in the butt,' she muttered, shouldering her way to a good position, right behind the rope that separated the photographers from the stars.

'Something stinks around here,' one of the guys said, directing his rude comment at her.

'Yeah, your breath when you talk,' she snapped back.

Personal hygiene had never been a big priority with Alison. She took a bath every couple of weeks when the smell got so bad even *she* couldn't stand it.

'Lara! Lara! Lara!' The cry of the crowds swelled like a mantra of adulation. Alison stood to attention as Lara swept into view wearing a green strapless dress that matched her startling eyes.

As soon as she saw what she was wearing, Alison scowled. The dress was too low cut for her liking. Lara wasn't some raunchy starlet desperate to show off the goods to get attention. She was Lara Ivory, the queen of Hollywood.

Somebody wasn't advising her right, and this made Alison mad.

'Take a look at the tits on Lara tonight,' one of the photographers remarked. 'Wouldn't mind suckin' on those juicy little cuties.'

Alison turned on him. 'Shut your filthy mouth,' she hissed.

'Get lost, freako,' he muttered.

Her temper flared and she kicked him in the calf.

'Crazy cunt!' he yelled, hopping on one leg. 'I'll fuckin' sue your fat ass.'

Lara glanced over, her attention attracted by the commotion.

She wants me to be with her, Alison thought. *Not trapped back here with these uncouth pigs.*

Without really thinking about it, she lunged forward, ducked under the rope, raced over to Lara and embraced her.

Everything seemed to happen in slow motion after that. Lara's publicist leaped forward, trying to shove Alison away. But she was too quick for him, she swung her right arm, hitting him hard across the face.

A woman moved in, attempting to pull her off Lara. Alison whacked her too.

Lara was completely stunned.

'I've come to save you,' Alison reassured her. 'I'm the only one who cares. I *am* your saviour.'

Before she could say or do anything else, two burly security guards descended on her, grabbing her under the arms, hauling her away from Lara. A cop rushed over, and she managed to kick him in the groin – even though the security guards had a firm grip on her.

Then she was struggling with all three of them, until she was hurled into the back of a police van, but not before she'd managed to kick and scratch and attack as many people as she could.

Alison Sewell was a very angry woman indeed.

21

The fish restaurant by the beach was candlelit and romantic. Lara couldn't remember when she'd had such a good time just talking – casual stuff, gossip about people on the set and their idiosyncrasies, more serious talk about acting. Since she and Joey were not involved in a relationship there was none of that intense *where are we going?* stuff. Instead they discussed movies, books, TV shows – it was delightfully relaxing, and yet while she was busy speaking, her inner voice was sending out all kinds of messages.

He's gorgeous. You like him. He's funny. He's sexy. Even better – he's nice. What are you planning to do about it?

Nothing, she told herself sternly. *Because most of all, he's taken.*

'Kyle's threatening to sue me,' Joey said, not sounding too upset. 'I told him to contact my lawyer – I could use the publicity.'

They both laughed. She sipped her wine and wondered when he was going to make a move. If he did, she'd have to say no – much as she didn't want to.

The waiter brought over the dessert menu.

'Not for me,' she said, shaking her head regretfully. 'Can't do it.'

'Tonight you're indulging yourself,' he said, taking charge.

'I am?' she said wryly.

'You am.'

At his insistence she ordered chocolate cake while he went for pecan pie. They shared each other's desserts, savouring every decadent bite.

'I'm outta here tomorrow,' Joey said, gulping down a cappuccino. 'There's nothin' else for me to do.'

She pushed a piece of chocolate cake around her plate with a fork. 'Where are you going?' she asked.

'Back to New York.'

She knew it wasn't her business, but she couldn't help herself. 'Do you and Phillipa share an apartment?'

'Right now we do,' he lied.

'That's good,' she said, nodding. 'It's always best to get to know someone before you marry them.'

'You an' Richard live together before you made it legal?'

'No. We should have.' She paused for a moment before continuing. 'Richard turned out to be a very complex and needy man. Now that he's married to my friend, Nikki – you met her at the party the other night – he's calmed down a lot.'

'Let me see . . . needy . . . needy . . . What exactly did he need? Other women?'

'You're very perceptive,' she said, her beautiful face serious. 'I caught him several times before it finally occurred to me that he had no intention of stopping.'

'Jesus! It's tough to believe any guy would screw around on you.'

She smiled wanly. 'I'm not that special, Joey.'

He stared at her, his dark eyes burning into hers. 'Don't ever let me hear you say that.'

She looked away, confused, and then began speaking again, much too fast. 'I'd like to meet Phillipa sometime. Maybe if the two of you come to LA you'll visit me. I have a small ranch off Old Oak Road. That's where I keep my horses and dogs.'

'An animal lover, huh?'

'I've always found animals more reliable than people.'

'Sometimes I think about gettin' a dog. Then I realize there's no way I can keep one locked up in an apartment all day.'

'No,' she said softly. 'That would be cruel.'

'Phillipa doesn't like animals anyway.'

'She doesn't?'

'Naw – she's a city girl.'

'You should try and convert her. Buy her a small dog.'

'And have her leave it alone all day? I don't think so.'

'Send it to me for vacations,' Lara joked. 'I'll take care of it.'

'Hey,' he said, looking at his watch, 'I promised I wouldn't keep you out late. You're working tomorrow.'

'That's OK,' she said quickly, not wanting the evening to end.

'No,' he said. 'I refuse to be responsible for bags under those beautiful eyes.'

Was it possible he *wasn't* going to make a move? This was a first. She was more than intrigued.

He snapped his fingers for the check, paid the bill in cash and helped her up.

Outside the restaurant they walked for a few minutes before Joey hailed a cab and gave the driver her address. She'd offered to bring her car and driver, but Joey had said it wasn't a good idea – too much gossiping would take place. And she'd agreed.

'Would you like to come in for coffee?' she asked tentatively, when the cab pulled up outside her house.

Before he could answer, her guard appeared. 'Evening, Miss Ivory.'

Was there no privacy?

Joey shook his head. 'You gotta get your beauty sleep.'

'You are coming by the set tomorrow to say goodbye to everyone, aren't you?' she asked, thinking she sounded a touch needy.

'*Not* a good idea,' he said, dutifully escorting her to the front door. 'You wouldn't want me and Kyle gettin' into it again.'

Her guard was hovering behind them. 'Thank you, Max,' she said crisply. He got the message and promptly retreated. 'Sorry about that,' she said, hoping he was at least going to kiss her good night.

'Don't worry about it. I like the fact you got people watchin' out for you. Wouldn't want to think of you bein' alone.'

'Are you sure about the coffee?'

God! How much more open could she be?

'Quite sure,' he said. 'Oh, an' by the way – if you ever get to New York, me and Philly would love to take you out.'

'She won't mind us having dinner tonight?'

'She knows she can trust me,' he said, leaning forward

and kissing her chastely on the cheek. 'Thanks, Lara – for everythin'.' Then he turned around and strolled back to the cab.

Lara was shocked. Was this it? Was he simply going to walk out of her life and she'd never see him again?

Yes, Lara, this is it.

She hurried into the house, hands trembling. She'd wanted him to come in so much, and yet, he obviously had principles – a quality she was forced to admire.

Why couldn't *she* meet a man like Joey Lorenzo? Handsome, charming, and most of all incorruptible.

She got undressed, slid between the sheets, closed her eyes and attempted to sleep.

After a few minutes the phone rang. She grabbed it, foolishly hoping it was Joey. 'Hi,' she murmured, husky-voiced.

'Well, hi to you, too,' Nikki said. 'Hope I'm not waking you.'

'No, no, I . . . I only just got in.'

'Hmm . . . out on a hot date, I hope.'

'Actually, I was having dinner with Joey Lorenzo.'

'You're *kidding*?'

'Don't start getting the wrong idea, Nik, it's purely a friendship thing.'

'Oh, a guy who looks like that, and it's purely a friendship thing. Yeah, yeah, I believe you.'

'How many times do I have to tell you he's engaged?' Lara said, exasperated. 'In fact, if you want the truth, I asked him in for coffee and he turned me down.'

'You *are* joking?'

'No, I am not. He's nice and I like him, but he's *definitely* not available.'

'Wow! That's really something.'

'Yes, isn't it?'

'Anyway, I called to fill you in on Mick Stefan. I met with him today.'

'How did it go?'

'He's kind of over the top – quirky – with a touch of the Quentin Tarantinos. I'm crazy about his work, and I'm sure he'll do an amazing job.'

'That's good news, isn't it?'

'Look, before I hire him, I need to get your take on something.'

'Yes?'

'He started asking how you felt about the rape scene. I told him you always use a body double, but he feels the scene is pivotal to the movie, and that you have to be completely into it.'

Lara considered her reply. 'If Mick does the movie, and he's as good as you say, then I guess I'm in his hands.'

'That's all I needed to hear,' Nikki said, sighing with relief.

Lara put the phone down. She couldn't sleep, and much to her annoyance she couldn't stop thinking about Joey.

Reaching for the TV remote, she tuned into a Sylvester Stallone, Sharon Stone movie, and tried to concentrate on the two actors as they writhed on the screen in a heated love scene, their perfect bodies naked and glistening with sweat.

Just what she needed. A steamy sex scene. She clicked the TV off. Try as she might, she couldn't get Joey out of her head.

One thing she knew for sure. Phillipa was a very lucky girl.

☆

Joey made it back to the hotel. He was revved, Lara had given him an opening and he hadn't taken it. The only sure way to score with a woman who could have any guy she wanted was to play hard to get. Right now she was sitting at home thinking that she couldn't have him, and that's exactly how he *wanted* her to feel.

A bunch of people from the movie were hanging out in the bar as he passed – Roxy, Yoko, and several members of the crew. Roxy waved, beckoning him to join them.

'I'm out of it,' he said, making a quick excuse. 'Gotta get some sleep.'

'We wanna buy you a drink,' said Freddie, the ginger-haired focus puller who'd danced with Lara at her party. 'You're our hero, man. Punching out Kyle Carson. That's good stuff.'

Everybody cheered.

'Yeah, well, I was only doing a public service,' he said modestly.

'C'mon,' Roxy said, smoothing down her clinging sweater, hard nipples thrusting through the flimsy fabric. 'We don't bite – not unless you request it! Have a drink with us.'

'Yes,' said Yoko, 'you can sit next to me.'

He wasn't even tempted to score with any of these women. They were nothing and Lara was everything.

'Gotta make some calls,' he said, excusing himself. 'I'll catch up with you guys in the mornin'.'

He went upstairs and stared at the phone, forcing himself not to call Lara. Had to make her wait. Had to make her yearn for him as he yearned for her.

He'd already decided that as soon as he got back to New York, he'd take the money he'd made from the movie, pay Madelaine back and move out. That way he'd be under no obligation, and she couldn't go around saying he was a thief.

Of course, that meant he'd be broke again, but so what? He'd survive. He always had.

For a moment he almost gave in and picked up the phone, stopping himself just in time.

He knew *exactly* how to make Lara want more.

She was his future, and he couldn't afford to screw it up.

22

'**That's no way** to behave,' Madelaine said, her pinched face tense with anger.

'What?' said Joey, not really listening as he idly switched TV channels. Why did he always get caught in these traps with women he didn't want to be with? Madelaine had been good to him, but now that he'd found Lara, he had to get out for both their sakes. It wasn't fair to string Madelaine along.

'What kind of a name will you get in the business if you go around punching people on the set?' Madelaine demanded, all steely-eyed and pissed off. 'Kyle Carson's a big star – you can't afford to have people like that mad at you. And let me assure you, Joey, word soon spreads if you're difficult. Then the work stops.'

'We had a fight scene,' he explained, clicking off the remote. 'Kyle Mr Fucking Big Star Carson was supposed to pull his punch. Instead he knocked me flat on my ass.'

'Kyle Carson is the star of the picture,' Madelaine stormed, dismissing his explanation. 'You should have accepted it.'

'Is that what you think I should've done?' he said sarcastically. 'Well, Jeez, Mad, guess what? I'm not in this business to get punched out – an' I don't give a crap *who's* doin' the punching.'

'You won't be in this business at all if you carry on like this.'

She'd been irritable ever since he'd gotten back. He knew it was because he'd refused to have sex with her. Of course he'd come up with a credible excuse, told her he might have herpes.

'What?' she'd asked, astounded.

'I've got this ridge on my dick – dunno *what* it is,' he'd lied. 'I'm worried about it. The girl I went with before you had kind of a dubious history.'

'I can't believe this!' Madelaine had exclaimed, the colour draining from her face. 'What if I've caught something?'

'Don't worry,' he'd said. 'I'm sure it's nothin', only I wouldn't wanna put you at risk. Here, take a look,' he'd added, unzipping his pants.

'No.' She'd shrunk back, horrified. 'Tomorrow you must see a doctor.'

The next day he told her he'd been to a doctor who'd informed him it was merely an abrasion, and that he should refrain from sex for a couple of weeks.

So now they were living in the same apartment and not having sex, and this did not please Madelaine one bit, since as far as she was concerned sex was his main attraction.

The third night he was home he waited until she was asleep, and then took off. He did not do his usual prowl around the mean streets, instead he went straight to a bar, found a pay phone and called Lara in the Hamptons.

She answered the phone herself. 'Remember me?' he said.

'Joey,' she responded, sounding pleased to hear from him.

'Thought I'd check in – see how it's goin' on the movie,' he said casually.

'Everything's great, thanks. Nice of you to think of us.'

'Kyle's gotta miss me like crazy,' he joked. 'Anythin' happen after I left?'

'He mumbled about you a lot, told Miles to be sure to cut you out of the movie . . .'

'Will he?'

'Not if I have anything to say about it. Our scene together is in the script I accepted. I fully expect to see it on the screen.'

He laughed. 'I like a woman with clout.'

She laughed back. 'You don't know the half of it.'

A short silence – then— 'Hey, Lara, it was really good spendin' time with you.'

'I enjoyed it, too,' she said softly.

'When are you off to LA?'

'Three weeks.'

'Bet you're lookin' forward to some down time.'

'Me? Down time?' she said ruefully. 'I'm making the most of it while I can, before I turn into an old hag.'

'Yeah, thirty-two's really gettin' up there.'

'Actually, my next project is Nikki's movie.'

'Nikki?'

'You met her at my party. She's producing her first film. In fact, she's signed Mick Stefan to direct.'

'Interesting choice. Although I heard somewhere he's a maniac.'

'It's a different type of role for me – something that will stretch me as an actress.' She paused for a moment, then added thoughtfully, 'You know, Joey, they're not going with stars – maybe there's something in it for you. Shall I ask Nikki if they'll see you?'

'That'd be great.'

'Problem is they're all on the West Coast.'

'I can fly to LA.'

'What about Phillipa?'

'Too busy, as usual.'

'I'll speak to Nikki – see what she says.'

'I'd appreciate it.'

'Consider it done.'

'Uh . . . Lara?'

'Yes?'

A long beat. 'Nothin' . . . I'll call again in a coupla days – don't wanna keep you up.'

'No, no,' she said quickly. 'I was watching television.'

'Well . . . it was good talkin' to you.'

'You too, Joey.'

He put the phone down, strolled over to the bar and had a beer.

Things were looking up. Lara Ivory *and* a role in her new movie – what could be a better combination?

☆

Lara hung up. She had to admit she was ridiculously pleased to hear from Joey. The truth was she couldn't get him out of her mind.

She called Nikki and asked her if there might be something for Joey in the film.

'Mick has very set ideas,' Nikki said. 'That's not to say I can't get him to meet with Joey as a favour to you. Is he coming to LA soon?'

'If there's a chance for him to see Mick Stefan, he'll be on the next plane.'

'Hmm . . .' Nikki murmured thoughtfully. 'Am I reading something into this? Let me see – the guy is engaged, you had dinner with him, invited him in for a coffee – he didn't go for it. Now you're trying to get him a part in *Revenge*. Could be you're taking a shot?'

'No way,' Lara said indignantly. 'We're just friends.'

'You're just friends 'cause *he* chooses to have it that way,' Nikki said knowingly.

'You think I couldn't get him?' Lara responded boldly.

'You're too nice to go after another girl's guy. It's not your MO.'

'Don't be so sure. You don't know *everything* about me.'

She put the phone down. Nikki could be so infuriating.

☆

'I think Lara's finally found herself a man,' Nikki said matter-of-factly.

Richard placed the copy of *Variety* he was reading on the bedside table, removed his glasses and looked up. 'What did you say?'

They were sitting comfortably in bed, propped up by pillows, surrounded by newspapers, magazines and the daily trades.

'I *said*,' Nikki repeated slowly, 'that Lara has found herself a guy.'

'What makes you think that?'

'She met an actor on her movie. He's supposedly engaged, but there seems to be something going on between them. She wants me to see him for *Revenge*. He's prepared to fly out. Now, would she go to all that trouble if she wasn't interested?'

'Have you met him?'

'I saw him when I was in the Hamptons. He's a looker – macho, dark. I don't know how talented he is, but hey – if it's what she wants, I may as well read him.'

'Why would she get involved with an actor?'

'It's really none of our business who she gets involved with.'

'Yes, it is,' he said irritably. 'I look out for Lara and her interests, she *needs* looking after.'

'She's your *ex*-wife, Richard,' Nikki reminded him. 'You don't have to watch out for her any more.'

'I thought she was your friend.'

'She *is* my friend and I love her. I'd like nothing better than for her to get laid – it's been almost a year.'

'God, you're vulgar!'

She moved closer to her husband, gently touching his thigh, her hand moving slowly up. 'Isn't that what you like about me?'

He picked up his copy of *Variety* again. 'I'm not in the mood,' he said, pushing her hand away.

'You always used to be,' she said, adding jokingly, 'in fact, for an old man you're extremely horny.'

'And I'm not old either,' he said, failing to see any humour in her crack.

'OK, OK,' she said, backing off because she realized he was age-sensitive. 'I stand corrected – middle-aged.'

'I hate that phrase,' he muttered.

'Well, that's what you are,' she said, continuing to needle him.

'Where's Summer tonight?' he asked, changing the subject.

'I've given up tracking her. The only person she'll listen to is you.'

'That's because *you* treat her like a baby. Give her more space, let her know you trust her.'

'I *don't* trust her, Richard. Every time I see her she's with a boy – kissing, groping . . . God knows what else.'

'Isn't that what you used to do when you were her age?'

'Yes, but not in front of my mother.'

'Ease up – then maybe you'll have a better relationship.'

Nikki realized that since Summer had arrived their sex life had definitely taken a dive. Usually when she made the first move, he was ready, willing and able. Not tonight. In fact, not for the last month.

She tried it again, deftly plucking *Variety* out of his hands, running her fingers lightly across his bare chest.

He reached over, switching off the bedside lamp. 'I'm tired,' he said.

She continued to work on him, her fingers travelling downwards, stroking his skin in little circles the way she knew he liked.

'Don't pressure me, Nikki,' he said, moving her hand again.

'Pressure you?' she repeated, amazed. 'I thought you *loved* me taking the initiative.'

He stretched out with his back toward her.

She moved up behind him, nuzzling against his comforting warmth. 'Tomorrow night,' she murmured, yawning. 'Let's go to bed early, then neither of us will be tired.'

'OK,' he said. 'Oh, and Nikki—'

'Yes?'

'Don't push Lara into anything.'

'*Me?*'

'Yes, *you*. You have a habit of forcing things. She's fine by herself.'

Nikki shifted away from him. He wanted Lara to be alone. He didn't like the idea of her being with a man. In some sick way he felt he still had a hold over her.

For a moment she was hurt and angry. Then she thought, *This is silly – he loves me, not Lara.*

And she closed her eyes and fell into a deep sleep.

☆

The next morning Lara realized she didn't have a number to contact Joey, so she sent Cassie into the production office to collect a cast and crew list. Sure enough he was listed, with a Manhattan address.

She took his number home with her that night and sat on her bed, contemplating whether to phone him or not. Finally she decided to do so, after all, she had a perfectly legitimate reason.

She dialled his number in New York. A woman answered. It had to be Phillipa. Panicked, she hung up.

Oh, great, she thought. *You really do like him, because if you didn't, you'd talk to his fiancée and explain why you're calling.*

To make matters worse, that night she had an erotic dream about him, awakening in the early hours of the morning flushed and aroused.

Nikki was right. It was time she got herself a man.

23

'**Your feelings** are showing up in dailies,' Miles said over a catering truck breakfast.

'Excuse me?' Lara responded, pushing two poached eggs around her plate because she wasn't hungry and the Swedish caterer – who harboured a big crush on her – had insisted on fixing her an enormous plate of food.

'We're making a love story,' Miles pointed out, removing his glasses and staring at her with faded blue eyes. 'And the chemistry between you and Kyle is fast running out.'

She pulled a face. 'Is it about the kissing scene yesterday?'

'You got it.'

'I'm sorry, Miles,' she said. 'Kyle had garlic for lunch and his breath stunk, plus he's *always* trying to shove his tongue down my throat.'

'I know he's a pain in the ass,' Miles agreed, nodding his shaggy mane of silver hair, 'only we're making a movie here, and on screen you two are supposed to be hopelessly in love. I have to see it, otherwise we're stone cold at the box office.'

'I'm trying.'

'Try harder. Weave your special magic, Lara, pretend he's someone else.'

Pretend he's Joey. The thought popped into her head completely unexpectedly. *Pretend he's Joey Lorenzo whom I haven't heard from in two and a half weeks even though I promised to get him an audition for* Revenge, *so shouldn't he be calling daily?*

'OK, Miles. I promise I'll do something about it,' she said, getting up from the table and heading for the make-up trailer.

Today they were shooting the big love scene, which

meant she'd have to summon all her acting skills and try her best to get into it.

As far as she was concerned, Kyle Carson was the worst kind of phony. He presented one image to the world – that of the poor hard-done-by movie star whose wife had abandoned him, while in true life he was an out and out womanizer who couldn't keep it zipped. Over the last few weeks his supply of females had accelerated – a new one arriving every other day. Roxy commented he was having a fuckathon – an apt description of his activities. Roxy also observed that he had a saggy butt and should hire a butt double – a pronouncement that broke everyone up.

Lara sighed – not only did she dislike kissing him, she was also nervous she could contact some dreaded disease. Thank God she had a body double replacing her for the more intimate moments of the love scene. It was sad that females on the screen were forced to show it all, whereas their male counterparts modestly got away with a brief flash of butt. Demi Moore was probably the only movie star who actually seemed to enjoy revealing everything.

The previous week three actresses had arrived from LA to audition for her body double. There was much ribald laughter and nudging on the set as the girls paraded into Miles' trailer for their interviews. Miles had asked her to sit in on the auditions. 'After all,' he'd said, 'it's *your* boobs that'll be up there. You want 'em to look good, don't you?'

'I'm sure you'll pick the best pair,' she'd replied wryly, wondering what it must be like to parade in front of a bunch of strangers exhibiting your breasts.

Barbara Westerberg stood in for her, and they'd finally hired Wilson Patterson, a veteran who'd doubled various body parts for Michelle Pfeiffer, Julia Roberts and Geena Davis. She wasn't knockout beautiful, but she did have a spectacular body and was not shy about showing it.

Today Wilson stood naked at the other end of the make-up trailer, having body make-up applied to every finely toned inch.

'Hello,' Lara said, as she entered the trailer.

'Hi,' Wilson replied, completely unembarrassed. 'Hope I'm gonna do you justice.'

'I'm sure you will,' Lara said, sitting in the make-up chair

– deciding that in her next contract she would not allow a body double, it was cheating of the worst kind.

'Have you seen the wig?' Yoko asked, cleansing Lara's face with a moist pad of cotton.

'What wig?'

'Roxy came up with this fantastic wig. From behind Wilson looks *exactly* like you.'

'I don't know why they have to do this,' Lara complained. 'It's embarrassing.'

'How come you allow it?' Yoko asked, patting a fine moisturizing cream onto her skin.

'Because they're paying me megabucks, therefore I'm expected to make concessions. And if I refuse to do it myself . . .' She trailed off. 'This is the last time.'

'I like Roxy's idea,' Yoko said, giggling slyly. 'A butt double for Kyle. How about a front double, too? You know, if an actor has a tiny dick, bring in a stuntman with a huge one – that'd be good for their egos, huh?'

'You're beginning to sound more like Roxy every day,' Lara said, laughing.

'God, no!' Yoko objected.

Lara closed her eyes, allowing Yoko's soothing hands to work on her face. As she lay back, her thoughts drifted once more to Joey. Nikki had called yesterday and said, 'Where is he? The movie's practically cast. I thought you wanted me to see him.'

'I've no idea,' she'd confessed a trifle sheepishly. 'I haven't been able to reach him.'

'Gee,' Nikki had said sarcastically. 'He must be really anxious to make a career for himself.'

She couldn't understand it, why *hadn't* he called? Maybe he and Phillipa had run off and gotten married. The thought disturbed her more than she cared to admit.

Kyle was waiting on the set with minty breath and an overly friendly smile. 'Ready for our big love scene, Princess?' he greeted.

'Do me a favour, Kyle,' she said vehemently. 'No more garlic for lunch.'

'Sorry about yesterday,' he said, not sorry at all. 'Did my breath offend you?'

'*I* wouldn't do it to you, so kindly return the favour.'

'Ah . . . Lara, Lara,' he said, shaking his head. 'You're so perfect. Don't you ever get wild? Let it all hang out? What d'you do for *fun*?'

'I work,' she replied, stony-faced.

'Work ain't fun. Getting down is fun.'

'From what I hear, you've been getting down every night.'

He gave a brittle laugh. 'What's a guy supposed to do when his wife walks? I was married for ever. Now it's getting out of jail time.'

'Aren't you worried about catching something?'

He regarded her as if she was crazy. 'Me? Worried? No way. All I have to do is look at a girl, and I can tell if they're clean.'

'That's kind of dumb, Kyle.'

'Are you calling me dumb?' he said, bristling.

'Not at all,' she said, realizing it wasn't worth a fight.

An hour later they were embroiled in a heavy love scene. She hated every minute of it, but she was an actress, so she closed her eyes and made believe he was somebody she yearned for. It worked. Their kisses took on a new intensity. *Now* Miles would be happy.

In the middle of the second take she felt Kyle's erection against the side of her thigh and tried to ignore it.

'Oh, baby, am I hot for you,' he muttered, right after Miles called cut.

Coldly she replied— 'Let's see if we can act like professionals, shall we, Kyle?'

'What are you – frigid?' he taunted, furious he couldn't get to her. 'Don't like guys?'

Why was it when a movie star couldn't score there always had to be something wrong with the woman?

'That's right,' she said, deliberately needling him. 'I'm lesbian of the year, didn't you know?'

By the time her body double took over, she was desperate to get out of there. Wilson sauntered into place wearing nothing but body make-up and a pleased smile. The entire crew went into a state of schoolboy excitement. Kyle immediately began making tit jokes.

Lara walked off the set, she had no desire to hang around watching all the guys ogle Wilson. It didn't take much to reduce grown men into horny little boys. They all acted like they'd never seen a pair before.

Her designated driver was sitting in the car outside. He could hardly wait to drop her off at her house and race back so that he could get an eyeful too.

She had the afternoon free, so she put on shorts and a T-shirt, took a towel and her script of *Revenge*, then set off down the beach. Finding a shady spot, she spread the towel out, lay on her stomach and began studying Rebecca's lines. *Revenge* was definitely the movie she'd been looking for – certainly the meatiest role she'd ever had.

She stayed on the deserted beach for a while, enjoying the solitude. When she returned to the house, Cassie greeted her on the back steps looking agitated. 'That actor's here,' Cassie said.

She frowned, hoping it wasn't Kyle and his erection paying a house call. 'What actor?'

'You *know*, the good-looking one. Joey something or other.'

'Joey's here?' she said, experiencing a small shiver of excitement.

'I know I should've sent him away,' Cassie wailed. 'Only he was very insistent, assured me you'd want to see him. He's sitting in his car.'

'You made him wait outside?'

'You didn't tell me he was coming. Were you expecting him?'

'Yes,' she said, hating that Cassie felt she had to know everything. 'I must have forgotten to tell you.'

'Oh,' Cassie said, not pleased to be left out of the loop.

'Invite him in,' Lara said, hurrying into the guest bathroom. She stared at her reflection, picked up a brush, ran it through her hair, then quickly dabbed gloss on her lips. All of a sudden her heart was pounding.

Trying to compose herself, she went out to the deck, sat in a chair and picked up a magazine.

When Joey walked out she was cool and collected.

'Hey,' he said, grinning at her. 'Don't you look cute in shorts.'

'Hey,' she replied, putting down the magazine and smiling up at him.

Cassie stood in the doorway, observing the two of them, wondering what was going on.

'Would you like a drink? Tea, coffee ... something stronger?' Lara asked, her voice sounding husky.

'I could use a beer,' he said, cracking his knuckles.

'Cassie – one beer, and I'll have a 7-Up.'

'Coming right up,' Cassie said, reluctantly going back into the house.

'So, Joey, this is a surprise,' she said, putting down the magazine. 'Have a seat.'

He flopped into a chair, long legs stretched out in front of him. He had on scuffed combat boots with ripped jeans, and a white T-shirt that defined the muscles in his arms.

'Guess you're wondering what I'm doing here,' he said.

'Weren't you supposed to call me?' she asked, trying to sound as if it didn't matter. 'I set up an interview for you in LA.'

'Had other things on my mind,' he said, taking a long beat. 'It's been a tough coupla weeks.'

'Really?' she said, once again admiring the darkness of his eyes, the faint stubble around his chin and the thrust of his finely etched jawline. Oh, God! What was going on here?

'Yeah,' he said, grimacing. 'Then today everything blew up. Hadda talk to someone – an' you always seem to understand me.' He threw her a long, penetrating stare, thinking she was even more beautiful than he remembered. 'You're not pissed I drove down to see you?'

'You came all this way just to see *me*?'

He nodded. 'Phillipa an' I finally broke up. We, uh ... couldn't work out our differences. She gave me back the ring an' here I am.' He laughed ruefully. 'Hey – *now* I can go to LA.'

'Is that what you were fighting about? Going to LA?'

'Naw,' he said, clearing his throat. 'She was so into her career, she didn't have time for me.' A long pause, another penetrating stare. 'I need somebody who's gonna put *me* first.'

'Of course you do,' Lara murmured sympathetically.

'I kinda figured that as we got deeper into our relationship, things would change,' he continued, drumming his fingers on the coffee table. 'Then I started realizin' her career came before me, an' that's no way to build a future – not when two people can't communicate.'

'Joey,' she said, understandingly, 'I know you're upset now, but if that's how things were, then you've probably made the right decision.'

Cassie returned carrying a tray with a bottle of beer, a can of 7-Up, two glasses and a dish of chocolate cookies. She placed the tray on a table in front of them, and hovered, dying to find out what was going on.

'Thanks,' Lara said, dismissing her.

Cassie had no choice but to go back inside.

Joey picked up the bottle of beer, flipping the top open with his teeth. 'You know what's so crazy about all of this?'

'Tell me,' she said softly.

His eyes met hers. 'How come I'm *here*?'

'I . . . I don't know . . .' she answered, feeling uncomfortably warm.

He took a couple of swigs from the bottle. 'It was like I *hadda* come,' he said intently. 'Like you're the only person I can talk to without feelin' I'm bein' judged.'

'I'm flattered,' she said, reaching for a cookie, even though she knew that right now she was incapable of swallowing.

'Hey, listen,' he said, rubbing his chin. 'I know you're a big movie star and all, but somehow I feel you're my friend.' Another long pause. 'Does that make me crazy, Lara?'

'No, Joey,' she said quietly. 'I am your friend.'

He jumped up, striding over to the edge of the wooden deck, staring out to sea, his back to her. 'I never screwed around on Philly,' he said flatly. 'Although believe me, I had plenty of opportunities. *Plenty*.'

'I'm sure you did,' she murmured.

'Y'see, I believed we were gettin' married. Now I can do what I like.'

'And what *do* you like?'

He spun around and their eyes met again for a long silent moment. 'I'd like t'fly to LA an' meet Mick Stefan. Whaddaya think – am I too late?'

'I'm not sure,' she said truthfully. 'I'll be returning to LA in a few days, the studio's sending a plane. If you want, you can hitch a ride with me and we'll see.'

'Sounds like a plan.'

'Where can I contact you?'

'Dunno,' he said with a vague shrug. 'Can't go back to our apartment, it's hers now.'

'So you have nowhere to live?'

He took another swig of beer. 'I rented a car an' stashed my two suitcases in the trunk. It's my new home.'

'Where will you stay until we leave?'

'I was thinkin' I'd check into the same hotel I was at before.'

'No,' she said quickly. 'Don't do that. Everyone will wonder why you're here.'

'Hey—' he said with a bitter laugh. 'Even I'm wondering why I'm here.'

She fixed him with her cool, green eyes. 'You told me why, Joey. I'm your friend.'

He grinned, marvelling once again at her outstanding beauty. 'OK, *friend*, you wanna have dinner tonight? I know a great little lobster place on the beach.'

She began to laugh. 'The same place you took me to before?'

'We had fun, didn't we?'

'Joey . . .' she said impulsively. 'Why don't you stay here? I'll have the maid set up the guest room, then you can fly to LA with me on Saturday.'

'C'mon, Lara, people will talk.'

'I'm over twenty-one, you know. And you said you needed a friend.' A beat. 'So . . . *will* you stay?'

'Well . . .'

They exchanged warm smiles.

'Good,' Lara said, and the butterflies in her stomach refused to calm down.

24

Richard realized he'd made a mistake sleeping with his assistant. Once sex entered the picture everything changed, and now Kimberly was after him with a vengeance, forever asking when they could get together again. He regretted bringing her back to his house and making love to her. He especially regretted Summer almost catching them together. She hadn't said anything, but she was a bright girl – she knew. He wanted to ask her not to tell Nikki he'd had Kimberly at the house – but if he did, it would be as good as admitting guilt. He simply had to hope she wouldn't open her mouth.

She caught him at breakfast one morning. 'Richard,' she said guilelessly. 'Will you talk to Mom for me?'

'About what?' he asked guardedly.

'Well . . . here's the thing. I uh . . . want to stay in LA. Don't want to go back to Chicago.'

'Tell her yourself.'

'She won't listen to me – we always get in a fight.' She gave him a winning smile. 'But if *you* do it . . .'

'OK,' he agreed, albeit reluctantly.

'Thanks, Richard,' she said, favouring him with a little hug. 'You're the best!'

And he knew she had his number.

☆

Actors trekked in and out of Mick Stefan's office at a lightning pace. He was not a patient man, and if someone started to read and he wasn't immediately sure they were getting it, he leaped to his feet, waved his gangly arms in the air, and yelled, '*Sayonara*,' before they could finish. There were a lot of pissed-off performers marching out of his office.

Nikki was in shock. He did not work like other directors – he certainly didn't work like Richard. Speed was his mantra – *get it done and get it done now!* And he didn't care whose feelings he hurt.

As a favour to her, Richard came to one casting session and left after twenty minutes, shaking his head in disgust. 'You can't treat people the way he does and live,' he said. 'The man's insane. One of these days he'll find an actor waiting in the parking lot with a loaded .45!'

Nikki felt she had to support Mick, this was her movie and it was absolutely necessary that she was in synch with the director, otherwise the film would run away from her. 'It's his way,' she informed Richard. 'Everyone has a different work method.'

She was worried about Lara's reaction to Mick. He was definitely an acquired taste, and once he and Lara got together she might balk at working with him. Even though Lara had verbally agreed to make the movie, she still hadn't signed a contract. Her agent was stalling. Nikki called him daily, but he always had an excuse. It was obvious that he didn't want his most important client starring in a small, low-budget movie – especially since his client had made the decision without consulting him.

Nikki was sure that once Lara got to LA Quinn planned on talking her out of it. *That's* why there was no signed contract on her desk.

Oh God! What a nightmare if Lara backed out.

She spoke to Mick. 'Listen,' she said. 'I'm not saying Lara's on a star trip or anything, only it's imperative that you treat her with respect.'

'Respect – what's that?' Mick said, smirking, the eternal cigarette dangling from his lower lip.

'For starters she hates cigarette smoke,' Nikki said briskly. 'And she won't appreciate you smoking on the set.'

'Don't do it when I'm working,' he said, crinkling his eyes. 'Freakin' problem solved.'

'Also, your language. Can you clean it up for her?'

'Are you out of your mothafuckin' mind?' he said, baiting Nikki because he got off on putting her on. 'I'm gonna treat her like I treat any other actor.'

'Great,' Nikki groaned. 'That'll go down really well.'

Richard couldn't wait to inform her that she'd hired the wrong director. 'He's a loose cannon,' he said ominously. 'I've checked him out.'

'You've also seen his work, so you know he's very talented.'

'*I'm* very talented,' Richard replied immodestly. 'And I don't run around screaming at people and acting like a maniac.'

'Let's give him a chance,' she said. 'I can always fire him.'

'That's a great attitude,' he answered with a derisive snort. 'Do you *know* how much it costs firing a director once you've started shooting? *Revenge* is a low-budget movie, and it's *your* job to keep it that way. If you want my opinion – you've made a *big* mistake talking Lara into doing this.'

'I didn't *talk* her into it,' she said defensively.

'I think you'll find that when she and your precious little genius director get together, it won't be a walk in the park.'

Richard was voicing her worst fears. 'Everything will work out,' she said, standing firm. 'You'll see.'

'I hope so,' he said grimly. 'For your sake.'

Mick persuaded her to hire Aiden Sean for the lead villain. Aiden was an edgy and dangerous actor – not conventionally good-looking, he had a certain sinister style that worked perfectly for the role of the main rapist. The problem was he'd been in and out of drug rehab so many times, he was almost uninsurable. Coke had been his pleasure, heroin his pain – supposedly he was now straight. The fact that he was an extraordinary actor was his only saving grace.

'Can you control him?' she asked Mick, before agreeing to hire him.

'*Me?*' Mick said innocently. 'I can control an army of ants parading up your cute little chick-babe ass!'

'We're on such a tight budget,' she worried, ignoring his sexist remark. 'We can't afford to be a second over.'

'You tell me every day,' Mick replied, with a wide-mouthed yawn.

'I tell you every day so that hopefully it'll sink in.'

'Y'know, I like you,' Mick said as if he'd just made up his mind. 'You're a tough chick-babe – but sexy with it. How'd you get into this business?'

'Don't worry about that,' she said sternly. 'All *you've* got to worry about is getting *Revenge* finished on time and on budget.'

☆

The next morning Summer got up early for once, catching Nikki on her way out. 'How's your movie going, Mom?' she asked, cute and pretty in rumpled cotton pyjamas.

Nikki had taken Richard's advice and eased up on her daughter. It wasn't like she was responsible. Summer lived in Chicago, and would soon be on a plane home. Still . . . she couldn't help regretting that they weren't closer.

'It's going great,' she replied, surprised, since this was the first glimmer of interest Summer had shown in her project.

'Like I'm kinda psyched,' Summer said. 'It's such a way cool thing to do.'

'Yes, it is,' Nikki said, pleased that her daughter was finally paying attention.

'Uh . . . Richard told me you signed Aiden Sean,' Summer added, trailing her to the door.

'That's right,' Nikki said, groping in her purse for her car keys. 'Do you approve?'

'Like he's totally bitchen!' Summer exclaimed, rolling her eyes. 'I'd give *anything* to meet him.'

So *that's* what this new-found interest was all about. *Hmm* . . . Nikki thought, remembering her own hero-worship days. She'd loved Robert Redford. Had a huge crush on Al Pacino. Been destroyed when John Lennon got assassinated.

'We don't start shooting for a while,' she said. 'But when we do, maybe you'll visit the set.'

'That'd be awesome!'

'I have to go now,' she said, checking in her purse to make sure she had her Filofax. 'What are your plans today?'

'The usual,' Summer answered vaguely.

'What's the usual?'

'Shopping, sunbathing. I met this girl – Tina – we hang out together.'

'Sounds fun to me.'

'It is!' Summer said with a big smile. 'Thanks, Mom.'

'For what?'

'Oh, I dunno. It's kinda way cool being here.'

Nikki left with a good feeling. When Summer wanted to, she could be adorable.

☆

That night Nikki and Richard had a quiet dinner at a small Italian restaurant in Malibu. Richard was still in a lecturing mood – carrying on about the do's and don'ts of movie making.

'Contrary to what you think, I *do* know what I'm doing,' Nikki said, fed up with his constant criticism.

'You've got a crazed director, a drugged-out leading man, and Lara for a leading lady,' he nagged. 'This is destined to be some fucked-up shoot.'

'Thanks, Richard,' she said flatly. 'I appreciate your words of encouragement.'

Later, they lay in bed, both keeping to their own sides. David Letterman was chatting with Sandra Bernhard on television – neither of them watched.

This movie is not good for my marriage, Nikki thought. *It's separating us. Driving us apart.*

Unfortunately there was nothing she could do. She had to proceed, there was no choice.

☆

And while Richard and Nikki were safely in bed, Summer was cruising the clubs on the Strip. Her vacation had turned out to be a total blast. It was so cool the way Richard kept on telling her mother to lay off – giving her the freedom she deserved. Things were way too complicated back in Chicago – what with her father and all. If only she could move to LA permanently.

At the Viper Room, Johnny Depp's club on Sunset, she sat in a corner with Jed, Tina, and a few other friends – most of them stoned or drunk.

'OhmiGod!' she suddenly exclaimed. 'Take a look at who just came in.'

'Who?' Tina asked, stretching her neck to see.

'Aiden Sean and Mick Stefan,' Summer said, her eyes swivelling to follow the emaciated-looking actor and the gawky director as they walked up to the bar accompanied by a drugged-out redhead in a black rubber tube dress and purple ankle boots. 'They're both so out there!' she said, flushed with excitement. 'I'm going over.'

'You can't do that,' Jed said, frowning. 'You don't even know 'em.'

'Who cares?' Summer said recklessly. 'Aiden's going to be in my mother's movie, and Mick's directing it – so it's *almost* like I know them.' Her blue eyes gleamed. 'C'mon, Tina, go with me.'

'No,' Tina said haughtily. 'I don't pick up men – *they* come to *me*.'

'That's right!' Jed muttered, not pleased Summer was chasing other guys.

'Well, *I'm* going over,' Summer said, jumping to her feet and sashaying across the room before anyone could stop her.

She went straight up to Aiden Sean. 'Hi,' she said, staring directly at him. He ignored her.

'Get lost, blondie,' said the drugged-out redhead.

'Hello, gorgeous!' Mick responded, lowering his glasses to gaze at this innocent teenage vision with the pouty lips and big blue eyes. 'How about a drink?'

She was carrying a fake ID Jed had given her, so why not?

'Martini,' she said, aware that it was a cool drink.

'One Martini comin' up,' Mick said, licking his rubbery lips.

'Uh . . . thanks,' she said, still staring at Aiden, who was taking absolutely no notice of her. A real bummer because she considered him killer. It was him she wanted, not the geek-faced director.

Three Martinis later she was feeling delightfully dizzy. Jed came over and said they had to go.

'I'll take her home,' Mick said.

'No way, man,' Jed replied.

''S OK,' she managed, even though the room was starting to spin. 'Mick'll look after me.'

Reluctantly Jed left.

'I'm gonna have a big hangover tomorrow,' she giggled. 'Big, big hangover.'

'I got a magic cure for hangovers,' Mick said with a knowing wink.

'What's that?' she asked boldly.

'Come outside to my limo an' I'll show you,' he offered.

Should she? Shouldn't she?

Why not? If she went with Mick, maybe Aiden would notice she existed.

'OK,' she said, suppressing a hiccup.

'OK!' Mick repeated with a wild cackle. And off they went.

By the time I was twenty-one I had a reputation for being a guy who could deliver the goods. And there were plenty of rich women in Hollywood who were into regular sex with a man who could actually get it up.

I had my own apartment, a new Corvette, and a slew of regular appointments. In a way I was living the good life, although I didn't have what I really craved, which was to be a movie star.

I was definitely leading a double life. I had a closet full of expensive clothes – most of them bought for me by grateful clients; and a separate closet filled with jeans and T-shirts.

On one hand I was the big stud. On the other – a guy who still went to acting class, mixing with people who were pumping gas and parking cars.

I even had a legitimate girlfriend, Margie – a sweet girl who didn't know shit about what I did on the side. She was under the mistaken impression I came from a rich family.

I liked Margie because of her innocence. Most of the girls I'd encountered in Hollywood were hard-nuts who'd gotten where they were by winning a beauty contest or some such shit, after which they'd high-tailed it out to Hollywood, done time at the Playboy mansion, fucked every sleazeball playboy in town, and ended up stoned out of their minds.

Margie was different. She lived in the Valley with her family. A former child star, she'd starred in a series until she was fifteen, when suddenly her career came to a sharp stop.

Now she was nineteen and trying to get back in the business.

Margie and I had fun together. It was the first time I'd had fun with a girl who wasn't handing me money.

I had one particular client, Ellie von Steuben, who I had a hunch could do me some good. Ellie was married to Maxwell von Steuben, a big-shot producer. Ellie and I met twice a week in a fancy penthouse on Wilshire Boulevard. I had no idea whose apartment it was, but I suspected it wasn't Ellie's since there was never anything personal around.

'This your place?' I asked her once.

'No,' she replied, refusing to reveal any more information.

Ellie was probably a real looker in her time, and even in her fifties she could still turn heads. She told me her husband hadn't touched her in years. 'He's too kinky for me anyway,' she confided, scratching my back with long talonlike nails. 'He prefers call-girls, so why shouldn't I have my own pleasure?'

No reason, sweetheart. Especially when you're paying me five hundred bucks a time.

Ellie was very businesslike. She made sure the money was always on the bedside table – five crisp hundred-dollar bills. And she wasn't into conversation, all she required was sex – and plenty of it.

I could do that. I could do it better than anyone she'd ever had before.

After a while she started recommending me to friends, which was how I built up such an exclusive clientele. The Hollywood women who weren't gettin' any – they were all mine. The big director's wife. The ex-wife of a superstar. The horniest old agent in town.

One day I asked Ellie if she'd help me with my career.

'I already have,' she replied coolly. 'I've given you more clients than you can handle.'

'That's not the career I'm talking about,' I replied.

She cupped my balls with a perfectly manicured hand and said, 'You don't want to be an actor, darling. Actors are jerk-offs – everybody treats them like garbage. You're king in your field. Stay a king.'

I was angry that she took my ambition so lightly. That night in acting class I got up and performed a scene with Margie. We kicked ass. The whole fuckin' class stood up and applauded.

Our acting teacher, an older man with flowing white hair and yellow skin, took me aside. 'It's time you got yourself an agent,' he said. 'You're ready.'

It was the first encouragement I'd ever gotten. He was telling me I was good enough to be a professional! He was saying I could do it. And fuck it – I could.

I made a decision. I was going to give up hustling and go for it. But first I had to get myself a stash of money. I'd already opened a bank account and taken out a safe deposit box, in which I had a few thousand cash. Now I had to concentrate on really piling it up.

I decided to spend six more months servicing women, then I'd say goodbye to that business. Maybe I'd even marry Margie, buy a little house in the Valley, have a couple of kids – live a normal life.

I started asking Ellie about agents. She started telling me to shut the fuck up and do what I had to do. She wasn't a nice woman.

One night I was doing what I had to do, when Maxwell von Steuben walked in on us. 'Jesus Christ!' he screamed, taking in the scene – Ellie with her legs clasped around my neck and me with my ass in the air. 'Jesus Christ! What kind of a whore am I married to?'

'What kind of a whore are you married to?' she retorted, wriggling out from under me. 'You're the worst whoremonger in this city, and you have the gall to criticize me?'

While they were screaming at each other I began scrambling for my clothes, not forgetting to scoop up the money sitting in its usual place.

Maxwell von Steuben ignored Ellie for a moment, turning his anger on me. 'Who are you?' he yelled, red in the face. 'Who the fuck are you?'

Oh, yeah, like I was gonna tell him.

'You'd better get your filthy ass out of this town. I never want to set eyes on you again.'

I grabbed my clothes and ran.

Ellie usually called me every Monday to set up our weekly appointments. The following Monday she did not call, nor did any of her friends.

The truth dawned. Ellie had been caught, and I was blacklisted. Fuck!

I decided it was a sign – I'd go straight.

So I sold my expensive suits, moved out of my costly apartment, rented a small place, and with my savings managed to keep it together while I did the rounds of agents, and spent more time with Margie – who, although she was very sweet, had begun to bore me.

I finally got me an agent who liked me as much as I liked

myself. A woman, naturally. Had to fuck her, of course, but then she started sending me on auditions, and that was a real kick. I actually landed a couple of small parts in TV shows. And I was good. One thing led to another, and one day I was sent out on an audition for a big action movie.

The day of my interview I sat in an outer office in Hollywood with seven other guys, all of us nervously sweating until it was our turn to go in.

Eventually I was called. I sauntered into the casting room determined to impress.

Sitting around were the usual casting people, a well-known director, and – wouldn't you know it – Maxwell von Steuben himself.

What kind of a lucky break was this?

Our eyes met. It took him a couple of seconds, but he recognized me. The old man leaped to his feet, waving his arms in a blind fury. 'Get him out of here!' he screamed. 'Get him the fuck out! You're finished in this town. Finished! Do you hear me, punk?'

The entire town heard him.

So once again my career as a movie star was put on hold.

25

Dinner with Joey was another memorable experience. Lara felt so comfortable with him – it was as if they'd known each other for years and were in perfect synch. Halfway through the evening he reached for her hand across the table and said, 'Something's happenin' here, Lara, an' I'm not sure what.'

'We're falling in like,' she said, smiling nervously – she who was usually so in control.

He smiled back. 'So *that's* what it is.'

'Maybe.'

They exchanged a long, intimate look.

She held her breath, lost in the moment. Kyle Carson chose that exact moment to enter the restaurant with his date for the night – an almost fully clothed Wilson, in a short orange tank dress that barely covered her ass, and pointy-toed stiletto heels. On her head was the Lara wig.

'Oh, no!' Lara groaned, spotting them and quickly sliding down in her chair.

'What?'

'It's Kyle – with my body double.'

Joey glanced over to where Kyle and Wilson were being seated at a nearby table. 'They seen us?' he asked, squinting across the room.

'I'm not sure,' she replied, dismayed they'd chosen the same restaurant.

'Somehow I got a feelin' you don't want them to.'

'Guess again.'

'Let's split, then. You slide off to the john, I'll grab the check. We'll meet outside.'

'Can we get away with it?' she asked hopefully.

'Yeah – if you go now, before they see you.'

She eased out of her seat and hurried to the ladies' room, hoping Kyle wouldn't spot her.

Safely inside, she leaned against the mirrored vanity unit studying her reflection. Joey had said it first: 'Something's happening here, I'm not sure what.'

Then she'd given him her flip reply. Nikki would be proud of her – she was coming up with lines!

Once again, her heart was racing. This was definitely the start of something, it was only a matter of time. Reaching in her purse, she removed her compact and began to powder her nose.

'Lara!' Wilson's reflection appeared in the mirror behind her. 'What are *you* doing here?'

'Oh, hi,' she said, furious at getting caught.

'Gotta say the scene went great,' Wilson boasted, tugging at her short dress. 'Boy! He's some sexy guy.'

'Who?' Lara asked quickly, hoping she wasn't referring to Joey.

'Kyle, of course,' Wilson said, fishing in her purse for a pot of jammy red lip gloss and a thick brush. She moved up beside Lara in the mirror and began applying the goo to her overly full lips. 'Do you happen to know what his situation is now? Somebody told me he's getting back with his wife. *I* don't think so. Let me tell you – he's *hot* to macarena – an' honey, I'm *into* dancin'!'

'I'm sure,' Lara murmured.

'Who're *you* with?' Wilson asked, dabbing on too much gloss.

'Friends,' Lara replied vaguely. 'We're on our way out.'

'Shame,' Wilson said. 'We could've all joined up.'

'Wouldn't that cramp your hot to macarena action?'

Wilson laughed. 'Right!'

Lara began edging toward the exit.

'See ya,' Wilson called out, heading into one of the stalls.

'Uh . . . thanks for doing a good job,' Lara said.

'Honey,' Wilson joked, 'your nipples never looked so good!'

Lara hurried outside to where Joey was waiting. 'I got cornered in the ladies' room,' she said.

'What're you worried about?'

'I don't want the whole set talking about us. Everyone

knows you're engaged, I'd be perceived as some kind of . . . you know . . . fiancé stealer.'

'Fiancé stealer?' he said, laughing at her.

She couldn't help joining in.

'C'mon,' he said, 'I'm taking the fiancé stealer home.'

'I have a better idea,' she said impulsively. 'Let's go for a walk along the beach. It's something I've been dying to do.'

'So how come you haven't done it?'

She laughed self-consciously. 'I'm scared.'

He regarded her quizzically. 'What of?'

She shrugged. 'I don't know, the dark, the unknown . . . There are times I don't feel . . . safe.'

'Lara,' he said, his handsome face serious, 'when I'm around, you need never be scared.'

She nodded, not sure how to respond.

'Anyhow,' he said, 'tonight I'm takin' you straight home. You've got an early call tomorrow.'

'What about our walk?' she asked, disappointed.

'Another time.'

'Promise?'

'We'll see.'

☆

'I got to fuck you last night,' Kyle said in a low-down dirty voice. It was early in the morning and he'd sidled up behind Lara's chair, taking her by surprise.

'Excuse me?' she said, not quite sure she'd heard correctly.

'And it was *goood*,' he said, making a smacking noise with his lips. 'Finger-lickin' *goood*!'

She gave him a cold look. 'Are you losing it, Kyle?'

'If you can't get the real thing, go for the substitute,' he said, laughing rudely. 'I put my hand over Wilson's face, and what with the wig and the body, I could've sworn I was fucking you.'

'You're disgusting,' she said contemptuously.

'No,' he replied, not at all put out. '*I'm* honest.' A short pause. 'By the way, I hear we were at the same restaurant last night. Who was *your* hot date?'

'I have to work with you, Kyle,' she said icily. 'I sure as hell don't have to talk to you.'

Roxy walked over. 'What's up?' she asked, noticing Lara was upset.

Kyle slouched away and began talking to Miles.

'The man's a pig,' Lara said vehemently.

'They all are,' Roxy sighed, like it was no big surprise.

'Kyle's the worst.'

'What'd he do now?'

'Believe me,' Lara said, shaking her head, 'you don't want to know.'

'Oh, yes I do!' Roxy replied, always up for juicy gossip.

'How come Wilson got to leave the set last night with the wig?' Lara asked.

'That bitch!' Roxy said, narrowing her eyes. 'I *told* her to come straight to the hair trailer with it, and she never showed up. This morning I found it stuffed in a bag outside my hotel room – and a fine mess it's in, too. God knows what she did with it!'

'Forget God, try Kyle,' Lara murmured.

'Oh, *really*?' Roxy said. 'And why should I be surprised, he's dicked everything else that has a pulse!'

Miles came over. 'Ready, my sweet?'

'Yes, Miles.' And she thought— *Only three more days and I never have to see Kyle Carson again.*

Forgetting about her personal feelings, she threw herself into the first scene of the day, hoping to get by with as few takes as possible.

Of course, Kyle blew it as usual, fluffing his lines and worrying about his hair.

At the lunch break she had one of the drivers take her to her house. Cassie was on the phone in the living room, surrounded by boxes, organizing everything for their imminent departure.

'What are *you* doing here?' Cassie asked, putting the phone on hold.

'Had to take a break, too much testosterone flying around the set,' Lara said, adding a casual— 'Uh . . . where's Joey?'

'Out,' Cassie said.

'Did he say where he was going?'

'Nope.'

Lara went into her bedroom, wondering why she felt so disappointed. She'd run home like a schoolgirl with a crush, and now he wasn't even here. Hmm ... Never expect anything in life and you'll never get disappointed.

A few minutes later Cassie knocked on her bedroom door. 'Lara,' she said, hovering in the doorway, 'is it OK if I say something out of line?'

'*Nooo*,' Lara replied, smiling faintly because she knew Cassie would say it anyway.

'This Joey guy—' Cassie said, a frown creasing her brow. 'What do you know about him?'

'As much as I need to.'

'Granted he's great-looking,' Cassie continued. 'But so are a lot of other guys.'

'Your point?'

'Are you sure it's wise letting him stay here?'

'It's only for a couple of days,' Lara said defensively. 'He's hardly an axe murderer. Don't worry, Cass, I know what I'm doing.'

'If you say so,' Cassie said, nodding unsurely. If she had her way Lara would get back together with Richard.

'I'd better return to the set,' Lara said. 'When Joey returns, tell him I'll be home later. Oh, and have the cook fix pasta tonight, we'll be eating outside.'

'It's done,' Cassie said.

☆

Shortly after Lara left for the studio, Joey had gotten in his rented car and taken a ride. He had to get out of the house, Cassie had her eye on him, and he was aware he hadn't won her over. She was suspicious, couldn't quite figure him out. Staying around was dangerous.

He drove aimlessly, stopping at the drug store to pick up a pack of cigarettes.

Madelaine had not been pleased when he'd announced he was moving on. 'Why are you leaving this time?' she'd demanded. 'I got you a job, gave you a place to live, what more do you want?'

'I can't make you happy, Maddy,' he'd said – the oldest line in the world, but it worked every time because there *was* no answer.

'You can try,' Madelaine had said, near tears of frustration.

'No,' he'd replied. 'I'll only make you miserable, and that's not good for either of us. I'm flyin' to LA – takin' a shot.'

'What about my money?' she'd asked, forgetting her tears for a moment.

'I'll pay it back.'

'When?'

'Keep my cheque for the movie when it comes in.'

'Don't imagine you can get around me again, Joey,' she'd warned. 'If you go this time – that's it.'

Yeah. Sure. I can walk into your life any time I want and you'll always take me back.

'I understand,' he'd said.

And so it was over and he'd hired a car, and driven out to see Lara.

He wasn't surprised that she'd asked him to stay. Some things were meant to be.

26

Early every morning Nikki left the Malibu house and drove to the *Revenge* production offices in the Valley. She had her own private office next to Mick's. He'd surrounded himself with a team of alarmingly young production people, while she'd brought in several thirtysomethings who knew what they were doing, and a very capable line producer. Hopefully, together, they'd make a cohesive group.

Everything was a go situation. The advantage of having Lara in the lead role was that they didn't require any other star names. Apart from Aiden Sean, the movie was cast with a group of talented unknowns; the financing was in place, and principal photography began in two weeks. Being a producer was very different from merely designing the clothes. Now she was in a boss situation, and it felt good when everyone came to her for answers.

Only another two days and Lara would arrive from New York, then she could meet with Mick. *Oh, God!* Nikki thought. *They're either going to hate each other or it will be a love fest.* She prayed it was the latter.

If only Richard would lighten up. She'd expected him to be proud of her for what she was doing, instead he did nothing but put her down.

So far she hadn't met Aiden Sean, although Mick kept insisting the three of them should get together, so today they were having lunch.

'I'm depending on you to keep him in line,' she reminded Mick sternly. 'Aiden's your responsibility. If he screws up, it's all your fault.'

'I got it, I got it,' Mick said, snapping his fingers in the air.

'Any trouble at all and he's out. I hope you've told him that.'

'Don't havta tell him. He knows.'

When Aiden turned up an hour late, Nikki was shocked at how pale and gaunt he was. White, almost translucent skin stretched across the fine bones of his haunted face, bleak ice-grey eyes, dusty brown hair pulled back in a scruffy ponytail, and a painfully skinny body decorated with various tattoos. In spite of being a scary presence, he was still attractive in an offbeat, drugged-out way. Like a world-weary rock star – he had the look.

He shook Nikki's hand, burnt-out eyes staring right through her. She noticed that his nicotine-stained fingers trembled when he went to light a cigarette immediately after their introduction.

Mick had assured her that Aiden was straight now – in all kinds of programmes – a guaranteed reformed addict.

No true drug addict is ever reformed, she thought – *they're merely taking a long pause before their next fix.*

If Aiden had not been an out-and-out junkie for so many years, he could have had a big career. As it was, he'd only managed to survive in the business because he was fiercely talented and always gave an amazing performance – in spite of being half crazy on drugs most of the time. Directors liked to employ him because he always delivered. Producers didn't because he was a major risk.

The three of them went to an Italian restaurant on Ventura. Aiden slid into the padded leather booth, immediately ordering a double Jack Daniel's on the rocks. Nikki observed that he smoked three cigarettes before the salad, even though the waitress – a pretty girl who was a fan – kept informing him there was no smoking in the restaurant.

'Fuck it,' Aiden said, his voice like cracked tar over gravel. 'A guy's gotta have *some* outlet.' Ice-grey eyes carefully checked her out. 'I gave it all up, Nikki,' he said mournfully. 'No coke, no speed, no fucking anything. I'm havin' a drink – don't let it bother you – I give up drinking when I'm working.'

'I'm *sooo* looking forward to being on the set with you two,' Nikki drawled. 'Mick doesn't smoke when he's working, *you* don't drink. Wow – this is going to be a blast watching the two of you control your addictions.'

Aiden smiled – a small, thin smile. 'You produced any-thing before, Nikki?'

'No,' she said, immediately on the defensive. 'However, I've worked in movies for the last six years. I've had plenty of experience.'

'Doing what?'

'Costume designer,' she replied, determined not to let him intimidate her. 'And of course, my husband's Richard Barry, so I've certainly had an education in all aspects of making movies.'

Now why had she told him *that*? He was supposed to be impressing *her*, she didn't have to give him her résumé.

'How old're you?' he asked, sucking on an ice cube.

'That's an extremely rude question to ask a woman.'

He expelled the ice cube back into his glass. 'You ashamed of your age? What are you – thirty-five – forty?'

'Thanks a lot,' she said indignantly. 'Thirty-two.'

He chuckled – a chuckle with a mean streak. 'Knew I could get it out of you.'

'Why?' she couldn't resist asking. 'Do I look older?'

'Just f-in' with you, darlin',' he said casually.

Shouldn't he be kissing her ass? This was the first job he'd had in eighteen months and, with his track record, he was lucky to get it.

'How old are *you*?' she demanded, not happy with his attitude.

'Thirty-four goin' on dead,' he said blankly.

'You're both old,' Mick said with a crazed cackle. 'Now me, I still got it goin'. Last week I had a babe who couldn't've been more than fifteen givin' me head in the back of my limo.'

'And you're *proud* of that?' Nikki asked, amazed.

Mick sniggered. 'It's a guy thing,' he said with a superior smirk.

'Yeah – probably a guy who can't get it up,' Nikki muttered.

'Now, now – don't go getting jealous,' Aiden said, mock-ing her.

Oh, God, she'd been worried about Lara meeting Mick, when this one was ten times worse.

She didn't want to think about the rape scene. Richard

had warned her to be absolutely sure about the people she hired – especially the actors – and she hadn't listened. Now he'd spend the next seven weeks saying, 'I told you so.'

She decided getting too friendly with these two misfits was not a good thing. Distance was good. A cool attitude would let them know who was boss.

As soon as she'd finished eating she consulted her watch, said a quick— 'I hate to eat and run, but I have an appointment.'

'Somethin' I should be at?' Mick asked, mouth twitching.

'No. It's uh ... personal,' she said, sliding out of the booth.

'See ya on the set,' Aiden said, looking her over in a way that made her uncomfortable.

She hurried from the restaurant, stood outside on the sidewalk waiting for her car, and took a big gulp of fresh air.

There was something about Aiden Sean that spelled trouble.

Nothing she could do about it now – his contract was signed, he was part of the team.

And yet ... in spite of everything, he did have a certain charisma – working with him would definitely not be dull.

Her car arrived and she jumped in, tipping the valet much too generously.

She had work to do. Time to concentrate.

☆

'I haven't called Mick and I don't intend to,' Summer said defiantly. ''Cause I didn't even like him. Aiden Sean's the hot one.'

'Then why'd you do stuff with Mick in the back of his limo?' Tina asked, ever practical.

'I *didn't*,' Summer answered indignantly. 'One sloppy kiss, and then he made me try to suck his you know what.'

'Did you?'

'No way. I thought going outside with him would get Aiden to notice me. I was into a stupid fit,' Summer admitted. 'Don't you ever do anything that even when you're *doing* it you know is dumb?'

They were sitting on the beach wearing minuscule bikinis

with thong bottoms, smoking a joint and working on their tans.

'Yes,' Tina agreed. 'When I was a hokey little kid.'

'You're not so old.'

'I've been around.'

'So have I,' Summer said, throwing back her head to catch the sun.

A fiftyish man, jogging along the beach, double-taked both girls and almost stopped.

'Married. Three kids. Cushy job,' Tina said, eyeing him up and down. 'I could have him any time I wanted.'

'Men!' Summer said.

'Pricks for brains,' Tina said.

'You've got it!' Summer agreed.

And they both rolled on the beach in fits of giggles.

27

Lara and Joey walked along the seashore hand in hand, barefoot and completely at ease with each other. They'd eaten dinner on the back deck – light pasta and a green salad accompanied by a bottle of red wine. After they were finished, Joey had said, 'C'mon, we're takin' that walk along the beach you were on about.'

'Great,' Lara had replied, her mouth dry with anticipation.

Now they were together, strolling along the damp sand, and she couldn't stop thinking about what would happen next. It was inevitable that he'd make a move, unless she was reading something into their friendship that didn't exist.

This was ridiculous, merely holding his hand was having a major effect. Talk about chemistry!

Halfway back to the house, he stopped and sat on the sand, pulling her down next to him. 'Take a look at the moon,' he said. 'Somethin', huh?'

'Beautiful!' she sighed.

'Like you.'

'Thanks,' she murmured, wondering why her pulse was racing and she felt so lightheaded.

'Hey, Lara,' he said, jumping up. 'Let's take a swim.'

'Don't be ridiculous,' she replied nervously. 'It's dark and cold. You won't see a thing.'

He laughed, stripping off his shirt. 'You think the fish care?' he said. 'You think they give a rat's ass whether it's dark or light?' He unzipped his pants, stepping out of them.

'You're crazy,' she said, shaking her head. 'You don't even have a towel.'

'Miss Practical,' he said, teasing her.

'Well, it's true,' she said, hating herself for sounding like the school prude.

'C'mon,' he said, pulling her up. 'There's nothin' like the ocean at night. It's like bein' in a big, dark, think tank.'

'I don't have a swimsuit,' she said primly.

'Your underwear will do,' he said, standing next to her in his jockey shorts, his clothes in a pile by his feet.

'What makes you think I wear any?' she asked boldly.

'Oh, *you* do,' he said, laughing at her. 'I'd bet a thousand big ones you do.'

'Why's that?'

''Cause all good girls wear panties.' She couldn't help laughing. 'Let's do it,' he urged. 'You gotta live dangerously some of the time.'

'I . . . I can't afford to catch cold.'

'Not into adventure?'

Her heart began racing. Joey had such an incredible effect on her, and she had no idea how to handle her feelings.

'OK, so *don't* do it,' he said, 'but I'm outta here,' and before she could stop him, he raced into the sea, plunging head-first into the breaking waves.

She stood on the moonlit beach, shivering. *Join him,* her inner voice urged. *If you want something to happen, then do it.*

She stepped out of her dress, tentatively approaching the cold water until the sea was lapping around her ankles. 'Joey,' she called, staring into darkness. 'Joey!' she shouted, edging further into the surf.

She was almost up to her waist in water when he pounced. 'Gotcha!' he yelled, grabbing her from behind.

'OhmiGod!' she shrieked, shivering uncontrollably. 'You startled me!'

'Follow me,' he said, taking her hand in his.

They waded out until the water was above her shoulders. 'Now start swimming,' he commanded.

'Not too far,' she said nervously. 'I . . . I can't see anything.'

'Don't sweat it,' he assured her. 'I'm right beside you.'

She wasn't the strongest swimmer in the world, but she trusted him, and he was right – this was an adventure. And why shouldn't she have fun instead of doing nothing but work?

They swam out in the dark ocean. They could feel the waves swelling around them, before lazily making their way inland and crashing on the shore. 'Uh . . . Joey . . . I want to go back,' Lara shouted, starting to get nervous.

'OK,' he yelled. 'Turn around an' follow me.'

She did as he said, and they began swimming toward the beach, struggling against a sudden undercurrent.

Lara swam strongly, but she soon found herself lagging behind.

'C'mon!' Joey yelled over the noise of the sea.

She was out of breath and on the edge of panic as she struggled to keep up. Oh, God! Tomorrow her hair would be full of salt water, her eyes red and bloodshot from the cold. She'd look a mess, and Yoko and Roxy would have to work hard to put her together. That's if she ever made it to shore.

Something brushed against her leg. She let out a startled scream, her eyes wide with fear. 'Are there sharks here?' she gasped.

'Sharks?' he yelled over his shoulder. 'Yeah. Tons of 'em!'

She began doing a frantic crawl, trying desperately to catch up with him.

'Hey – stop freakin' out,' he said, treading water until she drew alongside. 'Guess what? You can stand here.'

Her feet touched the bottom and she calmed down.

'C'mon,' he said, taking her hand again. 'We'd better get you outta here before a shark eats you up!'

'Very funny,' she said crossly, gasping for breath as they staggered out of the water onto the damp sand.

'How are we going to dry off?' she asked, once again shivering uncontrollably.

'Body warmth,' he said, wrapping his arms around her and hugging her close. 'It'll do it every time.'

It was then she realized that somewhere between going in and coming out he'd lost his jockey shorts.

She felt his hardness pressing insistently against her leg. 'Joey . . .' she began, 'I . . .'

He brought his lips down on hers, and all rational thought deserted her as he began exploring her mouth with his tongue.

It was finally happening, and she was powerless to stop it. What's more, she had no desire to do so.

They kissed for a long time, kisses the like of which she'd never experienced. One moment his lips were tender, the next – strong and assertive, his tongue slowly caressing her teeth, making her shudder with the anticipation of what was to come next.

He didn't rush things, he took his time, until she was silently begging him to touch her in other places.

Her nipples were erect, straining against the wet silkiness of her bra. She longed for him to undo the clip and touch her breasts. She'd reached the point of no return – a moment she'd been building toward for weeks.

He continued kissing her – long, sensual kisses that were beginning to drive her a little bit crazy.

Weak with desire, she moaned, reaching down to caress him.

He removed her hand as if to say – *Be patient. I'll tell you when.*

Although the wind was bitter, she didn't notice. Every inch of her was on fire, all she could think about was Joey being inside her.

He treated her with extreme care. Lara wasn't like other women – she was a beautiful Princess who made him feel like a Prince. *Her* Prince.

From the day he'd set eyes on her he'd given up casual sex, saving himself for her.

Her mouth was so sweet – she tasted of all things good and fresh.

Ignoring the urge to throw her down on the sand and make hard passionate love to her, he held back, curbing his appetite – because he knew he had to make this night extraordinary.

Very slowly he began touching her breasts.

She moaned again, thrusting toward him, silently urging him to release her from the confines of her bra.

He didn't. Instead he began teasing her nipples through the flimsy material, stroking them ever so lightly.

'Take ... it ... off,' she mumbled, unable to stop herself from begging, frightened that she'd come before him, because she couldn't recall when she'd ever been this aroused. *'Please!'*

He lightly brushed the tips of her nipples with his fingertips.

Feverishly she reached up, unclipping the front fastening on her bra.

Slowly he peeled her bra open, revealing her breasts. Beautiful, just like the rest of her. He cupped them in his hands. Then, pushing her to her knees, he began rubbing his cock against her erect nipples, moving back and forth between them, faster and faster.

'Joey!' she gasped his name, totally unaware of the cold wind and the gritty wet sand digging into her knees.

'What?' he asked. 'Tell me exactly what you'd like.'

'You!' she said, her breath catching in her throat. 'I . . . want . . . you!'

He put his hands under her arms, picked her up and began kissing her again – long, torturous kisses – more pleasurable than anything she'd ever known.

Next he raised her hands above her head, while he bent his mouth to her left breast and drew in the nipple as if he was suckling milk.

'Ohhh . . .' Before she could help herself, she came with a series of shuddering convulsions that shook her body from tip to toe. And he hadn't even touched her where she craved to be touched.

He released her hands, pulling her to him. She snuggled against his chest, her body tingling with a deep warm satisfaction.

'Was that good for you, baby?' he asked, stroking her hair. 'Was it special?'

'God, yes!'

'Tomorrow it'll be even better.'

'Forget about tomorrow,' she murmured, inhaling his salty masculine smell and loving it. 'Let's go home to bed.'

'No,' he said, firmly. 'You've gotta work tomorrow. Sleep comes first.'

'But, Joey . . .'

He placed a finger on her lips— 'Quiet,' he commanded. 'Let's get dressed before we freeze.'

They groped on the sand for their clothes, hurriedly dressed, and raced back to the house. She was expecting him to come to her bedroom, but he didn't. He kissed her chastely on the lips and bid her a fast goodnight.

She was completely stunned that he would leave her, and yet she knew he was right, she *did* have an early call, and if he'd come into her bed neither of them would have gotten any sleep.

She lay in bed, thinking about his face, his hair, his smell, the way he smiled.

Joey Lorenzo. Was he her destiny? Had she finally found the man capable of making her forget her past?

☆

Joey went to his room, restlessly paced around, and lit up a cigarette. So *this* is what he'd heard about all these years. *This* was love.

It didn't seem possible that it had happened to him. He'd never wanted it, never expected it. Women were women and getting laid was getting laid.

Now this. Christ! What was he supposed to do?

He waited until she'd left in the morning, and then took off.

It was the only way.

☆

Lara's alarm woke her at five a.m. She was so tired she could barely stagger out of bed. She immediately began sneezing and didn't dare look in the mirror.

At work Roxy greeted her with a caustic— 'What in *hell* happened to your hair?'

'I . . . I went swimming in the sea . . .'

'Shit, Lara,' Roxy said, running a hand through her own spiky locks, 'we're gonna havta shampoo.'

She sneezed twice in quick succession. 'OK.'

'Don't tell me you caught a cold?'

'Seems like it.'

'Great!' Roxy grumbled. 'Now we'll all get sick.'

'I promise not to breathe in your direction.'

'Yeah, yeah.'

Yoko was not much kinder; just as Lara had suspected,

her eyes were bloodshot from the salt water. Yoko noticed immediately and complained loudly, then she made her lie on a couch with cucumber slices over her eyes for fifteen minutes, and after that she smeared a thick mud treatment all over her face.

By the time Roxy and Yoko were finished with her, she looked her usual gorgeous self. Unfortunately she was an hour late hitting the set.

Kyle was in a sulk, while Miles paced up and down, mumbling ominously under his breath.

'Glad you could make it,' Miles said sarcastically.

'Yeah, Lara, nice of you to honour us with your presence,' Kyle added.

'This is the first time I've been late,' she pointed out, thinking that all she wanted to do was complete the day's scenes and hurry home to Joey. They needed to talk, discuss what was going on between them.

How had it happened so quickly? One moment they were casual friends – the next they were naked on the beach, and she'd wanted him so much she would have done anything he'd asked.

Oh, God – even thinking about him now she felt herself becoming aroused. The way he'd made her come . . . it was like he'd hardly touched her and she was ready.

Was she that desperate for a man?

No. She could have any man she wanted. It just so happened Joey was the one.

She thought about his muscled body, knowing eyes, and the way he looked at her with such direct intensity . . .

'What are you smiling about?' Kyle demanded, startling her back to reality. 'This is supposed to be a serious scene.'

'Uh . . . sorry . . . I was just uh . . . remembering something funny.'

'Didja get it on last night, Lara?' he asked slyly, nudging her.

She flushed. Was it written all over her face for the world to see? 'Excuse me?' she said, freezing him out.

'Guess not,' he sneered. 'The Ice Princess doesn't do it, does she?'

At lunch break she borrowed Jane's cellphone and called home. Cassie answered.

'Get me Joey,' she said, drumming her fingers impatiently on the side of the phone.

'He's gone,' Cassie said.

'Gone,' she repeated blankly.

'Told me he had an emergency in the city. He'll call you tomorrow.'

'*What* emergency?'

'Don't know.'

'Did he leave a number?'

'Nope.'

'Well, why didn't you get one?' She heard herself shouting and abruptly stopped. She shouldn't take it out on Cassie, it wasn't her fault.

'Sorry,' Cassie said, sounding hurt. 'I didn't realize it was that important.'

'It's not,' she said, and clicked off the phone.

'Something wrong?' asked Yoko, who was standing nearby.

'Nothing,' she said, wondering how she was going to get through the night without him. 'Nothing at all.'

28

After the incident outside the Directors' Guild, Alison Sewell appeared in court, and was sentenced to eighteen months in jail for stalking, aggravated assault and attacking a policeman.

Alison considered the whole thing grossly unfair. She wasn't stalking Lara. She was her friend. Didn't the morons get it? SHE WAS HER FUCKING FRIEND.

Why weren't the dumb cops out arresting real villains? Murderers and rapists, child molesters and thieves?

Some stupid private investigator, hired by Lara's business manager, had produced all the letters she'd written to Lara. Those letters were private, and were for Lara's eyes only. But the stupid investigator stood up in court and read extracts aloud for all to hear. Alison was furious.

Then Lara herself had gotten up and claimed that she, Alison Sewell, had been bothering her for months, turning up at her house uninvited, making over a hundred unwanted phone calls, trying to gain access to wherever she was working.

What bullshit nonsense. All Alison had done was try to be her friend, and look where it had gotten her. Prison. Locked up with actual criminals.

She shared a cell with some loony who'd poisoned all the cats in her neighbourhood – a nice old lady with white hair and a pleasant demeanour. Until one night, when Alison was dozing, the old cow had tried to strangle her.

Her new cell mate was a bottle-blond hooker who'd stabbed one of her johns and now refused to speak.

This suited Alison fine. She had a lot of thinking to do.

Because when she got out – Lara Ivory was going to pay.

29

The phone refused to ring. For two nights Lara stared at it feeling like a lovesick fool, until she realized that of course – there must be something wrong with the line.

She picked up the receiver. Perfectly normal dial tone. Slamming it down, she grabbed a book and attempted to concentrate.

Impossible. All the while a little voice kept chanting in her head – *Joey . . . Joey . . . Joey . . .* And she kept reliving their evening together in her head – fast-forwarding to the beach – the two of them running out of the ocean . . . falling into each other's arms . . . the way he'd touched her . . . the intensity of her orgasm . . .

Oh, God! All she had to do was think about him and she was completely finished. She'd never felt this way with Richard. And as for Lee – he'd merely been a comfortable interlude.

As far as she was concerned it had been magical. What was *his* problem?

Phillipa. That had to be his problem.

Phillipa. Could he have gone back to her?

She felt like an idiot. Joey Lorenzo entered her life and five minutes later she'd invited him into her house and practically begged him to make love to her on the beach. Now he was gone without a word of explanation. Joey Lorenzo. *Where the hell are you?*

The movie was finished. Cassie had packed up everything, tonight was the wrap party and tomorrow morning she'd be on a plane home to LA.

Without Joey Lorenzo thank you very much. And you'd better get used to it, he's definitely history.

She was Lara Ivory – movie star. And in spite of the adulation and vast rewards she was lonely. Achingly lonely. Haunted by her past and unable to forget. Somehow she'd thought Joey would change all that.

But no, he'd seen beneath the façade. He'd seen the ugly little slut . . .

Oh, God. How could she ever forget her father's harsh words. And his blood . . . splashing over her . . . the chunks of charred flesh . . .

Abruptly she put her book down and forced herself to start getting dressed for the party.

The phone rang. She reached for it.

'How's everything?' Nikki asked.

'Great!' she replied, falsely cheerful.

'Can't wait till you're here,' Nikki said. 'Mick's dying to meet you.'

'You're getting along?'

'Don't believe one word you hear about him. He's a touch eccentric, but that goes with the talent.'

They chatted for a few more minutes. Lara was tempted to confide about Joey, then decided she had nothing to gain from revealing her schoolgirl crush.

As soon as she put the phone down she began thinking about *Revenge* and the gruelling weeks of work ahead. Quinn was right – she should never have agreed to make the movie, the shooting schedule was a killer, and having just completed two major films back to back what she needed was a long vacation.

If it was anyone else but Nikki . . .

No. She refused to let her best friend down, it wouldn't be fair. Besides, making *Revenge* would take her mind off Joey.

She finished dressing for the party in a simple turquoise dress and strappy sandals. There would be dancing on the beach and all the guys from the crew would expect to have their picture taken with her.

She brushed her hair, then added gold hoop earrings and a wide gold bracelet Richard had given her shortly after their marriage. Satisfied with her appearance, she went downstairs.

Joey was standing in the living room talking to Cassie.

For a moment she was filled with confusion. Joey was back. Her Joey.

He's not your Joey. Get your head together and stop fantasizing.

She stood very still.

'Look who's here,' Cassie said, like it wasn't painfully obvious.

Time to return to her movie star roots. Chill him out. Nobody played Ice Princess better than Lara Ivory.

'Joey,' she said lightly. 'What are you doing here?'

'I'll go see if the car's outside,' Cassie said, hurriedly heading for the door.

'Don't!' Lara said sharply.

Cassie paused, unsure what to do.

'Uh . . . I'd kinda like to speak to you alone,' Joey ventured, giving her one of his intense stares.

'I'm sorry,' she replied, green eyes freezing him out. 'We're late for the wrap party. Maybe another time.'

He edged closer, speaking in a low voice. 'You're pissed, huh? Not interested in hearin' why I had to split.'

For a moment she weakened. Then her strong side took over and she thought, *To hell with him – he's stringing me along like some nothing little bimbo.*

'No, Joey, I'm not angry,' she said evenly. 'Why should I be?' And as she spoke, she moved toward the door, adding an off-handed— 'Right now you'll have to excuse us.'

'Phillipa tried to kill herself,' he muttered flatly. 'OD'd on pills.'

She stopped abruptly. 'Oh, God!'

'Don't you understand?' he continued. 'I *had* to leave.'

'Wait in the car,' she said to Cassie, who quickly left. 'Why didn't you call me?' she asked, turning on him accusingly. 'Why did you take off without a word?'

'Had to get my head straight,' he explained, running a hand through his thick dark hair. 'You've no idea what it was like – the guilt – sittin' in the hospital . . . knowin' that all I wanted was to be with you.'

'Oh,' she said, completely confused.

'Soon as she was strong enough, I told her there was someone else, an' came right back.' He moved closer, taking her hand in his. 'Didn't mean to let you down.'

A feeling of relief swept over her. Perhaps there was a future for them after all. 'It can't have been easy,' she said quietly.

'Hey—' he said, squeezing her hand. 'It wasn't.' And he knew, as he gazed into her eyes, that his plan had worked – she was all his. 'If it's OK with you, this time I'm stayin'.'

She felt the sheer physical thrill of having him close again, and her anger and disappointment slowly began to dissolve. 'Yes, Joey,' she said, with a little sigh. 'It's perfectly all right with me.'

☆

'Holy shit!' Roxy shrieked. 'Will ya get an eyeful of who Lara's comin' in with.'

'Who?' Yoko asked, craning to see.

'Joey whatever his name is. And Lordy, Miss Y – they are holdin' hands!'

'No!'

'See for yourself.'

'Thought he was engaged.'

'One sniff around our Lara, an' his engagement musta taken a dive.'

Roxy and Yoko weren't the only two observing Lara's entrance – the buzz was everywhere. Kyle, who'd flown in his estranged wife, Jean, for the party, noticed immediately. '*What* is Lara doing with *that* deadbeat?' he demanded of Jean – a pretty woman with curled brown hair and a long-suffering expression.

'What's wrong with him?' Jean asked, wondering if her unfaithful dog of a husband had slept with the exquisite actress.

'He's an extra, for Chrissakes,' Kyle said grumpily, non-plussed that Lara would show up with such a loser when she could've had him. 'Jesus Christ!' he added, conveniently forgetting about his own many indiscretions. 'Doesn't she get it? Hollywood Rule number one – *never* screw below the line.'

☆

'I got a hunch we're causin' a commotion,' Joey remarked.

'What?' Lara asked, clasping his hand.

'I'm tellin' you – we're exhibit number one. Everyone's starin'.'

'Really?' she said, completely unabashed. Let them stare, let them all stare. She was with Joey, and she didn't care who knew it.

'Your hairdresser's eyes are out on stalks!' he added, laughing.

'Hmm . . .' she said, with the trace of a smile, 'I've a feeling you were starring in a few of Roxy's fantasies.'

'I was?' he asked innocently.

'Come on, Joey,' she chided. 'You must know how women feel about you – they consider you prey.'

'You say the cutest things!'

'It's true,' she said, smiling broadly. 'I'm sure you're aware of your lethal effect.'

'I'm not interested in *women*,' he stated. 'Only you.'

'How gallant,' she said, shivering with anticipation, because tonight they'd surely consummate their relationship.

'Cold?' he asked, concerned.

'No. *Veree, veree* hot,' she murmured, teasingly.

'Hey,' he said, grinning, 'you're tellin' me? I'm the lucky guy who was on the beach with you – remember?'

Their eyes met, fusing a connection that blew her away. 'I . . . I've got to mingle,' she said, catching her breath. 'Y'know, take pictures with the crew, play nice.'

'Are we goin' to LA in the mornin'?' he asked casually.

'You're coming?'

He grinned again. 'Think I'd let you go without me?'

30

'**What in hell's** going on?' Roxy asked Trinee, raising her painted eyebrows.

'How would I know?' Trinee replied, irritated because she didn't.

'You were tight with the guy. You should be able to give us the scam.'

Trinee shrugged. 'Soon as he unglues himself from her side, I'll ask him.'

'Do that,' Roxy said. ''Cause I know men, and this one's a player.'

'Why do you say that?' Yoko interrupted. 'We never saw him screw around, and he sure had plenty of opportunities.'

'I got a hunch about him,' Roxy said, nodding knowingly. 'He's not for Lara.'

'You've got a hunch 'cause you wanted him for yourself,' Yoko said. 'Now our star has him and you're green, baby.'

'Not true,' Roxy objected. 'I'm *glad* Lara's landed herself a guy. I only hope he's the right one.'

'Tall, dark and handsome, something wrong with that?'

'Lara's not street-smart like us,' Roxy responded. 'She hasn't been around the block three hundred times.'

'Speak for yourself,' Yoko said crisply. 'Personally, I'm a one-man woman.'

'Yeah,' Roxy muttered. 'One man at a time.'

☆

Joey found a corner and settled back in a chair. Lara had fallen into position – no problem. Keep 'em wanting more and they'll always be there.

It occurred to him that maybe he hadn't needed to play games, but it had certainly been a smart move.

After taking off, he'd checked into a nearby motel and holed up for a couple of days doing nothing except stare at the TV. It had taken all his self-control not to call her. Now, as he watched her flit around doing her movie star thing – posing with the guys, smiling nicely and making conversation – he knew that she was his.

Every so often their eyes met and the connection between them was on fire. Tonight he'd make love to her. She was more than ready – although anticipation always added to the event.

'So,' Trinee said, flopping down in a chair opposite him, interrupting his flow of thought. 'I thought you were this engaged person – same as me. Now you're here with Lara. What's goin' on, man?'

He regarded Trinee through narrowed eyes. She had a nerve, coming over and pestering him with personal questions. Didn't she get it? Things were different now. 'It's like this, Trinee,' he said, feeding her the information he wished her to pass around. 'Do you believe in fate?'

'Fate?' she repeated blankly.

'That's what happened between Lara an' me.'

'Yeah?'

'Unavoidable.'

'What about your fiancée? Man, she must be pissed!'

'She'll get over it,' he said calmly. Across the room he caught Barbara Westerberg glaring at him. He avoided eye contact.

'You're somethin' else,' Trinee said.

'What I am is honest.'

Trinee flounced off.

Eventually Lara came back, face flushed. She was clutching a gardenia one of the grips had presented her with. 'Duty done,' she said breathlessly. 'We can go now.'

'Good. The natives are not exactly friendly.'

'Who's not friendly?'

'Barbara Westerberg's been throwin' me the cold-fish eye all night.'

'She wanted you,' Lara said lightly. 'They all wanted you.'

'And look who won the prize.'

'You know what they say about prizes?'

'Tell me.'

She laughed softly. 'They're to take home and play with.'

'Lara!' he said, pretending to be shocked. 'An' I thought you were a nice girl.'

'No, Joey, I'm not the perfect little prude everyone imagines.'

'Let's split,' he said. 'We got better things to do.'

She found Cassie and told her they were leaving.

'You sure you're OK?' Cassie asked, frowning slightly. This thing with the actor was beginning to worry her.

'OK?' Lara said, glowing. 'I feel absolutely wonderful.'

'If you say so,' Cassie said, thinking she'd never seen Lara so out of control.

'Oh, c'mon, Cass ... how long is it since I've been this happy?'

'I want it to be good for you, Lara,' Cassie said earnestly. 'If you think Joey's the right guy ...'

She laughed. 'I'm not *marrying* him, Cass, I'm merely having fun. Oh, and by the way, you'd better let the pilot know that Joey's coming with us in the morning.'

Now Cassie was really confused. 'To LA?'

'That's right,' she said, running over and kissing Miles. 'See you in LA, my darling.'

'Lara, you're the best,' he said, beaming. 'You make my job easy.'

'The same applies, Miles. We'll do it again.'

She nodded at Kyle and his wife, feeling sorry for the poor woman. 'Jean, nice to see you again. Kyle, I'm sure we'll meet in the dubbing rooms.'

'Be careful, Lara,' Kyle said, standing up.

'Excuse me?'

He leaned close to her ear so his wife couldn't hear. 'You got no idea where he's been, honey. Make sure you get him tested for AIDS.'

She drew away, flushed with annoyance. 'One rule for you, Kyle, another for me,' she said in a low voice. 'You give chauvinist pigs a bad name.'

Joey was waiting outside in the car. She slid into the back seat next to him. He took her hand and they rode in silence until they reached the house.

Once inside, he stopped her from switching on the lights by grabbing both her wrists, holding them above her head and roughly kissing her, bruising her lips. 'I've been wanting to do that all night,' he said, releasing her at last.

'And I've been wanting you to,' she whispered back.

'How long's Cassie stayin' at the party?'

'Does it matter?'

'Yeah, it matters. We should be alone here.'

'She'll be a while.'

'Lock the front door.'

'Joey . . . shouldn't we talk?'

'Not now,' he said, and began kissing her again – long deep soul kisses until she didn't care about anything except him.

Soon he began peeling down the straps of her dress, easing it off her shoulders. Then he roughly unclipped her bra, tossing it across the room.

She was faint with excitement. Trembling slightly, her hands grabbed the zipper on his pants, boldly pulling it down, reaching in to explore.

He yanked the rest of her dress down over her slender hips, taking her bikini panties along with it.

'Lie on the floor,' he commanded.

As if in a trance she did as he asked, watching as he stripped off the rest of his clothes.

She'd never wanted a man so badly in her life. With Richard things had always taken place in the bedroom; with Lee they'd been a little more adventurous; here with Joey, lying on the floor of her rented house in the living room, she was wild with passion.

Then he was on top of her – no foreplay this time, she didn't need any as he moved smoothly inside her, causing her to moan deeply in the back of her throat.

Soon they were in perfect rhythm, riding a giant wave, balancing precariously on the edge . . .

In the distance she could hear someone screaming. Vaguely she realized it was her.

They reached the peak together, climaxing with a frenzy of moans. And it was all she'd ever hoped for and more.

When they were finished he remained spreadeagled on top of her, neither of them moving. She was hot and sticky and totally ecstatic. 'Joey,' she murmured contentedly. 'Oh, God, Joey.'

'Was it good for you, baby?' he asked lazily, rolling off and throwing his arm across her.

'The best,' she whispered happily. 'The absolute best.'

'Tell me,' he urged.

'Tell you what?'

'Tell me that there'll never be anyone else for you. That I'm it. I'm your whole fuckin' world.'

'Joey . . .'

A week. All he needed was a week and she'd tell him anything he wanted.

31

'**I want you** to see a rough assemblage tonight,' Richard said. 'Meet me here at six, and we'll drive to the screening room together.'

'Can't wait,' Nikki responded, hoping she'd be able to get away from the production office early enough to accommodate him.

'You won't believe Lara's performance,' he raved. 'She's sensational.'

'I'm hardly surprised,' Nikki said, wishing that he wouldn't carry on about Lara quite so much. Besides, didn't he remember that it was *she* who'd designed every stitch of clothing that covered Lara's gorgeous body in the movie, making her a big part of the movie's success. It was a costume picture, after all.

They were eating breakfast out on the deck. Normally she would have left by this time, but as she was on her way out Richard had announced he had something important to talk about, so she'd delayed her early start, even though she was anxious to get to the office.

Impatiently she glanced at her watch. So far he hadn't come up with a subject that merited her staying any longer. 'Lara flies back today,' she said, making conversation. 'I thought we'd have her over for dinner tomorrow, and Mick, too, if that's OK with you.'

'Why *that* asshole?'

'It seems a good plan for them to meet socially. Kind of a get to know each other before the movie starts.'

'Lara will hate him,' Richard said flatly. 'She sees right through assholes.'

'She won't hate him.'

'Trust me, she will.'

'Richard,' Nikki said, feeling defensive, 'when I started this project you were very supportive – now, every day, you seem to get less so.'

'Because you're making the wrong choices,' he said, his voice a monotonous nag. 'You refuse to listen. You should *never* have cast Lara, nor hired Mick Stefan.'

'Why not? He's brilliant.'

'He might be brilliant, but he needs a producer who can control him. You've had no experience, Nikki. You *need* experience.'

'Oh, gee, thanks. I appreciate your confidence,' she said, checking her watch again. 'I have to get going, Richard. Was there anything else?'

'I promised Summer I'd talk to you.'

'What about?' she asked, annoyed, because if Summer had something to say, she should come out with it herself.

'She said that every time she tries to talk to you, the two of you end up getting in a fight.'

'Not so.'

'*She* seems to think it is.'

Nikki sighed. 'So what is it?'

He pressed his fingers together, staring directly at her. 'She wants to come and live with us.'

'Excuse me?' Nikki said, not sure she'd heard correctly.

'She doesn't want to go back to Chicago. She'd sooner go to school here.' There was a long silence. 'You should be thrilled,' he added. 'She *is* your daughter.'

'Yes, my daughter, whom I've had hardly anything to do with since she was eight. Quite frankly, I'm not sure if I can take on the responsibility now.'

'You're not being very understanding,' he chided, annoying her even more.

'You know, Richard,' she said, beginning a slow burn, 'I resent the fact that she asked *you* to speak to me.'

'I'm merely the messenger,' he said, sipping his coffee. 'You should sit down with her.'

'I will – when I've got time. Right now I'm late for the office.' Grabbing her car keys from the table, she set off, seething. How *dare* Summer run to Richard and persuade him to plead her case!

For a moment she was tempted to go back to the house

and roust her lazy daughter out of bed. According to the maid, Summer slept in every day until noon, then got up, met friends, and wasn't to be seen again until it was to put on a different outfit. Then Nikki changed her mind, suddenly overcome with guilt – after all, as Richard had so succinctly pointed out, she *was* Summer's mother. She decided the fair thing to do was discuss Summer's wish to move to LA with Sheldon.

When she arrived at the office, Mick was in the middle of a big production meeting. He'd started without her, which pissed her off even more.

She sat down next to him. He threw her a vague wave. She'd known making movies was hard work, but being involved on the production side was completely time consuming, there were so many decisions to make. Each department had questions, and it was imperative that every detail was in place before the start of principal photography.

As soon as they took a break, she instructed her assistant to send Lara flowers with a note welcoming her back and inviting her to dinner the following night.

Mick grabbed her at lunchtime. 'Aiden's nutto about you,' he said, sucking on his lower lip. 'You charmed the crap outta him.'

'How nice,' she replied, noncommittal.

'Yeah, he thinks you're a real cool chick-babe.'

'As long as he behaves himself I couldn't care less what he thinks.'

'How many times I gotta tell you?' Mick said, beaming. 'Aiden's a pussy.'

'Don't forget,' she reminded him, 'tomorrow night at my house. I know you and Lara will get along.'

He cackled. 'Yeah, well, we gotta, haven't we?'

'Try to remember, Mick, she's a star, treat her with respect.'

'Enough already – I'm getting the message. I'll even wear a tie – I got one, y'know.'

'You don't have to do that.'

'Yeah, yeah – kinda a respect move.'

She made it home before seven. Richard and Summer were sitting out on the deck playing a game of Scrabble. She felt like an intruder as she walked past them.

'Oh hi, Mom,' Summer said, sweet as apple candy. 'Did you have a good day?'

How come when Richard was around, Summer played the perfect daughter?

'I'm exhausted,' she said, flopping into a chair.

'Ha!' Richard said. 'If you think you're tired now, wait until you start shooting.'

Summer jumped up. She wore minuscule shorts and a cropped top. *Too much flesh*, Nikki thought. 'Gotta get changed,' Summer announced. 'I'm off to a party.'

'*Another* one?' Nikki said.

''S OK, Mom – Richard said I should enjoy myself while I'm young.'

'Did he?' Nikki said, throwing him a look.

'I'm having such an amazing vacation,' Summer said enthusiastically, throwing her arms around Nikki's neck. 'Thanks, Mom.' Then she ran over and kissed Richard, too, before vanishing into the house.

'Why do you always complain about her?' Richard asked, pushing the Scrabble board away. 'She's a lovely girl.'

'You only see the good side,' Nikki replied ominously.

An hour later they were settled in a small screening room watching a rough cut of *French Summer*.

Nikki forgot about *Revenge* and concentrated on the exquisite images playing on the screen before her. The cinematographer was a master, the period clothes she'd designed were perfect, and Richard was right – Lara's performance was incandescent; plus Harry Solitaire and Pierre Perez both gave charming performances.

When the lights came up Richard had a big smile on his face.

'You've excelled yourself!' she exclaimed. 'I love everything!'

'Couldn't have done it without Lara,' he said. 'She was the perfect leading lady.'

Great, Nikki thought, *what about me?*

They stopped at Dan Tana's on the way home, ordered steaks and salads, and Nikki listened while Richard talked endlessly about his movie. He really was obsessed. She tried to bring up *Revenge*, but he wasn't interested.

After dinner they drove to the beach.

'Let's go straight to bed,' she suggested as soon as they entered the house.

'What's your hurry?'

Maybe I'm feeling horny, she wanted to say, but she didn't. Instead she followed Richard into the bedroom, locking the door behind them.

'Why are you doing that?' he asked, pulling off his sweater and dropping his pants.

'For privacy.'

'Summer's out. And even if she was home, she wouldn't come in here unannounced,' he said, clicking on the television.

'Who can tell with Summer?' she said, going into the bathroom, emerging a few minutes later clad in a sexy black nightgown.

Richard was now lying under the covers staring at the television, mesmerized.

'Why is it,' she said, climbing into bed beside him, 'that I get the distinct feeling you're more into *Nightline* than me?'

'Don't be ridiculous,' he said, holding tightly on to the remote lest she try to grab it from him.

'We haven't made love in weeks,' she pointed out.

'That's because we've both been so busy,' he replied, seemingly unconcerned.

'When did that ever stop you?' she asked, reaching over and expertly stroking him until he became aroused.

After a few moments he moved on top of her, and without a word began pumping away until he was satisfied. Then he rolled off, closed his eyes and immediately fell into a deep sleep.

Nikki was outraged. Whatever happened to romance? Not to mention foreplay. One thing about Richard, he'd always been a considerate lover – now this. And the biggest insult of all was that he'd kept the television on.

She turned away from his snoring presence, burying her head in the pillow, hurt and angry.

When *Revenge* was completed, they were due to have a long talk, and not a moment too soon.

32

'I couldn't get in last night,' Cassie said, tight-mouthed.

'Sorry,' Lara replied guiltily. 'I must've locked the door out of . . . habit.'

'I had to break a window,' Cassie continued accusingly. 'We're responsible for a replacement, I've made a note of the damage.'

'Of course.'

'Everything OK?'

Lara smiled a beauteous smile. 'Yes, Cassie, everything's wonderful.'

Cassie handed her a folder. 'I've put together an LA schedule for you,' she said. 'It's tight, but as long as you don't come down with the flu or anything, you'll manage.'

Lara glanced at the hourly schedule and groaned. 'This is impossible,' she said. 'It barely gives me time to breathe.'

'You wanted to make *Revenge*. Quinn warned you.'

Lara frowned as she studied the crammed schedule. 'I'm sure we can cancel some of the things on here.'

'Not really,' Cassie said. 'It's all important. There's publicity for your last two movies. Dubbing on *French Summer*. TV commitments. Your charity work. Doctor and dentist appointments. PR stills. Magazine covers—'

'OK, OK, I'll go over it on the plane.'

Cassie nodded and left the room. Lara glanced out of the window. Her limo was outside the house, the luggage stacked beside it. Their driver was busy loading the trunk. Ten more minutes and they should be on their way.

She went back into the bedroom. Joey was in the bathroom, naked, staring at himself in the mirror.

She moved up beside him, dressed and ready for their flight. 'We've got to go,' she said, thinking how much she liked his body. He was muscular without it being too much. His shoulders were broad, his stomach washboard flat, and his legs long and athletic. On his chest was a smattering of black hair – exactly the right amount. He had the best butt in the world.

'I know,' he said, still studying his reflection.

She slapped him lightly on his ass. 'You'd better stop admiring yourself and hurry up, Mr Handsome.'

He turned around, leaning his bare butt against the sink.

She noticed he was hard and automatically her legs began to weaken. How had they gotten this intimate so quickly? She couldn't believe he was standing around naked in her bathroom as if they were an old married couple. She, who was usually so careful, had fallen into something like lightning. And she didn't care. She was enjoying every irresponsible exciting moment.

'Why don't you get down on your knees?' he suggested matter-of-factly. 'Why don't you do it *now*?'

'Why don't *you* get dressed?' she responded.

He smiled at her. 'See something you like?'

She smiled back. 'Yes, and I'm sure it'll still be there when we get to LA.'

He laughed. 'OK, OK – I'll get dressed.'

'Five minutes. The plane will be waiting.'

'It's a private plane, isn't it?' he said, reaching for his underwear.

'That doesn't make any difference. They have a flight schedule to keep to.'

'Yes, *ma'am*,' he said mockingly, pulling on his shorts.

She ran into the kitchen, alive and glowing. Through the window she saw Cassie standing by the limo chatting to their driver. She couldn't wait to confide in Nikki – shout out the news that she was in love – well maybe not love – but certainly lust.

She'd never fallen into bed with anyone so quickly. Richard had waited months before she'd slept with him; and she'd kept Lee hanging for six weeks. Now Joey. And it was instant. And the sex had never been so exciting and passionate. Nikki would understand totally.

Remembering last night, she shivered with pleasure, hugging her secret to herself.

Joey emerged a few minutes later. He'd put on worn jeans and a faded denim work shirt, his dark hair was ruffled and untidy.

'I'm taking you shopping when we get to LA,' she announced. 'You could use some Armani jackets and pants, socks and ties, and—'

'Wait a minute,' he interrupted, his expression hardening. 'If I was into that kind of shit – which I'm not – I'd buy it for myself. I don't need *you* to pay my bills.'

'I didn't mean I was going to buy you clothes because you *needed* them,' she said, flustered. 'I wanted to get you stuff simply because . . .' she trailed off. Why had she made such a stupid suggestion? She was acting as if he didn't have any money. Of course he was insulted, any man would be.

He stared at her. She looked so radiant with her luminescent skin and sparkling green eyes – how could he possibly be mad at her? 'C'mere,' he said, his tone softening. 'Have I told you lately you're the most beautiful woman I've ever seen?'

'And *you're* the most beautiful man,' she replied, happy again.

They walked out to the limo hand in hand.

The chauffeur opened the door for them. They sat in the back. Cassie chose to sit up front with the driver. Throughout the ride to the airport they only had eyes for each other.

Nikki will not *believe this*, Lara thought. *It's all happened so fast I can hardly believe it myself.*

The Gulfstream jet was waiting at the airport. The pilot greeted Lara personally, honoured to be flying her. An attentive steward escorted them aboard.

The plane was comfortably equipped with four armchairs placed around an oblong table, and several other luxurious seating areas. In the back of the plane there was a bedroom and a shower.

'Do we get to use the bedroom?' Joey whispered.

'I'm a star, I can do what I like,' Lara joked. 'However,' she added, more seriously, 'here's what I *think* we should do.'

'What?'

'Talk . . . take the time to get to know each other. I want

to find out all about you – where you're from – your family – what kind of cereal you like in the morning ... everything ...'

'How's this for a fantasy?' he interrupted. 'Our lives begin now, forget about the past.'

'I can go with that.'

'Then good – no talkin' – we'll spend all our time in the bedroom.'

'Joey!' she chided, laughter in her eyes. 'Are you a sex maniac?'

'C'mon,' he said persuasively. 'You know you want to.'

Yes, she wanted to. But the truth was she should be studying her script, preparing for her first meeting with Mick Stefan. Principal photography on *Revenge* was due to start in less than two weeks and there was much to do. She hadn't been home for nearly four months, and the last thing she'd planned on was an involvement.

Joey took her hand, placing it casually atop his growing erection.

She quickly pulled it away, motioning toward Cassie, whose face was hidden behind a copy of *USA Today*.

'There's enough for her, too,' he whispered.

'You're incorrigible!' she said, laughing softly.

The steward came by to take their drink orders. Joey requested a beer, and Lara went for a 7-Up. 'I need the sugar,' she said with a wry grin. 'You've sapped all my energy.'

'Yeah?' he said, pleased. 'An' we haven't even started yet.'

She smiled, thinking about the previous evening, once again shivering with pleasure.

'So,' Joey said. 'When do I get to meet Mick Stefan?'

'I think the movie's cast.'

'You're the star,' he said casually. 'Fire somebody.'

She laughed, sure he was joking. 'I can't fire anyone. I haven't even met Mick.'

'Hey,' he said, turning on the little boy charm. 'Surely if you want your boyfriend to have a part ...'

She tilted her head to one side, regarding him quizzically. 'Is that what you are, Joey? My boyfriend?'

'How about lover? It sounds sexier.'

'Works for me,' she said, still smiling. 'My . . . lover.' She paused for a moment. 'Oh, God! Wait till the tabloids find out.'

He leaned over, placing his hands behind her neck and pulling her close. 'Come here, you,' he said, running his tongue slowly over her lips. 'I got an idea,' he said in a low voice. 'Throw Cassie off the plane. Tell her to fly commercial—'

'I can't do that.'

'Yes, you can.'

'Joey – I can't,' she repeated, thinking he couldn't possibly be serious.

'OK, just a suggestion,' he said lightly. 'I always had an urge to run around naked on a plane. Can't do it with her on board.'

'You're crazy,' she said, smiling indulgently.

'Never said I wasn't.'

'That's true.'

'Let's see now,' he said, squinting at her. 'According to you I'm a sex maniac, crazy an' incorrigible. Anythin' else you wanna throw at me?'

'Not that I can think of.'

'Good.'

'Are you fond of dogs?' she asked curiously.

'Love 'em – from a distance. Why? You gonna set 'em on me?'

'I have three.'

'Big or small?'

'Mixed.'

'What else d'you have I should know about?'

'Horses. And a couple of cats.'

'You sure there's room for me?'

'Uh . . .' She didn't know what to say, they hadn't discussed where he was going to stay. Now it was obvious he assumed he was staying with her.

He caught her confusion. 'Don't sweat it,' he said quickly. 'I plan on checkin' into a hotel for a coupla weeks. Then if I decide to settle in LA, I'll rent an apartment.'

'Joey,' she said impulsively – thinking, *My God, it isn't as if we're strangers* – 'I'd like you to stay at my house for a few days until you find a place.'

'Naw,' he said, shaking his head. 'Wouldn't want to impose.'

'It's not an imposition, you'll be very comfortable,' she said, fastening her seatbelt as the plane began taxiing down the runway.

'Hey,' he said, breaking out another grin, 'as long as I'm with you, nothin' matters.'

And that was the truth, because he'd finally found the woman he could be with for ever.

Lara smiled. Yes, it was happening fast, but the good thing was that it all seemed so right. And best of all, it was great to be with someone who cared.

33

Nikki decided to cook; it wasn't often she spent time in the kitchen, but because Lara had been away for so long, she suspected a home-cooked meal would be appreciated. She was fixing roast chicken, creamed potatoes, broccoli, peas and English bread sauce – all of Lara's favourites.

Richard arrived home early for a change, and headed straight into the kitchen where Nikki was busying herself slicing avocado for the salad. He kissed her on the back of her neck.

'Guess what?' she said brightly, knowing he'd be pissed, but after his performance the night before she couldn't help needling him.

'What?' he said, picking up a slice of avocado.

'Lara's bringing someone.'

His eyebrows shot up. 'She is?'

'Yeah – remember I told you about that guy she was kind of interested in, the actor I met, Joey Lorenzo? Well, apparently she's more than interested.'

'How do you know?'

'I haven't had a chance to talk to her, but Cassie called to say she wants to bring him tonight. Naturally I said it was OK.'

'Didn't you mention to me that he was engaged?'

'Looks like he's disengaged now.'

'I don't get it,' Richard said, sourly. 'Why would she hook up with some unknown actor?'

'Why not? Who else does she meet?'

'And she's bringing him here tonight?' He shook his head. 'Who'd believe *this*.'

'Believe it, honey. Your ex is venturing out on her own again.'

Richard opened the fridge and took out a bottle of white wine. 'I'll talk to her,' he said.

Nikki snorted derisively. 'And tell her *what*? That she can't get laid without your permission?'

He threw her a steely glare and marched out of the kitchen carrying the wine just as Summer entered, wide-eyed and smiling. 'Mom!' she exclaimed, deliciously pretty in a pale pink sundress. 'Something smells way good!'

'Thanks,' Nikki said, wondering what Summer wanted. A car? The house? Richard?

You're not being very nice, she thought. *Lighten up and try getting through to her.*

'Nikki!' Richard yelled from the other room. 'Pick up the phone – it's Mick.'

Oh, God! Don't tell me he's cancelling, she thought, grabbing the phone.

'I got a big one to ask,' Mick mumbled. 'A bigeroonie.'

'Go ahead.'

'It's real important to me.'

'What is it?' she asked impatiently.

'Aiden's goin' through a bad time. He's livin' in a rented dump – got no friends.'

'Are you asking if you can bring him?' she said with an exasperated sigh, knowing she'd regret it.

'That's the deal.'

'Eight o'clock. Casual.' She slammed down the phone. 'Wanda!' she yelled. 'Set another place.'

'Is it OK if I stay for dinner?' Summer asked, bright blue eyes shining as she danced around the kitchen. She'd over-heard the conversation and couldn't believe her luck.

Nikki couldn't help herself. 'How come you're not going out?'

'What – and miss your yummy cooking?' Summer replied, dipping her fingers into the salad and plucking out a small red tomato.

What could she say to her daughter? *I'm expecting guests – you can't stay.* 'It's actually a business dinner,' she said lamely.

'Richard said Lara's coming. I like love Lara – haven't seen her in ages.'

'It's not only Lara,' Nikki said quickly. 'We're also having

my director, Mick Stefan. There'll be a lot of shop talk. You'll
be bored.'

'Don't you *want* me to stay home, Mom?' Summer asked
accusingly.

No. This was the one dinner she didn't want Summer to
attend. 'Of course I do,' she said, feeling the old familiar
guilt. Turning to the maid she said a brusque, 'Wanda, set
one more place, we're growing by the minute.'

'Thanks, Mom!' Summer exclaimed, racing out of the
kitchen.

Nikki made a mental note to check with Sheldon as soon
as possible. If Summer was serious about staying, then
maybe she'd give her a chance. Perhaps there was hope for
them after all.

☆

Summer rushed into her room. Mick Stefan coming to the
house was the best! She'd never told him who she was. He'd
freak when he spotted her! But the big news was Aiden Sean.
The babe himself. She couldn't be more excited.

What to wear, that was the problem. Something so sexy
he'd be unable to resist her. Yeah! Tonight was the night!

☆

Lara sat in front of her dressing table adding the finishing
touches to her make-up, thinking how good it was to be
home.

Yesterday, as soon as they'd arrived at the house, she'd
instructed Mr and Mrs Crenshaw, the elderly Scottish couple
who worked for her, to set up the guest room for Joey. Mrs
Crenshaw had nodded, slyly checking Joey out, which made
Lara smile. The Crenshaws – like everyone else – were very
protective of her.

Once Joey was settled, he'd begun exploring her house.
'Jeez! This is some place,' he'd exclaimed, roaming around.
'I didn't realize you lived like this.'

'It's where I spend all my time when I'm not working,'
she'd explained. 'I've tried to make it as comfortable as
possible.'

'You sure did a good job.'

He was like a kid let loose in Disneyland, fiddling with

the stereo system, checking out the many televisions, playing ball with the dogs, and when he discovered she had a gym he was in heaven.

In the evening they'd had a quiet dinner together outside in the garden. Later she'd waited for him to make a move. Disappointingly, he hadn't. He'd kissed her chastely on the cheek, remarked that they were both exhausted, and vanished into the guest room.

She was confused. One moment he was her lover, the next merely a house guest.

She'd lain in bed, unable to sleep, thinking about him. But he hadn't come to her, and she was too proud to go to him. One thing about Joey, he certainly didn't believe in pushing it.

They'd both gotten up early and met in the kitchen. After breakfast she'd taken him down to the stables to see her horses. 'Can you ride?' she'd asked.

'I can try,' he'd said.

Mr Wicker, the man who ran her stables, had chosen a horse for Joey to take out. He'd mounted it without faltering and they'd set off. He was a natural.

'Unbelievable!' she'd exclaimed. 'I've been riding for years, and you simply climb on a horse and get it immediately.'

'I can do anythin' I set my mind to,' he'd boasted, grinning. 'Anythin'.'

They'd lunched around the swimming pool and spent a relaxing day, thanks to Joey, who'd insisted she cancel all her appointments. 'C'mon, Lara,' he'd said. 'You deserve one day to yourself.'

Cassie was not pleased as she sat in her small office attempting to rearrange the already overcrowded schedule.

Now Lara was getting ready for dinner at Richard and Nikki's.

She wondered what Richard's reaction would be to Joey. Sometimes her ex-husband was too possessive – it would do him good to see her with another man.

Joey knocked and wandered into the room, looking very handsome in a black silk T-shirt, Armani jacket and black pants, a thin lizard-skin belt enclosing his narrow waist.

He'd taken his outfit from the film – too bad if they didn't want him to have it.

'I'm glad you're meeting Mick this way,' she said, adding a touch of blush to her high cheekbones. 'Better than going in for an interview. I promise I'll ask him if there's anything in the movie for you.'

'Don't *ask* – *tell*,' he said, picking up a Lalique perfume bottle and sniffing the scent.

'I can't force them to do anything,' she said, standing up and reaching for her purse.

'They can't force you, either,' he reminded her, unexpectedly plunging his hand down the front of her dress, enclosing her left breast, tweaking her nipple.

She gasped, taken by surprise.

'We'd better go,' he said, removing his hand.

All she really wanted to do was stay home and make love. Instead she followed Joey from the room.

Outside in the garage, he walked around inspecting her cars. She had a grey Range Rover, a sleek gold Jaguar XKJ, and a black Mercedes with dark tinted windows.

'Three cars?' he said, grinning. 'Lady – I like your style.'

'Which one shall we take tonight?' she asked.

'The Jag,' he answered quickly. 'I'll drive.'

He opened the door for her, and she got into the passenger seat. 'Do you have a car, Joey?'

'In New York? No way. Soon as I know what I'm doin', I'll lease somethin' here.'

It occurred to her that if he didn't get a part in *Revenge* he might have to go back to New York, and then when would she see him?

Stop it, she told herself sternly. *This is no big romance, it's a fling. Short and sweet.*

Or is it?

Maybe Joey's the man I've been waiting for. The man who's going to make a difference in my life.

No more lonely nights.

No more sickening nightmares.

She could only wish.

☆

So now her cosy little dinner for three was seven. *Great!* Nikki thought.

Two actors – who would probably hate each other; two directors – who couldn't be more different; a beautiful movie star; a difficult teenager; and herself. What a group! And on top of everything else, Richard had started drinking too much again – which wasn't a problem unless he took it too far. And from the look in his eyes she knew that tonight he'd definitely take it too far. He'd already consumed half a bottle of wine, and was now on to Martinis.

She put the CD player on shuffle – a selection of Sting, Jamiroquai and Jewel. Then she sampled one of Juan's lethal Margaritas. She'd sent for Juan at the last minute to help out at the bar; one quick inspection and she wished she hadn't. Juan – who was Wanda's son – had the look of a juvenile Antonio Banderas with his slicked-back jet hair, bedroom eyes and cocky attitude. Last time she'd seen him he'd been a boy – now he was eighteen and she shuddered to think what would happen when he set his horny eyes on Summer.

'Your son's certainly grown up in a short time,' she remarked to Wanda as they stood in the kitchen.

'Juan's a good boy,' Wanda said, beaming proudly. 'He no get involved with gangs. He wanna be singer.'

'A singer, huh?' Nikki said, checking on the chickens roasting away in the oven.

'Big talent,' Wanda said. 'Mebbe you and the Mister wanna hear?'

'Another time,' Nikki said quickly. Right now she had an evening to get through.

Running into Maxwell von Steuben did not help my career one bit. In fact, true to his word, the sonofabitch tried to have me blacklisted.

Here's what he didn't think of. He didn't think I could change my name, and that's exactly what I did. All of a sudden I was a new guy in town, and as long as I avoided going on any auditions where Maxwell might be, I was safe. The dumb shit was blacklisting someone who didn't exist any more.

Soon after the incident with Maxwell I dumped Margie. Had to. She gave boring a whole new meaning. My dreams of a little house in the Valley with a couple of kids vanished. Who gave a damn? There were too many women out there who needed my attention. Too many babes who had the money to pay for it.

Changing my name was an ace move. As far as my career was concerned, it changed my luck, too. After a few months, I landed the lead in a late-night TV action show. Kind of low-core porno on syndication, but it sure made me feel like a king. All of a sudden people were bowing and scraping, running to take care of my every command. There's nothing like being the star of a show, however bad the show. And I even got to direct a couple of episodes – a real kick.

My co-star was a nervous blond who'd done time around the track several times and then some. Once she'd been a contender, only she'd never quite got to the top. Now she was doing shit shows like mine, and lucky to get the job because she'd never see thirty-five again. And for a woman over thirty in Hollywood – unless you've already made it – it's finito.

Her name was Hadley. She had long legs and a voracious sexual appetite. I wouldn't fuck her, didn't want to mix business with pleasure. This drove her totally crazy, causing her to do everything in her power to turn me on. She came to my trailer *wearing nothing but a mink coat bought for her by her gangster boyfriend; paraded around the make-up room in stiletto heels and Frederick's of Hollywood lingerie; and sent me outrageous gifts from a sex shop she frequented.*

I didn't fall for her act. I was finally getting smart. But one day she pushed my buttons. We were shooting a night scene in Culver City, and she picked up one of the extras – an outrageously sexy black girl – and one thing led to another, and the three of us ended up in Hadley's trailer, bombed out of our skulls on straight tequila and very fine Mexican grass.

From what I can remember I must have fucked her, and not gone back for more, because shortly after she managed to get me fired. Bitch!

What the hell – I found myself a new agent and started doing the rounds again. An Australian company was making a series of low-budget action movies for Asia. They wanted an American actor, and they discovered me. I was into a little kick boxing, and with the help of a coach I soon honed the skill.

All of a sudden, I was a half-assed star in Asia. Big fucking deal. I went there for a promo trip, and spent the majority of time getting laid and drugged out of my head. Asian drugs, man, they are something else!

By the time I got back to the States I had myself a habit that wouldn't quit.

Truth was I was well and truly hooked.

34

Lara and Joey arrived first. Nikki took one look at her glowing countenance and didn't have to ask – they were definitely in bed together. And who could blame her? Joey Lorenzo was one of the best-looking men around.

She hugged Lara, said a cordial hello to Joey, then led them out to the deck where – much to Nikki's annoyance – Richard was on his third vodka Martini.

He immediately jumped to his feet when he saw Lara, enveloping her in a loving embrace. 'I've missed you, sweetheart,' he said warmly. 'I've *really* missed you.'

'You, too, Richard,' she said, extracting herself from his arms. She hesitated a moment, not quite sure how to introduce Joey. 'Say hello to my, uh . . . friend . . . Joey Lorenzo.'

Joey stepped forward, anxious to check out the ex-husband. 'Mr Barry, it's a real pleasure, sir.'

The 'sir' hung in the air like a dirty word. Nikki stifled a nervous giggle, Richard's annoyance was palpable. 'Let's not be so formal,' she said, hurriedly taking Joey's arm and steering him over to the small bar. 'I'm Nikki, he's Richard. What would you like to drink?'

'A beer'll do it,' Joey said, remembering that apart from being Lara's best friend, she was also the producer of *Revenge*, therefore he'd best be nice to her.

'One beer,' Nikki instructed Juan. 'And Lara – what can we get you?'

'Champagne,' Lara replied, completely incapable of wiping the dreamy smile off her face.

'Mick's on his way,' Nikki explained. 'He's bringing Aiden Sean, so you get to meet them both at once.' She noticed Joey reach for Lara's hand. This was love all right, she'd never seen Lara in such a trancelike state.

'So, you're an actor,' Richard boomed, joining them at the bar. 'What have you done?'

Lara laughed lightly. 'Now, now, Richard, Joey doesn't travel armed with his résumé.'

'Maybe he should,' Richard said nastily.

'Yeah, why's that?' Joey asked, challenging the older man with a long hard look. He wasn't about to take shit from anyone.

Fortunately Mick chose that moment to make his entrance. True to his word, he'd worn a tie – decorated with a nude Marilyn Monroe. He also wore an ill-fitting sixties-style white tuxedo, baggy pants, a frayed shirt and a goofy grin.

Aiden Sean shuffled in behind him – low-key in khakis and sinister impenetrable shades.

'Welcome to our home,' Nikki said graciously. 'I'm glad you could make it.'

'I bet you are!' muttered Aiden.

She pretended she hadn't heard as she effected introductions.

Joey checked out Mick and Aiden. A couple of big-time losers who'd struck it lucky. Shit! Why wasn't he directing movies and starring in them? He probably had more talent in his dick than these two had between them. And Lara – *his* Lara – was putting herself in their hands, it didn't make sense. He nudged her. '*This* is the boy wonder?' he whispered rudely. 'What a jerk!'

'Be nice,' she whispered back. 'Don't judge him on his appearance.'

Why the fuck not? he wanted to say. But he remained silent. He'd learned at an early age that the smart thing was to find out everyone's deal and then speak up.

'Lara,' Mick said, gulping down a frozen Margarita as if it was lemonade, 'gotta tell ya – I'm totally psyched you're doing my movie.'

Nikki caught the 'my movie' and didn't like it one bit. Since when was it *his* movie?

'Nikki's developed an excellent script,' Lara replied, dazzling him with a smile. 'How could I resist?'

'I got a lotta new ideas,' Mick said enthusiastically. 'Lotta bigeroonies.'

'Great,' she replied, 'I'm always open to suggestions – if they're good.'

That put Mr Big Shot Stefan in his place. Joey was proud of her, she knew how to handle herself around jerks. Not that he'd ever doubted her.

Aiden Sean hadn't said a word. After ordering a Jack Daniel's on the rocks, he'd slumped down on a lounge chair as far away from everyone as he could get.

Nikki contemplated going over, playing the polite hostess. Then she thought, *Why should I? He's the uninvited guest, let him put himself out.*

Summer timed her entrance five minutes before dinner. She sauntered outside, barefoot, in sprayed-on denim cut-offs, and a midriff-baring top. Her long white-blond hair was freshly washed, framing her pretty face. 'Hi, everyone,' she said, innocence personified. 'Gee, Mom – dinner smells good enough to eat!'

'Holy shit!' Mick exclaimed, his voice cracking.

'Meet my daughter,' Nikki said, hoping he wasn't into teenagers. 'Everyone – this is Summer.'

'Your daughter?' Mick croaked, arms flailing wildly.

'Yes,' Nikki said, noticing that Juan was standing to attention, completely mesmerized by Summer.

Fortunately she hadn't spotted him yet. With a little luck it would stay that way.

Ignoring Mick, Summer spotted Lara and ran over. 'Lara!' she squealed.

'*You've* certainly grown up,' Lara said, hugging her. 'And so pretty. Say hi to Joey Lorenzo.'

'Hello, Joey,' Summer said, checking him out.

'Hello,' he replied, staring jailbait in the face. If Nikki was smart she'd lock this one up and swallow the key until she was eighteen.

Summer edged her way over to Aiden Sean. He looked at her blankly. 'I'm a major fan,' she said, determined to get his attention. 'Seen all your movies like ten times! You're way, way the most genius actor around.'

No reaction from Aiden, who seemed more interested in nursing his glass of Jack Daniel's.

'Don't you *remember* me?' Summer demanded, lowering her voice so nobody else could hear.

He barely moved his head. 'Nope.'

'The Viper Club.'

'Sorry, kid,' he said, yawning in her face.

She glared at him. He'd pay for calling her kid.

☆

Across the deck Joey didn't miss a thing. 'How old's the nymphet?' he whispered to Lara.

'Fifteen. Frightening, isn't it?'

'She's sure made Mick's evening. Take a look – his eyes are buggin' out.'

'Don't be disgusting, she's a child.'

'This one grew up a long time ago.'

'What makes you think that?'

'I can tell.'

☆

Mick grabbed Summer's attention on the way into dinner.

'Whyn't you tell me who your mother was?' he demanded, mouth twitching.

'You didn't ask,' she retorted flippantly.

'And how come you didn't call me?'

''Cause I knew you'd be mad when you found out my mom was Nikki Barry.'

He looked perplexed. This little Lolita was confusing him.

Before he could say anything else, she'd moved away, and he found himself seated between Lara Ivory and Aiden.

☆

The conversation around the dinner table was dominated by Mick, who decided the only way to get Summer's attention was to spew forth his opinions on everything from politics to crime. 'We gotta bring back public hangin',' he said, distractedly circling Marilyn's left tit with his index finger, while managing to keep a keen watch on Summer, who so far had refused to look at him. 'Hang 'em up by the balls an' watch 'em squirm. *I'd* pay.'

'That's obscene,' Richard said, his face clouding over. 'We may as well all run around in loincloths carrying spears.'

'The law of the jungle – fuck 'em before they fuck you,'

Mick said, winking at Summer, who immediately looked away.

Joey observed the scene. Someone should tell the kid that directors were the ones with all the power, not actors – the little tease hadn't taken her baby blues off Aiden all night. He placed his hand on Lara's leg under the table, slowly moving it up her thigh.

'Are you aware of how many people are executed by mistake?' Richard demanded, banging his fist on the table.

'Hardly any,' Mick responded. 'An' y'know why? 'Cause bleedin' heart liberals like you wanna end the death penalty altogether.'

'The death penalty is *not* a deterrent,' Richard announced sternly, wishing everyone would get the hell out of his house.

'Bullshit!' shouted Mick, turning to Lara. 'What do *you* think?'

'It depends on the crime,' she said, determined not to get trapped in the middle of their fight.

Aiden stood up from the table. He had not removed his dark glasses all night and barely spoken a word. 'Where's the head?' he muttered.

'In the front hall,' Nikki replied.

'I'll show you,' Summer said, leaping to her feet and accompanying him from the room.

She led him all the way to the guest bathroom, and when they arrived she attempted to enter with him.

'What the fuck are you playing at?' he asked, blocking her at the door.

'Nothing,' she answered innocently. 'I had no idea you were in my mom's movie.'

'And I suppose you didn't know Mick was her director,' he said, as if he didn't believe her.

Ah, so he *did* remember her. 'Honestly, I didn't,' she said, trying to edge into the bathroom with him – aware that if she wrapped her long blond hair around *it*, and enclosed *it* with her sweet young lips, she could send a man to heaven. Mick had been susceptible, but it was Aiden she really wanted.

'Go away, little girl,' he said, slamming the door in her face.

Reluctantly she returned to the dinner table. Aiden Sean hadn't heard the last of her, she'd show *him*.

☆

Lara and Joey left shortly before eleven.

'Some night!' Lara exclaimed in the car going home. 'I must say – Mick's quite a character. And as for Aiden Sean . . .'

'Your ex has a major crush on you,' Joey remarked.

'Not really,' she said quickly.

'How come he let you get away?'

'I told you, he was unfaithful,' she said with a deep sigh. 'I finally realized I'd had enough.'

'Bet he regrets it now.'

'He and Nikki are very happy.'

'Don't be so sure.'

'They are,' she insisted.

'C'mon, honey,' Joey teased, 'you don't think he doesn't dream about you in bed? Your incredible skin? Your soft arms? Your long legs wrapped around his neck . . . ?' He took one hand off the steering wheel, and cupped her left breast. 'Take off your bra,' he ordered.

'What?' she replied breathlessly.

'You heard. Slip it out from under your top.'

'Joey,' she laughed nervously, 'can't you wait until we get home?'

'No,' he said insistently. 'I've been wantin' to touch you all night. Now do it.'

Her throat was suddenly dry with anticipation. This man was insatiable, and she loved it.

Reaching under her blouse, she unclipped her bra and slipped it off.

Immediately his hand snaked under her blouse, pressing her nipple roughly between his fingers.

She moaned, flooded with desire. He had such an amazing effect on her, she couldn't think straight when he touched her.

'Unzip my pants,' he instructed, staring at the road ahead. 'Take it out.'

'Joey,' she objected, 'we're on a public highway. People will see . . .'

'What people? We're in a moving vehicle. Do it!'

'Joey . . .' But in spite of her protests she found herself obeying. It was almost as if he had her under a spell and she was powerless to say no. The truth was she had no desire to refuse him anything. Releasing him from his pants, she caressed him, wishing they were home so he could make love to her properly.

'Suck it!' he commanded, pushing his hand firmly against the back of her head.

Oh, God! All he had to do was ask . . .

She bent her head, tasting him, enclosing him. And when he came, they were racing along the Pacific Coast Highway at seventy miles an hour, and the kick was so potent that she felt herself climaxing too.

'You belong to me, baby,' he said, his eyes fixed on the road. 'Don't ever forget it. You're mine, all mine. Right, baby. *Right?*'

And she nodded dreamily and leaned back in the seat and couldn't wait until they were home in bed together.

☆

As soon as Aiden Sean and Mick Stefan left her mother's stupid dinner party, Summer called a cab. Aiden wasn't treating her nicely, even though he now knew who she was.

God! Mick's face when she'd walked in and Nikki had announced she was her daughter. Talk about sudden panic! She'd almost laughed out loud. Mick had taken her for some little nymphet fan the night she'd met him at the Viper Club – nothing more than a teenage blow job. Big shock for him!

She didn't care about him anyway, he was too geeky. It was Aiden Sean she liked, and when Summer wanted something she was determined.

Before the party she'd called the production office and told them her mother needed Aiden's home address. Smart thinking, because as soon as he left she'd informed Nikki she had a party to go to, and now she was sitting in a cab on her way to his place.

He lived in a ratty little apartment in North Hollywood on a narrow dusty street. She paid off the cab and rang the doorbell.

Aiden came to the door stark naked, except for dark shades covering his eyes, and a pair of knitted slippers on his long callused feet. 'Aw, Jesus!' he groaned. 'You followed me home.'

'You're not very nice to me,' she said, pushing past him into his apartment. The television was blaring and there was a half-empty bottle of Jack Daniel's on the table. She remembered all the things she'd read about him in the tabloids and shivered with excitement. 'Are you *really* a drug addict?' she asked, wide-eyed.

'Are you *really* a fucking moron?' he responded, quickly pulling on a pair of pants. 'Where does Mommy think you are now?'

'Told her I had to go to a party. She doesn't care, she's too busy with her movie and Richard.'

'That old fart,' Aiden growled, taking a gulp of booze from the bottle.

'Richard's OK,' Summer said. 'I can get anything I want out of him, and he's like an *amazing* director – better than your friend Mick.'

Aiden lowered his shades and regarded her for a moment. 'What are you after, kid?' he asked, flopping down on a worn-out couch. ''Cause whatever it is, you're not getting it from me.'

'I'm into experiencing life,' she said ingenuously.

'You're treading a dangerous line. Fortunately for you, I'm not a bastard.'

She giggled disbelievingly. 'You're *not*?'

'Some people would've screwed the ass off you an' not given a shit. But I got principles.'

'Anyway,' she said matter-of-factly, 'that's why I'm here. I want you to . . . uh . . . do it to me.'

'Not me, kid – I got enough problems.'

'If you won't, I'll tell my dad you did, and the police'll arrest you 'cause I'm under-age.'

He stared at her for a long silent moment. 'You'd do that, wouldn't you?'

'My dad's a big-time shrink in Chicago,' she boasted. 'He's got real pull. He knows the Mayor.'

Aiden shook his head in disbelief. 'Get the fuck outta here or your mom's gonna hear about this.'

'She won't believe you, and you'll like get dumped from her movie.'

'You think I give a fast shit?' he said, hustling her to the door. 'Go home, little girl, an' don't come back.'

'You'll be sorry,' she said, shocked that he was rejecting her.

'So I'll be sorry. Big fucking deal.'

35

Lara and Nikki sat in the Chinese restaurant across the street from the production offices enjoying a sumptuous feast of wild rice, sweet and sour shrimp, egg rolls and won tons.

'I've never seen you like this, you're positively glowing,' Nikki said, reaching for an egg roll. 'And if you don't wipe that annoying smile off your face, I'll be forced to smack it off!'

'Isn't he great?' Lara said dreamily. 'And it's not only his looks – God knows I've passed up dozens of handsome guys.'

'Silly you,' Nikki murmured.

'You've got to understand,' Lara said, her green eyes burning bright, 'Joey is different. He's gentle and strong, smart and undemanding . . . and *soo* sexy.'

'Oh,' Nikki said, nodding wisely, 'now I get it. It's a sex thing.'

'No,' Lara objected quickly, 'honestly, Nikki, it's not just sex.'

'Yeah, yeah,' Nikki said disbelievingly. 'He's got you hooked sexually. And how is he in that department?'

Ignoring her friend, Lara continued, 'It's as if we belong together. Like we were out there alone and . . . somehow . . . we found each other.'

Nikki plucked a won ton off her plate and popped it in her mouth. 'Does he have money?'

Lara frowned. 'What does money have to do with anything?'

'Don't be so naive. Let us not forget you're a rich woman.'

'He's not asking for anything.'

'He doesn't have to. Not yet, anyway.'

232

Lara took a sip of black tea, attempting to remain calm. 'Why are you being so nasty?' she asked at last. 'You're the one who kept on begging me to sleep with someone.'

Nikki ran a hand through her short dark hair. 'I'm merely playing devil's advocate. A great fuck is one thing – but if you're falling in love, you need to know more about him. Like who he is would be a good start.'

'I know plenty.'

'Like what?'

'Like right now he's the perfect man for me.'

'I give up!' Nikki said, throwing her hands in the air. 'This is exactly what happens after a long dry spell.'

'Excuse me?'

'Getting laid again. Screws up your head quicker than anything.'

'Can't you be happy for me?'

'I am. It's just that this guy came out of nowhere. Dumped his fiancée and moved in on you big-time.'

'He didn't move in on me. I *invited* him to stay.'

'OK, OK, as long as you know what you're doing.'

They ate in silence for a few minutes, both busy with their own thoughts. Sometimes Lara resented Nikki's way of saying exactly what was on her mind. It was none of her business what she did or who she did it with.

'By the way, I need a favour,' she said, breaking the silence.

'Speak now.'

'I want Joey in the movie.'

Nikki groaned and stopped eating. 'You've *got* to be kidding.'

'We talked about it before.'

'That was weeks ago. Every role is cast.'

'You're the producer,' she said sharply. 'Find him something, he's an excellent actor.'

'I'm sure he is. But the truth is, you've left it too late.'

'Too late for what?'

'For Mick. He's meticulous about his casting. Every character is set.'

'Y'know,' Lara said, speaking in measured tones to be sure Nikki got the message, 'I'm doing this movie as a favour to you. A *big* favour.'

Nikki was shocked, this was not the Lara she knew and loved. 'So?' she said belligerently.

'So,' Lara responded, allowing her words to hang in the air. 'I'm requesting something back.'

'You're asking for something I can't do anything about,' Nikki said, furious at being put in such an awkward position.

'Yes, you can,' Lara countered. 'Be realistic.'

'I'll talk to Mick,' Nikki said resentfully.

'I'd appreciate it.'

They finished lunch barely speaking.

☆

Summer awoke in her own bed, late. She yawned and stretched, allowing her mind to wander over the events of the previous night. First the dinner party. Boring. Then her nocturnal visit to Aiden Sean. What a big fat disappointment he'd turned out to be. Just because her mother was Nikki Barry he hadn't wanted anything to do with her, he'd practically thrown her out – which really sucked.

Still . . . Aiden Sean was a movie star, and that had to count for something – especially in Chicago where she could impress everyone – including her dad's new wife, who thought she was such a hot number. Well, not hot enough – because *Rachel* hadn't almost made out with a movie star.

What would happen if she told Rachel the truth about the man she was married to?

The Monster Man.

My Daddy.

Suddenly Summer's eyes filled with tears as the truth came crashing back. She could never tell anyone. She was too ashamed.

Get over it, her inner voice screamed inside her head. *GET OVER IT!*

But it wasn't that easy.

☆

Back at the production offices, Mick stopped by to say hello to Lara, staring at her through his strange, magnified glasses. 'Lookin' forward to tomorrow,' he said, rubbing the tips of his long bony fingers together. 'The read-through's gonna be a happenin'.'

'I'm looking forward to it, too,' she replied, wondering what working with him would be like.

Later, after Lara had gone off to meet with the wardrobe people, Nikki cornered Mick in his office. He was on the phone having a conversation in which he appeared to be begging some woman to forgive him for a past indiscretion. 'C'mon, sweetie baby-love,' he wheedled. 'We'll have dinner, sex, a few laughs. You know you get off on me.'

Apparently the woman didn't, because Nikki could hear the loud dial tone on the other end of the phone as she hung up on him.

Mick pretended she was still on the line, mumbled a phony 'Goodbye,' put the phone down and turned to Nikki. 'What's up?' he asked, slumping back in his chair. She began pacing up and down in front of his desk, apprehensive about broaching such a delicate subject. 'Uh . . . this is the deal, Mick,' she said, dreading his reaction.

'Yeah?' he mumbled, checking out her legs.

'The truth is we're lucky to have Lara in our movie, on account of her being such a big star and all.'

'What're you telling me?' Mick asked irritably. 'She met me, doesn't like me, an' wants to walk? Is that it?'

'No, she thought you were charming,' Nikki said. Actually they'd been so busy discussing Joey, they'd barely mentioned him.

'Bull's-eye,' Mick sneered. 'I score charming award of the year.' He snickered wildly. 'That's before she's worked with me, right?'

Nikki sighed. 'She wants us to give her boyfriend a part.'

'Aw, shit!' he said, sitting up straight.

'I *told* her everything was cast.'

'You mean that creep she was with last night?'

'He's not a creep,' Nikki said patiently. 'He's her current boyfriend, and she wants him in the movie.'

'Who does she expect him to play? One of the freakin' rapists, for Chrissakes?'

'Maybe a detective?' Nikki suggested in her best *please do this for me* voice. 'Perhaps you can write another one in.'

'When didja ever see a detective that looked like him?' Mick grumbled. 'He's freakin' Mel Gibson twenty years ago – an' taller, too. Bastard!'

'That doesn't necessarily make him a bad guy,' Nikki murmured.

'It don't make him a good actor either.'

'The thing is, we'd like to have a happy star, wouldn't we?' She trailed off, hoping he got it.

'This is some fuckin' drag,' he mumbled. 'I never hadda compromise before.'

Well, you've only been in the business five minutes, she was tempted to say. But she didn't, knowing it wouldn't help matters.

'Will you think about it, Mick? For me? After all, I did you a favour with Aiden last night, who, I might add – wasn't exactly the life and soul of the party.'

'Do I at least get to read the boyfriend?' Mick asked, curling his lip.

'Of course.'

'Have him here at seven in the mornin' before the read-through. For you I'll check him out.'

'Thanks, Mick,' she said gratefully. 'I owe you one.'

'A blow job'll pay me back,' he said with an insane cackle.

'I'll tell Richard, he'll be flattered someone else wants me.'

'Not *you*,' Mick said scornfully. 'Your daughter.'

She gave him a long cold look. 'I take it you're joking.'

He laughed hysterically. 'Never joke about pussy.'

'Then I'll make believe I didn't hear you,' Nikki said, thinking that sometimes his pathetic attempt at humour was way out of whack.

'Whatever gets you through the night,' he said, with a manic shrug.

Yeah, she thought, *whatever gets me through the night. Richard's turning into a cold fish, Lara's in the throes of a love affair, Mick wants to get it on with my teenage daughter, and I'm left out in the cold trying to keep it all together.*

She went into her office, closing the door behind her, and immediately began thinking about the previous night's dinner party.

By the time everyone had left, Richard was completely plastered. He'd staggered into their bedroom, flopped on the bed, and she'd been forced to listen to his ranting and raving about *Revenge*, and Mick, and what a mistake Lara was making, before he'd fallen into a drunken stupor.

She had no respect for him when he drank too much – being loud and belligerent didn't suit him. What was it with these old guys she married? First Sheldon, now Richard. Was this marriage starting to crumble, too?

In the morning she'd left before he got up. And now she was at the office trying to get Lara's boyfriend a job. Producing a movie was not going to be as easy as she'd thought. Everybody had an angle – including Lara.

☆

When Lara arrived home, she found Joey in the den, watching sports on TV, looking perfectly content.

'Hi, beautiful,' he said, barely glancing up.

'I've got you an appointment with Mick tomorrow morning at seven,' she announced triumphantly. 'You cannot be late.'

'Seven!' he groaned. 'That's kinda early.'

She picked up the remote, clicking off the TV. 'I did as you asked, Joey,' she said quietly. 'I compromised myself.'

He stood up. 'How'd you do that?'

'I almost threatened Nikki I'd walk off the movie, which wasn't very nice of me.'

'Well, yeah, but we've both discovered you're not as nice as everyone thinks,' he said, putting his arms around her waist, pulling her close and running his hands over her body. 'You give out this aura of goodness, but underneath you're nothin' but a bad little sexpot!'

'Is that what you think?' she asked, shivering.

'C'mere, beautiful,' he said, bending her back and kissing her passionately on the mouth. 'Gotta tell you – I missed you all day.'

'You did?' she said, luxuriating in his kisses.

'Every second.'

'What did you do?'

'Worked out, swam. Mrs C. cooked me eggs, an' I took a look at your CD collection. You do know it's in need of serious work.'

'As if I have time to go to Tower and browse.'

'Hey – let's go together.'

'I get recognized in public places.'

'How 'bout we disguise you? Like Michael Jackson.'

'Michael Jackson is recognized everywhere he goes. And if I put on a white surgical mask and gloves, I'd be recognized too.'

'We'll get you a short black wig an' big shades. Or maybe we'll dress you up as a little boy.'

'A *little* boy?' she asked, laughing.

'Naw, a teenager. You could pass for a teenager, you're kinda flat-chested.'

'So now I'm flat-chested, am I?' she said, pretending to be exasperated.

'Not exactly.' He laughed, tweaking her nipples. 'They're big enough for me.'

She picked up a magazine, slamming him on the head.

He held up his hands, protecting himself. They both collapsed laughing on the couch.

He enfolded her in his arms, holding her close against him. He'd never had a relationship like this with anyone, and he liked it. Not only was Lara staggeringly beautiful and famous, she was genuinely nice. And warm and caring and sexy and fun. How had he finally gotten so lucky?

She snuggled into his chest, totally content. 'I usually get home from a day like this dead to the world,' she murmured. 'Now you're bringing out somebody in me I didn't know still existed.'

He looked at her with a quizzical expression. 'You tellin' me you'd forgotten how to have fun?'

'My past relationships were very staid. Richard's much older than me.'

'I noticed.'

'Lee was sweet.'

'Sweet don't cut it, babe,' he said, enclosing her breasts with his hands, working on her nipples. 'I bet he couldn't excite you the way I do, huh?'

She struggled to sit up. 'Joey – this is crazy. We've been together such a short time, and yet . . . sometimes I feel I've been with you all my life.'

'It's called soulmates,' he said, suddenly serious.

She stood up. 'Oh, that's what it's called, is it?'

He got up, too. 'What did Nikki say? Yes, I'll put Joey in the movie, I'll fire Aiden Sean and give him *that* role.'

'Oh, sure, I *really* want you playing the rapist.'

He walked over to the bar, opened the fridge and extracted a can of beer. 'I was readin' through the script today,' he said, flipping open the can. 'It's pretty heavy stuff.'

'I know.'

'Do you trust this Mick Stefan guy? He may be a hot director, but is he for you? You're playin' against your image big-time.'

'I know that, too.'

'You gotta consider your fans,' he said, swigging from the can. 'Why d'you think they go see you?'

'Because I'm a good actress?' she said flippantly.

'They go see you 'cause you send out this aura, this image.'

'I do?'

'You got it all, babe. You're beautiful an' nice. You're what every guy dreams about – the sexy good girl.'

'I'm glad you added sexy,' she said with a soft smile.

'Let's analyse it,' he said. 'Why was I so attracted to you? 'Cause – truth is – I've had a lot of women.'

'Before you were engaged, I presume,' she said archly.

'No question,' he replied seriously. 'I'm a big believer in fidelity – aren't you?'

'Yes,' she said, equally serious. 'I absolutely believe in it, Joey. After my experience with Richard, I vowed no man will ever cheat on me again.'

'What would you do,' he asked teasingly, 'if you'd come home today and found me in bed with a girl?'

'That's not a good question.'

'No, c'mon, tell me,' he urged. 'Would you have blown my head off? Kicked me out? Screamed at me? At *her*? What *would* you have done?'

'I'd have walked away,' she said calmly. 'Simply walked away.'

'Oh, no, baby,' he said confidently. 'There's no way you could walk away from me.'

For a moment her green eyes darkened. 'Don't bet on it, Joey. Don't ever bet on it. I'm stronger than you think.'

☆

By the time Nikki arrived at the Malibu house Richard was drunk again.

'This is getting to be a habit,' she said coldly. 'I thought your drinking days were behind you.'

'What's the matter?' he asked belligerently. 'Aren't I allowed to relax?'

Oh, God! Not another fight. 'You still working on post?' she asked, walking into the kitchen.

'Everything's done,' he said, following her.

'Where's Summer?'

'Out,' he replied, still bad-tempered.

'Listen, Richard,' she said, determined to clear things up, 'it was you who encouraged me to get involved in producing. I thought you wanted me to make this film.'

'I didn't tell you to drag Lara into it, put her together with a piece-of-shit director and ruin her career,' he said curtly. 'You're using your connections, and I don't like it.'

'Lara *wants* to do my film,' she said, opening the fridge and removing two steaks neatly enclosed in Saran-wrap.

'She's only doing it because of me,' he said, sourly.

'If that's what you think,' she said, placing the steaks on the grill.

'You wouldn't even *know* Lara if it wasn't for me.'

'What kind of remark is that?'

'The truth.'

'I'm sorry you feel this way,' she said flatly, not ready to get into another fight. 'Can we discuss it later? Right now I'm fixing dinner.'

Later, he was too drunk, and they went to bed not speaking.

☆

Summer and Tina went back to Club Pot, where they danced all night, sometimes with each other, sometimes with a selection of different guys. They finally sat down, their hard tanned young bodies glistening with sweat.

'Last night Mick Stefan and Aiden Sean were at my

mom's house,' Summer confided. 'Can you *imagine*? Mick almost crapped! While stupid Aiden pretended he so didn't know me.'

'*That* dick!' Tina said scornfully.

'And you know what I did?'

'What?'

'Took a cab to his stinky old apartment and told him what a phoney he was.'

Tina raised an eyebrow. 'You did that?'

'Well . . .' Summer giggled. 'Actually, I went there to get him to sleep with me. But he wouldn't do it. I think he must be gay.'

'Really?'

'I don't see why else he wouldn't.'

'Y'know, Summer,' Tina said thoughtfully, 'if it's a movie star you want, *I* can get you plenty.'

'No way,' Summer said.

'Way,' Tina boasted. '*And* – here's the kicker – they'll pay you to do stuff. Big big bucks!'

'Wow!' Summer responded, thinking that getting paid for anything at all was a really wild idea.

'If you're serious, I'll arrange it,' Tina said casually. 'Only if I do – you can't fink out on me.'

'Go ahead,' Summer said boldly. 'I'm up for anything.'

'Are you sure?' Tina asked. ''Cause I'm not playing games. This is the real thing, and if I bring you in, there's no way you can let me down.'

'I wouldn't do that.'

'OK. I'll set it up. Call me in the morning.'

Another adventure. Summer couldn't wait.

36

Unfairly incarcerated for stalking and attacking her best friend, Alison Sewell spent most of her time in jail plotting and planning the revenge she would wreak when she got out. Her eighteen-month sentence was automatically reduced to half. Nine months inside. Pregnant with hate for the woman who'd put her there.

Lara Ivory. Bitch. Whore. She wasn't a friend after all, she was the enemy, exactly like the rest of the morons Alison had to deal with.

Lara Ivory had fooled everyone with her beautiful face. But Alison realized the face was merely a cover for the evil woman who lurked within.

As soon as she got out, Alison knew she had to do something about the bad seed that was Lara Ivory.

Yes, she'd wipe the sweet smile off Lara's ugly face for ever.

Meanwhile she had prison to deal with, and no camera to hide behind. And as each day passed, her thirst for revenge grew.

37

'Where'd you study?' Mick asked, swinging back in the chair behind his desk, legs splayed in front of him, beady eyes behind his heavy glasses crinkled in a deep squint.

'Does it matter?' Joey asked, trying to figure out a way to get through to this asshole. He knew the guy hated him, had to hate him. He was too good-looking for most men, especially someone like Mick, with his wild hair, pointed face and geeky clothes. However, Joey knew there had to be a way to connect, there always was.

'LA, New York, where?' Mick pressed.

'I, uh . . . I kinda studied around New York,' Joey said, purposely keeping it vague. 'Actin' class, workshops, things like that. Then I got a break in *Solid*.'

'Thought I'd seen you somewhere before,' Mick said, squinting even more ferociously. 'How come nothin' happened after that?'

'Family problems took me back home for a while,' Joey mumbled. 'Soon as I hit New York again, I scored the role in *The Dreamer*.'

'An' that's where you met Lara, huh?' Mick said, wriggling his ankles. 'She's a real cool babe-chick. Some freakin' looker.'

'She sure is,' Joey agreed.

Mick leered. 'Pretty nice when you get 'em great looking *an'* they wanna get you a job.'

All of a sudden Joey got it, he knew exactly how to bond with this cretin. 'I'm fucking her, why shouldn't I be in her movie?' he said calmly.

This was the kind of talk Mick understood. 'Got it!' he said, a huge beam covering his pointed face. 'Hey – I can bump somebody if I gotta. There's like this older detective with a younger partner. I was into the younger guy being black, no reason it couldn't be you.' He tossed a script across the desk, burping loudly. 'Course, I'll havta dump the black actor, which means the NAACP'll cream my ass, but who gives a shit? Page fifty-two – wanna read?'

Joey held the script. 'Who'm I readin' with?'

'Me,' Mick said, getting up and walking around the desk. 'I'll play the older detective. Used t'be an actor, y'know.'

'Yeah?'

'You don't have much to say, but you'll be there, keepin' watch on your girlfriend.' He snickered. 'She's gotta be something in the sack, huh? Wild legs. Those classy ones got it all goin'.'

'You could say that,' Joey replied, searching for the right page.

Mick winked, happy with Joey's reply. 'Maybe when we're workin' together – hanging out – we can get down to details. Whaddaya think?'

'I think,' Joey said slowly, 'when I'm doing the movie, you and I can hang out as much as you want.'

Mick cackled again. 'OK, let's read the motherfucker.'

☆

'Richard?' Lara said, cradling the phone under her chin. 'Has Nikki left yet?'

'What's the matter?' Richard said. 'Don't want to speak to me?'

'You're always so busy.'

'Never too busy for you, sweetheart.'

'That's nice,' she said, wishing he'd put Nikki on the line.

'Wait till you see the movie, Lara,' he said enthusiastically. 'Your performance is impeccable.'

She remembered what Joey had said about Richard still having a crush on her, and knew in her heart that it was true. She wasn't flattered. The only reason Richard wanted her was because he couldn't have her any more.

'I'm excited about seeing it.'

'I'll arrange a screening.'

'Is Nikki there?'

'I was thinking,' Richard said, with no intention of getting off the phone, 'you and I should have lunch.'

'Sounds good, only right now my schedule's frantic.'

'Nobody understands that better than me. But think about it, Lara – how many people *really* care about you? You have no family.'

She'd told Richard the same story she'd told everyone else. Her family were all wiped out in a car crash. She'd been raised by a distant relative – now deceased. It was safer never to reveal the truth.

'I'm worried about you, Lara,' Richard continued. 'That guy you brought with you the other night – that actor – who is he?'

She was not in the mood for a question and answer session. 'Why does everyone keep on asking me who he is?' she said, exasperated. 'What am I *supposed* to do – get a Dunn and Bradstreet on every man I go out with?'

'For almost the last year you haven't been out with anyone. Before that it was Lee.'

'Keeping a score card?' she asked, annoyed that he was questioning her.

'Now Lee was an OK guy,' he continued, ignoring her acid comment. 'He'd been in the business for years and knew his way around. Nobody knows anything about this Joey guy. Where's he from? What's his story?'

'Richard,' she said, trying to keep her aggravation in check, 'I'm a grown-up. I don't need anyone watching out for me.'

'This isn't like you, sweetheart. We must sit down and talk face to face, just the two of us.'

'How about Nikki?'

'She won't mind,' he said, clearing his throat. 'We can do it tomorrow. Lunch. You and me, the Bistro Gardens in the Valley. It's important to me, Lara, don't let me down.'

'Well, all right,' she found herself saying. 'But no third degree, because I'm very happy. In fact, I'm happier than I've ever been.'

'I only want the best for you, sweetheart.'

'*Now* can I speak to Nikki?' she asked patiently.

'Hang on a moment.' He went off to fetch her.

After a few moments Nikki got on the line.

'What time are you leaving?' Lara asked.

'Soon. Why?'

'And the read-through is ten o'clock?'

'You're up for it, aren't you?'

'Of course.'

'Then *what*?'

'I'm anxious to know the outcome of Joey's meeting with Mick, so maybe you'll call me when you get there.'

'Listen,' Nikki said evenly, not sounding like her usual warm self, 'you gave me an ultimatum. I passed it on to Mick. He'll hire Joey, he has to.'

'Really?'

'You're the star, Lara, you made that very clear.'

'I didn't mean I'd walk if he wasn't hired.'

'Yes, you did,' Nikki sighed. 'But I understand.'

Nikki was pissed – too bad. She couldn't please everybody all the time.

She thought about Joey and smiled. Joey Lorenzo. He treated her like a woman, not a movie star – and she loved it. Joey. The man who excited the hell out of her. For the last two nights he'd slept in her bed, and they'd indulged in hot, exciting, incredibly intense sex. She hadn't realized that making love could be so inventive and different every time. Joey gave new meaning to passion.

She hadn't thought she'd ever find this kind of relationship, and now that she had – all everyone wanted to do was criticize him. What did she care about his background or where he was from? Although she had to admit she was a tiny bit curious about his ex-fiancée, Phillipa, whom he never mentioned, even when she'd tried to question him once.

But the truth was, keeping secrets was OK. She had her own, and those weren't to be shared either.

When she was almost dressed she found herself going into his room. His two suitcases were on the floor – stacked one on top of the other. She felt guilty invading his privacy, but somehow she couldn't help herself.

Opening the closet, she peered inside. He didn't have many clothes – not even a suit. She was prepared to buy him anything he desired – a car, clothes, it didn't matter to her. As far as she was concerned their future was together.

The thought never occurred to her that he might be with her because she was rich. Without false modesty she was well aware she could have almost any man she wanted, and not just because she was a movie star. No, her fame wasn't the main attraction. It was her beauty that made men desire her with such a longing.

Sometimes she called it her cursed beauty.

When she recalled her youth . . . the far-off dark days . . . the nightmare times nobody knew about . . .

Her face clouded over. No! She wasn't getting into *that* today.

She couldn't find anything personal in the room. No photos, papers, nothing. Her face flushed with guilt at what she was doing, she opened the top suitcase, coming across a jumble of dirty socks, T-shirts and underwear. The other suitcase was locked.

She looked around, but couldn't find a key. Hating herself for snooping, she quickly left the room, bumping into Mrs Crenshaw in the corridor outside.

'Everything all right, Miss Lara?' Mrs Crenshaw asked.

'Yes, thank you,' she replied, escaping to her bedroom.

She'd told Joey to call as soon as he got through with Mick. He hadn't done so yet. Hopefully things were going well.

She dressed hurriedly and left the house, arriving at the production offices early. When she walked into the main room she found Joey sitting at a table with Mick and a couple of crew members. They were laughing, drinking coffee and eating doughnuts. She presumed from his attitude that everything had worked out.

'Hi, baby,' he said, standing up and grinning.

'Hi, Joey,' she replied, a touch cool because he hadn't called her.

He grabbed her in an intimate hug, kissing her full on the mouth, letting everyone know she was his.

Mick lurched to his feet, a knowing leer all over his pointed face. 'Hiya, Lara,' he said, absent-mindedly rubbing his crotch. 'You're early.'

'Yes, I am,' she said with a tight smile. 'Joey, can we go downstairs for breakfast?'

'Sure, baby,' he said, winking at the guys. 'See ya.'

Why did she have this uncomfortable feeling that they'd been talking about her?

'You were supposed to call me,' she said, as soon as they were in the elevator.

'I couldn't get away from Mick,' he explained. 'After he gave me the part of detective number two, he kept on talkin'. What could I do?'

'So he hired you?'

'Course he did. An' the good news is it'll mean I'll be there to keep a watch on you.'

'I don't need anyone watching over me, Joey,' she said. 'When I'm working I'm *very* focused.'

'I bet you are, but you still need somebody around to protect you.'

'Cassie follows me everywhere,' she said, as they stepped out of the elevator. 'She's enough protection for anyone.'

'No, no, baby,' he said insistently. 'On this movie you're gonna need *me* around.'

'Well, anyway, I'm delighted it all worked out,' she said, squeezing his hand. 'You'd better call your agent, have him make a deal.'

Somehow he didn't think Madelaine Francis would appreciate his phone call. 'Don't wanna use the one I had in New York,' he said.

'Then go to mine. I'll have Cassie arrange an appointment.'

'Whyn't you call him yourself?'

'If that's what you'd like.'

They left the building, crossing the street to the coffee shop. Several cars nearly ran into the back of each other when the drivers spotted Lara. She didn't appear to notice.

As soon as they were seated, she took out her cellphone, contacting Quinn at his office. 'I have a new client for you,' she said crisply. 'Joey Lorenzo, a very good friend of mine. He needs you to negotiate a deal for him on *Revenge*.' She paused for a moment, tapping the side of the phone. 'Yes, Quinn, I *know* there's no money on this movie. Do the best you can.' She covered the mouthpiece. 'Joey, can you see him tomorrow morning?' He nodded. 'OK, he'll be there around ten. Thanks, Quinn.' She clicked off the phone. 'Done,' she said, pleased with herself.

Joey leaned across the table, fixing her with one of his looks. 'How come you're so good to me?' he asked.

'Because you're good to me, too,' she replied softly. 'It's a two-way street.'

'I try.'

'You're succeeding.'

The waitress came over, pad poised. Lara ordered an egg-white omelette and herbal tea. Joey went for coffee and a Danish.

'Did you see Nikki this morning?' she asked.

He shook his head. 'Naw. Why?'

'She's not very pleased with me – thinks I pressured her to get you in the film. But I *know* you won't let me down.'

'Now Mick knows it too,' he said confidently. 'I gave a pretty good reading.'

'I'm sure,' she murmured.

He reached across the table and took her hand. They smiled intimately at each other.

It was a physical thing. They couldn't keep their hands off each other.

38

Once again Summer awoke late, it was getting to be a habit, and why not? She didn't have school to go to or people nagging her to get up. Daddy's housekeeper, Mrs Stern, was just that – an ornery old witch who, if she ever knew what was going on under her pointed old nose, would drop on the spot.

It was so amazing being away from them all – living her life without the threat of her father molesting her ... the image of his face looming over her in the middle of the night.

She shuddered at the thought. Ah ... freedom ... She couldn't wait to get out permanently.

Last night she'd staggered home at four a.m., encountering Richard in the kitchen getting a glass of water – which is exactly what she'd planned on doing to counteract the major hangover heading her way. She'd had three or four potent drinks called Gangbusters – a mixture of vodka, fruit juice and rum – and she'd felt like she was about to throw up.

'Just getting in?' Richard had asked, crinkling his eyes.

Oh, no! Not a lecture. Please!

'I was staying at my girlfriend's,' she'd explained. 'Then there was like a huge fire in the kitchen, and everywhere filled with smoke, so I came home.'

Richard had laughed. 'Very inventive, dear. Save those kind of stories for your mother.'

She'd giggled. Richard never gave her a hard time. He was the best. She couldn't understand why he and Lara had gotten divorced, it seemed crazy. Lara was so sweet and beautiful, how could any man give her up?

She turned over in bed, then remembered she'd promised

to call Tina – who'd said something about meeting stars and making money. How radical would *that* be?

If she could only make enough money, she'd *never* have to go home.

☆

The actors gathered together at ten for the reading, which was taking place in a large conference room beneath the production offices. Lara was secretly thrilled Joey was now part of the production; the truth was she *did* feel more secure having him next to her.

Most of the actors were hanging around the coffee machine getting to know each other. Lara didn't recognize anyone, but she made eye contact and smiled, well aware that it was up to her as the star to create a friendly atmosphere.

Now that he was in the movie, Joey decided it might be a smart move to charm Nikki. He went over to her. 'I owe you a big thank you,' he said. 'I know you had a lot t'do with gettin' me this gig.'

'Thank Lara, not me,' she replied, a touch snippy.

'Oh, I will.'

'Make sure you do,' she said, heading for the coffee maker.

He fell into step behind her. 'You two are good friends, huh?'

'We certainly are.'

'That's great. Friendships are important.'

Nikki stopped, regarding him for a long silent moment. What did he want? Her approval? Obviously. 'A lot of people love Lara very much, including me and Richard,' she said at last. 'So, Joey, you should know that if you ever hurt her—'

'Hey,' he interrupted, 'I may be new in her life, but I love and respect Lara, I always will.'

Nikki nodded and walked away.

She wasn't easy, but Joey figured he'd better persevere – as Lara's best friend he needed her on his side.

Lara took her place at the head of the big conference table, motioning Joey to sit beside her. He did so.

Mick stood up, waving his gangly arms in the air. He then made an impassioned speech.

Nikki was impressed. A good director had to be a powerful leader, and with all his foibles Mick seemed to be just that.

Aiden Sean arrived late, clad in grungy jeans, a wrinkled T-shirt, and a black baseball cap emblazoned with a scarlet *Eat my sorrow*. Dark shades covered his eyes.

'Glad you could make it,' Nikki said coolly as he passed her chair.

He lowered his shades, peering at her over the top. 'Don't worry 'bout me,' he mumbled. 'You got problems closer to home.'

She frowned. Could he possibly know that she and Richard weren't getting along? 'What do you mean by *that*?'

'Forget it,' he said, slouching over to a chair at the end of the table.

The reading began.

Joey got off on the way Lara handled herself. As she read Rebecca, the schoolteacher, so she became the character. It was almost as if her glowing beauty slipped away and she *was* the plain, timid woman.

Twenty pages into the script came the rape scene. Lara handled it like the true professional she was. And Joey did well with the few scenes he had.

The script was extremely powerful – a real tour de force for Lara. At the end of the reading she was emotionally drained.

Mick rushed over, kissing her full on the mouth. 'You're the greatest,' he said, beaming and twitching. 'Never thought you could make it work this good, but lady – you're fanfuckingtastic!'

She was happy that she'd done the words justice. 'Thanks, Mick,' she said shyly, thinking how she couldn't wait to go home and be with Joey, snuggled in the safety of his arms.

Nikki hugged her, unable to stay mad. 'I'm so happy,' she said excitedly. 'You're so much more than just a movie star, and it's about time people realized it. This movie will finally bring you the recognition you deserve.'

'I'll do my best,' Lara said modestly.

'Your best is amazing!' Nikki replied, laughing.

They hugged each other again. 'I'm sorry if I've been on

your case,' Nikki continued. 'I realize that if you like Joey, he *must* be an OK guy. And he did fine today. He's actually very good.'

'I didn't mean to force you to hire him,' Lara said. 'It's only that how often does someone come along who's special? And if Joey wasn't working, he'd have to go back to New York, then you'd be stuck with one miserable actress.'

'It all worked out,' Nikki said cheerfully. 'Now – the big question. Are you comfortable with Mick?'

'He's no Richard, but I'm sure we'll get along.'

'I feel so much better about everything today,' Nikki exclaimed. 'Even Aiden's cutting it.'

'Richard asked me to lunch tomorrow. Will you come?'

'I can't, too busy.'

'You don't mind?'

Nikki laughed. 'You and Richard having lunch? Oh yeah, I'm *really* bent out of shape. Although it would've been nice if he'd invited me too.'

'He's *your* husband.'

'Yeah, lucky me,' Nikki said, grinning ruefully.

'Is everything OK?' Lara asked, picking up bad vibrations.

'Sure,' Nikki replied, determined not to throw her troubles in Lara's lap. 'Why wouldn't it be?'

'If you want to talk . . .'

'Yeah, yeah, I know – you've been there, done that. Thanks, anyway.'

Lara glanced around, searching for Joey. He was over the other side of the room talking to a young production assistant with long curly hair and a spectacular body. She felt a tingle of jealousy. Ridiculous! She'd never been jealous before. Joey had her emotions completely out of control.

'How's it working out with Summer?' she asked, forcing herself to turn back to Nikki.

'Considering I hardly ever see her, I guess it's fine,' Nikki said. 'I decided rather than nag her to death, I'd allow her plenty of freedom. She wants to move here.'

'Is that such a good idea?' Lara asked gently. 'This is a tough town for a teenager to be loose in.'

'I know,' Nikki said with a deep sigh. 'But right now I haven't got time to play mother.'

'Perhaps you should send her back to Chicago until you finish the movie.'

'You're right, that's exactly what I should do. I'll call Sheldon tomorrow.'

'She shouldn't be running around by herself.'

Nikki frowned. 'Did Summer tell you something I should hear about?'

'No, it's just that I remember when I first came to LA I was only nineteen, and believe me – I know how the sleazy guys in this town hit on young girls.'

'Ah yes,' Nikki said, with a smile. 'But I'm sure you handled it with your usual indomitable style.'

Lara's eyes clouded over. *If Nikki only knew*, she thought.

She glanced in Joey's direction again. He was on his way toward her. Grabbing her arm, he smiled broadly. 'Isn't she the greatest?' he said to Nikki. 'This woman is amazin'!'

'*I've* always thought so.'

He drew Lara close to him, his hand creeping down and squeezing her ass. 'My star. My baby. You're the best!'

Hmm, Nikki thought. *He wants everyone to know he has power of ownership.*

Lara didn't seem to mind; in fact, from the way she gazed up at him, Joey could do whatever he wanted and get away with it.

'Why don't we leave one of the cars here and go home together?' he suggested. 'Send Mr and Mrs C. to pick it up.'

'I can't make them drive all the way to the Valley,' Lara objected.

'Why not? They work for you.'

'Yes, but . . .'

'OK, settled. We're takin' the Jag.'

'I guess you're taking the Jag,' Nikki said drily.

'I guess we are,' Lara replied, perfectly happy to let Joey take charge.

In the parking structure, Lara got into the passenger seat of the Jaguar, while Joey sat behind the wheel. He leaned over and kissed her. 'I'm so proud of you,' he said. 'Whenever I look at you, an' realize you're mine, I can hardly believe it.'

'How about you?' she said, smiling. 'I'm proud too. You were great.'

'C'mon, I've hardly got anythin' to do.'

'What you did have was very impressive.'

'Flattery will get you the key to my dick!'

'I'll have it gold-plated,' she deadpanned.

'Show off!'

They both laughed as he steered the car out into the street.

'Y'know, I was thinking,' he said. 'After this movie's finished, we should take off – go to Bali, Tahiti, somewhere exotic.'

'I'm always too busy working.'

'I bet you've been everywhere, huh?'

'The only places I get to see are locations.'

'You wanna do it, then?'

'I'll check my schedule.'

'Lara,' he said, looking at her quizzically, 'tell the truth – before me, didja do *everythin'* by schedule?'

'As a matter of fact, yes,' she admitted sheepishly.

'Then as soon as you finish the movie, we're tearin' up your schedule, 'cause from now on it's a whole new life.'

She smiled contentedly. 'Whatever you say, Joey.'

☆

Summer met Tina at an outdoor restaurant on Sunset Plaza Drive. Tina was sitting with an attractive older woman who Summer reckoned was about the same age as her mother.

'Meet Darlene,' Tina said, introducing them. 'Darlene's cool. She organizes things.'

'Hi, Summer,' Darlene said with a pleasant smile. Her hair was dark blond and upswept, and her teeth white and even. She was expensively dressed in Chanel, and real diamonds glittered on her ears and fingers.

'Hi,' Summer responded, quite impressed with this woman's obvious sophistication.

'Sit down, dear,' Darlene said.

She sat in a chair next to Tina, noticing Darlene's perfect manicure and blood-red inch-long nails.

'Well, Summer,' Darlene said, 'I understand you might be interested in working for me.'

Summer glanced at Tina, who nodded reassuringly. 'It's what we talked about,' Tina reminded her. 'Y'know – the movie star thing.'

'Oh,' Summer said. 'Uh . . . yes.'

'It so happens,' Darlene said smoothly, 'that there's an extremely handsome young movie star who'd love to meet you.'

Talk about things moving fast! 'There is?'

'Are you interested?'

She had absolutely nothing to lose, and money and freedom to gain. 'Sure,' she said quickly.

Darlene licked her generous lips. 'How does five hundred dollars in cash sound to you?'

Summer couldn't believe this was happening to her. 'Uh . . . amazing,' she managed.

'Just one thing,' Darlene said. 'You're not a virgin, are you? You do know how to look after yourself?'

No, I am not a virgin on account of the fact that my dear daddy has been screwing me since I was ten.

'Yes, I know how to look after myself,' she said, thinking that a condom and a joint would get her through any tricky situation.

'Tomorrow night,' Darlene said, getting up from the table. 'I'll set it up. Tina will give you the details.' She nodded approvingly at Tina. 'You were right, dear. Summer's quite lovely.' And with that she walked over to a chauffeured Mercedes waiting kerbside, got inside, and the car slid off.

'Wow!' Summer exclaimed. 'Who is she?'

'Isn't she great?' Tina said admiringly. 'I want to be her one day. You should see her house!'

'Where did you meet her?' Summer asked, swiping a slice of pizza from Tina's plate.

'Around,' Tina said vaguely. 'I was doing a modelling job and one of the other models introduced us. Darlene's primo. I've made tons of money with her. You can, too, only whatever you do, *don't* tell her you're only fifteen – I said you're seventeen. Remember that.'

'I *know*,' she said. What kind of idiot did Tina take her for?

'And keep this to yourself,' Tina warned. 'No telling Jed or any of the others. This is our secret.'

'I'm good at keeping secrets.'

'Knew I could trust you.'

And Summer beckoned the waiter and ordered a whole pizza for herself, because soon she was going to be rich.

39

Richard snapped his fingers at the wine waiter and requested a bottle of Chardonnay.

'I'm not drinking,' Lara said, already wishing she hadn't agreed to lunch with him.

'Come on, sweetheart,' he said persuasively. 'For old times' sake.'

'Old times' sake?' she said, irritated. 'I thought the purpose of this lunch was that you wanted to talk to me about Joey.'

'Yes, but that doesn't mean we can't enjoy ourselves while we're doing it,' he said smoothly, turning on the charm. 'A glass of wine with your ex-husband – is that such a terrible thing?'

'I have to be truthful with you, Richard,' she said, glancing across the room, 'I'd be a lot more comfortable if Nikki was here.'

'How can you say that?' he complained, giving her a hurt look. 'I was *married* to you, for Chrissakes. It's not as if we're having a secret assignation.'

'I suppose you're right,' she said, gazing blankly around the restaurant. So far she'd had a busy day. She'd taped several TV interviews for Australia, followed by an hour with a reporter from *Premiere* magazine. And now lunch with Richard. Later she'd agreed to do even more print interviews at her publicist's office, something she hated, even though she'd done so many of them it was like being on automatic pilot.

She was half tempted to excuse herself from the table, go to the phone and cancel, but then she realized she'd be letting everyone down, and publicity was important, especially as she had three upcoming movies to promote.

The truth was she had no desire to spend a couple more precious hours sitting in her publicist's office when she could be with Joey.

Ah, Joey . . . Was she thinking about him too much? Was she getting in too deep too fast?

Who knew? Who cared? She was content for the first time in ages, and that's all that mattered.

'Are you happy?' Richard asked, as if delving into her thoughts.

'Very,' she replied firmly. 'Joey's allowing me the freedom to be myself.'

He stared at her, wondering how he could ever have let this woman go. 'That's an interesting statement,' he said. 'What exactly does it mean?'

'Oh, I don't know . . .' she said vaguely. 'Shedding my inhibitions, becoming totally free.'

His eyes gleamed. 'Sexually?'

'That's really none of your business.'

'Well,' he said, leaning back in his chair. 'Since we're being so truthful, that *was* one of the reasons I found myself seeking out other women.'

'*Excuse* me?' she said, frowning.

'Don't get me wrong,' he said, afraid he'd overstepped her tolerance level. 'But, sweetheart, you have to admit – you were never exactly adventurous in the bedroom. There are times a man needs more . . . spice.'

She glared at him, her green eyes suddenly cold. What gave her ex-husband the right to talk to her this way? If their sex life was so lousy it certainly wasn't *her* fault, *she* hadn't been the one out there screwing around. 'Y'know, Richard,' she said, her tone cool, 'I may not have been as adventurous as you might have liked, but did you ever consider that you seemed to prefer watching TV?'

Now it was his turn to do a slow burn. This was the second time he'd been told he preferred television to sex. First Nikki. Now Lara. Shit! He'd had more sex than they'd had hot dinners. 'If you want to get into reasons—' he began.

'I don't,' she interrupted, realizing the smart thing would be to make a move before they became embroiled in a real fight. 'This lunch was a mistake,' she continued, standing up. 'In fact, I'm leaving while we're still talking.'

'You can't do that,' he said, standing too.

'You tricked me into coming so you could talk about our past. You know what, Richard? I think you're jealous because I've found somebody I'm in synch with.'

'That's ridiculous!' he objected.

'Joey's young and good-looking,' she said heatedly. 'We're having a great time together, and it's sticking in your gut. So don't start telling *me* I was a dud in the bedroom. Let me tell *you* something – when a woman's not good in bed, it's because the man doesn't inspire her. So . . . no more cosy little lunches for two. Let's stay friends and out of each other's business, OK, Richard?'

And before he had a chance to reply, she was on her way to the door.

She stood outside trying to compose herself. How dare he criticize her performance in bed. Joey certainly had no complaints.

A hovering photographer began taking shots, which always made her nervous. As soon as the valet brought her car, she took off, realizing that she now had an hour to waste before going to her publicist's office. Not enough time to go home, so, after driving over the hill, she stopped at Neiman Marcus, indulging in some mindless shopping.

The attention she received from customers and sales people alike was stifling – one of the drawbacks of having a famous face. She smiled politely and signed a few autographs before reclaiming her car and heading over to her publicist's early, startling several assistants who couldn't do enough for her.

Linden, her publicist, a handsome black man in his early forties, was delighted to see her. 'How's my favourite client?' he asked, kissing her on both cheeks.

'Tired,' she replied, suppressing a yawn.

'You sure don't look it,' he said cheerfully.

Linden was a former stuntman who'd lost an arm in a stunt gone wrong on one of Lara's early movies. She'd helped him make the best of a bad situation by investing in the publicity firm he put together, and becoming his first client. Now, six years later, he was extremely successful and well liked in the business. He often told her he owed it all to her. She laughed, and refused to take credit.

'You're always so sweet, Linden,' she said.

'I try to please my clients at all times,' he replied with a smile.

'You certainly do that.'

Linden settled her in a private office and she called home. Mrs Crenshaw informed her Joey was out.

She didn't want him to be out. She wanted to talk to him, tell him she missed him and couldn't wait to be in his arms.

Last night he'd made love to her in the games room – bent her over the pool table, lifted her skirt and taken her just like that. It had been incredibly erotic.

Joey was never predictable sexually. Sometimes he made her feel like a whore and sometimes the perfect lady. The combination was dangerously addictive.

Merely thinking about him caused her a shudder of excitement.

She smiled. Joey always put a smile on her face, and that's exactly the way she liked it.

☆

'Thanks for seein' me, I appreciate it,' Joey said.

As if I had a choice, Quinn Lattimore thought sourly, running a hand through his dyed hair as he regarded Joey through suspicious eyes and asked too many questions.

Joey kept it vague as Quinn pressed for more information. 'I'm startin' fresh,' he explained.

I bet you are, Quinn thought, trying to figure out what was going on with Lara lately. First she'd insisted on making this cheapo movie *Revenge.* Now she'd gotten her boyfriend a part in it, and the capper was she expected *him*, Quinn Lattimore, to represent this unknown actor, even though she knew he was obsessively fussy about the people he took on, turning down good-looking actors every day. And Joey was a cagey one, refusing to reveal anything about his past, including what agent had represented him in New York. Quinn found this highly suspect.

He sat back, checking Joey out. He had to admit that the young man *was* extremely handsome, but who knew if he had talent?

'You'll need to get some new head shots,' he said, tapping his stubby fingers on the desk. 'I suggest you go to Greg

Jackie Collins

Gorman – he's the best photographer around for men. Not cheap, but definitely worth the investment.'

'How much is not cheap?' Joey asked casually.

'Have Lara call him,' Quinn said. 'Greg loves her. Maybe she can cut you a deal.'

Who doesn't love Lara? Joey thought. 'Listen, Mr Lattimore,' he said slowly. 'You should know I'm very fond of Lara.'

'I'm sure you are,' Quinn said.

'I'm plannin' on lookin' after her,' Joey added, staring at him intently.

'Does she *need* looking after?' Quinn asked, raising a cynical eyebrow.

'I believe so,' Joey said, wondering how much commission this fat cat had made out of her. 'Sometimes people are inclined to take advantage of a woman on her own – 'specially a famous woman.'

'I advised her not to do *Revenge*,' Quinn said pompously. 'I insisted she take a well-deserved break, but you know Lara – she's stubborn, wouldn't listen.'

'She's pushin' herself too hard,' Joey said. 'If I'd been with her I wouldn't have allowed her to do it. It's too tough a role. Plus it goes against her image big-time.'

Quinn decided it might be prudent to get Joey on his side. Better to be friends with the man who was in bed with his most successful client rather than enemies. 'Joey,' he said, warming up considerably, 'I'll get you what I can for *Revenge*, only I should warn you – they have a non-existent budget.'

'Yeah,' Joey said, standing up. 'Lara mentioned it.'

'Good. Because I wouldn't want to disappoint you.'

Joey nodded, at least Quinn was a straight shooter. 'I'll look into those head shots you mentioned.'

'The sooner the better,' Quinn said.

Joey left the office on Sunset Boulevard, and walked around the corner to Lara's car. A group of musicians were unloading their equipment outside a rock club. An outstandingly pretty girl in a skimpy outfit sat on one of the speakers, casually filing her nails. She glanced up as Joey passed, smiling invitingly. 'Hi,' she said.

'How ya doin'?' he responded, hardly noticing her.

'Wouldn't mind a coffee,' she said, all stoned eyes and exposed pink flesh.

Once he would have taken her up on her invitation, but now he had no intention of doing so. He'd finally discovered the woman he'd been searching for all his life, and no way was he screwing it up.

☆

Nikki sat behind her desk trying to get her head straight. Richard was behaving like a horse's ass, and she didn't know what to do. He was a big success, he had his own movie coming out – *French Summer*, which was going to garner nothing but great reviews and mega attention – and yet he seemed to be jealous of her modest film.

It didn't make sense. Last night they'd barely spoken again. Truth was he resented Lara appearing in *Revenge*. Well, too bad, she hadn't *forced* her to say yes. Lara was free to make her own choices, including Joey – whom Richard hated.

It startled Nikki that he was so concerned. She wanted to remind him that Lara was his ex-wife, and it was about time he let go.

A production assistant stopped by with a stack of memos. Nikki riffled through them, placed them on her desk, then picked up the phone and called Sheldon in Chicago, a task she'd been putting off.

'How are you, Nikki?' Sheldon asked in that supercilious tone she remembered so well and loathed so much.

'Fine,' she replied, waiting to see if he mentioned Summer first. He didn't. 'Nice vacation?' she asked, merely being polite.

'Pleasant,' he replied.

A short silence. Nikki broke it. 'Uh . . . Sheldon,' she said, plunging in, 'I'm calling to discuss Summer.'

'What about her?'

'She wants to go to school in LA.'

'Why?' he asked sharply.

'She likes it here.'

'I certainly hope you haven't been allowing her to run riot,' he said sternly.

'You know your daughter, she's hardly the easiest girl in

the world to keep tabs on. Besides, she told me you never gave her a curfew.'

'Surely you didn't fall for that?'

How she hated speaking to Sheldon, it brought back every bad memory from her past. 'So – what do you think?' she asked breezily. 'Is it a good idea or not?'

There was a long silence while Sheldon thought it over. 'Are you available to spend plenty of time with her?' he asked at last.

'Actually, right now I'm producing a movie,' she said, wondering how he'd take *that* piece of news.

He snorted derisively. '*You're* producing?'

'Is that so strange?' she said, immediately defensive.

'What experience do *you* have?'

'Enough, thank you.'

'No,' he said, abruptly. 'It's not a good idea. I want her home as soon as possible.'

'I'll tell her that's how you feel.'

'Do that.'

'She'll be disappointed.'

'I don't particularly care.'

No. Of course he didn't. Sheldon was as cold as a dead shark, with about as much personality.

'OK,' Nikki said slowly. 'Maybe when the time comes for her to go to college, we can consider her moving here then. She could attend UCLA or USC, both excellent choices.'

'That decision is *mine*, Nikki.'

'No,' she said heatedly, 'it's mine, too. We're both her parents.'

'You gave up that right when you left her with me.'

Fuck you, Sheldon. Who do you think you're talking to? The naive little girl you married? I'm a big girl now. I can stand up for myself.

'If you remember,' Nikki said, her voice a flat monotone, 'you *insisted* she stay with you. And you made her feel so guilty that she told me it's what she wanted.'

A cold laugh. 'Ah ... Nikki, Nikki, you always were adept at making excuses.'

The old familiar anger began to overwhelm her. 'How's your child bride?' she asked bitchily.

'That's right,' he said calmly. 'Try and get at me that way.' A brief pause. 'The truth is, my dear, it won't work. I've told you before – you're damaged, you need help.'

'Oh, screw you!' she shouted, suddenly snapping. 'You're *still* an asshole!' And she slammed down the phone, furious she'd allowed him to goad her.

Now she was stuck with the job of telling Summer she couldn't stay. Of course, if she was truthful, she knew it was for the best, considering she had neither the time nor the inclination to watch over her. Summer was better off with her father – even if he *was* major prick of the year.

For a brief moment she was tempted to call him back and tell him that. Sheldon, with his shock of thick white hair of which he was so proud; his smug expression; his perfectly capped teeth; and his small dick.

She couldn't help a vindictive smile when she recalled his tiny member. Sheldon was a big man everywhere except in the one place it really mattered. A psychiatrist with a small dick problem. Not the perfect combination. It forever pissed him off, which is why he went for young inexperienced girls who had nothing to compare it with.

She sighed. Sheldon and his small dick were part of her past, she'd moved on long ago. So why did he still bug her?

There was a tap on her office door and Aiden Sean wandered in looking like he'd just staggered out of bed – which he probably had.

'What's up?' she asked.

'You've got that tense face on,' he said, flexing a skinny arm.

'Me, tense?' she said lightly. 'Why would you say that?'

'I got a feelin' for emotions.'

'Can I help you?' she asked, determined not to fall into his *let's get intimate* trap, because she instinctively knew he wanted to get closer.

'Yeah. I need a coupla changes in the script. Wanna talk t'you about it before I go t'Mick. He can be an uptight bitch 'bout changin' stuff.'

'In other words, you'd like me on your side?'

'Why not? You're the boss.'

She grinned, forgetting about Sheldon and Richard and all her problems. 'Flattery will garner you my full attention.'

He nodded, like he'd known that all along. 'Let's get a drink,' he said. 'You look like you could use one.'

'I do?'

'Yes, boss-lady.'

She looked at him sceptically. 'How come you always treat me like I'm a hundred and two?'

He shrugged. 'Maybe I like t'bug you.'

'Why?'

''Cause you're so easy.'

She shook her head ruefully. 'Thanks.'

'OK, Nikki. Are we goin' for a drink or not?'

'You sure you're supposed to drink?'

He laughed drily. 'I was a druggie, not an alcoholic.'

'Well . . . I guess I could use a glass of wine.'

'Big boozer, huh?'

She ignored his remark and picked up her purse. It was past six, she should be heading home – but for what? To have another fight with Richard? She needed his support, not his constant criticism.

Besides, if Aiden wished to discuss the script it was her duty as the producer to be there for him.

40

Joey was lying on the couch in the den, watching sports on TV, when Lara arrived home. Laid out on the coffee table in front of him was a bowl of caramel popcorn and a plate of freshly baked cookies.

'I see Mrs Crenshaw is looking after you,' she said, pleased that he seemed to be settling in so comfortably.

He barely looked up. 'I got her under my voodoo spell,' he said, casually tossing a handful of popcorn into his mouth.

'They're all under your spell,' she replied, lightly touching his cheek. 'Women adore you, and you love it.'

'Whatever you say,' he said, eyes fixed firmly on the TV.

She wished he'd shut off the television and pay her some attention, she wasn't used to being treated in such a cavalier fashion. 'So,' she said, perching on the edge of the couch. 'Tell me what happened with you and Quinn.'

'Nothin' much,' he answered vaguely.

'Will he negotiate for you?'

'You told him to, didn't you?'

'Yes.'

'Well,' he said, a slight edge to his tone, 'when Miz Ivory tells people to do things – they do 'em. Right?'

She paused for a moment before saying— 'Aren't you pleased?'

'I dunno,' he said moodily. 'Sometimes I think I shouldn't be askin' you t'do stuff for me. You got me *Revenge*, then you got me your agent . . .'

'Joey,' she said softly, 'I can only open the door. Once you're in, you have to prove yourself.'

'Yeah,' he said, laughing sardonically. 'Like they're gonna

fire me if I don't deliver. There's no way they'd risk pissin' you off.'

'I didn't get you *The Dreamer*,' she pointed out. 'You did that by yourself.'

'Yeah, clever me,' he mumbled.

'Is something the matter?' she asked, treading carefully around his bad mood.

'I'm feelin' kinda down tonight,' he admitted, finally giving her his full attention, even though he didn't bother lowering the sound on the TV.

'Why?'

''Cause you deserted me today.'

'Joey,' she explained, sure he must be joking, 'I had to do publicity. I've got two movies coming out soon.'

'I know, I know . . .' A long beat. 'Truth is I'm feelin' kinda homesick.'

'Homesick?' she said, frowning.

'I miss the New York street action. I don't know anybody in LA.'

'I can introduce you to people.'

He gave an ironic laugh. 'Oh, yeah – like the people you'd introduce me to are gonna be interested in meetin' me.'

She decided this conversation was not taking a good turn. 'What do you want to do tonight?' she asked, changing the subject. 'We could go out, stay in – whatever you like.'

'What do *you* wanna do?' he said, turning the question around so that it was she who had to make the decision.

'I don't mind,' she replied.

'Then maybe I'll watch the end of the ball game,' he said, turning back to the television.

Was he dismissing her? She couldn't believe that she'd been thinking about him all day, and now that she was home, he was behaving this way toward her. 'Are you saying you want to be alone?' she said, trying not to sound upset.

'Is that OK with you?'

'Fine,' she said, 'I'll see you later.'

She hurried upstairs to her bedroom. They'd hardly been together ten minutes and all of a sudden he was pulling this moody stuff on her. Was it something she'd done? Had she offended him in some way?

How *could* she have offended him? As he'd pointed out, she'd gotten him an interview with her agent, a job in her movie. What else was she supposed to do?

Maybe it hadn't been such a good idea suggesting he stay at her house, a hotel might have been better.

For a moment her eyes filled with tears. She'd so wanted this to turn out to be something good, now she wasn't so sure.

She went into her bathroom, stopping in front of the mirror and staring at her reflection. Lara Ivory. Beautiful movie star. The woman who could have anyone. Yeah. Sure.

And the real truth is – Lara Ann Miller – you know who she is – the kid who watched her father butcher her mother and brother – then sat back while he blew his brains out.

Some nice little girl.

Some ugly little slut.

Dammit! She wasn't about to start feeling sorry for herself.

She went back into the bedroom, buzzed the kitchen and reached Mrs Crenshaw. 'Where are the dogs?' she asked.

'Mr Joey said they'd be better off spending more time outside in the dog run,' Mrs Crenshaw replied.

'Oh, he did, did he? Well, kindly let them back into the house right now.'

'Certainly, Miss Ivory.'

He'd told her he loved dogs, now he was banishing them outside the house. What was going on?

She was tempted to go down and confront him. But what if he split? What if he said, 'OK, this isn't working out, goodbye.' Was she ready for that?

No. She wasn't prepared to give up on this relationship. Not yet anyway. They were still getting to know each other – she had to give it time.

☆

Nikki and Aiden drove to the Chateau Marmont in her car. Aiden shut his eyes and slept all the way. *Hmm*, Nikki thought, *he's certainly not into being polite.* 'Wakey, wakey,' she said drily when they arrived.

'I'm beat,' he said, rubbing his eyes. 'Takes a crap-load of energy doin' nothing. Can't wait to start work.'

They sat at a small table. Aiden ordered his usual Jack Daniel's. She went for a glass of red wine. He lit up a cigarette, blowing a stream of smoke into her face. She coughed, clearing the air with her hands.

'Sorry,' he mumbled, not looking sorry at all.

'So,' she said, all business. 'What's your problem with the script?'

'It sucks.'

'Excuse me?'

'I wanna change my dialogue – do a rewrite, an' get compensated.'

'I presume you're joking.'

He dragged on his cigarette. 'Deadly serious.'

'Not possible, Aiden. We start shooting in a few days, no time for rewrites. Plus, everyone else is perfectly happy with the script.'

'It's corny shit.'

Now he was starting to aggravate her; *Revenge* was a great script. 'Then why did you accept the part?' she asked coldly.

He gave a mirthless laugh. 'Only game goin' on. I'm trouble – didn'tcha know?'

Fortunately she was used to dealing with actors, they were all insecure – this one more than most. 'Listen to me,' she said, as calmly as she could manage. 'Mick hired you. He promised me you were in good shape, now you're coming to me with this.'

'I'm fuckin' bored,' Aiden said, ice-grey eyes restlessly scanning the room. 'I'm fuckin' bored with everyone tellin' me what I can do an' what I can't. Right now I wanna get laid. You into fast sex?'

Why had she agreed to have a drink with him? Rule one for producers – stay away from actors. 'You're nuts,' she said, shaking her head.

'Bin told that many times. Wanna fuck or not?'

'Not,' she said, briskly rising from the table. 'I have to get home.'

'Hubby waitin' patiently?'

'What's it to you?'

'You're too young to set up house with such an old cocker.'

'Why don't you concentrate on getting your act together and leave me alone?'

''Cause I like you.'

'Really,' she said, feigning uninterest, although if she was truthful, she had to admit he did intrigue her.

'Somethin' about you,' he added, with a sly grin.

'It's not reciprocal,' she said sternly.

'Big word.'

She sighed. 'Go home, Aiden. That's what I'm doing.'

'What's it like living with someone twenty years older than you?' he asked, not finished with her yet.

What made him think he had the right to get into her business?

'No accounting for taste,' she said tartly. 'Didn't you tell me you had a fifteen-year-old giving you head the other day? Let me see – you're thirty-four – that would make her nineteen years younger than you. She's probably never heard of Bruce Springsteen. Doesn't that make you feel *ancient*?'

He laughed bitterly. 'You've got it wrong. Mick was the guy with the fifteen-year-old. Not me. I'm not into juveniles.'

'Of course not,' she said disbelievingly.

He took another gulp of Jack Daniel's. 'Then I guess you're not gonna help me do somethin' about the script?'

'Take it up with Mick. He's the creative genius.'

'I'd still like to fuck you.'

'Wow – Aiden, you're such a romantic! Your girlfriends must faint with pleasure.'

'What girlfriends?' he said sourly. 'I don't have any.'

'How about the fifteen-year-old?'

'Aren't you *listening* to me?' he said, burnt-out eyes watching her closely. 'It was *Mick*. 'Sides, she's major trouble.'

'Not to mention under-age,' Nikki said crisply. 'Aren't you *embarrassed*?'

'Aren't you?' he snapped back.

'Excuse me?'

'She's *your* daughter.' The words were out before he could stop himself.

There was a moment of deathly silence. The colour drained from Nikki's face and she sat down abruptly. 'What?' she said blankly, thinking that there was no way he could be telling the truth.

'Shit! I shouldn't've told you,' he muttered, taking another swig of his drink. 'Mick had no clue she was your kid. He told me she came on like a seasoned groupie – you know, the kind you trip over in this town. When he saw her at your house, he had a shit fit.'

'Oh, God!' Nikki said, suddenly feeling sick.

'Later she turns up at my apartment, an' starts tellin' me that if I don't screw her, she'll go to her dad and he'll have me arrested 'cause of her being under-age an' all. This is bad for my karma, Nikki. I'm tryin' to keep it together, which ain't easy – so do everyone a big favour an' warn her off.'

'Did you . . . sleep with her?' Nikki asked, her mouth dry with the anticipation of his reply.

'Who, me?' he said indignantly. 'No way. She's a fucked-up kid who's way out of her league. You'd better do something about her.'

For once Nikki wished that Sheldon was there to share this enormous problem.

'I don't understand,' she said wearily. 'Why are you telling me this?'

'Didn't mean to. 'Sides, if I was gonna fuck anyone in your family – it'd be you.'

'You're disgusting!' she said angrily.

'No – I*m* honest,' he said, watching her closely. 'How about you?'

Her heart was beating fast. Stress, stress, stress. She was too young to feel like this. What should she do?

She stood up, determined to gain control of the situation. 'Consider it taken care of, Aiden,' she said, as coolly as she could manage. 'And I'd appreciate it if you didn't mention this to anyone. Including Mick. I'll deal with it in my own way.'

'You got it,' he said, draining his glass.

She hurried from the hotel and waited impatiently for the valet to bring her car around.

Who could she turn to? Sheldon or Richard? Or maybe it was best to leave them both out of it and handle it herself.

Yes, she decided, that's what she'd do, deal with it herself.

☆

Lara was asleep, tossing restlessly, dreaming of the sea enveloping her, flooding her house, taking away everything. She cried out in her sleep, waking abruptly, covered in a thin film of sweat.

She lay very still for a moment, the heavy darkness wrapped around her. Her breathing was heavy – too heavy. With a sudden start she realized she was not alone. Seated in a chair next to the bed was Joey. She sat up, clutching the sheet to her chest. 'God!' she exclaimed. 'You scared me.'

'Maybe you should lock your door,' he said.

'Maybe *you* shouldn't sneak around,' she retorted, trying to take a peek at the clock on her bedside table.

'It's two a.m.,' he said obligingly.

For a moment she was afraid, perhaps Richard and Nikki were right to be concerned about Joey. What *did* she know about him? Exactly nothing. They'd had great sex for a few weeks, but tonight she'd encountered a stranger sitting in front of her TV, casually ignoring her. And now that stranger was in her bedroom and he was making her very nervous.

'What do you want, Joey?' she asked, keeping her tone even and noncommittal.

'We gotta talk.'

'Now?'

'I can't do this, Lara,' he said, speaking fast and low. 'Can't go for any kind of commitment. You're too nice for me . . . I wanna be here for you, but I'm not sure I can make you happy.'

'Joey, you *are* making me happy.'

'I could blow it at any time. That's me. I'm selfish, want my own way – I'm not into this relationship thing, it's too tough.'

'Are you saying you want to leave?'

'Dunno,' he muttered.

'Joey,' she murmured softly, understanding that he was frightened of commitment and not afraid to voice his fears. After all, he was coming out of a broken relationship and what had happened between them had taken place so fast –

a lightning connection that was enough to frighten anyone. 'I understand, I really do. We're *both* confused by what's happened between us.'

'It's not like I don't *wanna* be here for you,' he said. 'Trouble is there's nothin' I can give you that you don't already have.'

'Yes, there is,' she whispered.

'What?'

'You. I want you.'

'You got me. You got me all the way,' he said, burying his head on her shoulder, snuggling against her like a little kid seeking solace.

She stroked his thick dark hair, holding him close, and it was at that moment she realized she loved him. Not a sexual moment. Not a having fun moment. Just a pure connection that made her melt inside.

'Get into bed,' she said serenely, quite sure they belonged together.

'You sure you *want* me to stay?'

This was a different Joey, vulnerable and insecure. 'Yes,' she said, loving him all the more.

And he got into bed, and they held each other, and after a while they fell asleep in each other's arms, perfectly content.

Lara knew she'd finally found the happiness she'd been searching for all her life.

I call them the drug days. Although truth is I should call them the drug years, because time passed so quickly and I had no idea what was going on.

Drugs took over my life. Drugs were the only reason to get up in the morning. Drugs ruled.

I bought myself a shack on Zuma with the money I'd made from the action movies, and moved to the beach. Since I'd stopped working, the money didn't last long, so I hooked up with Christel, a beautiful swimsuit model who was also into the drug scene, and was not averse to performing a little extra money action on the side.

My life had gone around in a circle. But I didn't care. I didn't care about anything.

After a while the usual happened, Christel got fed up with supporting me and told me that I had to throw some money into the pot or she was gone. I was bloated and out of shape, couldn't get a job acting. Didn't want to anyway – who needed to work? Somehow I'd lost all ambition to be a movie star. The dream was gone.

One of my dealers sold me a gun. 'You need protection, man,' he told me. 'These are dangerous times.'

I liked the gun. It was my faithful companion when nobody else cared. It never answered back, and was always there when I needed comfort. I slept with it under my pillow, fully loaded.

This totally freaked Christel, who imagined it might go off one night and pierce one of her very expensive silicon breasts. She got on my case so often that I used to take it out and point it at her simply to piss her off.

Hey – when you're stoned out of your head you do strange things.

Eventually, Christel left me. Bitch! When you get right down to it, they're all bitches.

So there I was, a drugged-out beach-bum with no money, and boy, I needed money badly because I couldn't get through the day without a little help from my pharmaceutical friends.

Then I remembered Hadley. She owed me, because she was the cunt who'd gotten me fired.

Hadley lived in a mansion at the top of Angelo Drive, bought for her by her gangster boyfriend who resided in New York with his plump Sicilian wife.

I drove up there one night with good intentions. All I wanted was to borrow a couple of thousand until I got it together again.

There was nobody home except Hadley. Her boyfriend wouldn't let her have live-in servants on account of the fact that he didn't want anybody proving he stayed there when he was in town.

She answered the door herself, staring at me like she was seeing a ghost.

'Yeah, I know,' I said. 'It's been a coupla years. I don't look so hot, right?'

'You look like dog shit,' she said flatly. 'What do you want?'

'Missed you, too,' I said, not pleased with her snotty attitude.

'You're stoned,' she said in a disgusted voice.

'Does that mean you won't lend me money?'

'Get the fuck out of here,' she snapped.

A woman telling me to get the fuck out. Me! I couldn't believe it. Usually they were begging me to stay.

'Do you wanna repeat that?' I said belligerently.

'You heard me,' she said.

Enough was enough. I took out my gun, pointing it straight at her.

She went very pale and stepped back into the house, reaching for a conveniently placed panic button.

Not convenient enough. Quick as a flash I slapped her arm away and burst into the house.

She began to kick and struggle, somehow or other jogging my trigger finger. Anyway, I think that's what happened. The gun went off, blowing a gaping hole in her chest that seemed bigger than China. She fell like a fucking stone.

Jesus! Whatever else happens to me I'll never forget that moment. I was totally high, but even through the fog – I realized what I'd done.

I turned and ran from the house like a maniac – sweat pouring down my face.

Halfway along the driveway I remembered I'd touched the door handle, so I raced back, taking off my shirt and wiping off the handle – the only thing I could recall touching. Then I made it to my car and somehow or other drove to the beach.

Hadley's murder made the second page of the LA Times. Even in death she wasn't a star.

There was nothing to connect me to her, but just in case, I took off for Mexico where I spent the next couple of years drying out. It was the start of a new beginning.

41

Kimberly had to go. She was becoming a total whiner, and Richard didn't care to be reminded of his cheating nature every time he glanced in her direction. He'd slept with her no more than four or five times, now she wanted more. 'When are you telling Nikki?' she kept on nagging.

Telling Nikki? Was she insane!

Why did women have to place so much importance on sex? Casual sex was exactly that, and they should get with the programme and understand.

But how to get rid of her without a sexual harassment suit? Kimberly was the type who wouldn't think twice about trying to ruin a man's career.

The truth was he should have stayed married to Lara. She was beautiful, undemanding, and most of all, truly nice. But no, he'd had to screw that up too – systematically fucking his way through each year of marriage with a variety of different women.

What a jerk he'd been. He would never forget the look on Lara's face when she'd caught the make-up girl giving him head in his trailer. Her face had turned to stone. 'I want a divorce,' she'd said, and after that there was no going back.

With Nikki he'd managed to stay faithful for almost two years. Now Kimberly and her chewable nipples were giving him a hard time.

'I'd love to visit your house again,' Kimberly said, sneaking up behind him as he stood by the window in his office. 'Can I?'

'It's not possible,' he said, furious she would even ask. 'Nikki's in town.'

'When are you telling her?' Kimberly demanded, like she had a right to know.

'I'll get around to it,' he lied.

And so the dance continued.

☆

As Nikki drew up outside the house in Malibu, she noticed that Richard's Mercedes was not in his parking space, even though it was nearly nine. He'd probably gotten fed up with waiting for her and popped out for something to eat. She knew she should've called, but, quite frankly, he was the last person on her mind.

All the way home she'd been thinking about Aiden and the things he'd said. It didn't seem possible Summer could behave in such a way, and yet, why not? *She's my daughter*, Nikki thought, *and I was just as adventurous at her age. In fact, I married Sheldon at sixteen because he knocked me up.*

Like mother like daughter.

Oh, God! What was she going to do?

Send her back to Chicago, that's what. But first – even though she was dreading it, she had to accept her responsibility and talk to her. A mother–daughter talk was way overdue.

☆

Summer was due to rendezvous with Tina at the same open-air restaurant on Sunset Plaza they'd met at before. Earlier in the day they'd gone shopping on Melrose, and Tina had loaned her the money to buy a short purple tank dress – very sexy – and some high wedgie sandals. After their shopping jaunt she'd rushed back to the beach to work on her tan.

Things were looking up, as long as she could avoid going back to Chicago and the all-encompassing arms of her father, she'd be happy.

Just before she left to meet Tina again, Richard arrived home. 'Where are *you* going, all dressed up?' he asked with an indulgent smile.

'Another party,' she replied, surreptitiously tugging at her short dress, which barely covered the tops of her golden thighs.

'I thought you'd be partied out by now,' he remarked, fixing himself a vodka on the rocks.

'Oh, Richard,' she said, gazing at him wistfully, big blue

eyes drawing him in. 'I wish I could stay here for ever. You promised to talk Mom into letting me stay. *Please* do it, Richard. *Please*.'

'I'm trying,' he said, digging into his pants pocket and handing her fifty dollars. 'You'll need this for cabs.'

'Thanks!' she said gratefully.

Richard was so easy, especially now she had something on him. Of course, she didn't blame him for making out with his assistant while Nikki was away. She'd often wondered what he saw in her stupid mother anyway. OK, so Nikki was pretty, but she was also dumb. She *must've* been dumb to have left her with Sheldon in Chicago. Didn't she realize what a sicko pervert he was?

Whenever Summer thought about her mother she conveniently forgot the screaming fits she'd thrown – insisting she was happier with her father and would kill herself if Nikki didn't let her live with him. Those were distant memories she didn't care to revisit.

At the restaurant, Tina was already sitting at a table looking pleased with herself. 'Park your butt,' she said, patting the chair next to her. 'I've a shitload of stuff to tell you.'

'What?' Summer asked, adjusting her Guess sunglasses, which she'd purchased that afternoon.

'Darlene told me this movie star dude wants to meet *both* of us,' Tina said excitedly. 'How way out is that?'

'*Both* of us?' Summer questioned.

'You know,' Tina said, giggling knowingly. 'For fun. We're on our way to making megabucks, sister!'

The waiter came over. Summer couldn't help checking him out. He was typical LA, with long blond hair and a surfer's body. Another out-of-work actor waiting to be discovered, she thought. LA was full of them. That's what made it such an awesome place!

She ordered pizza and a milkshake, because she hadn't eaten all day and felt quite light-headed, while Tina went for an iced coffee.

'Will he take us out?' she asked, imagining a night at the Viper Room or some other happening club.

Tina screwed up her nose. 'You're a bit naive, aren't you?'

'I'm not naive,' she said flatly. 'I've done things you so wouldn't even dream about.'

'Then there's no problem,' Tina said, waving at a guy in a passing Ferrari. 'It'll be the two of us and him.'

Summer frowned. 'I don't get it.'

'Oh, *c'mon*,' said Tina, a touch scornful. 'Haven't you ever done it with a girl before? That's what all these guys are into – watching two girls together. Especially two *young* innocents like us. Ha! If they only knew!'

'You mean like . . . sex?' Summer asked hesitantly.

'Why are you even thinking about it?' Tina said irritably. 'You would've done it for nothing with that sleazy dog Aiden Sean, so what's the big deal?'

'At least I knew *him*.'

'So you'll know this other guy soon.'

'Who is he anyway?'

'Dunno, but Darlene said he's a major babe. And trust me, she knows major babes.'

The waiter delivered their order.

'The guys are gonna *love* us!' Tina said, giggling again. 'And it's not like you'll be doing anything you wouldn't do with a date. 'Cept this way you get paid, and you get a lot more respect.'

'How come?' Summer asked, slurping her milkshake.

''Cause they're *paying* for it, dummy. They know you're a pro.'

For a moment Summer thought about the road she was about to embark on. Sex with a stranger for money. Wouldn't that make her a prostitute?

No. Prostitutes cruised Sunset giving blow jobs to people like Hugh Grant in the back of cars. Prostitutes were cheap bimbos in vinyl boots and fake leopardskin miniskirts with bad hair.

'What time are we meeting him?' she asked, feeling excited and apprehensive all at the same time.

'Chill,' Tina said, sipping her iced coffee. 'We don't have to be at his hotel until nine. I'm psyched, aren't you?'

'You bet!' said Summer, not quite sure *how* she felt.

☆

No Richard to aggravate her. No Summer to drive her crazy. Neither of them were home.

Nikki didn't know what to do. Should she call Sheldon? It was past midnight in Chicago and he probably wouldn't appreciate a late-night phone call. Anyway, she could just imagine the conversation. *Hi, Sheldon. I'm sorry to tell you that your little golden girl has been going around giving out blow jobs. What shall we do about it?*

Of course Sheldon would blame her. *Why do you think I never allowed her to live with you?* he'd say. *It's your bad influence, Nikki. She learns from you.*

No, telling him would only complicate matters.

Why did this have to happen just as she was about to commence the biggest career move of her life? Producing a movie was not an easy job, she'd need every ounce of concentration she could muster to make sure it didn't get away from her – especially with a wild card like Mick Stefan directing, and an even wilder card like Aiden Sean starring.

Another thought occurred to her. Should she fire Mick before it was too late? Because once they started shooting it would be impossible.

No. Firing him now would create problems too big to contemplate. Much as she dreaded facing him – the movie had to go on. After all, it wasn't as if he'd *known* Summer was her daughter.

Oh, God! Decisions, decisions – maybe she should dump the whole thing on Richard and see what solution he came up with.

But Richard wasn't around. He hadn't even left a note saying where he'd gone.

She thought about calling Lara, then changed her mind. Now that Lara was with Joey, she wasn't as available as she used to be. Anyway, it wasn't fair to burden her with this.

Making her way into Summer's room, she stood in the doorway observing chaos. Obviously the maid had given up, because all she could see was a messy jumble of clothes, CDs, spilled make-up, magazines, 7-Up cans, dirty dishes, and several dried-up slices of pizza. What a mess!

She realized it was probably her fault. She'd been sixteen when she'd given birth to Summer, and never quite reconciled herself to the fact that she had the responsibility of a young child to raise. The truth was, she'd been happy to leave Summer with Sheldon in Chicago, enabling her to go off and have a life.

And yet, deep down she'd always wanted to be there for her daughter.

Unfortunately Sheldon had never given her the opportunity.

She found a yellow legal pad and wrote on it in large bold letters with a felt-tip pen.

MEET ME IN THE KITCHEN AT 8:00 A.M.
DO NOT LEAVE THE HOUSE UNTIL WE TALK.

Then she placed the pad on the centre of Summer's unmade bed, went into the living room and fixed herself a well-needed drink.

☆

Two hours later Richard arrived home.

'Hi,' Nikki said, now on her third vodka.

'Hi,' he replied, brushing off her hug.

'Everything OK?' she said, following him into the bedroom.

'Why wouldn't it be?' he said, removing his jacket and throwing it on the bed.

'Where did you go?' she asked.

He gave her an uptight look. 'Would you care for a written report?'

'No,' she said, holding her temper. 'That won't be necessary. I merely wondered if you'd eaten.'

'Yes,' he said, leaving the bedroom and going to his study. He'd taken Kimberly to a quiet restaurant further along the beach, and she'd blown him in the car. Now he felt guilty.

Nikki trailed behind him. He'd been drinking, she could smell it all over him. She could also make out the scent of another woman's perfume.

Suddenly she knew why he was being so distant. The sonofabitch was back to his old habits – he was screwing around on her!

This was all she needed. Goddamn it! Why hadn't she seen it coming? Why had she been so blindly self-confident that she'd thought he wouldn't do to *her* what he'd done to Lara?

She waited until he was settled at his computer, then she went back into the bedroom and did something she'd sworn she'd never do – rifled through his jacket pockets.

Bingo! A packet of condoms – one missing.

Bingo! A credit card receipt – dinner for two at The Ivy.

Bingo! A handkerchief with lipstick on – not her colour.

How could she have been so stupid?

Overcome with fury, she marched back into his study. 'I want you to pack up and get out,' she said, angrily.

He looked at her like she was totally insane. 'What?'

'Bad enough that you're drinking again,' she continued, her voice rising. 'But other women? Oh, no, I don't think so.'

'Are you crazy?' he said irritably.

Her heart was pounding like a sledgehammer. 'Yes, I'm crazy,' she said vehemently. 'Crazy to have imagined you'd ever change.'

'Calm down.'

'Fuck you, Richard,' she said, waving the packet of condoms in his face. 'Fuck you for reverting to your cheating self.' And she threw the dinner receipt on his desk, hurled the incriminating handkerchief on the floor and marched to the door. 'Get out, Richard. It's over. And don't come back.'

42

Norman Barton opened the door of his hotel suite with a rakish grin, holding a glass of champagne in one hand and clutching a joint in the other.

Norman was puppy dog handsome, with big brown eyes, a cowlick of muddy brown hair, and a wide toothy grin. He was in his mid-twenties and not very tall.

'Evening, ladies,' he said with exaggerated politeness, and a sweeping if somewhat drunken bow. 'Enter the land of good times.'

Summer recognized him immediately. He'd starred in a family TV series, then made it big in movies. He was constantly being written about in the tabloids and fan magazines. He'd been engaged three times, and when Heidi Fleiss got busted he was one of the famous names mentioned in her little black book.

Tina nudged her. 'Told you!' she whispered triumphantly.

Inside the hotel suite stood a small, skinny Hispanic man, somewhat older than Norman. Clinging to his arm was an exceptionally tall, sour-faced brunette, clad in slinky black leather.

'Park your butts, girls,' said Norman, indicating the couch. 'And tell me your pleasure? A joint? Champagne? Or how about a little nose candy?'

'I'll take a joint,' Summer said boldly.

Norman grabbed her hand. 'Now *that's* my kind of girl,' he said, with a boyish grin. 'And pretty, too. *Veree* pretty – just the way I like 'em.'

Summer breathed a little easier. She could get through this if all she had to do was be nice to this guy. He was cuter than Aiden Sean any day, although Aiden had that dangerous edge she hankered after.

She sat down on the couch next to Tina. The Hispanic man ignored them, so did his girlfriend.

'Listen, Norman,' the Hispanic man said in a low growly voice, 'I gotta get outta here. You have my money?'

'What's your hurry?' Norman grumbled. 'You're always in such a freakin' hurry. Whyn't you stay an' join the party?'

'He don' wanna join no party,' his girlfriend said, scowling. 'We have places to go. Give him what you owe, an' let's get the fuck outta here.'

'OK, OK,' Norman said, throwing up his hands. 'Don't get in a blue funk.' He winked at Tina and Summer. 'You two sit tight while I go take care of business.' He beckoned the Hispanic man and his bad-tempered girlfriend, and the three of them vanished into the bedroom, closing the door.

'Darlene told me we've got to get paid up front,' Tina said, speaking fast. 'The guy has a house account, but Darlene says he's way behind. And after what I just heard, we'd better make *sure* we get the cash first.'

'Well, we can't just like . . . *ask* for it,' Summer said.

'Why not? Those people did.'

'Who are they?'

'How do I know?' Tina said, pulling a face. 'Probably his drug dealers or something.'

'He has drug dealers to score pot?'

'Where do *you* get it?'

'Boys on the beach. They're always so ready to give me anything I want.'

'Oh, you're such a little princess,' Tina giggled. 'It's all that blond hair, and those perky tits!'

'I've been meaning to ask,' Summer said. 'When you left home – how could you afford to?'

Tina grinned. 'Scammed five thousand bucks from my stepfather's safe. Figured he deserved to give me *something* for all the trouble he put me through. Then I took off.'

'What about your mother?'

'She didn't give a shit. She's an actress.'

'Famous?' Summer asked, surprised because Tina had never mentioned her mother before.

'Who cares,' Tina said, defiantly tossing back her curly brown hair. 'I rented an apartment, and started doing a few modelling gigs. Then I met Darlene and everything changed.'

'Didn't your mom send people looking for you?'

'Ha! The old bag was thrilled I beat it. No more competition. Besides, I was sixteen and legal.'

'Wow!' Summer exclaimed, wishing she could do the same.

'When will *you* be sixteen?' Tina asked, scooping up a handful of nuts from a dish on the table and cramming them in her mouth.

'In a couple of months,' Summer said.

'Then do it,' Tina said matter-of-factly, taking out a mirrored compact and studying her pretty face. 'In fact, you can stay with me. We'll work as a team. Guys *really* get off on baby pussy.'

'If only I could,' Summer sighed, knowing that if she vanished her father would have the whole of Chicago searching for her.

Norman re-entered the room, trailed by the Hispanic man and his sulky girlfriend. They headed for the door. 'Next time don' make us wait,' the woman warned, slamming the door behind them.

'Bye,' Norman said, with a jaunty wave at the closed door. 'Sorry you don't wanna stay and party.'

Once they were gone, he focused his attention on the girls. 'OK, ladies,' he crowed, grabbing the champagne bottle. 'Everybody naked and in the bedroom, it's *way* past gettin' it on time!'

'Now?' Summer asked innocently.

'Yes, *now*!' Tina said, jumping up.

'We hardly know him,' Summer whispered, finally coming to the conclusion that maybe this wasn't such a good idea.

'He's over twenty-one, famous and rich,' Tina said, ever practical. 'That's all we need to know. Come on,' she added impatiently. 'Let's go do it!'

Reluctantly Summer trailed her into the bedroom.

43

Summer was confused. Sex was supposed to be getting one over on someone else, and yet Norman was treating her so nicely. After the debasing experiences with her father, she'd always regarded sex as dirty – something you used to get your own way. But Norman wasn't like that. Norman wanted to laugh and have fun and make her feel good. Not to mention plying her with champagne.

By the time she and Tina had to do some sex stuff, she was completely giggly and drunk. And it wasn't so bad. Although being naked with another girl was kind of icky.

Norman didn't join in. He sat in a chair and watched, as if he were viewing a particularly engrossing movie.

Tina kissed her all over, which made her want to giggle even more. And then she had to do the same to Tina, which kind of grossed her out.

When it was all over she couldn't wait to wriggle back into her clothes. Then Norman took her to one side, handed her a piece of paper with his phone number on, and said, 'Call me. We can do private business. No reason we gotta go through Darlene. Right, cutie?'

'It . . . it's not for me to say,' she stammered, staring at his familiar face that she'd seen on the cover of countless magazines.

He favoured her with his famous puppy dog smile. 'You're a very sweet girl,' he said. 'Kinda special.'

'Thank you,' she said demurely.

'Make sure you call me soon,' he said.

'Oh, I will,' she said, eyes shining.

Then he ordered two cabs, and sent them both home.

She sat in the back of the cab thinking about how wonderful he was, and what a perfect life they could have together.

He was a movie star and rich. He'd be able to keep her father away from her permanently.

When she crept into the Malibu house, she spotted Nikki, asleep on a couch in the living room. Trying hard not to wake her, she tiptoed into her room, shut the door, and fell into bed with all her clothes on.

Yes, she could be Mrs Norman Barton. That would suit her nicely.

☆

Lara awoke first and rolled over into Joey's arms. He groaned in his sleep. She nuzzled against his neck, inhaling his seductive masculine smell. God! She really did love him.

He opened one eye. 'Wa's goin' on?' he muttered sleepily. 'There a fire?'

'A fire?'

'Yeah . . . got caught in one once.'

'When?'

'Oh, years ago in a . . . hotel.'

'Guess you escaped.'

'Guess I did.'

'Lucky me.'

'Lucky you.'

They both started laughing. He threw open his arms and she snuggled into them.

'Where *are* you from, Joey?' she asked, lightly stroking his chest. 'I was thinking . . . I hardly know anything about you.'

'Florida,' he answered casually. 'Parents dead. No other family. Your turn.'

'The Midwest,' she replied, revealing as little as he did. 'Parents dead. No other family.'

'Jesus!' he exclaimed. 'We really are soulmates.'

She snuggled closer. 'Joey?'

'Yes?'

'Let's make love. Let's make wild passionate love.'

'*Now?*' he said, surprised at her unexpected boldness.

'No, next week,' she deadpanned.

'OK, OK – sex maniac,' he laughed. 'Get me in the mood.'

'Not a problem,' she said – thinking that Joey was bring-ing out a whole new her.

'Got an idea,' he said. 'Pretend you're the maid.'

'Joey!'

'Not into role-playing, huh?' he teased.

'Well, I never . . .'

'Never *what*, Lara?' he asked, hands reaching for her breasts, tweaking her nipples, making her cry out with pleasure.

'I never did that kind of fantasy thing,' she said shyly. 'You know, role-playing and all of that. Richard wasn't into it.'

'How many men have you had?' he asked, curiously. 'Was Richard your first?'

'How many women have *you* had?' she responded.

'Let's see . . .' He pretended to think. 'Guess you must be number two thousand and one.'

'Ha!' she said, sitting up in bed, crossing her arms across her breasts. 'You *know* women love you. I see them watching you all the time.'

He rolled onto his back. 'Like guys don't watch you.'

'It's not the same.'

'You know something, beautiful? In my world there's only you.'

'Really?' she asked breathlessly.

'Yup. You're the only good thing that ever happened to me.'

'I am?'

'You am,' he said, pulling her down on top of him, then kissing her so hard she thought he'd split her lip.

She didn't care. When she was with Joey she didn't care about anything except him. He was her life, her love, and she would do anything for him.

☆

Nikki awoke at first light, feeling lousy. After throwing Richard out, she'd managed to get through half a bottle of vodka – not usually her style, but she'd been forced to do *something* to relieve the tension. And on top of everything, Summer had failed to come home.

She got up from the couch and went into Summer's room.

Her daughter was buried under the covers, asleep. She marched straight over to the bed and shook her awake.

'Wa's goin' on?' Summer mumbled, flinging out her arms.

'What time did you get home last night?' Nikki demanded.

'Oh hi, Mom,' Summer said sleepily. 'Why're you waking me? Isn't it like *really* early?'

'Yes, it's *really* early,' Nikki said flatly. 'And you obviously got home *really* late. Where were you?'

'Oh, um . . . a party,' Summer said, attempting to gather her thoughts.

'Whose party?'

'Friend of mine.'

'And I thought you were with an enemy,' Nikki said sarcastically.

'Funny, Mom.'

'I don't intend to be funny,' Nikki said brusquely. 'I don't intend to be funny about anything.'

'S' what's up now?' Summer asked, sensing bad vibrations.

'Well . . .' Nikki said, struggling for the best way to put it. 'I've been told something extremely disturbing . . .'

'Like what?'

'Look, honey,' Nikki said, sitting on the edge of the bed. 'You're young and unsophisticated. People will try to take advantage of you – especially in this town. Don't live your life too fast.'

Oh, God! Her mother had found out about Norman Barton and now she was in big trouble.

'Summer,' Nikki said, taking a deep breath, 'I know what you did with Mick Stefan, and it's not right. First of all, it isn't the kind of . . . uh . . . thing you should do with anyone, unless you're . . . uh . . . married. There are diseases out there . . . not just AIDS, all kinds of other terrible things.' She paused; discussing sex with her daughter was excruciating. 'LA's a tough town,' she continued, quoting Lara. 'There's a lot of men here who are into using young girls. You're far too naive to be out on your own.'

Summer rolled her eyes. 'Mom, I'm nearly sixteen.'

'Didn't you hear what I just said? I *know* what you did with Mick Stefan.'

Summer was silent for a moment. Was getting in the back of Mick's limo *that* bad? It wasn't as if she'd done anything, but all the same she was obviously in deep trouble. 'Who told you?' she demanded, wishing she had a joint to lighten the lecture.

'It doesn't matter.'

'Was it Mick?'

'No. It wasn't.'

'Anyway, whatever he said, it's not true,' she muttered sulkily. 'Nothing happened.'

'I'd be happy if it wasn't,' Nikki said. 'But since I know it is – here's my decision. I've booked you on a noon flight home to Chicago.'

That woke Summer up in a hurry. 'No!' she shrieked, her blue eyes filling with tears of frustration. 'I can't go back there.'

'Yes, you can,' Nikki said firmly. 'And you will.'

'Why do I have to?' Summer yelled. '*Why?* Why? *Why?*'

'Because you're only fifteen, and you must finish school and do what your father tells you. Perhaps next time you visit, you'll behave in a more responsible fashion.'

'This isn't fair!' Summer shouted, jumping out of bed.

'Fair or not, that's my decision,' Nikki said, her expression grim.

Later that day, she drove Summer to the airport, personally putting her on a plane. In the evening she called Sheldon to make sure their daughter had arrived safely.

'What did you do to her while she was in LA?' Sheldon demanded, sounding pissed off. 'She looks dreadful.'

'I didn't do anything,' Nikki retorted, forcing her voice into neutral. 'You sent me a kid who was out of control.'

'Not when she left here she wasn't,' Sheldon thundered.

Nikki held her temper in check. '*I'm* not the parent figure here, Sheldon – *you* are. So it's up to you to do something about her.'

And that was that. Mission accomplished.

Her daughter was off her hands and now she could concentrate on work.

44

They'd been shooting *Revenge* for five weeks, and although Lara was tired, she was also exhilarated. It was the most exciting film she'd ever been involved with, even though Mick was insane – his manic energy dominating the set as he raced around encouraging his actors to fly – arms waving in the air, huge glasses falling off his nose. He was truly obsessed, his unbridled enthusiasm encouraging everyone to do better.

Her life was making the movie and Joey, who since the night they'd discussed commitment had been there for her all the way, a constant reassuring presence.

She loved him so much. He made everything easy, cushioning any problems, so that all she had to do was concentrate on her work.

The people who usually surrounded her were not pleased. Cassie was relegated to sitting in the office at home, unless Joey said it was OK for her to come to the set. Nikki was around, but always busy. So her only close contact was Joey.

The fact that he was in the movie was a big plus. They even had scenes together and she loved working with him. They rehearsed at home, running lines, critiquing each other, getting into it. He taught her how to handle a gun – which wasn't an easy thing for her to learn, because it dredged up so many bad memories. However, with his help she mastered it, which was good, it meant she'd be prepared for the upcoming scene where she got to shoot Aiden's character.

In return she taught him certain tricks to use in front of the camera, and all about lighting. They made love every night, and each time it got better.

Most evenings they sat up in bed, side by side, watching

old movies or *Seinfeld*, sending out for food, never feeling the need to go anywhere, perfectly content. Sometimes Mrs Crenshaw cooked, and on those nights they ate outside on the patio. Other times they rode the horses along the beach, or played with the dogs.

As far as Lara was concerned, things couldn't be more idyllic. She was making a powerful movie that meant something to her, and she had a man beside her who was everything she'd ever wanted. The nightmares were becoming more and more distant. It was amazing that they'd found each other.

She awoke with a flutter in her stomach, because today they were shooting the rape scene. There was hardly any dialogue, mostly action. Mick had told her he planned on tracking the action with three cameras, so there'd be no mistakes. Still . . . she couldn't help dreading it.

Joey walked in from the bathroom in his new white terry-cloth robe, his jet-black hair damp and slicked back. He sat on the edge of the bed and said, 'Maybe you should smoke a joint – take the edge off.'

'You know I don't do grass,' she admonished, thinking how handsome he looked.

'I know, babe, but trust me, you might need it today.'

'Rebecca wasn't stoned,' she said, shaking her head. 'So *I* can't be.'

He got up and went over to the window. 'I dunno if I should come to the set today,' he said moodily.

'I want you there,' she said. 'I need your support.'

'If I havta watch those assholes attackin' you, I'm liable to kill 'em,' he said, vehemently. 'Tear the fuckers to pieces.'

'Honey,' she said soothingly, 'you're so dramatic. After all, it's only acting.'

'Yeah, yeah,' he said, coming back to sit next to her. 'I still wish you didn't have to go through it.'

'That's very thoughtful,' she said quietly.

'I'm not thoughtful, but thanks anyway,' he said, holding out his arms. She fell into them, and they rolled around on the bed, lost in a tight embrace.

'There's somethin' I've been meanin' to tell you,' he mumbled, crushing her until she almost couldn't breathe. 'Somethin' important.'

'What?' she gasped, feeling so secure and content in his arms, wishing she could stay there for ever.

'You're gonna think I'm crazy.'

'I'll let you know.'

'It's somethin' I should've told you before.'

'*What?*' she asked, attempting to sit up.

'It'll sound stupid . . .'

'Will you *tell* me?' she said, exasperated.

He hesitated for a moment. 'Naw . . . can't.'

She struggled into a sitting position. 'Yes you can.'

He stared at her, dark eyes fusing with her brilliant green ones. 'OK . . . OK,' he said at last. 'Here's the deal.' A long beat. 'I guess I kinda like . . . love you.'

She caught her breath, taken by surprise. 'You kinda like *love* me?' she repeated, thrilled that he'd finally said it.

He frowned. 'Hey – I told you it'd sound stupid.'

'Joey,' she said, gently reaching up to touch his cheek, 'it's not stupid.'

'No?'

'No.'

'How come?'

'Because . . . since we're being truthful, I . . . I love you, too.' A long pause. 'In fact, Joey, I think I've loved you since we first met.'

He broke out in a big grin. 'No shit?'

'Joey! Please! This is supposed to be a romantic moment.'

'Hey – you wanna see romance,' he said, easing her nightgown off her shoulders, fondling her breasts until she began gasping with pleasure.

One touch and she was his.

Nikki was right, he did have her hooked sexually, only their relationship was much more than sex. It was caring and loving and being together.

They made love slowly in the traditional way, and when it was over, she stretched luxuriously, murmuring a satisfied— 'Umm . . . that was better than grass any day.'

'What would you know about grass?' he teased, tickling her stomach.

'Oh, you think I'm such a little goody-goody, don't you?' she said, half serious. 'Let me tell you – there was a time I was wild.'

'What?' he said mockingly. 'You smoked a joint once –
that was wild?'

'Joey,' she responded quietly, 'you don't know *everything*
about me.'

'Why – you got secrets?'

'Maybe . . .' she said mysteriously.

He grinned. 'I'll tell you mine if you tell me yours.'

She smiled, perfectly happy. 'Whatever you want.'

But they both knew that neither of them were prepared
to share their secrets.

Not yet anyway.

☆

Nikki arrived at the street location in time for an early
breakfast. Mick was already there, sitting at a table near the
food truck, diligently working on his laptop while shovelling
down a huge plate of ham and eggs.

Although she considered him a degenerate jerk, she
couldn't help admiring his work ethic; he was always prepared, and totally passionate about the film.

They were both aware that today could be difficult.
Yesterday she'd sent Lara flowers and a note of encouragement, because although Lara was doing a wonderful job,
everyone knew today was the real test.

Nikki hadn't heard from Richard since she'd thrown him
out. Something had died between them – which was probably the reason he'd reverted to his old ways. In her heart
she knew it had to do with Lara and the unhealthy obsession
he still harboured. It was blatantly obvious he couldn't stand
his ex-wife being in a sexual relationship, so he'd turned to
another woman. Ah, yes, Richard's big solution – screw your
troubles away.

Ha! I should've been a shrink, she thought wryly. *Sheldon
and I would finally have something in common.*

Summer was back in Chicago, which was a big relief.
She'd called her a few times over the last few weeks, and
they'd had several stilted conversations.

'Maybe you'll visit at Christmas,' she'd suggested.

'OK,' Summer had replied, sounding listless.

In a way Nikki was relieved to be by herself. No Richard
to get in her way. No Summer to run wild. She was able to

concentrate on *Revenge* and nothing else. As soon as the movie was finished she'd consider her next move. Divorce was on her mind.

'Morning, sexy,' Mick said, glancing up from his laptop. 'What's goin' on?'

'How do you feel about today?' she asked, flopping down beside him.

'Don't worry,' he said confidently. 'Lara's got it together. She'll be cool.'

'You'd better warn the actors to go easy on her,' Nikki said, frowning. 'Make sure they don't get carried away.'

'Right,' Mick replied, sarcastically. 'I'll tell 'em to make it a *gentle* freakin' rape. Is that what you'd like?'

'You know exactly what I mean,' she said irritably, hating it when Mick waxed facetious. 'I'm worried about Aiden.'

'Aiden's fuckin' ace,' Mick said, cracking his knuckles. 'Didn't I tell you he'd stay clean?'

'Yes, I must admit you did.'

'C'mon, chick-babe, lighten up. We're three-quarters through the shoot, an' not one scamoose. You should be singin' your socks off.'

'Don't tempt fate, Mick.'

'We're way ahead of schedule,' he said, letting out a crazed cackle. 'Get with the freakin' ball game an' relax.'

What an asshole!

However, he was *her* asshole. The asshole who was going to deliver one fine movie. And until that time came she had to stay on good terms with him, much as it pained her.

Producer's Rule Number One. The film comes first.

Nikki considered herself an excellent producer.

45

The day after Alison Sewell was released from jail she received a mysterious phone call. Mysterious because only the tabloid editors she'd dealt with in the past had her number. Mysterious because the man on the other end of the phone refused to identify himself.

'I have a proposition that I know will interest you,' he said.

She was lying in bed at the time, gorging on Snickers bars and watching Michelle Pfeiffer on the *Rosie O'Donnell Show*.

While she'd been locked up in jail her mother had passed away, so now she had the luxury of answering to no one. They'd let her out for the funeral. Two hours of guarded freedom. Big deal.

'Who is this?' she demanded.

'A friend,' the man replied. 'A friend who wants to do you a favour.'

Sad fact of life. She didn't have any friends. Only Lara Ivory, who'd turned out to be a Judas. And yes, Lara *would* be punished. And soon.

'What kind of favour?' she asked, reaching for the powerful whistle she kept in a bedside drawer, because if this was a dirty phone call, she'd blast this sicko's eardrum straight through his asshole.

'I know why you were in jail,' the man said. 'And in my eyes it was injustice.'

'How do you know anything about me?' she asked suspiciously.

'Let's just say we have a mutual interest.'

'What mutual interest?' she snapped.

'Are your cameras in working order?'

She lowered the sound on the TV. 'You from one of the tabs?'

'No. But I do have an assignment for you. Something you should relish.'

'What's that?'

'Let me explain . . .'

46

Heart pounding wildly, Lara walked down the dimly lit
street, dressed in a simple blouse and skirt, sensible shoes,
hair pulled back in a ponytail. Clutching a bag of groceries
to her chest, she hurried along the deserted street, leather
purse slung casually over one shoulder.

She *was* Rebecca Fullerton, a schoolteacher who worked
hard at a job she loved, and took care of her elderly mother
with whom she lived.

The real Rebecca was on the set today. Watching. Observing. This made Lara even more nervous, painfully aware
that every detail had to be right.

Suddenly she heard footsteps behind her.

*Mindset Rebecca. Did she realize she was being followed? No.
Was she frightened? No. The real Rebecca had said she was
thinking about what she was going to cook for dinner.*

Taking a deep breath, she concentrated on walking as if
nothing was about to happen.

How would *she* react in a situation like this? Rebecca had
fought back, fighting and clawing until her strength deserted
her. Even after she'd stopped fighting, she'd been beaten
repeatedly.

They'd blocked the scene out before shooting just to make
sure every move was in place right up until the attack. After
that Mick had told the actors they were on their own – he
was going for total reality with no set dialogue. 'Improvise,'
he'd informed them.

Earlier she'd sat with the real Rebecca, asking questions.
'I was fighting for survival,' Rebecca had told her quietly,
her thin face impassive. 'It was surreal, almost like a dream
happening in slow motion to someone else. I'll never forget
it.'

Thrill!

Yes. Lara could understand that.

They were working on a dusty street in the seedy part of town. Beyond the lights and cameras, onlookers and fans were cordoned off behind police lines. Mick had wanted a closed set, but since they were shooting on a public street it was impossible. Nikki had suggested they film this scene in a studio, but their production manager had informed them that it upped the budget prohibitively. Besides, Mick wanted the authenticity of being out on a real street.

Lara kept walking, trying not to tense her body in preparation for the attack she knew was coming any second. *Act natural!* a voice screamed in her head. *Go with whatever takes place.*

Joey had said he wasn't coming to the set, but in the end he'd relented and she knew he was lurking somewhere behind the main camera. Now she regretted asking him to be there.

Suddenly she felt the presence of the three actors as they fell into step beside her.

'Hey, cooze – what's a fine piece a ass like you doin' out alone?' Aiden jeered, shoving his hand in her grocery bag. 'Whatcha got for big daddy? Somethin' hot an' juicy? 'Cause, honey, that's what big daddy's got for you.'

'Go away,' she said, repeating the words Rebecca had said on that fateful night. 'Go away and leave me alone.'

'Don' wanna share what you got with big daddy?' Aiden mocked, circling her like a snake, while the other two men laughed and crowed.

She could smell him, he hadn't bathed for several days because Rebecca had mentioned how badly the men smelled. Aiden was nothing if not a method actor.

She quickened her step, trying to escape. But as she passed the opening to the alley, Aiden's character struck, putting his arm around her throat, spinning her off balance and dragging her into the alley.

The bag of groceries fell to the ground, vegetables and fruit rolling everywhere.

Rebecca was right – no time to scream. Concentrate on survival.

She kicked out, and as she did so she felt one of the actors run his hand up her skirt.

In the distance she heard the whirr of the camera. Everything was surreal – just as Rebecca had said – like she wasn't being watched by hundreds of eyes – like this was actually happening to her and there was no way she could think about anything except getting through it. *Just like real life*, she thought.

Aiden flung her up against the side of a building, hurting her back. His smell was all over her as he began clawing at her clothes.

Mick had promised to shoot in such a way that her body would be hidden from the cameras. 'But like you gotta be in the moment,' he'd said. 'We gotta feel your pain.'

He meant that when Aiden ripped the clothes from her body, she'd be totally naked, apart from the flesh-coloured G-string she wore under her panties. And that she shouldn't let nudity hamper her performance.

One take, she kept on thinking. *I only have to do this once and then it's over.*

Aiden tore off her blouse, tipping her breasts out of her bra before dragging it from her body until she was totally naked and exposed.

In a daze she wondered what the camera could see and what it couldn't. She didn't wonder for long, because she was too busy defending herself. The man on top of her wasn't Aiden Sean any more – he was scum from the streets, violating her body, hurting her, exposing every secret she possessed.

He faked a violent slap across her face, then his hands were moving under her skirt, and she was frantically struggling and screaming, while the two other actors spread her legs, held her down, and dragged her skirt off. Next they went for her panties, and she felt the G-string come off with them, but there was nothing she could do, because if she called 'Cut,' they'd have to start all over again, and she couldn't take it a second time.

Aiden was on top of her, simulating fucking. The camera was behind him. He was breathing hard, his stink enveloping her.

She recoiled in horror. Why had she asked Joey to come to the set? She didn't want him seeing her like this – degraded and used. This might be a movie, but she was still the victim – just like she'd been once before . . . an innocent victim caught up in a wild frenzy of unspeakable violence.

'Dumb cunt!' Aiden screamed, faking another hard slap across her face. 'Tell me you love it, bitch. Tell me you're gettin' off!'

Aiden wasn't acting any more. She felt his hard penis between her legs. If he dropped his pants she'd be forced to scream, 'Cut!'

The other actors were all over her, faking slaps and punches, yelling vile obscenities.

She began to struggle and scream in earnest. This was too much – she wanted out. Why had she agreed to make this movie? She should have listened to Quinn and Joey, they'd both warned her it was a mistake.

She continued screaming, but it wasn't doing her any good, they still kept at her, swarming over her like locusts.

And somewhere, three cameras were busy covering her humiliation and degradation.

She felt Rebecca's rage and pain burning through her like a firestorm. And she screamed – an explosive scream of fury and frustration.

Finally Mick stepped forward and shouted— 'Cut!' The pack of rats retreated.

Rebecca and Nikki moved in next to her, comforting her, while the wardrobe woman threw a silk robe across her shoulders, covering her nakedness.

'You OK?' Aiden asked, his long thin face nothing more than a vague blur.

She nodded, still in a daze.

Mick dashed over, arms going like windmills. 'Unbelievable!' he enthused. 'Freakin' unbelievable!'

Without any warning she suddenly bent forward and began to weep, unable to hold back the unexpected flood of tears.

And she couldn't stop sobbing until Joey was beside her, scooping her up in his arms, carrying her to her trailer and safety.

Finally her ordeal was over.

47

'That's it,' Joey said, scowling darkly. 'They've got their scene. No close-ups – nothing. Your stand-in can do the rest. That's fucking *it*!'

'Joey,' she murmured, 'if Mick wants close-ups, I'll have to do them.'

'No,' he said ominously. 'I'm taking you home.'

'I can't leave. I must finish.'

'Why the fuck did I let you do this?' he exploded, black eyes full of rage. 'I *knew* they were out to exploit you.'

She couldn't believe he was mad at *her*. What had *she* done?

'Joey—' she began, but it was no good reasoning with him – he was on a roll.

'How fuckin' stupid can you get?' he raged. 'How fuckin' dumb? This'll blow your whole career.'

Nikki knocked on the trailer door, entering tentatively. 'Spectacular!' she exclaimed.

'Yeah,' Joey said, turning on her, 'spectacular for your fuckin' movie. What do you think this'll do for Lara?'

'It'll get her an Oscar nomination, that's what,' Nikki said tightly.

'Yeah, *sure*.'

'Don't be so negative, Joey,' Lara said, attempting to keep the peace. 'It's OK, really it is.'

He turned on her, still furious. 'Negative? *I'm* tryin' to protect you. Can't you see what these people are doin' to you?'

'What are we doing to her?' Nikki asked, ready for battle.

'Screwing her, that's what,' he yelled.

'And what do *you* think *you're* doing?' Nikki retorted angrily, pushing a hand through her short dark hair.

'You *asshole!*' he muttered. 'All *you* wanna do is make money.'

'What the hell do you mean by that?' she blazed.

'You're exploitin' the shit outta Lara in the name of friendship.'

'How dare you!'

'Stop it!' Lara shouted, shivering uncontrollably. 'Get out of here – both of you. I can't take this.'

'Are you talkin' to me?' he said, turning on her – his dark eyes cold and hard. 'Are you tellin' me to get out?'

'It was my choice to play this role,' she said weakly, 'so don't make a big deal of it.'

'Fuck you,' he said angrily. 'Fuck *you.*' And he marched from the trailer.

'What's *his* problem?' Nikki said, still angry.

'He's upset. I shouldn't have forced him to come to the set, it was selfish of me.'

Nikki was amazed. He'd just screamed at Lara for no reason, called her stupid and God knew what else, and she was *defending* him!

'Why are you putting *his* feelings first?' she asked, exasperated.

'I'd react in the same way if I had to watch *him* getting beat up.'

'You're too understanding for me to fathom,' Nikki said, shaking her head in disbelief. 'The guy's with *you*, for Chrissakes – he should be kissing your ass.'

'Don't criticize him,' Lara said, clutching her robe around her. 'He treats me wonderfully.'

'Yeah, well, *I* haven't seen it.'

'You know what?' Lara said, wishing Nikki would vanish. 'It's really none of your business.'

'I'm your friend,' Nikki said earnestly. 'How do you know Joey's not just another bum actor hanging around for the glory?'

'I suppose you got that little speech straight from Richard. It sounds exactly like him.'

'No,' Nikki snapped. 'Richard and I have split up. I didn't want to tell you before, in case it upset you.'

'So now I guess it's all right because I'm upset anyway?'

'No. I didn't mean—'

'This isn't the time to get into it,' Lara said wearily. 'If you don't mind, I need to be alone.'

'Fine,' Nikki said, and left the trailer, disappointed Lara wasn't more concerned about her news.

As soon as she was by herself, Lara began shivering uncontrollably. She was in shock that the people closest to her were acting like this. First Joey walking out. Then Nikki and her problems. Just when she needed tender loving care, they'd both seen fit to dump on her.

She felt shut off from everyone – alone and frightened. Exactly the way she'd felt when she was six years old and the tragedy had taken place . . .

She hated remembering, but sometimes – in moments of trauma – it was inevitable.

She buried her head in her hands, and before she could stop it – the memories came flooding back.

☆

'Lara Ann, you're going to live with your Aunt Lucy.'

The policewoman who spoke had ruddy cheeks and several hairy warts on her face. Lara Ann concentrated on the warts. If she stared at them hard enough, maybe all the bad things would go away.

For over a week she'd been kept in a child care facility while the authorities tried to track down a relative who would care for her. They'd finally come up with Aunt Lucy, her father's second cousin, who lived in Arizona.

Aunt Lucy didn't come to fetch Lara Ann herself, she sent Mac, her big strapping son. He drove a pick-up truck, chewed gum nonstop, and was quite ugly. He scooped up little Lara Ann, tossing her into the back of the truck as if she was a rag doll. She remained there for most of the long drive to Arizona.

Aunt Lucy, a dour widow woman with a long miserable face, owned a small motel, which she ran with the help of her son. Aunt Lucy was not at all affectionate, and certainly not pleased to be stuck with Lara Ann. She greeted the child with a curt nod, showed her to the tiny storeroom in back where she was to sleep, and the next morning packed her off to the local school.

Lara Ann was utterly traumatized. Nobody mentioned the tragedy to her. Nobody spoke to her about the loss of her family.

It was like they'd ceased to exist and not one person cared to address it.

Aunt Lucy certainly didn't mention it. Neither did Mac. Although one day his best friend said to her— 'Are you batty? Mac says you are, 'cause your daddy killed your mom. So you gotta be a loony, too.'

Lara Ann was frightened and confused. She couldn't understand what had happened, only that her life was in shatters.

She soon realized that Aunt Lucy didn't want her, and even though she was very young, she also sensed that she didn't fit in at the motel. She withdrew into silence – the only safe place – speaking only when spoken to. At school she kept to herself, desperately trying to fade into the background. Unfortunately, as she grew, it was not possible to stay unnoticed, for she was incredibly pretty. By the time she was thirteen, boys were chasing her, even though she gave them no encouragement.

After school and all during summer vacations she helped out at the motel doing the work of a maid – cleaning rooms, scrubbing floors, folding laundry. Mac's best friend worked as a handyman at the motel. He had his eye on her, and even though she was only thirteen and kept to herself, she knew he was watching her.

One day he trapped her in the laundry room, pinned her up against the wall and tried to kiss and grope her. He wanted to do more, but when she started to scream he got nervous and ran.

Aunt Lucy appeared at the door of the laundry room, her long face livid. 'Why are you encouraging him?' she yelled. 'What are you? A tramp like your mother?'

'My mama wasn't a tramp,' Lara Ann whispered.

Aunt Lucy didn't listen. Stern-faced, she proceeded to give her a lecture about how lucky she was that they'd taken her in, even though they could ill afford to, and she was a terrible burden.

A burden? She was doing a full-time job for no wages. Fervently she vowed that one of these days she would get away from Aunt Lucy, and never speak to her again, because she was a hateful woman.

Sometimes Lara Ann felt like Cinderella. She had no friends, nobody to love and cherish her, nobody who cared. Many nights she'd sob herself to sleep in her little room. School was not much better. She was too pretty to fit in, and they all let her know it. The other girls hated her, and the boys wanted to jump her. Her only solace was reading, and she haunted the school library, getting hold of every book she could. Reading took her to another place – another life. It proved to her that things could be better.

When she was fifteen a tenant shot himself in one of the rooms. Lara Ann discovered the body when she went in to clean, and became hysterical.

Aunt Lucy slapped her across the face and told her to shut up and pull herself together while she called the police.

Two hours later the police arrived, took photographs, hauled the body away, and when the task was completed, Aunt Lucy told her to go in and clean up the mess.

'No!' Lara Ann shrieked, horrified. 'I can't go in there. I can't!'

'Pretty little miss doesn't want to get blood on her hands?' Aunt Lucy sneered. 'You get in there and do as I say.'

That was the day Lara Ann knew she couldn't take it any more. Unfortunately, she had no choice – there was nowhere for her to run.

And then, one Friday afternoon, a man called Morgan Creedo checked into the motel. Morgan was a half-assed country singer, twenty-nine years old, thin as a whippet, with long blond hair and a weather-beaten, heavily tanned face.

To Lara Ann he was glamour personified. She hovered outside his room, listening to him sing and play his guitar.

'Is he a movie star?' she whispered to Mac.

'No, he's not a goddamn movie star,' Mac snapped. 'Why'd you think that?'

''Cause he's so . . . special,' Lara Ann replied.

'Oh, you're just a dumb kid, what do you know?' Mac sneered.

He was right. She was a dumb kid. An ugly little slut. She didn't know anything. Aunt Lucy was always telling her how stupid she was. Mac called her a retard and a loony. Even the kids at school steered clear of her because she wasn't like them.

Maybe I am crazy, she thought to herself. Maybe I'm crazy to have stayed with these people all these years. Because when she remembered her beautiful mother, and her fun-loving brother, and all the cuddles and love she'd received from her father before that fateful night when everything had blown up in her face – she knew life could be good.

Morgan Creedo was appearing in a concert nearby, and she wanted more than anything to go. 'It's not like he's the star,' Mac said. 'There's about ten other acts, and he's appearing first – which means he's a nobody.'

'I'm going to ask him if I can go,' Lara Ann said.

'Ask away. Lucy won't let you.'

But she had no intention of getting Aunt Lucy's permission.

Later that day when she delivered clean towels to Morgan Creedo's room, she found him lying on the bed watching a Western on television.

''Scuse me, sir,' she ventured.

He barely glanced up. 'Yeah – whaddaya want?'

'I was wondering if you had a spare ticket to your concert,' she said boldly.

He laughed. 'You wanna come see my concert, little girl?'

'Yes, I'd like that a lot.'

'Well, well, well.' He sat up with a broad smile on his face. 'Heard about how good I am, huh?'

'I hope it's not rude, but I've been standing outside your door listening to your singing. You sound real good to me.'

'Yeah, I'm pretty damn good, kid. Trouble is I'm the only person who appreciates me.' He got off the bed and stretched. 'I'll get you a ticket. You got a name?'

'Lara Ann.'

'Lara Ann, huh?' He looked at her like he was seeing her for the first time. 'How old're you?'

'Fifteen.'

He laughed. 'Old enough, huh?'

'Do you have to be a certain age to come to your concert?' she asked, her beautiful face completely innocent.

He laughed again. 'Not what I was talking about, kid. Tell you what – I'll leave you a ticket in the room. The concert's tomorrow night. Come backstage after, I'll buy you a lemonade.'

The next day she found the ticket he'd left for her on the dresser in his room. She stuffed it in her pocket, barely able to conceal her excitement.

That night, after dinner was finished and she'd washed the dishes, she left the kitchen as if she was going to bed as usual, and snuck out the back door, making her way by bus to the concert hall where Morgan Creedo was appearing, her precious ticket clutched tightly in her hand.

The theatre was vast, but Morgan had gotten her a seat right *at the front. She was so excited she could barely breathe. Most of the audience had come to see the star act, a female country and western singer, but when Morgan hit the stage, Lara Ann felt butterflies in the pit of her stomach.*

He sang two songs. The audience didn't seem too interested, but Lara Ann clapped until her hands hurt. As soon as he was finished she got up her courage and approached a guard standing at the side of the stage.

''Scuse me,' she said, 'can you tell me how I get back to see Mr Creedo?'

'Mr Who?' the guard said.

'He was just up there singing.'

'He was, huh? You got a backstage pass?'

'No, but he gave me my ticket, and told me to go backstage after.'

'OK,' he said with a dirty laugh. 'Guess there's nothin' wrong with another groupie gettin' it on. Go on back, sweetie.'

He didn't move, forcing her to squeeze past him. As she did so, he pinched her bottom.

Backstage there were dozens of people running around. She spotted the star of the show with her big lemon-coloured hair, sequined dress and toothy smile. She stopped a girl with magenta curls, carrying a hairbrush.

''Scuse me,' she said politely. 'I'm looking for Mr Creedo.'

'Oh, you mean Morgan? He's outta here already.'

'I was supposed to meet him. Do you know where he'd be?'

'You're a little young for Morgan, aren't you?' the girl said, looking her up and down.

'I'm a friend of his.'

'Sure you are. Guess he'd be in the bar next door, sweetie, but I wouldn't pursue it if I were you.'

'Excuse me?'

'What I mean is, whyn't you go on home. You're too young for a reptile like him.'

Lara Ann didn't appreciate the girl calling Morgan a reptile. She made her way out of the stage door, and hesitated on the street. There were two bars in sight, one across the street and one next to the theatre. She decided the one next to the theatre might be where he was.

Pushing the door open, she was swept into a crowd of beer-drinking, card-playing men. She looked around, finally spotting

Morgan at the bar nursing a glass of tequila. She went over and tapped him on the shoulder.

'What the fuck you want?' he said, turning around and staring at her with bloodshot eyes.

'I'm from the motel, remember? You left me a ticket. Told me I could come see you tonight. My name's Lara Ann.'

'Ah Jesus, kid.'

'You were so wonderful,' she said, her green eyes shining.

'I was shit,' he replied bitterly. 'I'm always shit. Did you hear? Those bastards didn't even listen to me. They're not interested – they just wanna eyeball that fuckin' fat blond with the big tits.'

'I thought you were wonderful,' Lara Ann repeated.

He squinted at her. 'You're a pretty little thing,' he said. 'How old you say you were?'

'Fifteen. But I'll soon be sixteen.'

'Big enough and old enough, huh?'

'Beg your pardon?'

'Nothin', darlin' – come here.' She moved closer to him. 'You think I'm wonderful, huh?'

'Oh yes,' she muttered adoringly.

They were married three weeks later on her sixteenth birthday. Aunt Lucy did not attend.

It wasn't until after they were married that Lara Ann realized Morgan had no home, only the cramped trailer attached to the battered old Cadillac he drove around the country. 'It ain't luxury, honey, but you'll get used to it,' he informed her.

She didn't care. She finally had somebody who knew she existed and whom she could look after. She'd learned to cook by watching Aunt Lucy; her ironing was impeccable; and she knew how to sew, keep house and clean.

What she didn't know was anything about sex. But this didn't bother Morgan.

'I'm gonna teach you everything you need to know, honey,' he said. 'This is what you do. You get down on your knees and you suck my dick till I come. That's all there is to it.'

'That's all?' she said, thinking about all the things she'd read about kissing and cuddling and making love.

'Yeah, so get goin', honey – I'm gonna teach you how to do it like a pro.'

They never did make love in the proper fashion. Morgan told her people only did it that way when they wanted to have kids.

She wasn't sure she believed him, but what could she do? He wasn't interested in anything other than her getting down on her knees.

Morgan Creedo was a sonofabitch. He made Lara Ann into his love slave. And because he wasn't a star, he let out all his frustrations on his young innocent bride. Lara Ann had no one except him, and he liked that. He kept her to himself, never allowing her to speak to anyone else.

As she grew older, so she became more beautiful – which Morgan considered an added bonus. When he hit her – and he did so often – he made sure he never touched her gorgeous face. In the back of his mind he thought that one day – when his career was over – he'd get her a job in porno movies. With her looks she could make enough money to keep them both in luxury.

'Ever thought about acting?' he asked one day.

She shook her head.

'You got what it takes, hon,' he said, unzipping his fly and pushing her to her knees.

The following week he started taking her to movies so she could study the famous actresses on the screen.

She fell in love with the moving images and the actors she observed. Meryl Streep and Robert Redford. Al Pacino and Jessica Lange. They were all so magical. They inspired her – making her realize that there was another life out there. Oh God, how she yearned for another life.

By the time she was nineteen, Morgan was fed up. She might be beautiful, but she was also boring. She never answered back; let him get away with anything; serviced him whenever he wanted. He needed fire in a woman, not docile obedience. Maybe if he put her on the road to porno stardom she'd become more exciting.

Lara Ann was also fed up – but for different reasons. She'd thought Morgan really cared for her, but as each day passed she understood that she was no more than his servant. The way he treated her, she might have been better off staying with Aunt Lucy.

One day he informed her they were going to Hollywood. 'I've got the number of a producer who's promised to give you a break.'

'A break at what?' she asked.

'To be a movie star, dummy. That's what you want, isn't it?'

'If you say so.'

They got in his old Cadillac and set off.

Halfway to Los Angeles, he stopped the car in a lay-by and told her to service him the way he liked.

'No,' she said.

'"No"?' he repeated, as if he couldn't believe she was turning him down. 'Do it, bitch. An' don't argue.'

'I don't want to.'

Once again he repeated her words. '"You don't want to."' Then he grabbed her by the hair with one hand, unzipped his fly with the other, and forced her head into his lap.

The novelty of her saying no made him come even faster than usual, and when he released her, she got in the back of the car and curled up on the seat, tears in her eyes, planning in her mind that when they reached LA she had to get away from Morgan and start afresh.

God made it easy for her.

Ten miles outside of Barstow, Morgan fell asleep at the wheel. Seconds later their car skidded under a huge truck parked illegally on the highway.

Lara Ann woke up in a hospital two days later.

'Where's Morgan?' she asked. 'Where's my husband?'

Morgan was dead. He'd been decapitated in the accident.

Once again she was by herself.

☆

'Are you all right, Lara, dear?' The English wardrobe woman stood in front of her, a concerned expression on her homely face.

She glanced up, leaving the vividly real memories behind. 'I'm fine,' she murmured.

'I was knocking on the door for ages.'

'Guess I must've fallen asleep.'

'Mick says you're finished for the day. Can I help you get dressed?'

'That's OK. Can you please make sure my driver's outside.'

'He's there, dear.'

'Thanks.'

She couldn't wait to get home to the safety of Joey's arms. He was the only one she could truly depend on.

48

Joey prowled around a fashionably rundown pool hall on Sunset. Most of the guys were intent on the game, except a few who were checking out the eager girls sitting in a row at the bar, hoping to be picked up.

Joey was edgy – for the first time in his life he realized he cared about someone, and this completely threw him. How had it happened? The instant he'd seen Lara he'd known it was going to be a whole other trip.

And yet, he was using her – living in her house, going to her agent, allowing her to get him a part in *Revenge*. Before, when he'd been with a woman, he'd always had a reason. Now everything was different. Shit! He didn't *want* to use her in any way.

What was he going to do? Harden himself against her? Get it back to where it should be?

He eyed the female talent at the bar. There were some pretty girls, but none of them came close to Lara.

He zeroed in on the prettiest, a curly-haired brunette in a white micro-dress sipping a Margarita. She was very young – too young.

'Hi,' he said, approaching her.

She looked him over, liking what she saw. 'You'd better not hit on me,' she warned, flirting anyway. 'I'm with my date, and he gets real mad.'

'Which one's your date?'

She pointed out a short balding guy across the room, intent on the game.

'I've seen competition,' Joey said with a dry laugh, 'an' I got a feelin' he ain't it.'

She giggled, fluttering her long eyelashes, getting off on the attention. 'I'm Tina. Who're you?'

'Bob,' he lied.

'Hi, Bob,' she said, small pink tongue snaking out to lick the rim of her Margarita glass in a suggestive fashion.

'Hi, Tina,' he replied, giving her intense eye contact.

Could this vampy little brunette persuade him to forget Lara? Could she make him fall out of love?

He sincerely doubted it. 'What's your phone number, Tina?' he asked, deciding he'd pursue it anyway.

'I can't give you that!' she said, shrieking with laughter. 'I told you, I'm with my date.'

'Yeah, but what if you break up with him tonight?' he said, giving her the full intense stare. 'Wouldn't you be sorry you hadn't given me your number?'

She thought that one over. 'Well ... OK, but if he sees, he's gonna kill me. *And* you.' Furtively she scrawled her number on a packet of book matches and handed it to him.

Score one. He'd probably never call her. Who gave a shit?

He left the pool hall and drove to a strip club several blocks down the street, paying an exorbitant price at the door.

The strippers were lacklustre, contemptuous of their patrons, undulating and gyrating with a distinct lack of energy. He concentrated on a sloe-eyed blond, lowering her quivering thighs up and down a steel pole wearing only a G-string and nippleless bra. She didn't do a thing for him.

'Take it off, honey-pot,' yelled a fat guy sitting to his right. 'Get naked so's I kin get a real good look at those big bouncy jimmy-jammies!'

The girl slithered across the floor to the man who was doing the shouting. 'A hundred bucks'll buy you a private dance,' she said, provocatively sliding her tongue across pouty lips.

'Honey-pot, I'm *buyin'*!' the fat man crowed, sweat beading his upper lip.

'Back room, ten minutes,' the stripper said, taking a long sideways look at Joey. Their eyes met for a moment. He saw the interest start to rise. 'How 'bout you, baby?' she crooned, with a slight lisp. 'Wanna visit paradise?'

He didn't bother replying. Strippers. They were all into each other, anyway. The ones he'd known harboured a deep hate for the guys who sat and ogled them, referring to them as losers and dorks – guys who couldn't get it up in normal life.

He wondered what Lara was doing now. She must have arrived home and found he was not there. He knew she'd be upset.

Why was he treating her this way? She was so good to him, she didn't deserve it.

Insurance. To make sure she stayed interested.

He got up and left, not even glancing at the sumptuous redhead with giant knockers who was doing unbelievable things to a steel-backed chair.

He sat in Lara's car for a moment before taking out the matchbook with Tina's number scribbled on the flap. Disgusted with himself – he threw it into the gutter.

Why sabotage something so perfect?

☆

Sitting in the back of her limo on the ride to her house, Lara attempted to calm down. Not only had she gone through the ordeal of the rape scene, but when the memories came flooding back, she'd felt a deep sense of sadness and desperation. Over the years she'd become adept at shutting out the nightmares – closing down the moment her mind went in a bad direction – a trick she'd learned to protect herself. Today it hadn't worked.

Enough! a voice screamed in her head. *Enough! I'm not thinking about any more of this today.*

She inspected her arms, both badly bruised from the mauling Aiden had given her. Maybe Joey was right. Maybe she shouldn't have agreed to appear in *Revenge*. Still . . . it was completely unfair of him to get mad at her.

The dogs greeted her when she arrived home, racing out of the house, barking and wagging their tails, jumping to lick her face, delighted to see her. She fussed them for a minute, thinking that you never had to worry about animals – they always loved you, no matter what.

Mrs Crenshaw came to the front door. 'Everything all right, Miss Lara?'

'Yes, thanks, Mrs C.'

'Will you be eating home tonight?'

'Yes. I'd like dinner served in the bedroom on trays. Is Mr Joey upstairs?'

'No, he's not home yet.'

'Oh,' she said, disappointed. 'Did he call?'

'Not that I know of.'

She was overwhelmed with a sudden feeling of emptiness. Why wasn't Joey here to say he was sorry for the way he'd behaved, and to tell her he loved her? She had no desire to spend the evening alone, she needed him beside her.

More than a little disturbed, she went upstairs into her bathroom and ran a tub, slowly pouring bubble bath under the running taps. Then she lit scented candles and put a Sade CD on the player. *Smooth Operator* serenaded her as she pinned her hair on top of her head and slid into the tub, allowing the warm water to soothe her aching body.

It had been some day.

☆

When Nikki walked into the house she found three irate messages from Richard on the answering machine, each one more angry than the last. The gist of his fury was that he'd heard how graphic the rape scene was, and how could she and her amateur director have put Lara through such an ordeal.

It was like he didn't get it. They weren't together, she was contemplating divorce, yet he acted as if this was merely a temporary separation and he could still tell her what to do.

She wasn't in the mood to call him back. In fact, until the movie was finished, she didn't care to do anything about him at all. Yes, it was lonely in the house without him around, but it was better than putting up with a man who couldn't stay faithful.

She was anxious to see the dailies, her job now was to protect Lara in the editing room, where she planned on looking over Mick's shoulder the entire time.

The phone rang. She reached for it.

'What the *fuck* is wrong with you?' Richard yelled, causing her to hold the phone away from her ear. 'Are you trying to ruin Lara's career?'

'What the *fuck* is wrong with *you*?' she responded heatedly. 'She'll get nominated for this role.'

'You're full of shit, Nikki. You have no idea what you're doing.'

'Don't talk down to me,' she answered coldly. 'You remind me of Sheldon.'

'Oh, I see. Every time I say something you don't like, I remind you of your ex.'

'I don't appreciate being told what to do. I make my own decisions.'

'Yes, you do. Decision number one: ruin Lara Ivory's career.'

'Why do you keep on saying that?'

'Because it's all over town that she's flashing her snatch in your crummy little movie.'

'Excuse me?'

'You don't think there wasn't some spy on the set with a hidden camera?' he taunted. 'The pictures will be front page on the tabloids next week. You think it'll do *my* movie any good? My beautiful, gentle romance, and let's take a look at Lara Ivory with her snatch in the air.'

'Bullshit.'

'For Chrissake, Nikki, wise up. This is Hollywood in the nineties, there are spies everywhere. Jesus Christ! Lara's supposed to be your friend. Why are you doing this to her?'

'I'm trying to make a movie, Richard. I'd appreciate it if you'd leave me alone.'

'You're so naive,' he said, completely disgusted. 'I was under the impression you knew what you were doing, but it turns out you're nothing but an amateur.'

'I don't have to listen to this.'

'Then *don't*.' And he slammed the phone down, which infuriated her even more.

A repeat performance, she thought. *The older man talking down to me. Exactly like Sheldon.*

Why did I marry two old guys, anyway?

Sheldon always said I was searching for Daddy – at least he made one correct call.

She was just about to phone Lara when the doorbell buzzed. Could it be Richard in person, all set to berate her some more?

'Who's there?' she called out.

'Aiden.'

She flung open the door and Aiden Sean ambled in, looking gaunt and worn and quite attractive in a grungy rock star sort of way. Kind of a younger Mick Jagger morphed with Tommy Lee.

'Y'know,' he said irately, rubbing his unshaved chin, 'I was in that scene today, too.'

She wasn't in the mood for Aiden and his complaints. 'Huh?' she said vaguely.

His bleak eyes scanned her face. 'Everybody's all over Lara like she's the President's wife. *I'm* what makes that scene real. I give it the power. Don't I get any credit?'

Actors! She'd forgotten to praise him and he was pissed. 'You were great, Aiden,' she murmured soothingly. 'You make the perfect rapist.'

He laughed drily. 'Thanks.'

'What's that smell?' she asked, wrinkling her nose.

'Me,' he said, utterly unfazed. 'Haven't had time to go home. Thought I'd use your shower.'

She frowned. Boy, he sure was different. 'You drove all the way to Malibu to use my shower?'

'No, I drove all this way to see you.'

A moment of silence while she tried to figure out if this was his way of flirting. 'Was that so I could tell you how great your performance was?' she asked lightly.

'I *wanted* to see you – is that allowed?' he said, fixing her with his burnt-out eyes. She fell into them and found herself admitting to herself that, yes – she *was* attracted to him, even though she'd been trying to bury her feelings.

'Uh, Aiden,' she said, thrown by the realization, 'I don't know how to tell you this, but uh . . . I'm married.'

'Separated,' he said, still pinning her with his mesmerizing eyes. 'It's all over the set.'

'I guess nothing's private when you're making a movie,' she said ruefully.

'Nothing,' he said, yawning and stretching. 'I worked hard today, now I feel like a piece of shit. Can I use your shower or not?'

His behaviour was bizarre, and she knew she should say no, but she wasn't in the mood to throw him out. She was in the mood for excitement and adventure, two things he seemed to offer. 'One shower and you'll go home?' she questioned.

A thin smile. 'Whyn't you be a good girl and fix us a drink while I'm in there.'

'Why don't you be a good boy and fix us a drink when you get out.'

He laughed, peeling off his work shirt. 'Lead me to the bathroom, Nikki. I can't even stand my own stink any more.'

And she knew that whatever happened next was inevitable.

☆

Richard Barry paced furiously around his hotel suite. How come *he* always ended up in a hotel, while his wives stayed put in the house that *he'd* paid for? He should never have married Nikki, she was too headstrong – full of her own importance now that she considered herself a 'producer'. As far as he was concerned, she couldn't produce shit. It was *his* fault for encouraging her, he should have known she wouldn't be able to cut it.

He should have stayed married to Lara. Getting divorced from her was the biggest mistake of his life. Now she was wasting her time with Joey Lorenzo – a first-degree loser. And he, Richard Barry, was sitting alone in a hotel room.

Thinking of Joey reminded him of a phone call he had to make. He fumbled in his pocket for a piece of paper with the number written on it, picked up the phone and dialled.

A woman answered.

'Ms Francis? This is Richard Barry,' he said smoothly. 'I'm sorry to bother you at home. I believe my assistant alerted you I'd be calling.'

'It's no bother, Mr Barry,' Madelaine Francis replied, wondering what this was about. 'In fact, it's an honour to speak with you. How can I help?'

He cleared his throat. 'I understand you were the agent for Joey Lorenzo on *The Dreamer*.'

'That's right.' A slight pause. 'Of course, I'm not responsible for anything he did after that, because he left my agency.'

Richard sensed tension in her voice and knew exactly

what to say next. 'Actors . . .' he said understandingly. 'One little break and they dump everyone who helped them get there. I've seen it happen a thousand times.'

'You've got that right,' Madelaine said, her tone bitter.

'Ah, well, that's the way it goes,' Richard said sympathetically. 'So . . . Ms Francis – what exactly can you tell me about Joey Lorenzo?'

'Are you interested in using him in one of your films?' Madelaine asked. 'Because I have other people I can recommend. In fact, I have tapes of several very talented young actors I'd appreciate you viewing.'

'Joey's working in LA at the moment,' Richard remarked.

'I didn't know that,' Madelaine replied, realizing that she mustn't sound too interested, even though she was anxious to know where the little shit had run off to this time. 'What's he working on?' she asked casually.

'A low-budget movie. Nothing important.'

'I see.'

'I have a suggestion, Ms Francis,' Richard said briskly. 'I'll pay for you to come out to the coast. Bring the tapes of your actors, and we'll sit down and discuss everything. I have several projects in development, I'm sure I can use a couple of your clients.'

'I . . . I'd like that,' she said, still trying to figure out why Richard Barry was so interested in Joey Lorenzo.

'The sooner the better,' Richard continued. 'One of my assistants will make the arrangements. My casting people are excellent, but occasionally I enjoy meeting with agents, especially New York agents, who have a knowledge of all the new young talent.'

'That's nice to hear, Mr Barry. Not many directors in your position feel that way.'

'I look forward to meeting you, Ms Francis.'

'Likewise, Mr Barry.'

He put the phone down and nodded to himself. It was about time he concentrated on finding out more about Mr Lorenzo.

Mexico City *welcomed me with open arms – this murdering, drug-addicted, dumb American. I slept on the plane with the help of half a bottle of vodka and a couple of joints. The whole thing was surreal. A fucking slow-motion trip of disaster. I kept on seeing Hadley's face, her look of surprise when the gun went off. Had anyone seen me at the house? Were there any witnesses? Was I going to get caught?*

The first thing I did was change my name again. Then I took a job at a gas station in a small town outside of the city. I rented a room and proceeded to dry out. Cold turkey. For once I was by myself. No woman to hold my hand and pay my bills. I wanted it that way. I wanted my life back.

After a couple of months I began to feel like a human being. I was punishing myself for what I'd done. No drugs. No booze. No sex. Working a dumb shit job. Sleeping when I wasn't working.

It was my punishment.

It cleared my head.

I was twenty-eight years old and a total fucking failure.

I met a woman. An American tourist searching for adventure. We travelled to Acapulco together. I paid my own way. She missed her husband. It was two weeks of nothing much.

After that I went back to being on my own. And it was then that I started to take stock of my life, my sad and sorry life. And I vowed that everything was going to change. Everything.

When I finally returned to LA I planned on being a totally different person.

49

'Hi,' Joey said, slouching into the bedroom.

Lara was sitting up in bed, watching *The Larry Sanders Show* on HBO, hair piled on top of her head, face devoid of make-up.

'God, you look beautiful!' he said, flopping down beside her. She ignored him as he edged nearer. 'You pissed at me, honey?' he asked.

'Can you wait until this programme is over?' she said coolly, her eyes following the actors on TV.

Oh, she was giving him a hard time. Well, she was entitled. 'Sure,' he said, reaching over and taking her hand. 'I can do anythin' you want.'

She allowed her hand to be limp in his, determined not to forgive him too fast.

'I'm sorry, baby,' he said with a deep sigh. 'I got crazy. Couldn't help myself.'

'I really appreciated you walking out,' she said accusingly.

'Didn't mean to.'

'Whether you meant to or not, that's exactly what you did.'

'Guess sorry doesn't cut it.'

'You *knew* how difficult the rape scene was for me. How could you act like that?'

''Cause I couldn't stand seein' you with those assholes crawlin' all over you,' he muttered. 'I warned you I shouldn't be there, it was you that insisted.'

'So now it's *my* fault?'

'In a way.'

'You're funny,' she said, shaking her head.

'Yeah, I'm the funny guy who doesn't wanna see you hurt. Is that so bad?'

'You didn't have to take it out on me.'

'Jeez! How many times do I havta say I'm sorry?'

'It's Nikki you should be apologizing to.'

Christ! Now Nikki! Wasn't it enough that he was back? That he hadn't fucked up her head by screwing around on her?

'Your so-called friend is way too possessive of you,' he said. 'Did you know the reason she split with Richard is 'cause he's pissed you're in her movie?'

'I don't believe that.'

'Hey – I'm fillin' you in on the set gossip. Believe what you like.' He rolled towards her, his tone drawing her in. 'C'mon, baby, let's not fight. You've been on my mind all night.'

'I have?' she asked, unable to stay mad at him for long.

'It's the truth.'

She gave a deep sigh, there seemed no point in fighting. 'I'm glad you came home,' she said softly.

'So am I,' he said, removing the remote from her hand and clicking off the TV.

'I was watching that—' she objected, none too strenuously.

'Y'know,' he said, stroking her hair, 'while I was thinkin' about you, I came up with a great idea.'

'You did?'

'Yup.'

She snuggled closer to him. 'Are you going to tell me?'

'Dunno,' he said, teasing her. 'Haven't decided.'

'Well, while you're deciding, shall I get Mrs C. to bring up dinner?'

'Sounds good t'me.'

☆

Aiden emerged from the shower and padded into the kitchen with only a thin bath sheet knotted around his narrow waist.

Nikki gave a low mocking whistle. 'Sex . . . ee!' She was trying to play this real cool because she wasn't sure *how* she felt. And what kind of nerve did this guy have anyway – parading naked around her house?

'Where's my drink?' he asked, perfectly at home.

'Aiden,' she said, 'a joke is a joke, but can you please put your clothes on and go home.'

'Can't.'

'Why?'

'They stink. Thought you could throw 'em in the wash.'

Oh God, how had she gotten involved in *this*?

'You're too much,' she said, shaking her head.

Ice-grey eyes met hers. 'Not the first time I've bin told that.'

She stared back at him. He was so thin that she could make out the outline of his ribs, and on his left shoulder he had a snake tattoo wending its way down his upper arm. Something drew her to it – she couldn't resist reaching out to touch.

Wrong move. Or maybe the right one. He grabbed her wrist, pulling her forcefully towards him, pressing his lips down on hers.

She kissed him back. What the hell – if it was OK for Richard . . .

Aiden was extremely passionate, hardly giving her a moment to think. So unlike Richard, who'd moved at a leisurely pace, an older man's pace.

'First time I saw your lips I couldn't wait to suck 'em,' Aiden said, breathing all over her. 'Fuckable lips . . . fuckable you . . .'

His hands were everywhere. Under her sweater, up her skirt, sneaking around the elastic of her panties. Long inquisitive fingers exploring new territory.

'Slow down,' she gasped.

'Fuck slowing down,' he responded. 'I've wanted to do this ever since that first lunch.' And then he began kissing her again, his tongue jamming deep into her mouth.

She found herself responding with a sexual zeal she hadn't felt in a long time. He tasted of cigarette smoke and booze and forbidden excitement and she wanted him desperately.

After a few feverish minutes, he ripped off her bra – breaking the clasp. Her breasts tumbled free as he pushed her up against the kitchen counter, raising her hips so that she was half sitting, tearing at her panties until they too were history. Her skirt was around her waist, her sweater around her neck, the rest of her exposed to his probing eyes.

With one hand he untied his towel, letting it drop to the floor. With the other he crushed her breasts together playing with her nipples.

Then he put his cock between her legs – pausing for a moment before plunging in.

She let out a scream of pleasurable pain. Aiden might be thin – but he made up for it in other places.

And finally they were into a wild ride that lasted for a very long time. And after that, sleep – a deeply satisfying sleep.

☆

'I can't remember ever being more content,' Lara said with a big smile. They sat in bed, trays in front of them – having recently finished a delicious dinner.

'Yeah,' Joey said. 'Mrs C.'s cookin' does it for me every time.'

'Will you stop!' she said, laughing. 'You know exactly what I mean. The two of us – here together – nobody to bother us. It's like being in our own little world.'

'You're right,' he said. 'Truth is – I've never been happier either. Who needs to go out?'

'We're so alike,' she said, sighing contentedly.

'Yeah, two loners wanderin' around lost – then we got lucky an' found each other. Right?'

'You said it, Joey.'

He grinned. 'An' now—'

'We're together.'

'Like you said – soulmates.' A long beat. 'In fact . . .'

'Yes, Joey?'

'You ready to hear my great idea?'

'What is it?' she asked with an indulgent smile. 'Dinner in bed for two?'

'No, smart-ass.'

'I'm waiting.'

'Well . . .' He paused before plunging ahead. 'I kinda had this crazy thought that when you finish the movie – we should take off . . . an', y'know, kinda get married.'

'Married?'

'Yeah, that's what people in love do, y'know.'

She regarded him for a long silent moment. 'They do?' she finally managed, filled with mixed emotions.

'You an' me, somewhere quiet, where no one can find us. What d'you say, baby?'

She hesitated for only a second, and then she realized how right it all was. 'I say ... whatever you want, Joey. Whatever makes you happy.'

'No,' he responded – staring at the most beautiful woman in the world, 'whatever makes you happy. I love you, Lara, an' I'm gonna make *you* happier than you ever imagined possible.'

And then they kissed – a long deep soul kiss. And Lara knew she was making the right decision. They truly belonged together, and they always would.

50

The mystery voice had delivered. Yes, Alison Sewell knew she finally had a friend, someone she could trust.

The voice had told her exactly where to go to get the pictures of Lara Ivory that nobody else would have. A seedy hotel room overlooking the alley where *Revenge* was shooting the next day. A hotel room booked and paid for in the name of Mrs Smith. All Alison had to do was to go there with her cameras and telephoto lenses and wait.

'If I get the pictures you say I will,' Alison had said, 'and I sell 'em to the tabs, what d'you get out of it?'

'Satisfaction,' the mystery voice had replied.

All had come to pass. Alison had done exactly as instructed, and sure enough she was centre stage for the rape scene, with an unobstructed view of the action.

God! She could hardly shoot fast enough as the scene progressed. *Snap snap* – as Lara was shoved to the ground; zoom in for close-up as Aiden Sean ripped off her bra; automatic reflex – five shots a second – as they spread her legs and ripped off her panties.

Alison was breathing hard. These were the pictures a photographer of her calibre dreamt about! Naked celebrities fetched top price – especially a celebrity who was supposed to be so sweet and nice. Lara Ivory. Miss Incorruptible. *Well, look at you now, bitch. That'll teach you to cross Alison Sewell.*

By the time she was finished, Alison was drenched with sweat. She hurriedly packed up her equipment and raced home, anxious to see what treasures her camera had brought her.

When she viewed the results she was in heaven. The photographs were so raunchy, so bad, so sellable . . .

Lara Ivory exposed for everyone to see.

Revenge was sweet as pie.

And this was just the start.

51

When Lara reported for work the next day, Mick started jumping all over her, spewing forth compliments. 'Couldn't've asked for more,' he said enthusiastically, pushing his heavy glasses back on his nose. 'That was some freakin' kick-ass performance.'

'I'm so glad it's over,' she said crisply. 'It was quite an ordeal, but I think we got it.'

'You bet we did,' he crowed. 'Thanks to you.'

'Do I get to shoot someone today?' she asked calmly, quite confident that when the gun was in her hands she could handle it.

'Lara!' Mick exclaimed. 'What happened to you?'

'Oh, I can be tough too,' she said with a wicked grin.

He grinned back. 'Oooh, baby, I get off when you're *bad*.'

'Then I'll try to be bad more often,' she said, still smiling.

'We brought in a weapons expert for the scene today,' Mick said. 'He'll show you how to handle a gun.'

'Joey already did that.'

'Nothin' like expert advice.'

'If you insist,' she said, heading for the make-up trailer, unable to stop thinking about Joey. Last night they'd decided that as soon as the movie was finished they'd take off and get married. He'd made her promise not to mention it to anyone – which wasn't easy because she wanted to tell the world. But he'd convinced her it was the only way if they didn't want a circus.

She hugged the secret to herself and couldn't stop smiling.

☆

Mick was already setting up the first shot when Nikki arrived – later than usual. 'What happened to *you*?' he said cheerfully. 'You're usually the early chick-bird on set.'

'I, uh . . . had a restless night,' she replied, wondering if it was written all over her face that what she'd actually had was great sex with Aiden and then overslept. 'Uh . . . Mick, do you know anything about anyone shooting photos yesterday?'

'"No press allowed" rule. Remember?'

'I heard a rumour someone might have gotten shots of Lara.'

'No way.'

'Are you certain?'

'On my set?' Mick said, arms flailing wildly. 'They would've been spotted and shot on the spot.'

'I guess you're right,' she said unsurely. 'Is Lara here yet?'

'In make-up.'

She headed for the make-up trailer, expecting to find Lara in a bad mood. But to her surprise Lara was smiling and chatting to the make-up woman, looking amazing as usual, in spite of yesterday's ordeal.

'Hi,' Nikki said, not quite sure where they were at.

'Morning,' Lara responded amiably.

'You look great.'

'I *feel* sensational. Now that the rape scene's over I can relax. This was a tough shoot, Nik. But I'm sure it's all going to be worth it.'

'You bet.' A pause. 'Uh, is Joey around?'

'He'll be in at noon. Why?'

'I was out of line yesterday, thought I'd apologize.'

Lara nodded her agreement. 'Truth is, you *both* behaved badly,' she said.

'I know, I know,' Nikki admitted. 'And I'm sorry. It's just that it hasn't been easy, what with Richard obsessing over you, plus my problems with Summer – which I won't even get into.'

'More problems?'

Nikki glanced at the make-up woman diligently doing her job. 'Uh . . . I'll tell you later.'

'How about lunch?' Lara suggested, feeling that maybe she'd been neglecting their friendship.

'Just the two of us?'

'Yes.'

'I'd like that.'

'So would I,' Lara responded warmly. 'It seems we never get a chance to talk any more.'

Nikki leaned over, impulsively kissing her on the cheek. 'You're my best friend,' she said. 'We'll always stick together, huh?'

Lara nodded. 'Of *course* we will, Nik.' And she wished she could confide her secret.

☆

The weapons expert was a beefy ex-cop who turned to mush in Lara's presence. He had difficulty explaining what she had to do, because her closeness rendered him speechless. She was gentle with him – knowing the effect she had on most men. Mick thought it was hilarious.

'Don't you *dare* embarrass him,' she said sternly. 'He's so sweet.'

'Sweet my ass!' Mick guffawed. 'He's a big old hairy pisser who'd jump you soon as look at you!'

Gingerly she held the gun and didn't feel a thing. No bad memories today. Little Lara Ann was safely tucked away in the back of her mind. No visual images of blood and gore and torn flesh . . .

When Joey arrived they embraced, completely oblivious that everyone was watching them.

'I booked the airline tickets,' he said, close to her ear. 'Under assumed names. We leave the morning after you wrap.'

'Shouldn't we wait a couple of days?'

'For what? We gotta do it fast, babe.'

'Where are we going?'

'Tahiti. I heard about a place where nobody'll bother us.'

For a moment she felt a frisson of anxiety. 'You're sure we're not rushing into this?'

'Do you *feel* as if we're rushin'?'

'No.'

'Then why're you givin' me a hard time?'

She smiled softly. 'I *never* give you a hard time.' And she gazed into his eyes and knew it was the right thing to do.

'That's what I like about you,' he said. 'That and your sexy body.'

'Hmm . . . right back at you.'

They both laughed.

'You wait until I get you alone on a tropical island,' he said in a low voice, nuzzling her neck. 'I'm gonna make love to you like you've never been made love to before.'

'You are?' she said, her voice husky with desire.

'Bet on it.' A beat. 'In fact, if we go to your trailer right now . . .'

'Uh . . . Joey, I promised I'd have lunch with Nikki today. You don't mind, do you?'

'Don't wanna have sex with me, huh?' he teased. 'Takin' me for granted.'

'It's just that Nikki needs to talk.'

'As long as you don't plan on telling her.'

She put her arms around his neck and kissed him. 'As if I would.'

He was pissed, although he didn't show it. Nikki had too strong a hold over Lara. Now that he'd made the final commitment he wanted her all to himself with no outside influences.

Still, only a few more days of filming, then she'd be all his, and there'd be nobody around to get in their way.

☆

'I can't believe you threw Richard out,' Lara said, pushing her fork around a bowl of cottage cheese and fruit. 'The two of you seemed so happy.'

'I can't believe it either,' Nikki replied. 'But I always harboured the philosophy that if he screwed around on me, I'd do it back to him.'

Lara shook her head sadly. 'And I thought the three of us would always be such good friends.'

'I'll be honest,' Nikki said, picking at a salad. 'Maybe I could have dealt with his infidelity. The thing I *couldn't* deal with was his obsession with you.'

'He doesn't have an obsession with me,' Lara said, stubbornly refusing to admit what everyone else seemed to know.

'Oh, yes he does,' Nikki insisted. 'I truly believe that if I hadn't asked you to be in *Revenge*, he wouldn't have gotten like this.'

'Could be he's jealous,' Lara said sagely.

'Of *what*?' Nikki snorted.

'Well ... Richard makes big expensive Hollywood movies. *Revenge* is a small, low-budget film – something he'll never get an opportunity to do again. Perhaps, deep down, he'd welcome the chance.'

'Who, Richard?' Nikki said derisively. 'He loves the fame and glory. Big budgets are his life. Surely you know that?'

'I suppose so.'

'The only thing *he's* jealous of is your relationship with Joey.'

'Well ... he'd better learn to accept it if he wants to stay friends.'

'I don't get it,' Nikki sighed. 'Men and their dicks. Is there no way they can keep them zipped up?'

'You *knew* Richard was a risk going in,' Lara said.

'True,' Nikki agreed. 'If he screwed around on you – what made me think *I* had a chance?' She laughed ruefully. 'Dumb me. I guess my ego told me I was different.'

'At least *you* didn't catch him in the act.'

'Small compensation,' she said, sipping a glass of apple juice. 'Anyway, the good news is I had fun with Aiden last night.'

'At last!' Lara exclaimed with a smile. 'Someone *not* old enough to be your father!'

'Yeah,' Nikki said wryly. 'Better I should be with a reformed druggie.'

'As long as he's reformed.'

'He *tells* me he is. Who knows? I'm not planning on sticking around long enough to find out.'

'So,' Lara said, reaching for her sunglasses. 'What's going on with Summer?'

'It's complicated,' Nikki said, not quite sure how much to reveal. 'Well ...' She hesitated a moment before plunging ahead. 'Aiden told me he saw her in a club one night coming on to Mick. Obviously it was before Mick knew who she was.'

'Coming on in what way?'

'How can I put this? She wasn't just flirting. Apparently Mick told Aiden she gave him a blow job in the back of his limo.' Nikki sighed, as if she couldn't quite believe it herself. 'Isn't that nice? Fifteen-year-old girl and crazed director. *My* director.'

'Are you sure?'

'Aiden wouldn't lie. Mick must've gone into shock when he came to my house for dinner and discovered who she was.'

'Did you talk to her?' Lara asked.

'I sent her back to Chicago. Sheldon's in charge, it's not for me to get into.'

'Yes, it is,' Lara said forcefully, remembering her own miserable teenage years. 'If *you* can't talk to her, at least fill Sheldon in. She needs guidance.'

'He'd throw a fit.'

'Don't let it go, Nik. She's only fifteen.'

'I know, I know, I've got to deal with it. Actually – there's more.'

Lara sighed. 'What now?'

'Nothing happened – but she came on to Aiden, too.' A long beat. 'I thought I'd bring her back here at Christmas, spend time with her then.'

'How can you do that if you're with Aiden?' Lara asked, frowning. 'What if this is the start of something you don't want to stop? *That'll* make her feel really comfortable – knowing he's probably told you.'

Nikki shook her head. 'It's not going anywhere with Aiden.'

'How do you know?'

' 'Cause we're too different.'

'Could be a challenge.'

'I've had enough challenges to last a lifetime,' Nikki sighed, pushing her plate away. 'Anyway,' she continued, 'enough about me. How's *your* big romance?'

Lara's face lit up. 'Joey's wonderful,' she said dreamily. 'He makes me feel secure. In fact . . . he makes me feel like I've never felt before.'

'Great sex'll do it every time!'

'Don't you ever think about anything else?'

'Not if I can help it!' Another long pause. 'Y'know, since Joey's obviously a keeper – isn't it time you found out more about him?'

'Why?' Lara said defensively. 'What he did before me has nothing to do with us.'

'I know that. But surely a person's background is important?'

'No,' Lara said firmly. 'The past is exactly that. I know everything I need to know about Joey.'

And Nikki knew it was time to shut up.

☆

Much to Summer's disgust, Chicago was caught in a cold spell. Every time she ventured outdoors she was assaulted by strong winds and sleeting rain. It was bad enough on schooldays – but weekends, too? *Not that I have anywhere to go,* she thought, staring glumly out of her bedroom window, watching the relentless rain dribbling down the window pane, wishing she was still in sunny LA.

She'd been home almost a month, and back in school a week – which was the drag of all time, because she didn't belong any more, she was way ahead of everyone. *I've almost had sex with a movie star*, she wanted to yell at the boys who came chasing after her. *Get lost, you retarded little dicks!*

The only good thing was that since she'd been back, her father hadn't touched her. Rachel kept him so busy that he didn't have time for his nocturnal visits, or maybe he was backing off now that she was old enough to complain.

Not that she'd ever complained. Who would she tell? Her absentee mother, who obviously didn't care? Her step-mother, Rachel? No way.

Her sixteenth birthday was coming up and Rachel had offered to throw her a party. She wasn't sure if she wanted one. Who would she invite? The geeks from school? None of them would be Aiden Sean or Norman Barton – so what was the point?

The night with Norman and Tina remained vivid in her mind. Norman had been so sweet and full of fun. And on top of having a good time, she'd actually gotten paid!

God! How she'd love to tell her father. Let him know that what he took from her without permission, she was now charging for. It would drive him insane, his sweet little girl having sex for money. A fitting punishment for him.

Sometimes she daydreamed about Norman setting her up in her own apartment in LA, visiting once a week and paying all the bills. What an awesome trip that would be!

The fact that her mother had shipped her back to Chicago without giving her a chance to contact him wasn't fair. She'd spoken to Tina a few times. 'Get your butt back here,' Tina had said. 'There's money to be made and mucho babes *panting* to pay us.'

'I'm trying,' she'd said.

'Try harder,' Tina insisted.

Rachel knocked and poked her head around the door. She was pretty, but not in a Hollywood way – she had none of the dazzle and style of Tina or Darlene. Actually she resembled a very young Nikki.

'What are you doing?' Rachel asked.

'Nothing much,' Summer replied listlessly.

'Want to go shopping? Spend a little of your daddy's hard-earned cash?'

'I'm always up for that,' Summer said, trying to dredge up some enthusiasm.

'Let's go, then,' Rachel said. 'I'll meet you by the car in five minutes.'

Summer peered at herself in the mirror. Her tan was fading, which really pissed her off because she didn't look half as good without a tan. Would Norman still like her all pale-faced and miserable?

She thought about Tina and Jed and the group of friends she'd hung with at the beach. Most of all she thought about Norman, and his cute puppy dog smile. They made a perfect couple.

What a blast she'd had in California. Why did she have to be stuck in Chicago?

And the big question – what was she going to do if her father ever came near her again?

52

For several days Nikki managed to avoid having contact with Aiden, until one afternoon he cornered her on the set. She didn't know what to say, everything had happened so fast the other night, and when she'd awoken in the morning, he was gone.

'*Finally*,' he said, looking perplexed.

'Oh, hi,' she said, quite flustered.

He leaned close, speaking intimately in her ear. 'You were somethin' the other night. A real wild woman!'

'I don't regret it, Aiden,' she said quickly, backing away, 'only please – take it as a one-off.'

He regarded her through narrowed eyes. 'A one-off?'

'It's too difficult for me right now.'

'I'm not askin' you to *marry* me, Nikki,' he said, his mouth curving into a thin smile.

'Gee – thanks. What *are* you asking for?'

He gave a noncommittal shrug. 'Thought you'd drop by my place later – fix a hungry man dinner.'

Well, he certainly had nerve. 'You thought that, did you?' she said, irritated.

'Don't you wanna see how the other half lives? Not everyone has a beach house in Malibu.'

'And what would I cook for you?'

'Pasta, a steak, whatever you're into.'

'Tempting offer. I'm passing.'

'Didn't imagine you'd say yes.'

His tone of voice indicated she was predictable. 'What does *that* mean?' she asked, a little bit angry.

'Nothing,' he said vaguely.

'No,' she said heatedly, 'I want to know what you meant.'

'It's your vibe.'

'What *vibe*?'

'Like you're only into money.'

'That's the *last* thing I'm into,' she said indignantly. 'The very last thing.'

'You married two rich guys, didn't you? The shrink in Chicago must have big bucks, and Richard's not exactly hurting.'

'Money has nothing to do with any of my relationships,' she said stiffly.

'Then come spend the night with a bum actor. I won't invite you again.'

'Fine, I'll be there.' And as she said it, she realized he'd caught her in a trap.

☆

Lara decided to surprise Joey when they returned from their honeymoon. She knew how much he loved the ocean, and when they were married it seemed like a great idea for them to have a romantic hideaway to run to whenever they needed to be alone. A year ago she'd rented at the beach for the summer – an old-fashioned Cape Cod style house perched on the edge of a bluff overlooking the ocean, located past Point Dume, and quite remote. She'd loved it so much that she'd tried to buy it. At the time it wasn't for sale. Recently she'd heard it was on the market, and she'd instructed her business manager to make an offer. The offer had been accepted, and the house was now hers, but she wasn't going to tell Joey until they got back. It would be her wedding present to him.

The only two people who knew about it were her business manager and Cassie, and she'd sworn them both to secrecy.

Thank God nobody had any clue that she and Joey were planning on getting married. She could just imagine the furore if it became public knowledge. Her lawyer would insist on a prenuptial and everyone else would worry that Joey was after her money.

How could people enter into a marriage like that? This wasn't a monetary deal. This was two people getting married because they loved each other.

The wonderful thing about Joey's love was that it had

nothing to do with her being a movie star and all the trappings. He wasn't interested in publicity or being seen with her, he preferred the simple pleasures of life. And great loving insane sex.

Every time she thought about the sex she became aroused. She'd never encountered a man who could turn her on the way Joey did, one glance and she was his. Richard was right about her not being exciting enough in bed – with him she probably hadn't been, because the magic hadn't existed. Joey had the magic. And as far as she was concerned, they'd be together for ever.

☆

Later, Nikki rode in Aiden's truck to his apartment, stopping at a supermarket on the way to pick up a couple of steaks and some salad.

They stood side by side at the checkout line. When it was time to pay she waited for Aiden to make a move. He made no attempt to do so. 'I don't know why I'm doing this,' she grumbled, fishing out her credit card.

'Yes, you do,' he said, picking up the grocery bag and carrying it to his truck. ''Cause you want to.'

'No, I don't,' she responded, trailing after him. 'I told you – what we had was a one-off.'

'Glad I made such an impression,' he said, throwing open the passenger door.

'I'll fix you a steak,' she said, climbing into his truck, 'then I have to go home. Richard's bugging me, I think it's time I spoke to my lawyer.'

'You're going for a divorce?'

'That's the plan.'

His apartment was a dump. She walked around in shock. 'How can you live like this?' she demanded.

'Wanna move me into the beach house?' he joked.

'Yeah, right,' she said, inspecting the tiny kitchen, noticing that the grill had not been cleaned in months. 'No maid service?'

'Doesn't cut it, does she?' he said, ruefully.

'*That's* the understatement of the year,' Nikki replied, going to work – cleaning the grill, washing the steaks and placing them on it.

While the meat was cooking she chopped up tomatoes, lettuce and cucumbers, tossing everything into a big wooden bowl. 'Where's your olive oil?'

'You think I cook?'

'How am I supposed to fix a salad dressing? You'd better run out and pick up a bottle.'

'Jeez! This is so friggin' domesticated,' he complained, but he went anyway.

As soon as he left she took a more thorough look around. Aiden was obviously not into possessions. His bed was a futon on the floor, his closet was almost empty, and the only personal things were stacks of scripts piled everywhere. What kind of man was he, anyway? Interesting for sure. Different. And a pretty sensational lover.

She couldn't help herself, she opened the top drawer of his dresser just out of curiosity. Tons of mismatched socks, all mixed up. And a gun.

She shut the drawer as quickly as she'd opened it. Dangerous territory. What was Aiden doing with a gun?

I am not getting involved, she told herself sternly. *No way.*

By the time he got back the steaks were nearly done. 'Clear some of those scripts off the table, and we'll eat,' she said, searching in a cupboard for a bottle of steak sauce. 'Then I'd appreciate it if you'd drive me back to my car.'

'You're really pissy for somebody who had great sex,' he remarked. 'One orgasm doesn't do it for you, huh?'

'I hate to burst your ego,' she said quickly. 'It didn't mean a thing.'

'No?'

'I can be exactly like a guy in that respect.'

'Fuck and run, huh?'

'I've always thought that anything a man can do, a woman can too. It was retribution – pure and simple.'

'Oh, I get it,' he said, a little bit pissed off. 'It was a revenge fuck. And the fact that you and I have this kind of electric thing between us had nothing to do with it – am I right?'

'What *are* you talking about?'

'I'm talking about hot . . . lustful . . . *sex.*'

And before she could stop him, he spun her around and grabbed her, pressing his lips down on hers, his hungry mouth devouring her, while the steaks burned on the grill and neither of them cared.

She made a feeble attempt to push him off.

It was useless. She was as into it as he was.

☆

Shopping with Rachel was fun, although not as much fun as cruising Melrose with Tina. Summer yearned for LA. It was like a sickness, being there was all she could think about as she trailed Rachel through Saks. Rachel spent Daddy Dearest's money at a pretty fast pace – throwing her credit card in Summer's direction whenever she needed it.

Idly Summer wondered what Rachel would do if she told her the truth. Freak out and cry. She didn't have much backbone.

When she got home she called Tina again and they had the same old conversation. 'When are you coming back?' Tina demanded.

'Maybe for Christmas. I'll be sixteen then. If things work out I can stay.'

'Darlene says you got rave reviews from Norman. He keeps asking where you are.'

'Wow!' she said. Norman Barton, an actual movie star, wondering where she was. This was too amazing!

A few days later Rachel came into her room crying. 'It's my mother,' Rachel sniffed. 'She's sick. I have to fly to Florida.'

'Want me to come with you?' Summer offered.

'No, I'll be all right.'

Summer didn't much care if Rachel would be all right or not, she dreaded being left alone in the house with her father. It had been over a year since he'd touched her, but what if he started again?

Rachel departed the next morning. Summer watched her go from her bedroom window, fervently hoping she'd be back soon.

An hour later she set off for school, but before she could make a clean getaway her father strode out of his study, blocking her by the front door. 'You and I will dine together tonight,' he said. 'The two of us – it'll be like old times, sweet pea.'

'Uh . . . I already have a date, Daddy,' she stammered – the words 'like old times' striking fear within her.

Sheldon did not look pleased. 'Who's the lucky young man?' he demanded.

'A boy at school,' she lied.

Sheldon stared at her for a moment, his thin lips twitching. 'I would like to meet him,' he said. 'Make sure you bring him in when he collects you.'

Oh no! What was she going to do now?

As soon as she got to school she approached Stuart, the school geek, who had a mammoth crush on her. 'Wanna go to a movie tonight?' she asked, cornering him by the lockers.

Stuart swallowed three times, so impressed was he by the invitation. 'Y . . . yes,' he stammered.

'OK, pick me up at seven, and don't make me wait around.'

Stuart was right on time, washed and brushed and eager as a frisky race horse. Summer marched him in to meet her father.

Sheldon looked him over with a cold eye. 'Be sure to have my daughter home by ten. And no monkey business.'

Monkey business! Was her father under the impression they were living in 1960?

'Yes, sir!' Stuart said, standing ramrod straight.

Ass-kisser, Summer thought.

Stuart took her to an action adventure epic starring Jean-Claude Van Damme. Halfway through the movie he attempted to hold her hand.

She snatched it away. 'Like get a life, Stuart,' she said in disgust, crushing any hope he might have had.

After the movie, they stopped for a hamburger and milkshake. Summer wolfed her burger, sipped her milkshake and barely spoke to Stuart. When they were finished he drove her home in his secondhand Buick.

She got rid of him with a brusque, 'G'night,' and rushed inside.

Her father was waiting in the front hall – a bad sign.

'Did you have a nice evening, dear?' he asked, puffing on a big stinky cigar.

'I'm really tired,' she said, feigning a yawn.

'I want to talk to you,' he responded. 'Come into my study.'

She didn't want to talk to him. She didn't want to be alone in the house with him. She didn't want to ever see him again.

Unfortunately she had no choice, so she reluctantly trailed him into his study.

'We haven't had much opportunity to chat since you got back,' he said, reaching for a glass of brandy – a *really* bad sign. 'Sit down, dear, and relax.'

She balanced uncomfortably on the edge of one of his stiff leather chairs, while he settled behind his desk, slugging back big gulps of brandy. 'You know, Summer,' he said, 'since you returned from California, you haven't been the same.'

'Yes, I have,' she answered defiantly.

'There's something different about you. I sense an unrest.'

'No, there's not.'

'I'm a professional when it comes to human behaviour, dear, and I feel that being with your mother was not good for you. She's hardly a positive influence.' A long pause. 'You see, I care about you, Summer. I should have insisted you came to the Bahamas with Rachel and me, instead of running off to LA.'

Ha! If he cared about her so much, how come he'd done all those vile things to her while she was growing up?

He refilled his brandy glass, fixing her with a penetrating stare. 'Did you go out with boys in LA, Summer?'

'I ... uh ... I dated a bit,' she stammered, wondering where this was leading. 'I'm nearly sixteen. I can do that.'

'I *know* how old you are,' he said sonorously. 'You're my daughter.'

'I'm allowed to date, aren't I?' she said boldly. 'Everyone else does.'

'I don't care what everyone else does.' Another sip of brandy. 'Tell me, pumpkin. Do these boys you go out with try to get fresh with you?'

Wow, he really is living in the sixties. 'No,' she lied, saying what he wanted to hear. 'I never let them touch me.'

He puffed on his cigar. 'How about kissing?'

'No ... I don't let them kiss me either.'

He nodded to himself, satisfied with her reply. 'You're a good girl, Summer,' he said. 'I always knew you were a good girl.'

She twisted restlessly in her chair, hating every minute of this stupid inquisition. 'Can I go to bed now, Daddy?' she asked, biting her nails. 'I'm really tired.'

He nodded again, and before he could stop her, she leaped up and ran upstairs without looking back.

There was a lock on her bedroom door, but no key. Where was the key? She searched frantically, but couldn't find it.

She was scared, for tonight he was bound to come to her room, she'd recognized that horrible look in his eyes. And yet – if he dared to do so, she was determined to repel him, because she didn't have to take it any more, there were laws against incest and sexual abuse. Besides, she was big enough to fight back.

She quickly put on her pyjamas and got into bed, pulling the covers up around her neck, watching television until she fell into an uneasy sleep.

She didn't know how late it was when she heard the click of her door opening. By the time she was fully awake, he was sitting on the side of her bed stinking of expensive cigars and too much brandy. *He always has to have alcohol*, she thought, her heart sinking. Alcohol and abuse. The two had gone together for as long as she could remember.

'Wass it like, kitten,' he asked, slurring his words, 'when boys kiss you? Whyn't you show Daddy 'xactly how they do it?'

'Daddy,' she said, reverting to the frightened little girl she once was, 'please don't do this any more. *Please*, Daddy, you know it's not right.'

'*C'mon*, sweet pea,' he mumbled, 'tell me what boys do to you. Do they put their tongue in your mouth? Touch your breasts? Your vagina? All your private places.' His big clumsy hands began unbuttoning her pyjama top. 'You can tell Daddy. Daddy's entitled to know.'

'No!' she shrieked, shrinking away from him. 'I warned you – you can't do this to me any more!'

'Wassamatter?' he slurred, his big hands fondling her breasts. 'Aren't you Daddy's little angel any more?'

'No! No! No!' she yelled, shoving him away with all her strength.

'But Daddy loves you,' he said, brandy breath enveloping her. 'You're my baby. My own little baby girly.'

And as his hands started to fondle her again, she leaped from her bed, raced into the bathroom, slamming and locking the door in his face.

Then she slid to the floor and burst into tears.

Enough was enough. She had to get out.

53

Alison Sewell had more money than she'd ever dreamed of. Her photographs of Lara Ivory were making her a fortune – especially the more explicit ones, too detailed for a weekly tabloid. Although she didn't believe in sharing her new-found wealth, she'd gone to an agent who specialized in selling the more sensational type of photos. He'd cut a deal with one of the monthly men's magazines, and now she was about to become even richer.

How proud Uncle Cyril would be of her. She regretted his demise *and* the death of her mother, who'd always said she'd never do as well as Uncle Cyril. She'd shown both of them. Pity they were ten feet under.

Now that she had Lara Ivory back in her sights, she thirsted for more. Staking out her house from a distance – because it wouldn't do to get thrown back in jail – she'd soon observed there was a new man in residence.

Tramp! Did she have to sleep with everyone?

Alison soon found out who he was. Joey Lorenzo – some small-time actor. He was good-looking. Big deal. Alison hated him too.

She kept far enough away that they couldn't spot her, and took a series of pictures of them coming and going.

While she was waiting for *Truth and Fact* to run, she discovered that if she climbed a nearby tree she could get a clear shot into Lara's bedroom. This so excited her that she nearly fell out of the tree, only saving herself by clinging to a protruding branch.

She called her new-found agent. 'What if I can get shots of Lara Ivory screwing her boyfriend?'

He promised her a hefty cheque and a Cadillac. Incredible! Uncle Cyril had never gotten a Cadillac.

The night before *Truth and Fact* hit the stands she almost got the shot. Lara and Joey were in the bedroom, talking; then Lara walked into the bathroom, and Joey pulled off his T-shirt.

Click. Click. This was shaping up nicely.

Joey began flexing his muscles. *Click click click.*

He walked toward the window. Even better.

He pulled down the shades.

Bastard! How could he do such a thing?

But she'd get 'em, no doubt about that. All she needed was patience.

If there was one thing Alison excelled at, it was waiting around.

54

Early Friday morning, photos of Lara taken from the set during the rape scene were front page on *Truth and Fact* – a particularly down and dirty tabloid.

Lara Ivory – skirt up around her waist.

Lara Ivory – topless.

Lara Ivory – lying in the gutter almost totally naked.

Nikki was the first to see them, because when she woke up in Aiden's rumpled bed and checked with her answering machine at home, there were several messages from an angry Richard yelling and carrying on.

She immediately woke Aiden and asked him to run out and get her a copy of the paper. He pulled on his jeans and obliged.

When he came back and handed her the offending tabloid she stared at it in horror. For once Richard's information was right. Somebody had gotten extremely graphic photographs of Lara.

Aiden inspected the photos over her shoulder. 'Hey, we should've been paid for these,' he remarked, like it was no big deal. 'I don't show off my ass for free.'

'Lara will freak,' Nikki groaned, dismayed. 'I'd better call Mick, find out how this happened.'

'It doesn't matter,' Aiden said. 'The photos are out there now. Look at it as good publicity for the movie.'

'You don't understand,' Nikki said. '*I* feel responsible. I should've posted guards on the set.'

'Fuck it,' Aiden said. 'I never believe anything I read, you shouldn't either.'

'It's not a question of believing. The pictures are *there* for everyone to see,' she said, reaching for the phone. 'I have to tell her myself.'

Mrs Crenshaw answered, informing her that Lara had already left and was on her way to work.

'I've got to go,' Nikki said, frantically gathering up her clothes from the floor and quickly dressing.

'I'll drive you,' Aiden offered.

She nodded. 'Can you break speed records? I have to get to her first.'

'We're on our way,' he said. 'I'm gonna give you the second greatest thrill ride of your life!'

☆

'Come in, make yourself comfortable,' Richard Barry said, ushering Madelaine Francis into his bungalow at the Beverly Hills Hotel.

'This is quite lovely,' Madelaine said, inspecting every detail.

'They recently refurbished the hotel,' Richard said. 'I like hotel living. Takes a lot of the daily responsibility out of life.'

'I thought you were married,' Madelaine remarked, placing her Prada purse on a table.

'Separated,' Richard replied, heading for the phone. 'What can I get you?'

'A decaf cappuccino would be nice.'

'Two decaf cappuccinos,' Richard said into the receiver.

Madelaine sat down. There was something vaguely familiar about Richard Barry, she felt as if they'd met before. But she couldn't remember where or when, which irritated her, because she prided herself on a brilliant memory. Of course, he was a famous director, so maybe he struck her as familiar because she'd seen his photo and read about his movies over the years. Yes, she decided, that was it.

True to his word, he'd made all the arrangements to fly her to LA. She'd arrived yesterday from New York, and was staying at the Beverly Regent Hotel for three nights. Well aware that this free trip had something to do with Joey, she was most curious to find out what. Patting her briefcase she said, 'I've brought tapes of several young actors whose talent I'm sure you'll appreciate. And if you care to see any of them in person, I can arrange to fly them out. Shall we view the tapes now?'

'No,' Richard said, wasting no time. 'Put them on the table. I'll take a look with my people later.'

'They're for you to keep,' Madelaine said. 'I had copies made.'

'You're very organized.'

'I have to be in my business,' she replied, thinking how charming and attractive he was – not what she'd expected at all.

'So,' he said, getting right to it, 'tell me about Joey Lorenzo.'

'What is it you wish to know?' she asked carefully.

Richard fixed her with a purposeful gaze. 'Everything,' he said.

For one wild moment she wondered if he was gay, and *that's* why he wanted information on Joey.

No. At one time he'd been married to Lara Ivory, and was now married to Nikki Barry, the costume designer, so he couldn't possibly be gay. Although you never knew in Hollywood, there were always surprises.

'Everything is a very all-encompassing word,' she said slowly.

'I'll be truthful with you, Ms Francis—' he began.

'Please call me Madelaine,' she interrupted.

'OK, Madelaine, allow me to be frank. I'm looking forward to seeing the tapes of your actors, and I'm sure that sometime in the future we'll do business together. But right now I have a problem with Joey Lorenzo, and I need information.'

'You do?' she said, wondering if Joey had stolen money from him, too. 'And what might that problem be?'

'Unfortunately he's attached himself to my wife,' Richard said, his face grim.

'Oh,' Madelaine said, quite surprised.

'Nobody seems to know anything about him,' Richard continued. 'And the truth is – I'm extremely concerned.'

And so you should be, Madelaine thought. *Joey Lorenzo is a thieving sonofabitch*. 'Did he meet Mrs Barry on a movie?' she asked politely.

'It's not Nikki he's with,' Richard answered impatiently. 'It's my ex-wife, Lara Ivory.'

For a moment Madelaine was completely speechless.

Joey with Lara Ivory? Impossible!

Then she thought about it and suddenly everything made sense. Joey was devastatingly handsome with charm to spare – not to mention sensational in bed. Women chased him wherever he went. Why *wouldn't* Lara Ivory want him?

'I . . . I don't know what to say,' she said, shaking her head. 'Joey's quite volatile. You're right to be apprehensive.'

Richard leaned towards her. 'Can I ask you an extremely personal question, Madelaine?'

'I suppose so,' she said, thinking it wasn't fair. How could she, Madelaine Francis, compete with one of the most beautiful women in the world? Not that she wanted him back, no way.

His voice was low and intent. 'Did you and Joey have an intimate relationship?'

She felt herself blushing. 'Look, Mr Barry, I realize Joey's quite a bit younger than me, but . . . sometimes, men of my age only want twenty-two-year-olds.' A long pause. 'Yes,' she admitted, refusing to make any more excuses. 'Joey was there, and very responsive. We lived together for a while.'

Right, Richard thought triumphantly. *He's the hustler I imagined he was. Living with an older agent to further his career. Madelaine Francis has to be at least twenty years his senior, and she's hardly Jane Fonda.*

The room service waiter knocked on the door and delivered two cappuccinos. Richard signed the check.

'Can I get you anything else, Mr Barry?' the waiter asked hopefully – really wanting to say— 'Will you read my screenplay? I act, too.'

'No,' Richard said curtly.

Reluctantly the waiter left the room. As soon as he was gone Richard turned back to Madelaine.

'Exactly how long were you and Joey together?' he asked, his voice tense.

She hesitated for a few seconds, then decided that she might as well tell him *something*, after all she had nothing to lose and everything to gain if she could win Richard Barry's friendship. 'Joey was twenty-four when we first met,' she began, remembering the moment only too well. 'He was a young actor trying to make it in New York and not getting very far.' She let out a long weary sigh. 'Believe me, I did plenty for him. Landed him a substantial role in *Solid*, a movie for which he received fabulous reviews. After that stellar beginning his career was all set to rise. Then he vanished.'

'What do you mean – vanished?' Richard asked, his interest aroused.

'He left town,' Madelaine said, sipping her cappuccino. 'Nobody heard from him. Nobody knew where he'd gone. Six years later he reappeared, told me he'd had family problems. Like a fool I took him back, and shortly after, I sent him up for the role in *The Dreamer*, where he obviously met your ex-wife. That's the last I saw of him.'

Richard drummed his fingers on the edge of his chair. 'Where was he for those six years?'

Madelaine shook her head. 'I have no idea.'

'What about his fiancée?'

'Fiancée?' she said, frowning. 'I know nothing of a fiancée.'

'He told everyone on *The Dreamer* he was engaged.'

'To whom?'

'A woman called Phillipa?'

'Knowing Joey – my guess is he probably made it up to make him appear more substantial.'

'He'd do something like that?'

She gave a bitter laugh. 'Joey would do anything.'

'Didn't you ever try to find him when he ran off?'

She shrugged. 'Not my style, Mr Barry. I'm hardly a detective.'

'Were you living with him when he made *The Dreamer*?'

She nodded, her anger building. Dumped twice. It wasn't fair. Joey Lorenzo was a cheating no-good bastard and she hated him for the way he'd played her.

She managed to hold her anger in check, it wouldn't do to let Richard Barry know how dumb she'd been. 'Perhaps, Mr Barry, you can do *me* a favour,' she said, fumbling in her purse for a cigarette, desperate for a nicotine fix.

'What would that be?'

'Give me Joey's address. There's a business matter I need to discuss with him.'

Richard leaned over and lit her cigarette, noting her

trembling hands. He felt sorry for her, she was his age, but everyone knew it was different for men. Men could get away with going out with girls twenty or thirty years younger than them, and nobody said a word. However, if a woman did it, she was considered a pathetic old desperado.

'He's living with my ex-wife,' Richard said. 'He's also in the movie she's shooting – *Revenge* – a low-budget piece of crap. I'll give you her number. In fact,' he added, as if the thought had only just occurred to him, 'it might be helpful if you told her personally about you and Joey.'

'I can do that,' Madelaine offered, filling her lungs with soothing smoke. *I'd love to do that.*

'Lara knows nothing about him,' Richard continued. 'If she did, maybe she'd see things more clearly.'

'Perhaps you'd like to arrange a meeting between us,' Madelaine suggested helpfully. 'I'm available.'

Hmm, Richard thought, *nothing like a cooperative vengeful woman.* 'As a matter of fact,' he said, 'I'm visiting the set this morning. Would you have time to come with me?'

'I'm sure I can make time.'

'Good.'

Madelaine Francis understood exactly what Richard Barry wanted her to do. And, she decided, it would be her pleasure. Her own personal way of getting back at Joey.

55

Linden, Lara's publicist, got to her before anyone else, handing her the offending tabloid in the privacy of her trailer. She stared at the two-page spread of revealing photographs and felt sick. Who'd allowed a photographer to capture the most intimate of scenes? Why wasn't anyone protecting her?

'I don't believe this!' she said, utterly dismayed. 'How can this have happened?'

'Somebody on the set with a hidden camera,' Linden replied. 'Mick or Nikki should've had everyone on alert. If they'd been aware – this couldn't't've been done.'

'It's simply not fair,' she whispered, her voice breaking. 'I feel so, so . . . *violated*.'

'It's a scene from a movie, Lara,' Linden said, trying to reassure her. 'It's certainly not you.'

'Of course it's me,' she answered vehemently, eyes flashing danger. 'You'd need a magnifying glass to read the small print that says the photos are from a movie.'

'I'll get into damage control. We'll put a whole other spin on this story.'

'How do I know they didn't release these pictures to get publicity for *Revenge*?' she asked flatly.

'You think Nikki would do that?'

'I don't know *what* to think any more,' she replied, feeling totally betrayed. 'Richard was right, he said they were using me. So did Joey.'

'There's nothing you can do about it now,' Linden said, taking the tabloid out of her hands. 'The best thing is to ignore it.'

'Thanks a lot,' she said, indignantly. 'You try ignoring it if these pictures were of you.'

'I don't think anyone would pay to see me in the buff,' he deadpanned.

'It's not funny, Linden.'

'I know, I know. Honestly Lara, I understand how difficult it is for you.'

No, you don't, she wanted to respond. *You have no idea what it's like to be humiliated this way. Reduced to nothing more than tits and ass.*

'OK,' she said, dismissing him. 'Go do damage control.'

He nodded. 'I'll check with you later.'

When he was gone she sat down, wondering how she was going to explain it to Joey. He was at an all-day photo shoot, so hopefully no one would mention it to him. She'd tell him tonight when she'd calmed down.

Shortly after Linden left, Nikki arrived. Lara didn't take a beat. 'What in hell happened?' she demanded coldly. 'How did these pictures get out?'

'Oh, God!' Nikki groaned. 'You saw them.'

'*Saw* them? I've had Quinn on the phone doing his "I told you so" number. Thank God Joey hasn't seen them yet, he'll go ballistic when he does. Richard's on his way over.'

Nikki could barely contain her annoyance. 'Why?'

'Because he called and I asked him to,' Lara answered defiantly. 'He *cares* about what goes on in my life, unlike *some* people.'

'I'm so sorry,' Nikki apologized. 'I don't know how anybody could've gotten those shots.'

'When I agreed to make *Revenge*, I expected to be protected,' Lara said, her voice an icy blast. 'The studios always protect me. Why can't you?'

'Believe me,' Nikki said earnestly. 'It's not my fault.'

'*You're* the producer of *Revenge*, that makes the responsibility yours.'

'Can't argue with that,' Nikki said sheepishly.

'Quinn's furious. He says this could have a very negative effect on my career.'

'I'm sure he's overreacting.'

'I understand your ambition, Nikki,' Lara continued. 'But I didn't expect I was the one who'd end up getting used.'

'Now you're being unfair.'

'I'm too angry to be fair,' Lara responded. 'I mean, how

would you like to be out there in the tabloids – naked for everyone to see? I've never done nude photographs in my life, and now I find myself in this position because of your damn movie.'

Richard arrived shortly after, just as Nikki was leaving the trailer. They exchanged abrupt hellos.

He hurried over to Lara, put his arms around her and held her close, breathing in her seductive scent. 'Wouldn't listen to me, would you?' he said, hugging her tightly.

She pulled away with a helpless shrug. 'What can I say? You were right.'

'If it had been my set, you can rest assured it would never have happened.'

'I know,' she said ruefully.

'This is what you get when you work with amateurs.'

'I guess so,' she replied, sitting down. 'Thanks for coming, Richard, it means a lot to me.'

'Sweetheart, I have only your best interests at heart.'

'I know.'

'You're on my mind all the time.' He paused, gauging her mood. 'I'm sure you know the main reason Nikki and I are no longer together is because you and I still have a very special connection? A connection that can never be broken.'

'Don't start, Richard—' she said, hoping he wasn't going to get too caught up in this.

'No,' he said sharply, 'hear me out, Lara. Screwing around on you was the biggest mistake of my life. And I want you to know that if you can ever forgive me, and think about us getting back together, then I'm always here for you.'

'That's very flattering,' she said, picking up a cold mug of tea and sipping it anyway. 'But, Richard, I'm with somebody now. I'm very involved.'

'How involved?'

'Well . . .' She hesitated for a moment. 'Joey and I are thinking of getting married, only please keep it to yourself. No one knows.'

He stared into her clear green eyes and wondered how someone so beautiful and nice could be so fucking naive. 'Are you serious?' he said disbelievingly.

She nodded. 'Very.'

'Listen to me carefully, Lara,' he said in measured tones. 'I warned you what would happen on this movie. Now I'm warning you what will happen if you marry Joey.'

Why did he always have to try to run her life? Why couldn't he just be her friend? 'Richard,' she said, attempting to remain calm, 'please don't tell me what to do, because it's really none of your business.'

He began pacing. 'Did Joey ever mention Madelaine Francis?'

She shook her head.

'He used to live with her – in fact, he was with her when he met you.' He checked out her reaction. She looked surprised. 'You should talk to Madelaine,' he added, striking fast.

'Why would I want to do that?' she asked, her eyes two stubborn pinpoints of light.

He kept going, knowing exactly how to get to her. 'Scared of what you might find out?' he challenged.

She stood up, wishing he'd leave. 'This is ridiculous,' she said impatiently.

'Do it for me, sweetheart,' he said, using his best powers of persuasion. 'Meet the woman, if only for a few minutes.'

'There's no reason—'

'For old times, Lara.'

'Oh, all right,' she said, agreeing reluctantly, her curiosity aroused. 'But I can assure you, it won't make any difference.'

He smiled to himself. *Wanna bet?* 'She's in my car,' he said. 'I'll go fetch her.'

56

Greg Gorman was a master photographer with several coffee-table books full of photos of stars. Joey was impressed. And the good thing was that Greg liked him, encouraged him to shine. So there he was in Greg's Beverly Boulevard studio, centre stage, under the lights, the camera clicking away, and Toni Braxton belting out a sexy love song on the stereo.

Joey got off on being the centre of attention. Getting primped and fussed over was his idea of a good time. And the good news was he hadn't even had to pay for the session, because Lara had spoken to an executive at Orpheus Studios – the studio responsible for *The Dreamer* – and gotten them to pay for it.

Greg stopped to change film, and the make-up person, hairdresser and stylist all descended on Joey at once.

This is how it should be, he reflected. *Me – on a star trip. It's about time.*

He grinned and stretched. He had a career. He had a fantastic woman he planned to marry. After all the shit, things were finally turning his way.

☆

Richard ushered Madelaine into Lara's trailer. She was sitting on the banquette seating, tapping her fingers impatiently on a plastic table. 'Hi,' she said, a little cold and a little tense.

'Hi, honey,' Richard said warmly. 'Say hello to Madelaine Francis.'

Lara nodded brusquely.

Madelaine stared at the beautiful actress. She was even more gorgeous in the flesh than on the screen.

Richard edged towards the door. 'Why don't I leave you two alone,' he suggested.

'Fine,' Lara replied, wondering why she'd agreed to do this. Oh yes, she knew – Richard and his persuasive ways had struck again.

As soon as he was gone, she shifted uncomfortably. 'I feel most awkward about this,' she said.

'So do I,' Madelaine agreed.

'It's Richard's idea,' she added. 'And quite frankly, if you have anything to say about Joey, I think he should be here to listen.'

'Wouldn't bother me,' Madelaine said, sitting down. 'In fact, he *should* be here.'

'Richard doesn't like Joey,' Lara stated with a weary sigh. 'He's busy digging for dirt.'

'Perhaps he's trying to protect you.'

'From what?' she answered sharply, appalled at the woman's nerve.

'Just a thought,' Madelaine murmured.

'Anyway, how do *you* fit into this?' Lara asked, her tone abrupt. 'Did you know Joey's fiancée?'

'Why does everyone keep mentioning a fiancée?' Madelaine said, irritably. 'When I got him the part in *The Dreamer*, he was living with *me*.'

'You?' Lara said, hardly able to conceal her surprise. The woman was old enough to be his mother. 'When Joey and I met, he was engaged to a girl called Phillipa. Are you Phillipa?'

'No,' Madelaine said, adding a dry— 'And I'm not a girl, as you've probably noticed.'

'I didn't mean—'

'Look, Miss Ivory,' Madelaine said brusquely, 'Joey Lorenzo and I were lovers until he met you. After that, it appears I was no longer useful.'

Lara took a long deep breath. *Why is this happening to me?* she thought. *Why?*

Because you're an ugly little slut and you don't deserve any happiness.

Her father's words came back to haunt her. So harsh. So unforgettable.

'Did Richard put you up to this?' she asked at last.

'Not at all,' Madelaine said. 'I've been an agent for twenty-five years, I have an impeccable reputation. You can ask anyone about me.' She began searching in her purse for a cigarette. 'Mind if I smoke?'

'Go ahead,' Lara said flatly.

'Unfortunately, several years ago I foolishly got involved with Joey,' Madelaine said, lighting up. 'We were together almost a year, then he took off for six years. I have no idea where he went. When he returned, he moved back into my apartment.' She dragged deeply on her cigarette. 'And this is something I *didn't* tell your ex – when Joey left the first time, he stole seven thousand dollars of my money.'

Lara felt a queasy sensation in the pit of her stomach. Instinct told her this woman was speaking the truth. 'What about Phillipa?' she asked in a strained voice.

'There *is* no Phillipa,' Madelaine said, waving her cigarette in the air. 'He made her up. Joey has a very lively imagination.'

'Why . . . why would he do that?' Lara stammered.

'Who knows with Joey? I can only assume he didn't want to tell you about me.'

'He could have,' Lara said bravely. 'There's nothing wrong with living with an older woman—'

'Be realistic, dear,' Madelaine interrupted. 'He was with me for what I could do for him. The ungrateful bastard *stole* my money, and *I* let him get away with it. If you'd found that out, you might have regarded him differently.'

Lara got up and began wandering aimlessly around the trailer. 'What else do you know about him?' she asked.

'Not very much. Joey was always secretive about his background – didn't want me prying.'

Lara remembered the number she'd called in New York – Phillipa's number. If it was the same as Madelaine's that definitely meant she was telling the truth. She asked Madelaine for her home number, then buzzed Cassie and had her check it with the call sheet from *The Dreamer*.

It was the same number.

She turned back to Madelaine. 'Are you sure he stole your money?'

Madelaine nodded. 'No doubt about it. When he returned, he gave me back three thousand dollars. The rest

I recovered from the cheque he got from his work on *The Dreamer*.'

Lara's mind was in turmoil. So Joey – *her* Joey – was nothing more than a cheap opportunist – a thief who used women for what he could get out of them. Her head was spinning. 'I ... I don't know what to say, Ms Francis ... this is information I'd sooner not have heard. But now that you've told me, I suppose I'll have to deal with it.'

'I understand,' Madelaine said, bobbing her head sympathetically. 'It's not easy. Joey's *very* charming, he has the knack. And of course he's also an extremely talented lover – as I'm sure you know. When Joey makes love to you, you feel as if you're the only woman in the world.' She chuckled wryly. 'And believe me – at my age, that's quite a feat.'

'I'm sure,' Lara murmured, while her idyllic world spun out of control, crashing around her in tiny fragmented pieces.

☆

Early in the morning Summer complained of a stomach ache, staying safely in bed until her father had departed for his office. As soon as she heard his car leave the garage, she leaped out of bed and raced downstairs.

Mrs Stern, their housekeeper, regarded her in surprise. 'I thought you weren't feeling well, missy,' she said accusingly.

'I'm much better now,' Summer said, all blond innocence. 'Gotta get to school. Major test today.'

'Shall I prepare your breakfast?'

'No, thanks, Mrs Stern.'

'If you're sure ...'

'Absolutely.' A very brief pause, then— 'I think I left some of my school work in Daddy's study. I'd better go take a look.' She dashed into his private domain, slamming the door behind her. As soon as she was sure Mrs Stern wasn't about to follow her, she began searching his desk. Tina had the right idea, find money and run. And if she did find some, she planned on running all the way to LA because there was no way she was staying around for any more nocturnal visits.

One by one she frantically ransacked his desk drawers,

until hidden under a pile of matching folders in the bottom left-hand drawer she discovered a large manila envelope containing a stack of pornographic pictures – most of them featuring young schoolgirls. What a stinking pervert! Why had Nikki left her with him? Why hadn't she cared enough to take her along?

On impulse she grabbed the envelope and ran upstairs, where she went straight to his closet, rifling through the pockets of his suits, remembering that when she was a kid that's where he'd kept his money. Her eager hands dived in and out of various inside pockets, finally coming across two thousand dollars secured with a rubber band.

She couldn't believe her luck. That much money should easily buy her a cheap ticket to LA.

Not wishing to alert Mrs Stern, she hurried into her room, quickly putting on her school clothes. Then she stuffed as much as she could into a large duffel bag, which she managed to smuggle out of the house before Mrs Stern noticed.

She lugged the heavy duffel bag to the corner of the street, hopping a bus into the centre of town. From there she hailed a cab to the airport.

LA – here I come! she thought. *And not a moment too soon.*

☆

'So Lara was really pissed with you?' Aiden asked, scratching the light stubble on his chin.

'Yes,' Nikki replied ruefully, as they stood by the Kraft service stand picking at a bowl of fruit. 'Then Richard turned up.'

Aiden bit into an apple. 'What did *he* want?'

'I told you, he's obsessed with Lara,' Nikki said, shaking her head. 'I must've been crazy to marry him. I didn't even see it. Although I do remember that on the South of France location he was always worried about where she was and what she was doing. Silly me – I thought he was merely being nice – y'know, the concerned ex.'

'Fuck Richard. Who needs him?' Aiden said, leading her over to a couple of high-backed canvas director's chairs. 'Let's talk about us.'

'What about us?' she asked, slightly breathless.

'I was kinda wondering,' he said, scratching his chin again. 'What happens after the movie? You and I gonna hang out? Be friends? Lovers? What's the deal here, Nik?'

Even though she liked him a lot, she wasn't in the mood to be pressured, everything was happening too fast and she needed time to think. 'Uh ... well ... I'll be shut away in the editing rooms for the next six weeks, trying to put this movie together with Mick.'

'Sounds like an experience,' he said drily.

'I'm looking forward to it,' she said. 'If *Revenge* is successful, I hope I get a chance to do it again.'

'You're really into this whole producing deal.'

'It's exciting – in spite of the setbacks.'

'Guess it beats sittin' around.'

'Aiden, I've been meaning to thank you—'

'For what?'

'For giving such a brilliant performance.'

'Hey,' he smiled faintly, pleased with her praise, 'it's what I do. And y'know something – Lara was pretty good, too. Surprised everyone.'

'She did, didn't she?'

'This movie's gonna get a lot of attention.'

'Do you think so?'

'Two thumbs up everyone's ass.'

She laughed, suddenly realizing she was going to miss him. 'So,' she said tentatively, 'what are your future plans?'

He shrugged like it didn't much matter. 'If anybody'll insure me, there's a few independents who're willing to take a chance. Course, once you're a known druggie, it's a bitch gettin' work.'

She watched him carefully. 'Tell me the truth, Aiden. Are you really straight now?'

'I take it day to day,' he answered restlessly. 'Course, it ain't easy, on account of the fact temptation's in my face every single minute. There's a shitload of actors into heroin – an' coke is like Sweet 'n' Low – you want a little snort with your breakfast – no freakin' problem. It's everywhere I go.'

'That must be difficult.'

A cynical grin. 'You could say that.'

'I *do* want to see you,' she said shyly. 'But first I need time for myself.'

'Hey—' a sly smile – 'as long as I'm not taken by the time you're ready.'

She smiled back. 'You're much nicer than you want people to think.'

'That a compliment?' he asked flippantly.

'I'll leave you to decide.'

Lara passed by on her way to the set, her expression grim. *Richard probably hasn't made things any better*, Nikki thought. *He's getting off on the drama. Damn him!*

'Need anything?' she called as Lara rushed past.

'Yes – a new life,' Lara snapped.

Nikki started to follow her. 'You *are* coming to the wrap party tonight?' she asked, hopeful that Lara would say yes.

'I wouldn't count on me if I were you,' Lara replied, not stopping.

Nikki knew when to back off.

☆

Lara had no intention of attending the end of filming party. She went to the set, performed her scene, then got on her cellphone to Cassie. 'We're taking a trip,' she said, her mind still in turmoil. 'Pack me a couple of bags, and meet me at the studio as soon as possible. I'm not coming home. Whatever you do, *don't* mention anything to Joey.'

'I take it he won't be coming with us?'

'You've got that right.'

'Where are we going?' Cassie asked curiously.

'To the house at the beach. Not a word to anyone.'

'It's done,' Cassie said.

Yes, Lara thought. *It's done. My life with Joey is done, too. Over. Finished. History.*

And she was filled with an overwhelming sense of sadness and loss.

57

'**How did** it go?' Richard asked, when Madelaine returned to his hotel as he'd requested.

'I'm sure it went exactly as you planned,' she responded crisply as he ushered her inside. She was not stupid, she knew the result Richard was after. He wanted his exquisite ex-wife back, and who could blame him?

He was cradling a hefty vodka on the rocks. 'Want one?' he asked.

'No, thank you,' she replied, walking over to the couch and sitting down.

He joined her. 'Did you tell Lara everything?' he asked intently.

'Yes.'

He nodded to himself. 'Excellent.'

'I also told her about the seven thousand dollars Joey stole from me.'

Richard sat up straight. Seven thousand bucks! Jesus! This was better than he'd thought. 'What did she say?'

Madelaine shrugged. 'She didn't have to say anything. It was all in her eyes. Disappointment, betrayal . . .'

'Good,' he said, before he could stop himself.

Madelaine raised a cynical eyebrow. 'Good?' she questioned.

'Uh . . . I mean it's good she found out the truth before it's too late.'

'I suppose so.'

'They were planning on getting married, you know.'

'Really?' Madelaine wasn't surprised. What did Joey have to lose by marrying Lara Ivory? Exactly nothing.

'Yeah. I'm sure you've persuaded her to change her

mind,' Richard said, taking a hefty swig of vodka. 'When she gets over being hurt she'll thank both of us.'

'I'm glad I could be of service,' Madelaine said.

He jumped up; she'd served her purpose, now he was ready to see her on her way.

It was at that moment Madelaine's memory nudged her into almost remembering where she knew Richard Barry from. The walk, the eyes, something about the voice . . . 'Tell me,' she asked curiously, 'were you ever an actor?'

'No,' he said quickly. 'Never.'

'There's something so familiar about you . . .'

He prodded her towards the door. 'Actors are treated like cattle,' he said abruptly. 'I prefer the other side of the camera.'

'Well . . .' she said, 'don't forget to take a look at my actors. I handle some good ones.'

'I'll view your tape tomorrow with my people.'

'I shall look forward to hearing from you.'

He closed the door on her before she had anything else to say. Why did women always want to talk? Jabber jabber jabber. Their gossipy little mouths going full tilt. Why couldn't they just shut the fuck up?

Were you ever an actor? Was she insane?

☆

I am Richard Barry, famous director. I have been Richard Barry for almost thirty years. I took the Richard from Mr Burton, and the Barry from a storefront opposite a movie theatre playing Caesar and Cleopatra.

Richard Barry. When I came back to America from my two-year sojourn in Mexico, that's who I was. The name had stature, dignity. The name represented the kind of life I aspired to. No more fucking my way to the bottom. What with the accidental killing of Hadley and my out-of-control drug days, I knew I couldn't sink much lower.

It was 1970. I was thirty years old and determined to make my mark. Since being thrown out by my father at sixteen, I'd fucked around for fifteen years. Now the fucking around was over, and Richard Barry was born.

I re-entered the States with a totally new agenda, plus papers proving who I was, and an attitude geared toward success. I also looked different. Thinner, fitter, with a neat beard and short hair. I did not resemble the stoned hustler who'd fled to Mexico, scared shitless he'd be arrested for murder.

After my married friend returned to America, I stayed in Acapulco – got myself a job working bar in a small place down by the water. The bar was owned by a long-retired film director, Hector Gonzales. Hector was a friendly man who loved to talk – especially to Americans. He owned a fishing boat, and one day he invited me to go out with him. After that first time we'd go fishing every weekend, and during our long hours of idly sitting there, waiting for a fish to bite, he'd regale me with tales about his life. And what a life he'd had. Married five times – twice to beautiful movie stars. Fourteen children. Twenty-six grandchildren. The recipient of many awards. The director of thirty-four movies.

It wasn't long before Hector invited me to his house, where he showed me books of yellowing press clips and photographs from the movies he'd directed. It was fascinating stuff and he was a fascinating character. Although he'd worked in Mexico most of his life, he'd directed one American film, and the tales he had to tell about that experience were quite something.

Listening to Hector was totally absorbing. I told him about directing a couple of episodes of a TV show in Los Angeles, and how much I'd enjoyed it.

'That's clever,' Hector said, with a knowing laugh, followed by a hacking cough. 'Everyone wants to be an actor. Don't they understand? The director is the one with the power.'

I began picking his brain, thinking that maybe I'd been pursuing the wrong profession all these years. I loved film, knew a lot about it – why couldn't I direct? The two times I'd done it had been fulfilling experiences, and I was certainly smart enough.

Every night after work, I'd go over to Hector's and view some of the movies he'd directed, learning about every aspect of filmmaking from the old man. After we'd finished with his films, he made me watch the great movies of other directors. Billy Wilder, John Huston and the like. Hector supplied me with the education I'd never had. The education I found I craved.

When I finally returned to America I was ready. I knew exactly what I wanted to do.

Hector had given me a couple of names to call, and I used his connections immediately. I'd put together an interesting fake résumé on the work I'd done in England over the past five years, and the first person I showed it to believed every word. I got a job as an assistant editor.

Since I'd temporarily given up women, work became my passion. From assistant editor it took me only a year to rise to main editor. And then an acquaintance of mine who read scripts for one of the big agencies let me have dibs on his rejection pile. One day I read a script called **Killer Eyes**. It was way before its time, but I immediately knew that here was the vehicle that would enable me to start my directing career. I hired a writer, and together we restructured the script. Then – with a little help from Hector's connections – I raised the money to make an extremely low-budget film. **Killer Eyes** became an underground hit. And I became a force to reckon with. After that I never looked back.

By the time I married Lara Ivory I was as big as they could get, and nobody ever recognized me from my nefarious past. I'd successfully managed to kill off the man I once was – the murdering stud who lived off women, did drugs, sold his body. I was totally reborn.

So what the hell did Madelaine mean by asking me if I was ever an actor?

No, sweetheart, I was never an actor. That person ceased to exist long ago.

And anyone who tries to bring him back will be severely punished.

58

'Hi,' Summer said.

'Hi,' Tina responded.

Then they both burst into giggles before awkwardly hugging each other.

Summer had called from the airport and Tina had insisted that she come stay.

'Enter chaos,' Tina invited, flinging open the door of her perfectly tidy apartment. 'Good flight?'

'As if!' Summer exclaimed, with a fake shudder. 'I was squeezed in next to a gruesomely fat lady with two whiny little geeks and a brain-dead husband.'

'At least you're here. Wait till Norman Barton finds out – according to Darlene, he's been asking for you ever since our one night of dirty lust!'

'He has?' she said, perking up.

'Yeah, but I didn't tell Darlene you were on your way back,' Tina said. 'Thought we'd work a deal for ourselves – knock out the commission factor. Whaddaya think?'

'Excellent,' she responded, the realization hitting her that she'd *finally* made a break and now she was free – totally out on her own! No more Daddy Dearest's midnight visits or Nikki's nagging to put up with. It was frightening, but at the same time extremely exhilarating. 'I'm starving,' she gulped.

'So'm I,' Tina agreed, leading her into the spare bedroom. 'Dump your stuff an' we'll go get food, scope out the action.'

Summer looked around. The room was filled with stuffed animals and glassy-eyed porcelain dolls; on the wall were giant posters of Brad Pitt and Antonio Sabbato, Jr. 'Didn't know you got off on Antonio,' she remarked, squinting at the posters.

'Oooh . . . those big sexy eyes!' Tina said, making a suggestive sucking noise with her lips. 'Maybe if I'm lucky I'll get to find out if he's got a great big zoomer to go with 'em!'

'Sex maniac!' Summer giggled.

'Course I am!' Tina agreed, cocking her head on one side. 'Who do *you* like?'

She didn't hesitate. 'Norman Barton.'

'*That's* convenient,' Tina said, rolling her eyes.

'OhmiGod, it's so amazing to be back in LA,' Summer sighed, flopping down on the bed. 'Just walking through the airport made me feel as if I was coming home.'

'How'd you manage the daring escape?' Tina asked, darting into the hall and dragging Summer's duffel bag into the room.

'I ran. Just like you. Discovered two thousand bucks hidden in one of my dad's suits and grabbed it.'

Tina wrinkled her pretty nose. 'D'you think he'll come looking for you?'

' 'Spect so,' Summer replied matter-of-factly. 'Unless he's nervous I'll tell.'

'Tell what?' Tina asked casually.

'You know,' Summer answered uneasily, not sure if she was ready to reveal her dirty little secret.

'*What?*' Tina demanded, her curiosity aroused.

'The sex stuff,' Summer muttered. There, now that she'd said it, she felt better.

'Sex stuff!' Tina exclaimed in surprise. 'I thought he was your *real* father.'

'He is.'

'Gruesome!' Tina shuddered. 'What a vile old perv. You could have him *arrested*.'

'I could?' Summer said, flashing on a mental picture of Sheldon being dragged off in handcuffs – a most satisfying image.

'Yes. That's incest – it's against the law.'

'Didn't you tell me your stepfather used to come on to you?'

'Stepfathers!' Tina spat. 'They're a whole other deal.'

'I hate my father,' Summer said, feeling a strange sense of euphoria at having finally revealed her secret.

'No shit?'

'I *really* hate him,' Summer added, hammering home the message.

'You told your mom what he's been doing to you?' Tina asked curiously.

'She'd say I was making it up. Like I mentioned before – my dad's this big-time shrink in Chicago, nobody would take my word against *his*.'

'*I* would,' Tina said staunchly.

'That's 'cause you don't know him. He's scary business. Like Mr Authority.'

'Yeah – Mr Authority with a big fat hard-on for his innocent little girl,' Tina sneered in disgust. 'What a retard! How long's he been doing it to you?'

'I don't want to talk about it any more,' Summer mumbled, clamming up.

'OK, OK,' Tina said, nodding understandingly. 'But you should've told your mom, then you wouldn't've had to go back to the old degenerate, you could've stayed here.'

Tina was right, she should have gone to Nikki when it first started. But she'd been ten years old, and totally confused, plus her father was all she had.

And then there were the threats . . . *If you ever tell anyone what we do, sweet pea, they'll take you away and lock you up in a home for bad girls . . . You wouldn't want that, pumpkin, would you?*

She wasn't a bad girl then. But now she'd show him exactly how bad she could be.

He deserved punishing. He deserved punishing big-time.

☆

The session with Greg Gorman lasted several hours, and after they were finished Joey was so elated that he hung around the studio for a while talking to Megan, the pretty stylist, Teddy Antolin, hairdresser supreme, and a couple of Greg's assistants before driving home. *Finally* it was happening for him. It had taken a while, but he was almost there.

Comfortably settled behind the wheel of Lara's Mercedes, he put his foot down as he cruised along Sunset, feeling surprisingly relaxed considering he was getting married any moment.

Joey Lorenzo and Lara Ivory. Fuck! He'd hit pay dirt and found the perfect woman. And their life together would be perfect, he'd make damn sure of that.

When he reached the house he spotted Cassie in the driveway getting into her car. Cassie was never very nice to him, although he'd certainly tried with her. If she didn't change her attitude, after they were married he'd persuade Lara to let her go and hire someone who showed him more respect.

'Where're you off to?' he asked, leaning out the car window.

Cassie jumped guiltily. 'What?' she said, squeezing behind the wheel of her Saab.

He got out of the Mercedes and strolled over. 'If you're headin' to the set, ask Lara if she wants me there early, or is she gonna come home before the wrap party?'

'Yes, Joey,' Cassie said, wondering what he'd done to make Lara so mad that she was planning on taking off without him.

'Oh, and tell her to put her cellphone on, I can't seem to get through.'

'Certainly.'

'See ya,' Joey said, turning and walking into the house.

Not likely, Cassie thought, quickly setting off for the studio, Lara's bags safely stashed in the trunk.

☆

The action at the restaurant on Sunset Plaza Drive was hot and heavy as Summer and Tina made their entrance – an entrance that did not go unnoticed. Two delectable, sexy young girls always caused men to stare. The open-air tables were jammed with rich young Italians, French and Iranians. It was like a dating fest – everybody checking everybody else out.

'Eurotrash city!' Tina exclaimed, grabbing an empty table. 'I'm psyched *I* don't have to date any of these guys. They're all creepos.'

'How come?' Summer asked.

'Take a look – they all drive the same expensive sports car Daddy bought them; they all have too much spending money; and they're all into getting their dicks sucked.'

'*What?*' Summer said with a nervous giggle.

'No, thank you!' Tina continued, wrinkling her nose. 'If *I'm* sucking dick, *I'm* getting paid big bucks.'

Summer hoped she wasn't as cynical as Tina by the time she was her age. 'Do you think getting paid for sex is wrong?' she asked innocently.

'Wrong!' Tina shrieked, causing several heads to turn. '*Shit*, no! Why do it for free if you can get major bucks? I'd feel bad if I screwed a guy and *didn't* get paid. Then he'd really be scoring off me.'

'Right,' Summer said hesitantly, wondering if her father had discovered her absence, and if so – what was he going to do about it? 'When do I get to see Norman?' she asked, anxious to close the deal.

'Mustn't seem antsy,' Tina replied, as if she'd been giving it a lot of thought. 'We gotta have a plan. I was thinking I'll call him myself and set up an appointment. I filched his number from Darlene's Rolodex.' A maniacal giggle of triumph. 'She'd have a shit-fit if she knew.'

'I bet she would,' Summer agreed.

'*I* could do what she does,' Tina mused, nodding to herself.

'Like what?'

'Set girls up,' Tina said airily. 'Send them out on dates and pocket a big chunk of commission.'

'Why don't you?'

'Oh, I dunno – too much trouble. Who needs paperwork? Not me.'

Summer pushed back her long blond hair. 'But like if you only go with guys who *pay* you,' she said, frowning, 'how do you ever get into a proper relationship?'

'Ha!' Tina said. 'Take a look around this town. There's *plenty* of women who started off getting paid, an' now they're big-deal hostesses. Married to hot-shit lawyers and studio guys – all that crap.'

'You mean some men don't mind if they have to pay for it?'

'What do they care? As long as they get what they want. And from what I hear, once they marry you they don't want it at all. So *then* you've got it made.'

'I believe in falling in love.'

'Get over it!' Tina said with a rude laugh. 'There's no such thing as love.'

Summer disagreed. She'd read about it enough times to know it did exist, and she'd decided she was *definitely* making Norman Barton fall in love with her.

A young Iranian with blue-black hair and a conceited smirk cruised by their table. 'You girls wanna hit the club circuit tonight?' he offered, flashing his gold Rolex.

'With *you*?' Tina said, her voice holding just the right amount of disdain.

'Me and my friend,' he replied, indicating a shorter version of himself hovering nearby.

'Are you *paying* for it, honey?' Tina enquired with a putdown smile. He backed off quickly. She shrieked with laughter. 'Do I know how to get rid of them or what?' she said triumphantly. 'No guy likes to think he *has* to pay. The *real* smart ones are the movie stars and the big businessmen. They know it's the only way to go.'

'Really?'

'Yeah, really. And don't you forget it. If I'm gonna train you – you'd better start listening to me.'

'Oh, I will,' Summer murmured. 'I want to learn – honestly I do.'

Anything was better than going home to her father. And if Tina was prepared to teach her, she'd be the best pupil ever.

59

Lara knew what she had to do and she didn't falter. Everyone thought she was so sweet and nice, but when she made up her mind, there was very little anyone could do to change it. She'd been a doormat over half her life – filled with guilt over her family's death; serving Aunt Lucy like a maid; a slave to Morgan Creedo. Until finally she'd gathered her strength and found her vocation – pursuing it with a steely passion. Now today everything seemed to be falling to pieces. First the revealing pictures spread all over a cheap tabloid. Then Joey.

Nobody could take her success away from her. It was her achievement in spite of horrible odds. And nobody was ever going to use her again.

☆

'Your husband's dead,' the nurse said, her expression a mixture of fake sympathy and Why do I have to give people bad news when it's the doctor's responsibility?

Lara Ann nodded. Bad news was nothing new; besides, during the four years she'd been with Morgan, she'd grown to hate him. He was no knight in shining armour come to save her from the rigours of working for Aunt Lucy. He'd turned out to be a shiftless, controlling bully – with minor talent – who'd never so much as kissed her.

They'd been married almost four years, and she was still a virgin, because Morgan only required her to service him with her lips. Once, when he was very drunk, he'd told her why. 'My mama warned me that puttin' it in a woman's pussy weakens a man,' he'd said with an embarrassed snigger. 'Makes him no better than a stallion servicing a mare. I come inside you – you got me trapped for ever.'

She hadn't argued with him. By that time it was the last thing she wanted him to do.

After the nurse informed her of Morgan's demise, the doctor appeared. He was young, hardly more than a student, and quite serious.

'You had a slight concussion,' he said, studying her chart. 'Nothing serious. In fact, I'm letting you go home.'

'I don't have a home,' she said in a low voice. 'My home was the trailer behind the car. It's gone.'

'I'm afraid so,' he said. 'You're lucky to have survived. If you hadn't been asleep on the back seat . . .'

My head would've come flying off along with Morgan's, she thought. Gallows humour. She was allowed.

'Do you have family?' the doctor asked.

'No,' she answered softly. 'I have no one.'

'No one,' he repeated, clearing his throat.

'That's right.'

He looked into her appealing green eyes, and before he could help himself he'd offered her the use of the couch in his small apartment for a few days, until she decided what she was going to do.

'I won't have sex with you,' she said.

'It never occurred to me,' he lied.

And so she moved into his place with only the clothes she'd been wearing at the time of the accident, and her purse, which contained all of their savings – five hundred dollars – and the phone number of Elliott Goldenson, a producer Morgan had said was prepared to give her a job in the movies. She wasn't quite sure she trusted Morgan's judgement – he hadn't even met Elliott Goldenson – but she called anyway, and a male secretary gave her an address in Hollywood and told her to come right over because Mr Goldenson was auditioning.

She decided this was a sign, and hurried to the address as fast as she could get there.

When she walked into the waiting room, she knew she was in the wrong place. A gaggle of blonds everywhere, yammering away at each other. They all had one thing in common – enormous breasts.

A young man with a bright red ponytail sat behind a large desk strewn with pictures.

She went over to him. 'I'm Lara Ann Creedo,' she said. 'I called and you told me to come over. Am I in the right place?'

He looked up at her. 'Honeybunch, you couldn't be more wrong.'

'This isn't the place?' she asked, dismayed.

'You're not the kind of girl he's looking for,' he said, pursing his lips. 'Why are you here?'

'Because you said Mr Goldenson was auditioning.'

'I know. But what fool gave you this number to call?'

'My husband.'

'Oh,' he nodded knowingly, 'one of those deals.'

'Can I ask you something?' she said, leaning across the desk.

'Ask away.'

'If I'm not right for this role, is there another one coming up?'

He spoke in hushed tones. 'Sweetie bunch, you're in the wrong place. Mr Goldenson makes porno movies. I don't think that's what you're looking for.'

She stepped back. 'Oh!' she said, startled. 'But . . . my husband . . . he had this number. He said I'd be perfect.'

'Hmm . . . I'd have a word with your husband if I was you. Anyway, don't look so disappointed, at least I didn't send you in there to strip off in front of a bunch of dirty old men.'

'I wouldn't do that anyway.'

'I take it you're new in town?'

'Yes.'

'Well, precious, this is my advice. Find yourself a legitimate agent, and start doing the rounds. You're certainly beautiful enough.'

'How do I find a legitimate agent?'

'Look in the yellow pages. Go to William Morris, ICM – one of the big ones.'

'Who's William Morris? Do you have his phone number?'

He threw up his hands in despair. 'The girl is a total novice. William Morris is a huge agency. Don't you know anything?'

'I guess not.'

'I suggest you go back to your husband and bite his butt for sending you here.'

'I can't do that.'

'Why not?'

'He's dead.'

'Oh, my God – it's a sob story! Please, whatever you do, don't make me feel sorry for you. I'm sorry enough for myself, having to do this shitty job. The only reason they employ me is because they know I'm not about to hit on the girls. Girls not being my style, if you know what I mean.'

'Are you . . . gay?'

'Honeybunch, do rabbits mate?'

And so a friendship was born. His name was Tommy, and two days later she moved out of the doctor's apartment and into Tommy's place above a restaurant on Sunset Boulevard.

He was mother, father and brother to her. He guided and protected her; sent her to acting class; introduced her to a proper agent; fed and clothed her; counselled her on all subjects; got her a job as a waitress while she was waiting for her first break; and made sure nobody took advantage of her innocence.

And in return she nursed him after he got sick with AIDS, and sobbed at his funeral when he died ten months later.

A week after his death she landed her first big movie. Tommy never got to see her become a star.

☆

Lara sighed deeply, remembering her friend Tommy, and all the fun they'd had. It wasn't fair he'd been taken from her, but it had made her all the more determined to succeed. Tommy had given her warmth and comfort and most of all – the right guidance on how to handle herself in Hollywood. He'd taught her well. He'd also taught her never to put up with any shit.

She recalled the day she'd left Richard – the day she'd actually *caught* him getting a blow job, and he'd *still* thought he could talk her out of leaving.

Richard and his charm. In that respect he was exactly like Joey, they both had the same kind of masculine power they thought made them irresistible to women.

Well, when it really mattered, she *could* resist. And even though she loved Joey – she did not wish to continue in a relationship with a man who was a fake. He'd *used* her. Invented a fiancée, and reeled her in like a fish. God! He probably thought she was so easy. Easy and desperate for a man. Poor little frustrated movie star. How he must have laughed behind her back.

Thank God she'd found out before marrying him. What a mistake *that* would have been.

And yet, she thought sadly, *what am I going to do without his strong arms to hold and protect me? His insistent lips that brought me such unbelievable pleasure?*

Was everything about him a lie? She'd never bothered to find out. It hadn't mattered. But now that she knew, it did.

Maybe you should listen to his side of the story, her inner voice suggested.

Why? So he can lie his way out of it exactly like Richard used to?

No. She was too wise to go down that street.

As soon as Cassie arrived, she was ready to go. She'd completed her final scene, promised the cast and crew she'd see them later at the party, and managed to avoid Nikki – whom she didn't feel like confiding in.

'I brought *my* car,' Cassie said, her cheeks flushed. 'Thought if I called the limo company, people could easily track us.'

'Good thinking, Cass,' Lara said, stuffing her golden hair beneath a Laker's baseball cap, and covering her eyes with Jackie Kennedy blacker-than-black shades.

Cassie was dying to ask what was going on, but she didn't, because she knew her boss well enough to understand that she'd explain the situation when she was ready and not before.

'What did you tell the Crenshaws?' Lara asked, getting into the passenger seat and fastening her seatbelt.

'Nothing,' Cassie replied, starting the engine. 'I figured if you wanted them to know anything you'd call them later.'

Lara nodded. At least she could always depend on Cassie.

60

Joey dressed carefully in a black silk Armani shirt, black slacks and a classic Armani blazer. Lara liked him in black, plus it suited him dressing against his looks. Casual yet hot.

He stared at his reflection in the mirror and remembered what he'd been doing a year ago. It wasn't a good memory – caused him sleepless nights and hot sweats. Thank God it was behind him. One day he'd tell Lara. In fact, when they were married he'd tell her everything – finally cleanse his soul to the one person he knew he could trust.

She hadn't called, which meant she was expecting him to meet her at the studio. Cassie had obviously forgotten to mention he was trying to get through on her cellphone, because the damn thing was still turned off.

He missed her, which was pretty ridiculous considering they'd only been apart one day.

That morning he'd held her in his arms stroking her into a state of almost orgasmic ecstasy. 'I'll finish the job later,' he'd joked.

'Since when did it become a job?' she'd laughed, flushed and breathless.

'You're gonna have to wait,' he'd said, kissing her soft inviting lips. 'But trust me – the wait'll be worth it.'

She'd smiled. 'Oh, I know that.'

Then he'd lain on top of the bed, hands propped behind his head, watching her dress.

She was so goddamn beautiful. How did he ever turn his life around and get this lucky?

Lara Ivory. *His* Lara.

Plucking the car keys off the dresser, he headed for the studio, a happy man.

☆

It started raining lightly as Cassie drove down Sunset toward the Pacific Coast Highway. All day there'd been storm warnings on the radio, but this was the first sign of bad weather.

Lara closed her eyes, agonizing over whether she was doing the right thing. As she relived the progression of her romance with Joey, she realized it had all been based on lies. He'd made up a fiancée, never told her about the money he'd taken, hadn't told her about living with Madelaine, hadn't told her anything really.

But then . . . what had she told him? Exactly nothing.

So, they were even. It was great fun, but it was just one . . .

'Another half-hour and we're there,' Cassie said, after she'd been driving for a while. 'I hope this rain stops. People in LA don't know how to drive when it rains here.'

'I'd forgotten how far it is,' Lara remarked.

'You wanted isolated.'

Cassie was right. She enjoyed being away from everyone and everything. Especially now.

She leaned back, desperately trying to shut out the jumbled memories that in times of stress always came flooding back.

There was so much of her past she'd never revealed to anyone. So many secrets . . .

One day she'd hoped to share them with Joey. Now it was not to be.

And that thought made her very desolate.

☆

'Anyone seen Lara?' Nikki asked hopefully, although she knew it was highly unlikely Lara would show.

'Saw plenty of her in *Truth and Fact*,' one of the grips sniggered.

Nikki threw him a disgusted look. She spotted Linden, and stopped him as he walked past. 'Is Lara coming?'

Linden shrugged. 'Don't know, Nikki. Sorry.'

The cast and crew were gathered on Sound Stage Four. A rock 'n' roll band blared fifties classics, while everyone tried not to look self-conscious in their fifties outfits and bouffant hairstyles. The fifties theme was Mick's idea – he was very into that period.

Clad in black stove-pipe jeans that made his skinny legs even skinnier, and a Marlon-in-his-thin-days white T-shirt, Mick made the rounds, dancing with everyone from the nineteen-year-old prop girl to the sixty-year-old accountant.

'I'm pissed at Lara,' he said, sweeping Nikki into a quick jive. 'She should be here.'

'She's upset about the photos,' Nikki explained, as he swung her in a wide circle. 'So am I.'

'Shit happens,' Mick said totally unconcerned. 'Tell her to move on, and get her fine movie star ass down here. The crew's disappointed.'

'Maybe I'll call her, see what I can do,' Nikki gasped, as he somehow or other lowered her between his legs, then pulled her up in an elaborate arc. She spotted Aiden watching her with an edgy grin. Fuck it! He was making fun of her. 'Bye, Mick,' she said, managing a quick escape. 'I'm not in a dancing mood.'

As she hurried toward Aiden, one of the production assistants came at her with a cellphone. 'It's a Mr Weston calling from Chicago. Says it's urgent.'

Like she didn't have enough problems. She grabbed the phone. 'Yes?'

Sheldon's voice sounded indistinct and panicky, unlike his usual in-control self. 'Is she with you?' he demanded.

'Is *who* with me?'

'Summer.'

'What are you talking about, Sheldon? She's in Chicago with you.'

'No, she's gone. Vanished. Please tell me she's with you.'

'No,' she said, her stomach dropping. 'She's not here, Sheldon. So where the hell is she?'

61

The thrill of the chase had always appealed to Alison Sewell. She'd followed movie stars home on many occasions, right up to the point where they shut their great big gates in her face. However, following someone who was unaware they were being tracked was even more of a kick. It was a cat and mouse game. Alison considered herself the big powerful cat and Lara the poor little mouse.

Alison had been trailing Lara all day. She'd followed her from her house in the morning, then sat in the parking lot near the location, watching as they shot the last day of *Revenge*. She'd had a perfect view of Lara's trailer – popping off roll after roll of film as Lara came and went.

Miz Ivory looked upset. And so she should. *Truth and Fact* had done Alison's pictures proud. Her photographs were on the cover, *and*, as if that wasn't enough, there was a double-page spread inside.

That would teach Lara Ivory to mess with Alison Sewell, spurn their friendship and haul her up in court like a common criminal. Who exactly did the bitch think she was?

Late in the day when Cassie arrived to pick Lara up, Alison was surprised. Usually the big movie star sat in the back of her chauffeur-driven car and was taken home that way. But not tonight. Tonight her driver was sitting across the street reading a Frederick Forsyth paperback behind the wheel of his car, unaware his star was leaving by other means.

Hmm . . . Alison thought. *Something's up.*

She drew out of her parking place and slid her station wagon behind Cassie's Saab as it left the location.

I would have been the perfect assistant for Lara, Alison thought. *I could have protected her better than anyone. Certainly better than that one-armed stupid publicist, or that dumb hand-some boyfriend. All she needs is me.*

When Cassie's car hit Sunset, Alison was right on her tail. Earlier she'd managed to have a conversation with one of the grips, acting real casual, as if she was a fan. He'd let slip that tonight was the wrap party. Surely the party wasn't at the beach, which is where Cassie seemed to be heading?

Alison hummed softly under her breath. She got a charge following the car, sure that she was the only person who knew Lara Ivory was in it. There were no other photographers around to bother her. No stupid men to deal with.

Truth was she was smarter than all of them. And the proof was that she'd made a fortune in the last week. Now she was rich, and could do whatever she liked. She'd made more money than Uncle Cyril ever did.

She switched on her windshield wipers to clear the sudden rain, so unexpected in sunny California. Then she reached in the glove compartment for a Snickers bar.

Unfortunately she now had a criminal record, thanks to Miz Ivory.

It didn't matter. She was rich. And she planned on getting even richer.

How much would pictures of Lara Ivory *dead* be worth?

How much could she score for pictures of a beautiful corpse?

62

Tina and Summer walked back from the restaurant, laughing about the guys who'd tried to come on to them.

'Bunch of pathetic dogs,' Tina sneered. 'Now do you see why it's so stupid to go out with somebody and not get paid? These dudes are only looking to get into your pants. The ones that pay are like *real* men.'

'Doesn't getting paid mean we're prostitutes?' Summer asked, trying not to yawn.

'Prostitutes?' Tina shrieked. 'What kind of an old-fashioned word is *that*? We're . . . service givers. Very *expensive* service givers. Being a prostitute is like grabbing a Big Mac. What we do is like dining out in the coolest restaurant in town. Get it?'

'I guess so,' Summer said, thinking how ready she was to crawl into bed and sleep.

Tina was in an ebullient mood. 'I'll tell you what we're gonna do,' she said, breaking into a jog as it began to lightly rain.

'What?' Summer asked, hoping it was bed time.

'We're gonna call Norman,' Tina said, as they reached her nearby apartment.

'*Now?*'

'Yeah, why wait till tomorrow?'

'I thought you said we shouldn't rush into anything.'

'Who's rushing? He doesn't even know you're here. It's definitely time we told him.'

'OK . . .' Summer said unsurely.

'I'm asking for *big* bucks,' Tina said excitedly, her eyes gleaming. 'I'm gonna tell him you don't put out any more. Only for special johns.'

'Can I listen in?' Summer asked, anxious to hear the sound of his voice.

'Yeah, pick up the second line,' Tina said, dialling his number. She got right through. 'Hi, Norman,' she said, putting on a low, sexy voice. 'Remember me? Tina? I was over at your place a few weeks ago with Summer, that gorgeous blond you were so wild about. Darlene sent us, remember?'

'Sure do,' Norman answered, sounding stoned.

'You were *really* into Summer,' Tina continued. 'Kept asking Darlene when she'd be back. But you know what? Bad news. Summer gave up the business, and she'll only do it for very special clients. Now the good news – *you* happen to be extra special.'

'Whyn't you come over,' Norman said. 'Both of you.'

'Well . . .' Tina said, pretending to hesitate, 'if we do, you'll have to pay us direct, and not mention a word to Darlene, 'cause like I told you – Summer's no longer in the business. So you'll be dealing directly with me. OK?'

'I can do that, cutie.'

'Oh, and it has to be cash. And it'll cost more—'cause, like I just said—'

'I know, I know—' he interrupted, with a jolly chuckle. 'Your friend's not in the business. So quit with the talking and get your cutie-pie asses over here.'

'We'll be right there,' Tina said, hanging up the phone with a triumphant grin. 'See? Easy pickings.'

'It's past ten,' Summer said, yawning again. 'I'm kinda beat, what with the flight and all.'

Tina was already at the mirror fluffing up her hair. 'Too beat to have fun with Norman?'

'I was like thinking maybe tomorrow.'

'Don't sweat it,' Tina said, picking up her shoulder bag, reaching inside and producing a small white pill. 'Take this. It'll rev you up.'

'What is it?'

'Nothing serious. See,' she said, reaching in her purse again, 'I'm taking one, too.'

Not wanting to look like a baby, Summer quickly swallowed the innocuous-looking pill.

'Good girl,' Tina said. 'It'll make you feel seriously better.'

'Uh . . . another thing,' Summer ventured.

'Yes?'

'Shouldn't it be Norman and me alone together?'

'I didn't notice him saying, "Just send the blond,"' Tina retorted huffily. 'Are you up for it or not?'

Summer nodded. She knew that once he saw her again, he'd realize how much he'd missed her, send Tina home, and from then on everything would work out just fine.

☆

The first thing Nikki did was have Aiden drive her to the Malibu house to check if Summer was there.

'Do you think she's in LA?' she kept asking him.

'I hardly know her,' he answered. 'But from what I've seen – she can look after herself.'

'She's fifteen, Aiden,' Nikki fretted. *'Fifteen.'*

'What can I tell you? She's *your* kid.'

'What if she's *not* here?'

'Could be she's staying with a girlfriend in Chicago. Your ex check into that?'

'Knowing Sheldon, he checked into everything. He's on a plane right now. You'll get to meet him, he's a real treat.'

'She leave a note?'

'No . . . the housekeeper told Sheldon she left late for school this morning, and that some of her clothes are gone. Oh, and apparently there's money missing.'

'Shit!' Aiden exclaimed, swerving to avoid another car that had skidded across the road.

Nikki put on her seatbelt. 'Please drive carefully. I *would* like to get there.'

'She have a boyfriend?' Aiden asked, slowing down.

'Not that I know of. Sheldon spoke to the boy who took her to a movie last night – Stuart something or other. He didn't know anything.' She let out a long, weary sigh. 'Oh, God, Aiden. I can only hope she's at the house.'

'I don't get it. If she *was* coming back here – why wouldn't she call first?'

'How do I know?' Nikki said irritably.

'Don't get pissed. You're gonna find her.'

'Maybe Richard knows something. They were kind of close when she was here.'

'Call him.'

She took out her cellphone and punched out his number. 'It's Nikki,' she said when he answered.

'How come you're not at the party?' Richard said. 'I'm going there now. Lara told me to drop by.'

'Why would she tell you to do that?' Nikki said, before she could help herself.

'Guess she wants to see me,' Richard replied, purposely needling her.

'You're out of luck, Richard, Lara's not there.'

'How do *you* know?'

'She's not, OK?'

'No need to get bitchy.'

She refused to let him get to her. Some other time, but not now. 'Sheldon called from Chicago,' she said brusquely. 'Summer's missing.'

'What do you mean, *missing*?'

'It's pretty clear, isn't it? She's taken off, run away.'

'So . . . what do you want from me?'

'Thanks for your concern, Richard.'

'No, I mean if there's anything I can do—'

'Do you have any idea where she might go?'

'No.'

'She hasn't called *you*?'

'If she does, I'll let you know.'

'I'm on my way to Malibu. She could be there.'

'Then I guess I won't see you later.'

'You won't see anybody later. I told you – Lara's not at the party.'

'Where is she?'

'How would I know? If you hear anything call me.' She cut the connection and began biting her nails – a bad habit she only reverted to in times of extreme stress. 'He's such a cold sonofabitch,' she said. 'All he cares about is seeing Lara.'

'Why'd you marry him, Nik? And why'd you marry Sheldon? They both seem like assholes.'

'Yes, I know,' she said sarcastically. 'I would have been better off with a druggie like you, right?'

'That's not very nice,' he said, shaking his head as if he couldn't believe she was being so nasty. 'I'm getting it back together. I was kind of hoping you'd help me.'

'I can't help anybody right now. I'm too upset.'

'Calm down,' he said soothingly. 'Summer's probably sitting at the house waiting for you.'

☆

Nikki's call annoyed Richard. He did not appreciate her attitude, telling him that he wasn't going to see Lara. Showed how much *she* knew. Not only was he going to see her, he was going to divorce Nikki, and get back together with Lara the way it should be.

He knew Lara better than anyone. With Joey out of the picture, she'd be lonely and vulnerable. And he, Richard Barry, would be right there to console her.

Before anyone knew it, they'd remarry.

Yes. That's exactly what was going to happen, whether Nikki liked it or not.

☆

'I hope he still *likes* me,' Summer said. She'd taken a quick shower and put on one of Tina's skimpy dresses. Now they were standing in the elevator taking them up to Norman Barton's hotel suite, where he resided permanently.

'Of *course* he'll still like you,' Tina said, adjusting her stretchy tank top to show even more cleavage. 'According to Darlene, he asks about you all the time.'

'At least that's good news,' Summer said, shivering slightly, not sure if it was from nerves, the air-conditioned elevator, or the stupid pill Tina had forced her to take. 'I'm totally psyched about seeing him again.'

'Little Miss Romantic,' Tina teased. 'It must be true love!'

'I think it is,' Summer giggled.

Norman did not open the door of his suite himself. This time a girl did – a stunning black girl with a provocative smile and sinewy body.

Tina quickly nudged Summer. 'OhmiGod!' she whispered. 'It's that big-time model, Cluny.'

'Hi, girls,' Cluny said with a shimmering smile. 'Come in, join the party.'

Summer had no intention of joining any party, she was only interested in seeing Norman.

'Absolutely!' Tina said. 'This is Summer – I'm Tina, and you're Cluny. I recognized you, you're so beautiful.'

Cluny had huge quivering lips and seductive cat eyes. 'Why thank you, darling,' she said, clutching Tina's arm. 'You can be my new best friend.'

They entered the room. There were girls everywhere and no Norman in sight.

'*Sir* is in the bedroom,' Cluny said with a throaty chuckle. 'He'll be out shortly. In the meantime, take off your clothes, get comfortable.'

Most of the girls lounging around on the couches and floor were half naked. Summer was horrified, this wasn't what she'd expected at all. 'What's going on?' she whispered to Tina.

'Looks like an orgy to me,' Tina said, not too put out.

'I thought he wanted to see *me*,' Summer said mournfully.

'Apparently along with dozens of others.'

'I'm going home,' Summer said, deeply disappointed.

'Don't be such a baby,' Tina scolded. 'What did you *think* he was doing while you were in Chicago – sitting around pining for you? We're here now, let's get with the action.'

'I'm not staying,' Summer said stubbornly.

'At least see what he has to say,' Tina said. 'We showed up, he's gotta pay us.'

'I'm not taking off *anything*,' Summer said, close to tears.

'You don't have to,' Tina answered, guiding her over to one of the couches where they squeezed on the end, next to a short, busty redhead who was snorting cocaine from the glass-topped coffee table. 'Want some?' the redhead asked with a friendly smile. 'It's free.'

'Sure,' Tina said agreeably.

'What are you *doing*?' Summer hissed, as Tina picked up a small straw and began imbibing the white powder.

'Takin' a little snort,' Tina whispered back. 'Why don't you do the same? You're so uptight.'

'I don't want to be here,' Summer moaned. 'I like *really* don't.'

'Oh, for God's sake – stop whining,' Tina snapped. 'You *said* you couldn't wait to see him.'

'Not this way.'

A few minutes later Norman emerged from the bedroom, clad in nothing but a pair of red candy-striped shorts. He had a big shit-eating grin on his face and a girl on each arm, both of them totally naked. 'Cluny!' he yelled. 'I need more money!'

'Honey,' Cluny replied, digging into her shoulder purse and pulling out a stack of hundred-dollar bills, 'you are *wailin'* tonight. No stoppin' *you*.'

Summer jumped to her feet. 'That's it,' she said. 'This sucks. I'm out of here.'

'Don't be such a pain,' Tina retorted.

'Give me the key.'

'*What* key?'

'To your apartment. I'm going home.'

'If you're baling on me – then you can forget about going to my place.'

'Thanks a *lot*.'

'Hey, Norman,' Cluny said, 'before you vanish again – take a peek at dessert. Two juicy little pieces of fresh. I bag me the baby blond. Can I have her? Please? Pretty please?'

'She's all yours, babe,' Norman said, not even glancing in Summer's direction, too stoned to concentrate on anything.

Summer stood up. 'I'm gone,' she said, furiously heading for the door.

'Then you're on your own,' Tina shouted after her.

'Fine,' Summer said, tears pricking her eyelids. 'I'll pick up my things tomorrow.'

She rushed from the room. To her chagrin, Norman didn't even notice.

63

There was a Marvin Gaye tribute on the radio. Joey listened to the veteran soul singer all the way to the studio. The music soothed him. Marvin Gaye sure had style – not to mention an incredible voice.

He recalled that when he was growing up, his mother had often played tapes of Otis Redding and Teddy Pendergrass. She was into soul. Ah yes, Adelaide was into a lot of things.

He flashed on his mother for a moment, picturing her dancing around their living room – so strikingly pretty with her black curly hair, dark eyes and startling wide smile. He'd inherited his looks from his mother. God, she'd been a beauty.

As he pulled into a parking place outside the sound stage, he could hear the music blaring away. 'Rock Around the Clock' by Bill Haley and the Comets. Oh, Jeez, he'd forgotten, it was a fifties party, and he was supposed to be in some kind of rock 'n' roll outfit. Well, what did it matter? They'd probably only stay a short time. Then he'd take Lara home, and tomorrow they'd be on their way to Tahiti and a whole new life.

He strolled into the sweaty noisy throng, stopping to greet a couple of sound guys, smiling at the hairdresser and make-up woman. Then he began looking around for Lara.

'Seen Lara?' he asked the continuity girl.

She shrugged. 'Haven't.'

He wandered over to one of the second assistants. 'Is Lara around?'

'Don't think she's here, Joey.'

'How about Nikki?'

'Saw her dancing with Mick a while back.'

'Thanks,' he said, edging around the dance floor, finally managing to attract Mick's attention as he staggered off the floor with his arm around a pretty props girl.

'Hey, it's the Joey man,' Mick said, swaying on his feet. 'How's it goin'? Where's the love of your unworthy life? You lucky bastard.'

'I was just about to ask you,' Joey said.

'Ain't spotted the lovely Lara,' Mick said, pushing up his glasses. 'Guess she's still freaked over the photos.'

'What photos?'

'Oh, man – you mean you haven't seen *Truth and Fact*? Everyone's favourite weekly tabloid. Lara's pissed city. Go ask Linden, he's by the bar.'

Joey went over to Linden. 'What's this about some photos?' he asked, frowning.

'You don't know?' Linden said.

'No, I don't fuckin' know,' Joey said, starting to get aggravated.

'Some . . . uh . . . unfortunate photographs of Lara turned up in *Truth and Fact*,' Linden said. 'Somebody sneaked 'em while they were shooting the rape scene. They're *very* explicit, and Lara's *very* upset.'

'Jesus!' Joey said. 'How'd it happen?'

'That's what everyone would like to know.'

'So she's gone home, right?'

'I would think so,' Linden said. 'I'm positive she won't show up here tonight.'

'Does Nikki know about this?'

'She's upset too.'

'No shit?'

'I'm sorry it happened.'

'I bet you are,' Joey muttered, hurrying back to the Mercedes, where he picked up the phone and tried the house. Mrs Crenshaw answered. 'Lara back yet?' he asked.

'No, Mr Joey.'

'When she gets there, tell her I'm on my way.'

☆

The rain was getting heavier as Cassie turned off the Pacific Coast Highway onto a deserted dirt road. 'We're almost there,' she announced. 'Do you have the key?'

'No, *you* do,' Lara replied, still in kind of a daze.

'No, *I* don't,' Cassie replied, slowing down.

'Why not?' Lara asked, exasperated.

'Because nobody ever gave me one. I assumed when you said we were coming here that *you* had it.'

'Shit!' Lara exclaimed.

Now Cassie knew she was *really* upset, because Lara rarely swore. 'Shall I turn around and go back?' she questioned.

'No,' Lara said sharply. 'We'll get in somehow. There's probably an unlocked door or window. After all, nobody's living there.'

'If you ask me, we should stay in a hotel overnight, and have the realtor drop off the keys tomorrow.'

'We're here now,' Lara said flatly. 'Not having a key is the least of my problems.'

'You're the boss,' Cassie sighed, spooked by the heavy rain, the unlit road and the empty house ahead. She was surprised Lara had bought the place. Even when Lara was renting she'd never thought much of it – the house was too remote and quite gloomy, with none of the charm of the Hamptons house.

The Saab hit a bump in the road. 'I can't see a thing,' Cassie complained, switching on her bright lights.

Lara wished Cassie would stop bitching. She wasn't in the frame of mind to put up with anyone's complaints. One of the advantages of being a star was that she didn't have to – if she said jump, that's what people were supposed to do. *So shut up, Cass, we're staying whether you like it or not.*

She wondered if Joey had realized she was missing. It would take a while before he understood she was not coming back. In a couple of days she'd have her lawyer call to tell him to move out of her house. And that would be that.

The big iron gate leading to the property was open. 'Nice,' Cassie said, making the turn, the wheels of her car crunching through pebbles and thick mud. 'They're *really* security conscious.'

'It's a good sign,' Lara said. 'Means we'll have no trouble getting in.'

'Very reassuring!' Cassie sighed, fielding off hunger pangs. 'Can't wait to spend the night.'

☆

Joey pulled the Mercedes up outside a 7-Eleven store and ran inside. He picked up a copy of *Truth and Fact*, and stared in disbelief at the revealing photographs on the cover. Jesus! What had they done to his beautiful Lara? He knew how private she was, how closely she guarded her good reputation – these sleazy pictures were enough to drive her crazy.

Slamming down money, he stormed back to the car. It was all Nikki's fault, she'd probably set it up to get publicity for her goddamn movie.

He started the engine and roared off. Why hadn't Lara called him? Too upset, of course.

The sooner he was with her the better.

Nobody knew more than he how soul-destroying it was to get set up.

☆

'I need money desperately, Joey.' So spoke the lovely Adelaide, his mother, always asking for something.

Adelaide was seventeen when she met Joey's father, Pete Lorenzo – a small-time wise guy who was sixty when he knocked up the pretty teenager. Two years later he'd finally married her. He was getting on in years, it was time to settle down with a woman who'd look after him.

Only Adelaide wasn't that woman. Adelaide had no intention of looking after anyone except herself. Once she'd hooked Pete she hired a sitter to watch Joey, and proceeded to accompany her husband wherever he went. His hang-outs were the racetrack, the fights, poker games and pool halls. Adelaide was by his side every step of the way.

One weekend they took three-year-old Joey with them to Vegas. He nearly drowned in the hotel swimming pool while they were busy playing craps. Another time, in Atlantic City, they left him in a hotel room where he nearly got trapped in a fire.

It was a hell of a childhood, neither parent had much time for him.

By the time he was ten, his father was seventy and tired; Adelaide was twenty-seven and sleeping with any good-looking jerk who came her way. When Pete complained, Adelaide laughed in his face. Pete Lorenzo had lost his power – he was too old to control her, and she was too wild to be controlled.

Joey, an introverted kid, watched it all. He adored his pretty mother, but he soon realized she was untrustworthy; therefore, he figured, all women were the same.

When he was eighteen, his dad suffered a massive heart attack at the racetrack and died on the spot. After that Adelaide went through a series of live-in boyfriends – each one worse than the last. She was into hoods and low-lifes. Con-men and hustlers. She'd also started drinking and gambling big-time.

Joey decided he'd better distance himself before he beat up one of her dumb boyfriends, so he moved out, trying a variety of jobs – busboy, waiter, car mechanic, limo driver. And a different girl every week. Girls went for him because he was so good-looking, but he never let them stay around long enough to get close.

After a while he took the big step and moved to New York, where he immediately got the acting bug. One day he walked into Madelaine Francis' office, and there she was – his big opportunity. An agent with clout.

She'd gotten him a couple of great movie roles, and everything was looking good until the phone call from his mother.

'I don't have any money, Ma,' he explained, feeling guilty anyway. 'I've only had two acting jobs. When I make more, I'll send you plenty.'

'You don't get it,' she replied, sounding drunk and none too friendly. 'This time it's different. This time it's life or death.'

'What about Danny?' he asked, mentioning her current boyfriend. 'Get him to help you.'

'Danny's a no-guts loser,' she spat. 'He can't help shit. And I need ten thousand, otherwise they'll kill me, Joey, they'll kill me.'

'You're crazy, Ma.'

'So help me, it's the truth.'

He didn't know what to do. He loved Adelaide, but she was a degenerate gambler who was never going to quit. Now she was coming to him to pay her debts.

Where the fuck was he supposed to come up with ten thousand bucks? He'd tried to distance himself, make a new life. So he was living with a woman almost thirty years older than him. He'd finally gotten smart and found himself someone who could do him some good. Madelaine was OK, she didn't hassle him about making a commitment – unlike his contemporaries who made him extremely nervous with their clinging ways and petty demands. Besides, none of them were ever as pretty as his mother – his gorgeous mother, who was such goddamn trouble.

He called her back the next day. 'Can't get my hands on any money right now,' he said.

'Then you can kiss your poor mama goodbye.'

'Don't snow me with that dramatic crap, Ma.'

'I told you,' she said, her voice hardening. 'Unless you come up with the money, I'm dead.'

He wrestled with the problem. Madelaine kept cash in the apartment. Could he ask her for a loan?

No, she wouldn't buy it.

So what if he just took it? Helped Adelaide out for the last time, then came back and explained everything to Madelaine.

Yeah, that was the way to do it. Madelaine would understand.

As soon as she left for the office the next day, he broke into her safe. He felt bad doing it, but what choice did he have?

He found seven thousand dollars stashed in her safe. It wasn't enough, but he took it all.

Adelaide had to quit with the gambling. This was positively the last time he was bailing her out.

☆

A car horn blared, making him jump. He realized he hadn't been concentrating, and quickly swerved the wheel, almost skidding, taking no notice as the other driver gave him the finger.

Lara needed him more than ever. He had to hurry home.

64

As Summer stood outside Norman Barton's hotel in the pouring rain, it occurred to her that she had absolutely nowhere to go. Tina, who she'd thought was such a good friend, had dumped on her big-time. Well, she didn't want to be friends with Tina anyway, not if she was into doing coke. Smoking grass was one thing, but getting into coke could lead to nothing but trouble.

She hovered outside the hotel entrance in her skimpy little dress, shivering.

'Can I get you a cab?' a young uniformed doorman asked.

'No, thanks,' she said, shaking her head.

'You one of those girls from the Norman Barton party?' he asked, edging nearer.

'Excuse me?' she said, freezing him out with a cold glare. 'I'm staying at the hotel with my *parents*.'

'Sorry, miss,' he said, backing off.

A limo slid kerbside and Summer watched in awe as Johnny Romano, the famous movie star, got out. Although he was with three girls he threw her a moody look and a slight wink. 'Hi, chickie,' he said as he slinked on by.

What was it with all these stupid movie stars? One girl didn't do it for them? Apparently not.

She tried to take a peek at the limo driver. If it was Jed she'd be saved. But no, it wasn't Jed, it was some gnarled old black man. And the annoying thing was she couldn't remember Jed's number.

She sighed, feeling let down and disappointed – not to mention slightly giddy. God knew what was in the pill Tina had forced her to take. Norman had *told* her to call, he'd insisted he wanted to see her again, causing her to fantasize about them having a future together. Now he'd turned out

399

to be nothing more than a coked-out bum. Well, it was good she'd found out before she'd gotten even more involved.

She shivered again and wrapped her arms across her chest. What was she going to do? She was alone in LA with nowhere to sleep and all her possessions – including her money – at Tina's.

'Where are your folks?' the young doorman asked, coming over again. 'Do they know you're out here?'

'Have you ever heard of minding your own business?' she said haughtily.

'Excuse *me* for talking to the princess,' he snapped back.

'I could report you,' she said indignantly.

'Go ahead – like losing this job would ruin my day.'

'If you *must* know,' she said, 'I had a fight with my parents.'

'You shouldn't wander around this town by yourself,' he said. 'Not a girl who looks like you. I get off in an hour. If you want to go to the coffee shop and wait, I'll drive you wherever you're going.'

'I don't have anywhere to go,' she admitted.

'You could stay at my place.'

'As if!' she said in disgust.

He laughed. 'Do I look like a crazed rapist?'

She took another look at him. He was not traditionally handsome. He had a Tom Cruise look, with a toothy grin and spiky hair. He wasn't Norman Barton, but what choice did she have. 'I suppose you're an out-of-work actor,' she sighed.

'Wrong,' he replied. 'I'm an artist, doing this to make my rent.'

'What kind of artist?' she asked, not quite believing him.

'I paint portraits. In fact, I'd quite like to paint you.'

'In the nude, I suppose.'

'You offering?'

'Get a life!' she said scornfully.

'You want to camp out at my place tonight or not?'

She didn't see any other alternative. 'OK.'

He nodded. 'I'll meet you in the coffee shop in an hour.'

☆

'Maybe Mick knows something,' Nikki said, close to tears. 'Where does he live?'

'Calm down,' Aiden said. 'Knowing Mick, he's left the party and gone clubbing. Leave a message on his machine.'

'I can't just sit here doing nothing. She's my child – out there on her own.'

'Hey, Nik, with all due respect, you're coming on like the concerned mother a little late, aren't you?'

'Are you saying I haven't been a good mother?'

'What's *your* take?'

'I know I could have given her more attention. But when she insisted on staying with Sheldon, I guess my feelings were hurt.'

'She's a kid – you abandoned her. Have you considered the fact she was angry?'

'Richard didn't give a rat's ass, he can be such a cold sonofabitch.'

'Hey – get with the programme, Richard has his own agenda.'

'She could have gone to Lara's.'

'Call her.'

'We're not exactly on good terms right now.'

'Call her anyway.'

'You're right,' she said, dialling Lara's house.

Mrs Crenshaw informed her nobody was home.

'Is Sheldon coming here from the airport?' Aiden asked.

'Yes, then we should call the police.'

'He hasn't done that?'

'Apparently you have to wait forty-eight hours before you can report a missing person.'

'Summer's a minor – doesn't that make a difference?'

'I don't know, I'll have to talk to Sheldon.'

'Hey.' He held open his long, thin arms. 'Come over here, you need a hug.'

'This isn't the time.'

'I said a hug, nothing else.'

She allowed him to embrace her. He was right – she was in dire need of love and affection. 'How come you're so understanding?' she sighed.

''Cause I've been everywhere and back,' he said with a

wry laugh. 'If I was you, I'd probably be imbibing every drug known to man. There's no way I could handle this. You're doing great, Nik. Just hang in there, we'll find her.'

☆

'Before I go with you, you'd better tell me your name,' Summer said, staring at the young doorman who looked even cuter out of uniform. If she hadn't felt so sick and dizzy, she might be enjoying this new adventure.

'Sam,' he said. 'And you're—'

'Summer.'

'Summer and Sam. What a team!'

'You're *sure* I can trust you, Sam?'

He laughed and took her arm. 'What's your choice? Me or the streets, right? Guess you're gonna have to trust me.'

And with his words ringing in her ears she left the hotel with a total stranger.

65

Alison Sewell often dreamed about what it would be like to be famous. As she turned off the lights on her station wagon and followed Lara's car down the dirt road, she couldn't help reflecting on the excitement that world fame would bring. Charles Manson and his cohorts were as famous as any President; John Hinckley was a name everyone knew because of his attempt to assassinate the President; Robert Bardo had made world headlines by killing Rebecca Schaefer; and Mark Chapman had waited outside the Dakota in New York, and shot John Lennon dead.

Because of their actions, these men would go down in history. They'd become icons themselves – appearing on the covers of *Time* and *Newsweek*. They were written about constantly, interviewed from their jail cells, fêted and acclaimed. Everyone knew their names. They were as famous as any movie star.

It occurred to Alison that she, too, could be famous. And why not? Was she supposed to be a nobody for ever? Pushed around and treated like dirt? No. She could do something about it.

Uncle Cyril would be so proud of her if she did. And the other cretins she'd worked alongside all those years – well, they'd be *fighting* to take *her* picture.

A smile spread across her face at the thought. Alison Sewell on the cover of *Newsweek*. She'd have to do something pretty outrageous to get that kind of coverage.

Was killing Lara Ivory outrageous enough?

There is a very thin line between love and hate. Alison Sewell had crossed that line.

She'd loved Lara Ivory with an absolute passion. Now she hated her enough to kill.

Tonight Lara Ivory was going to pay.

Tonight Lara Ivory was going to die.

66

The big old house was deserted, dark and cold. Cassie had gained access through an open kitchen window, and then let Lara in through the back door. 'There's no power,' she complained. 'Lara, if you don't mind me saying so, this is *not* a good idea.'

'We're here now,' Lara said stubbornly. 'All we're going to do is sleep.'

'Oh,' Cassie said, unable to hold back a twist of sarcasm, 'like eating went out of style, I suppose. Not to mention heating.'

'I can tell you never camped out,' Lara said. 'A little hardship is good for you.'

Screw hardship, Cassie wanted to say. NYPD Blue *is on TV and I want my dinner*. But she didn't, because Lara was in one of her weird moods. The photo-spread in *Truth and Fact* had obviously freaked her. But why was Joey being punished?

'I'll get the flashlight from my car,' she said.

'Good idea,' Lara answered, thinking that all she really wanted to do was get into bed and shut out the world. Joey Lorenzo had completely fooled her, making believe he cared, while all the time he was waiting to score off her and then who knows?

She'd never had much luck with men; foolishly she'd thought Joey was different, but it was not to be.

The house was freezing. Maybe Cassie was right – a hotel might be a better idea.

But no, if she checked into a hotel she'd be recognized, and before she knew it Joey would find her. She wanted complete anonymity. In a way she was punishing herself for having been such a lovesick idiot.

She thought wistfully of Tommy and his wise advice. He'd tell her the photographs were yesterday's news and to forget about them. And as for his take on Joey— 'All men are pigs,' he'd say. 'It depends on what degree of piggery you're prepared to put up with.'

If only Tommy had been straight, she thought with a wan smile, *we could have gotten married and lived happily ever after*. That's if he hadn't gotten sick and died on her.

Cassie came back with a flashlight and they began looking around. Although she'd bought the two-storey house furnished, everything was covered in dust sheets.

As they started upstairs, Cassie said, 'It just occurred to me – there'll be no linens, so I guess my hotel suggestion is the only way to go.'

'Will you *stop* carrying on about a hotel,' Lara said sharply. 'God, you're such a complainer.'

Unfortunately Cassie was right, there were no linens on the beds.

'You see,' Cassie said triumphantly.

'No, I do not see,' Lara said, throwing open the big linen closet in the hall. It was stocked with everything they needed. 'Sorry, Cass,' she said. 'It seems we're going to be making beds after all.'

'I can't spend the night here unless I get something to eat,' Cassie muttered.

'OK,' Lara said, 'here's the plan. You go find a supermarket and stock up, while I stay here and make our beds.'

Cassie raised an eyebrow. '*You're* going to make the beds?'

'I'm capable, Cass. Besides, I feel like it.'

Cassie had no idea she used to be a maid at Aunt Lucy's motel and could make a bed in record time. Anyway, she didn't mind, sometimes housework was therapeutic.

'OK,' Cassie said, 'if you're sure. I'll buy food, batteries, candles. Anything else?'

'Nope,' Lara said. 'Don't worry, we'll be perfectly comfortable here.'

'What can I get you for dinner?' Cassie asked. 'How about a couple of Big Macs?'

'Hmm,' Lara scolded, 'we're really going to have to do something about your eating habits.'

'I can't help having a healthy appetite,' Cassie said defensively, well aware she was fifty pounds overweight.

'Healthy is the wrong word if you're talking Big Macs.'

'It's oral satisfaction.'

'Don't get me started, Cass. You should look after yourself.'

'I will,' Cassie promised, knowing she wouldn't. 'But not tonight. Now, what would you like to eat?'

'I'm not hungry,' Lara said, feeling depressed and sad. 'You pick up whatever you want.'

'I'll be quick,' Cassie promised.

'No need to rush. Who needs television or lights? If it stops raining I might even take a walk along the beach.'

'Don't even *attempt* to go down those rickety stairs,' Cassie said sternly.

'You worry too much,' Lara answered lightly. 'I've got a new policy – I'm doing what I want whenever I want, and I refuse to worry about anything.'

'Can I ask you a question?' Cassie said curiously. 'Will Joey be joining us tomorrow?'

'Joey?' Lara looked at her blankly. 'Who's Joey?'

☆

The dogs greeted him before Mrs Crenshaw.

'Is she back yet?' he asked.

'Not yet, Mr Joey.'

'Jesus! Where is she?'

'I'm sure I don't know,' Mrs Crenshaw said, a touch officiously. 'I've prepared dinner if you're hungry . . .'

'No, thanks.' He stared at the old housekeeper. Was she telling him the truth? 'You're certain she didn't leave a message?'

'Quite certain.'

He went upstairs. The bedroom was empty. It was almost ten o'clock. He could understand Lara was upset about the pictures, but why hadn't she called?

He went back downstairs to the den and put on the TV. *NYPD Blue* was just starting. He watched moodily for a while. Jimmy Smits, smooth as silk; Dennis Franz, crotchety as usual; Kim Delaney, edgy and wild. It was one of the few programmes he enjoyed, in fact, he'd decided to talk to

Quinn about maybe getting him a guest shot. Of course, he wasn't into doing TV, but appearing on a show as good as *NYPD Blue* wouldn't be a bad thing.

He had no intention of becoming Mr Lara Ivory simply because they were married. Oh no, Joey Lorenzo was planning on making a name for himself.

As far as he was concerned, he hadn't even started.

☆

Cassie drove away from the big house. If Lara wasn't so damn secretive, she could've called Linden and instructed him to get his ass out there, so that he, too, could babysit Lara and put up with the inconvenience of spending the night in an empty house with no power. It was dark, frightening and plain stupid.

The first market she came to was fifteen minutes away and did not have anything she wanted. Plus an oversize biker with yellowing teeth, stringy grey hair and multiple leather crosses and chains hanging around his neck was eyeballing her like he wouldn't mind having her for supper. Even Cassie, who was constantly on the lookout for a man, was not tempted.

Getting back in her car, she drove all the way to the big supermarket in Malibu, where she suddenly had a brilliant idea – Granita, one of Lara's favourite restaurants was right there. She could order something special for Lara – a Wolfgang Puck pizza being a much better deal than something she'd pick up in the market. Before parking and going into the restaurant she called her sister with whom she shared a small house.

'Where are you?' Maggie asked.

Cassie explained the situation, finishing off with— 'I hope you're taping *NYPD Blue*.'

'Of course!' Maggie said.

'Hopefully I'll see you in the morning.'

She left the car and entered Granita. As soon as Wolf heard she was there for Lara, he came over, greeting her personally, promising to fix Lara's favourite chicken dish. Then he insisted she sit at a table while she was waiting, and a few minutes later he sent over one of his delicious smoked salmon pizzas.

She tried Lara on her cellphone. Unfortunately it was out of range.

Oh, well – Lara had seemed perfectly happy alone in the house. Cassie didn't think she'd mind if she took longer than expected.

☆

Lara explored the big old house with only Cassie's flashlight to guide her way. First she went upstairs to the master suite where there was a spectacular view of the ocean. Not that she could see much tonight, only the stormy sky and the ocean down below, everything a raging mass of darkness.

Next she returned to the living room with its vast terrace perilously overhanging the edge of the cliff. From the terrace there was a gate, leading to a rough wooden staircase that went all the way down to the beach. When she was renting the house she'd taken a walk along the beach every morning at six, and loved the freedom.

She ventured onto the terrace for a moment. Too wet, cold and windy. She hurried back inside.

Somehow being in the house alone fit her mood – she wasn't planning on feeling sorry for herself, but she liked the idea that nobody could reach her.

In the morning she'd start making decisions about her future. As everyone couldn't wait to tell her – she'd been working too hard – nonstop, in fact. Was that why she'd fallen into Joey's trap, instead of treading carefully as she usually did?

Nikki was right, he'd hooked her sexually, damn him. *Good old Nikki. She certainly knows her stuff. Sex does it every time.*

It occurred to her that she'd probably been too hard on Nikki, putting the full blame for the photographs on her. *Revenge* didn't need cheap publicity, it was a powerful movie that could stand on its own merits.

I haven't been much of a friend, she thought. *Nikki's going through a tough time and I should be there for her.*

Reaching into her purse, she took out her cellphone. Unfortunately the battery needed recharging and she couldn't get a signal.

Now she felt really isolated. But that was good, it gave her time to reflect, and most of all, to regain control of her life.

☆

Joey paced restlessly around the house. It was past eleven and he had a bad feeling that something must have happened to Lara. He had no idea where to start looking. The only person he could think of to call was Nikki, so he found Lara's book and looked up her number.

Aiden answered the phone. Recognizing his voice, Joey said, 'Hey, man – I need to talk to Nikki.'

'About Summer?'

'Summer?'

'She's missing. You didn't know?'

'No, I'm tryin' to find Lara. Is she there?'

'Sorry.'

'Maybe Nikki knows where she is.'

'I'll see if she can talk.'

Nikki came on the line a few moments later. 'I have no idea where Lara is, Joey.'

'Aiden told me about Summer. What happened?'

'She took off. We don't know where she's gone.'

'Could she be with Lara?'

'I don't see how. Didn't Lara leave you a message?'

'No, nothing. She wasn't at the party, they said she never showed.'

'I wish I could help you.'

'Yeah, well, I'm sorry about Summer.'

'Wait a minute,' Nikki said. 'I just thought of something. Richard was on the set this morning.'

'With Lara?'

'Yes – he was busy putting in his ten cents about the tabloid photos.'

'Are you sayin' she might be with him?'

'No . . . but he was up to something. He had an older woman with him – he took her into Lara's trailer and left them alone together for a while.'

'Who was the woman?'

'I don't know. She was in her fifties, smartly dressed, reddish hair.'

The description chilled him. Could it possibly be Madelaine Francis?

No. Inconceivable.

And yet . . . Richard hated him and still lusted after Lara. Maybe he'd found out about Madelaine. If that was the case he was in deep trouble.

'Thanks, Nikki,' he said, clicking off the phone.

If Madelaine Francis was in LA he'd find her. And if Richard Barry had put her in touch with Lara, he was going to pay.

Something was wrong. And he'd better find out what, before it was too late.

67

It was cold sitting in her car watching the big house, but Alison Sewell was fired with energy. She leaned over, reaching into the back seat of her station wagon and grabbing a warm parka which she kept for just such occasions – the occasions when she had to track stars and sit outside their houses all night.

However, tonight was different. Tonight she wasn't hanging around waiting for a photo opportunity. Tonight she was getting it for herself, and Lara and her dumb assistant were making it very easy. A house with no electricity, shrouded in darkness, and now Cassie driving off without her boss. What could be better?

As soon as she saw Cassie leave, Alison exited her car, carefully making her way through the open gate, approaching the house warily. Many times she'd been attacked by guard dogs, or some tiresome security guard with a gun had jumped out demanding to know what she wanted.

Just in case she always carried her own weapons: a large hunting knife – similar to the one used in the Nicole Simpson/Ron Goldman murders; a couple of sharp knitting needles: thick leather gloves to protect her hands; a screwdriver; and a special credit card that could get her through any door.

Once she'd been lying in wait for a particularly outrageous rock star when his vicious dog had come sniffing around her crotch. Before the mutt could make a sound she'd slit its throat with her hunting knife. She remembered the way the knife had sliced through the dog's jugular vein, and how its blood had spurted all over her. It hadn't upset her at all. In fact, it had given her a strange thrill.

What would Lara look like when that happened to her?

What expression would she have on that beautiful face?

Alison wondered if Lara Ivory realized how lucky she was to have been born with such a perfect face. Stardom had fallen upon her like a golden mantle, and because of that face she'd led a charmed life.

As if the bitch deserved it. She deserved nothing, because she didn't know how to give. She was a selfish self-obsessed movie star like all the rest of them.

Well, Alison planned to change that.

The night was dark and murky, the rain pounding down.

Alison didn't need light. The rain didn't bother her. She knew exactly where she was heading.

The cover of *Time* and *Newsweek*, that's where she was heading.

68

The moment Nikki set eyes on Sheldon she was overcome with that old familiar sick feeling in the pit of her stomach. It was years since she'd seen him – years of freedom and being away from his overbearing, pompous, full-of-shit presence. Now he was back and to her annoyance he still affected her physically.

He did not look his usual pulled-together self. He seemed more shopworn and weary, clad in a rumpled sports coat, open-neck shirt and creased pants. His face was lined and old. His grey hair dry and too long for a man his age. His thin lips tighter than ever.

'Is she here?' were the first words out of his mouth.

'No,' Nikki said. 'She's not.'

'I need a drink,' he growled.

From the smell of him she could tell he'd had quite a few on the plane. 'Help yourself,' she said, gesturing toward the bar. 'Uh, Sheldon, this is Aiden Sean.'

Barely glancing in Aiden's direction, Sheldon mumbled a curt, 'Good evening.'

Aiden exchanged glances with Nikki. 'I told you,' she mouthed behind Sheldon's back. 'Total asshole.'

Sheldon fixed himself a large snifter of brandy.

'Well, Sheldon, what happened?' Nikki asked.

'She ran away, that's what happened.'

'She wouldn't go without a reason. Did you have a fight?'

'Summer and I never fight. We are extremely close.'

'Then what was it?'

'Ever since she came back from Los Angeles she's been a different girl. It obviously has something to do with *you*.'

'Why *me*?' Nikki said indignantly.

'Because it was you who allowed her to run wild, let her go out with boys, and God *knows* what else she got up to while she was in your care.'

'Hey, listen,' Aiden interrupted, 'it's not my plan to get in the middle here, but shouldn't you both be concentrating on finding your kid?'

Sheldon threw him a frosty look. 'Who are you?' he said rudely.

Nikki bristled. 'Aiden's the man in my life,' she said, adding a terse 'Not that it's any of your business.'

'What happened to Richard?'

'We're getting divorced.'

'Oh, *he* couldn't put up with you either.'

'Screw you, Sheldon!' she said, unable to control herself.

'Is that all you have to say?' He gave her one of his supercilious smiles. 'I hoped you would have mastered a more intelligent vocabulary by now.'

'Fighting won't solve shit,' Aiden interrupted. 'One of you should contact the cops. You checked her friends here, Nik?'

'Right,' Nikki said, glaring at Sheldon. 'I'll go through the stuff she left here, see what I can find.'

☆

Sam rode a motorbike, not exactly a Harley, but it was kind of a fun ride. Summer sat behind him, her arms clasped firmly around his waist, pressing her body up against his back – not by choice, but because she didn't fancy falling off.

Thank goodness there's some nice guys left in the world, she thought, *guys who don't hit on you the second you look in their direction.* She leaned her head against his back, her eyes almost closing. She was so tired, it was a big effort to stay awake.

Sam drove too fast for the rainy streets. It didn't bother her, she liked speed, it was exciting. Every time they stopped at a red light he turned his head and asked if she was having fun.

'Oh, yes,' she replied drily. 'Never had a better time.'

'You're a sarcastic little bitch, aren't you?' he laughed.

'Not so little,' she mumbled.

Sam lived in the guest cottage of a sprawling house in the Valley. His cottage consisted of two big rooms; one was his bedroom/living room, and the other his studio, filled with many paintings – mostly portraits.

She did an obligatory walk around. 'You really got it going,' she said admiringly. 'Cool stuff.'

'I know,' he responded, Mr Modest. 'One day I'll make it. Then no more parking cars for me.'

'Thanks for rescuing me tonight, Sam,' she said. 'Guess I should confess – I was at the Norman Barton party, only I couldn't stay there with all these lame hookers. I had *no clue* it was going to be like that.'

'I kinda figured that's where you were,' he said. 'No parents, right?'

'Not at the hotel.'

'Where?'

'My dad's in Chicago, mom's here. They're divorced.'

'My parents did that when I was five.'

Yes, but I bet you didn't have a father who came into your room at night and molested you, she wanted to say. Only she kept her mouth shut, telling Tina was bad enough.

'I haven't got much in the way of food,' he said. 'Help yourself to what's there.'

She checked out his fridge. There was a half-eaten pizza and a rancid piece of cheese.

'I'm not hungry,' she said. 'Just tired. Is it OK if I like crash on the couch in the corner?'

'Take the bed,' he said generously. 'I've got work to finish – probably won't get any sleep tonight.'

'You're sure?' she said, too exhausted to argue.

'It's all yours,' he said generously.

'Wow – *thanks*.'

'The bathroom's over there,' he said, pointing. 'You'll find pyjamas behind the door.'

She hurried into the bathroom, slipped out of her dress and put on the pyjamas he'd mentioned. Even though they were several sizes too big, they were better than nothing. Then she got into bed, thinking that tomorrow she'd collect her bag from Tina, and maybe stay in a hotel for a couple of days before deciding her next move.

Whatever happened, she was *never* going back to Chicago.

☆

Leaving Sheldon and Aiden alone together was not a great idea, but Nikki did it anyway while she scoured the guest room, searching through the few things Summer had left behind.

After a few minutes she found the name Jed scribbled on a piece of paper, with two exclamation points next to his name.

She tried the number, getting an answering machine. 'Hi, this is Jed. You need me, I need you, so leave a message at the sound of the you know what.'

She waited for the tone, then said, 'Uh ... my name's Nikki Barry. I'm calling about Summer. It's urgent that I talk to you as soon as possible. Please call me back.' She left her phone number, then tried Mick at home. He was there. 'Oh,' she said, 'I thought you'd still be at the party.'

'Nice of you to stay around,' he drawled sarcastically. 'Jesus, Nik – that's no way to make friends and influence your crew.'

'I had an emergency.'

'What? Like the big movie star throwin' a blue freakin' fit about those photos?'

'It's my daughter, Summer. She's run away from home.'

'Oh.'

There was a long pause. Nikki broke it. 'Mick, I *know* what happened between you and Summer.'

'Huh?' he blustered.

'I'm aware you made her commit a ... sexual act, even though you must have known she was a minor. So ... if you have any information about her whereabouts, you'd better tell me right now.'

'Jesus, Nik – I had no freakin' clue she was your daughter, or that she was only fifteen ...'

'So you haven't heard from her?' Nikki interrupted coldly.

'No. And the truth is we didn't do a damn thing.'

'That's not what you told Aiden.'

'Guys boast,' he said sheepishly. 'Guess I got carried away.'

Nikki wasn't sure whether to believe him or not. 'Anyway,' she said, 'her father's flown in from Chicago, and when he contacts the police, I wouldn't want him telling them what you made her do.'

'Are you *insane*?' Mick shrieked. 'You'd get me thrown in jail for something I *didn't* do? Is that the kind of publicity you want for our movie?'

'This is not about the movie, Mick. It's about my daughter. And I want her back.'

'Listen, chickie-babe,' he said, rolling his eyes as he clung on to the phone. 'I swear on my life, *my mother's life, Quentin Tarantino's* life – and you know he's my idol – I never touched her and I haven't heard from her.'

'If you're sure.'

'Dead sure.'

She was unconvinced. What if Summer *had* contacted him? What if she was sitting in his house even as they spoke?

Back in the living room she took Aiden to one side. 'I've got a feeling about Mick,' she said. 'I have to make sure Summer's not there. Can we go over to his place? We'll leave Sheldon here.'

'C'*mon*, Nik,' Aiden said, shaking his head. 'You gotta control your paranoia.'

'If he has nothing to hide, he won't mind us dropping by.'

'Jesus! You're serious.'

'Sheldon,' she said, going over to her ex, 'Aiden and I have to go out. We'll be back as quickly as possible.' She watched as he poured himself another hefty brandy. 'Oh,' she added sarcastically, 'and do make yourself at home.'

☆

Summer was asleep in the middle of Sam's big bed dreaming about running on the beach with Norman Barton and seven naked hookers when she felt her father's hands on her.

'No!' she screamed, opening her eyes in horror. 'Get off me, Daddy! Get *off*!'

But it wasn't Daddy. It was Sam.

'Come *on*,' he said impatiently. 'Gimme a piece of what you gave Norman Barton. You know you want to.'

'Drop dead, you horrible pig!' she yelled, trying to wriggle out from under him. 'Pretending to be my friend. I *trusted* you!'

'Lesson number one,' he said, pinning her arms above her head. 'Never trust anyone.'

'You'd better leave me alone,' she warned, struggling ferociously, 'otherwise I'm screaming rape.'

'Scream away,' he said. 'Nobody'll hear you.'

'This sucks!' she shrieked.

'Didn't your mommy warn you? Never go home with a stranger,' he said, tearing at the buttons of her pyjama top. 'Why'd you come with me if you didn't want it? Pushing your little titties up against me on the bike. You *know* you want it.'

He had one hand on her left breast. She kneed him in the groin as hard as she could.

'*Jesus!*' he groaned. 'What the hell do you think you're doing?'

'Getting out of here – that's what!' she shouted, rolling off the bed, grabbing her dress and shoes from the floor, and racing for the door before he could do anything about it.

She made it outside, and began running down the muddy garden path toward the front of the house.

A dog started to bark, she didn't care – she kept running as fast as she could.

Oh God, this is like the nightmare day of all time, she thought, hiding behind a tree, trying to shelter from the rain as she shimmied into her dress.

In the distance Sam emerged from his house and began calling her name. She stayed silent. After a while he went back into his house, slamming the door behind him.

What a loser geek! Him with his Tom Cruise smile and spiky hair. Brad Pitt he wasn't.

She waited until she saw the light go out in his house. Then she crept back down there, picking up a sharp piece of glass on the way, puncturing the tyres on his precious motorbike. That would teach the moron not to mess with Summer Weston.

Now it was past midnight and she was freezing to death,

starving hungry, wet, tired and miserable. Maybe leaving Chicago hadn't been such a good idea after all. Although anything was better than life with Daddy Dearest. Shivering, she set off down the street.

By the time she reached Ventura Boulevard, unexpected tears were rolling down her cheeks mingling with the rain. She'd thought she could handle being out on her own, only now she had no money, couldn't trust anybody, and had nowhere to go.

She hesitated on the corner of the street. A truck shrieked to a stop.

'Wanna ride?' a man said, leaning out his window, a big leer spread across his ruddy face.

'Come on,' his companion encouraged, 'We ain't gonna bite – jump in – we'll show ya the sights. Get ya outta the rain.'

'Yeah,' the first man sniggered. 'We'll even throw in ten bucks if you're a *real* good little girlie.'

She turned and ran in the other direction, not stopping until she reached an all-night deli.

'Is there a phone I can use?' she said to the Mexican parking valet.

'Over there,' he said.

'I, uh ... don't have money,' she said. 'Can you lend me a quarter to make a call? I'll bring it back tomorrow. Promise.'

The valet shrugged. He felt sorry for the young girl. She was soaked and miserable. 'Looks like you can use it more than me,' he said, handing her the change.

Gratefully she took the quarter and ran to the phone booth. She'd made a momentous decision. She was telling Nikki everything.

She dialled her mother's number, praying she was home.

Someone answered the phone. Unfortunately that some-one was her father.

'Oh God no!' she gasped, slamming the phone down and bursting into tears.

What was she going to do now?

69

If **Madelaine Francis** was in LA, Joey figured she had to be registered at a hotel. He tried the Beverly Hills Hotel first, they'd never heard of her. Next the Hilton – same thing. Then the Beverly Regent. 'One moment, please,' the operator said, 'I'll connect you.'

Fuck Richard Barry. The prick wanted Lara back and he'd go to any lengths to get her, including tracking Madelaine Francis.

'Hello?' Madelaine's voice, sounding sleepy.

'Madelaine?' he said, hardly able to believe it.

'Who's this?'

'Joey.'

'Oh.' A long pause. 'What do *you* want?'

What the fuck did she think he wanted? 'Did you go with Richard Barry to see Lara Ivory this morning?'

She took her time before answering. 'Who told you that?' she said at last.

'*Did* you?'

'Yes,' she admitted, refusing to be intimidated. 'I was there.'

'Couldn't accept me being happy, huh?'

'Get real, Joey,' she snapped, suddenly losing it. 'I'm thrilled you're happy. Not so *thrilled* that you stole my money. What would you *like* me to do? Sit back and let you trample all over me twice? Oh no, young man, Lara Ivory deserves better than you.'

'You've got your money,' he said.

'I waited six years for the first payment,' she said curtly. 'And no thanks to you, I deducted the rest from your *Dreamer* cheque.'

Jackie Collins

'What did you tell Lara?'

'I simply made her aware of who you are. Good God, Joey, you certainly fed her a crock of shit. A fiancée indeed! Frightened to mention you were living with an old bag like me? Did I embarrass you that much?'

'Where's she gone?'

'I have no idea. But I'm delighted to hear that she *has* gone. At least she has sense.'

'I don't suppose it matters to you, Madelaine – but you've ruined my life.'

'Don't mention it, Joey. You've already ruined mine.'

And she slammed the phone down.

He stared into space for a moment. Richard Barry had screwed him, destroyed the only chance of happiness he'd ever had. And the slick sonofabitch was probably with Lara now, consoling her, telling her what a lousy no-good bastard Joey Lorenzo was.

Well, yeah, maybe he was a bastard. And yes, he should have paid Madelaine back long ago.

But what opportunity had he had when he was locked up in jail for a crime he didn't commit?

What fucking opportunity?

☆

The same day Joey took Madelaine's savings, he hopped a plane to St Louis, where he got a cab to Adelaide's apartment.

When she opened the door he was shocked. He hadn't seen her in three years. Her long dark hair was matted around her shoulders, her face puffy, with dark circles under her eyes, and orange lipstick smeared crookedly on swollen lips. She wore a stained pink peignoir, from which peeped a torn white bra. She also had a black eye and a chipped front tooth.

Who was this addled old woman? It certainly wasn't the beautiful mother he'd left behind.

'I knew you'd come, son,' she said. 'Knew you wouldn't let me down.'

Why was she calling him son? She'd never done so before.

'OK, what's the deal here?' he said.

'I . . . I got into trouble playing the ponies. Borrowed money at the track. You know what it's like when you're on a roll. You think it'll never end – then it all falls to pieces, and the people I

422

borrowed from – they're not very nice ... and these threats have been coming ...'

There was something not quite honest about her story. She was stammering too much, eyes downcast, unable to look at him.

'Where'd you get the black eye, Ma?'

'I fell,' she stammered.

'Who are these people you owe money to?'

'A ... a syndicate. You know – they send collectors. A couple of guys came to the door. I'm frightened, Joey.'

'What's Danny got to say about it?'

'Danny!' She called out her boyfriend's name.

Danny wandered in from the bedroom clad in the definitive gangster outfit. Black shirt, white tie and spiffy black suit. Like Pete Lorenzo, Danny was a petty hood, only instead of being forty years older than her, he was ten years younger. 'Hey, Joey,' he said. 'How's it goin'?'

'Not so great,' Joey replied. 'Not when I see my mother lookin' like this. What happened to her?'

Danny shrugged. 'Beats me.'

'You live with her. Aren't you supposed to be watchin' out for her?'

'The broad's a drunk – what can I tell you?'

'Don't call my mother a broad.'

Danny shrugged. 'Whatever y'say, Joey.'

'So tell me about the gamblin' debts?'

'All I know is she's gotta pay. You bring us the money?'

Joey resented the way he said 'us', since when was Danny involved?

'I saw you in Solid, son,' his mother ventured, lower lip quivering. 'I was so proud, watchin' you up there on the screen.'

'How come you didn't call?'

'I was going to, and then I was uh ... busy.'

Oh, yeah. She wasn't too busy to call when she needed money.

'How'd you chip your tooth?' he asked. 'Another fall?'

Danny sniggered. 'Yeah, the cunt can't walk straight when she's drunk.'

Joey threw him a long hard look. 'What did you say?'

'I tell it like it is,' Danny said, picking his teeth with a matchbook. 'Don't sit well with you, Joey boy? Well, fuck you. You're not the one stuck here lookin' after the old broad.'

'You'd better watch your mouth,' Joey said.

Danny narrowed his eyes. 'The pretty actor boy's gonna tell me *what t'do?'*

'You're an asshole,' Joey said.

'Now, now, guys,' Adelaide interrupted, like she was Lana Turner in some old gangster movie. 'Don't want you fighting over me.'

Joey felt like crying. She didn't get it, did she? This pathetic old woman was his mother, his once beautiful Adelaide – the shining light of his life, who'd never given a shit about him. Now she was this drunken crone, with a boyfriend from hell.

'I'll tell you what I'm gonna do,' he said. 'I'll meet with the guys you owe. Make a deal with 'em. OK?'

'Not OK,' Danny said quickly. 'We need cash now.'

'Back off,' Joey said. 'You're not gettin' shit till I straighten this out.'

'There's only one way to straighten it out,' Danny said. 'And that's t'hand me the money.'

'Yes, Joey,' Adelaide said anxiously. 'Give Danny the money, then you can go home.'

What did they take him for – a fucking bank? Give them the money and get the fuck out. What was going on here?

'You have it, don't you?' Adelaide asked.

'Some of it,' he answered cautiously.

'Hope you didn't leave nothin' at your hotel,' Danny said.

'I'm not at a hotel.'

'Then you got it on you?'

'Maybe.'

'Hand it over, Joey boy.'

'Do it,' Adelaide encouraged, wringing her hands.

'The only way you're gettin' the money is when I pay it to the people she owes.'

'Dumb prick!' Danny exploded. And before Joey knew what was happening, Danny had pulled a gun and was pointing it in his direction. 'Drop the wad on the table, sonny, and get out.'

Adelaide said nothing. She watched.

'What kind of a set-up is this?' Joey demanded.

'I'm sorry,' Adelaide murmured.

Sorry didn't cut it. He was burning up. He certainly hadn't come back to St Louis to be told what to do by some broken-down hood. And the motherfucker was holding a gun on him. *No way was this prick getting away with this crap. Besides, Danny was too much of a coward to use it, Joey could see the yellow in his eyes.*

He kicked out like he'd seen in the movies. Danny fell, and the gun went flying out of his hand.

'Dumb punk,' Danny roared, scrambling across the floor for his weapon.

'I'm a punk, huh?' Joey said, kicking the gun away. 'Wanna show me what kinda punk I am?'

'Stop it,' Adelaide groaned. 'Please stop it.'

Danny staggered to his feet and threw a punch. Joey retaliated – catching him on the chin.

'Cocksucker!' Danny yelled. 'You got no idea who you're dealin' with.'

'Who gives a shit?' Joey responded, struggling with the man. 'I want you out of my mother's life.'

'You call her your mother,' Danny sneered. 'I call her a dumb hooker cunt.'

Now they were rolling on the floor, exchanging blows. And then Danny pinned Joey down, grabbed a bookend from a nearby shelf, and smashed the side of Joey's head with such force that he lost consciousness for a moment. In the distance he heard a shot and thought that was it – he was gone.

He managed to open his eyes. Danny was slumped on the floor – blood pumping from a hole in his neck. Adelaide was standing next to him, shaking from head to toe, holding the gun.

'Oh fuck, Ma,' Joey groaned, staggering to his feet. 'What've you done now? Oh, fuck!' He snatched the gun out of her hand and made her sit down. Then he ran into the kitchen for a bottle of brandy and forced her to take a couple of swigs.

Neighbours began hammering on the door. A rough male voice. 'Everything all right in there? What's goin' on? We've called the cops.'

Without really thinking about it, he grabbed a cloth from the kitchen and wiped the handle of the gun clean. Then he put his own prints on it. 'You didn't do it, Ma,' he said, sweat mixing with the blood trickling down his face. 'Remember, you didn't do it – I did. I was defending you. OK?'

'Yes, son,' she repeated in a quavery voice. 'I didn't do it. You did.'

'Take the money,' he said, pulling the wad from his jacket pocket. 'Somebody must've called the police. I'm not runnin'. I'll tell 'em it was self-defence.'

Self-defence – sure. He got eight years for manslaughter – out in six for good behaviour – and that's why Madelaine didn't get her money.

His mother never visited him in jail. When he got out he discovered she'd moved to Puerto Rico with a lounge singer and left no forwarding address.

He got on a plane and went back to New York.

☆

Six years of his life locked up for a crime he didn't commit. Six lost years of harsh punishment he had nightmares remembering.

And then Lara had entered his life, and everything changed. He had a chance at genuine happiness. A chance that Richard Barry had taken and ground underfoot.

Screw Richard Barry and everything he represented. Screw the jealous prick who'd trashed his future.

Determined to find Lara, he picked up the phone and called the sonofabitch.

'What do *you* want?' Richard asked, cold as a three-day-old corpse.

'Where is she?' he demanded

'Looking for Lara?' Richard taunted.

'Where the *fuck* is she?'

'Y'know, Joey, I'd love to tell you she's with me,' Richard said, continuing to taunt him. 'But unfortunately, I have no idea where she is.'

'You had to screw it up, didn't you?'

'Excuse me?'

'I made her happy. We were together like you and she never were. You couldn't stand it, could you?'

'Spare me the sob story,' Richard said. 'I know what's best for Lara. I always have. And when she comes back, it's *me* she'll be with, not a two-bit loser like you.'

Joey slammed the phone down, he'd heard enough. The important thing was to get to Lara before Richard poisoned her against him even more.

Where would she go? That was the question.

Cassie. Yes, Cassie would know.

He frantically scanned Lara's phone book until he found her home number.

A woman answered her phone. 'Cassie?' he said.

'No, I'm Maggie, her sister. Who's this?'

'Joey Lorenzo, Lara's uh . . . fiancé. Is Cassie around?'

'She won't be home tonight. She's spending the night with Lara. Didn't they tell you?'

'Yeah, I uh . . . forgot. Lara left me a note, guess it got thrown out. *Where* were they going again?'

'The house at the beach.'

'You mean Nikki's house at the beach?'

'No. The one Lara rented last year.'

'That's right. I'm supposed to meet them later. What's that address?'

'Let me see . . . You go to the first turning past Point Dume Road, and it's the big house at the end.'

'Is there a phone number?'

'No, but if Cassie calls, shall I tell her you're coming?'

'Don't bother, Maggie. Thought I'd surprise 'em.'

Within minutes he was in the Mercedes and on his way.

☆

Lara was getting restless sitting in the dark, waiting for Cassie to return. She remembered waiting once before – huddled in a chair in a motel room – waiting until her father shot himself to death.

Joey had helped her get over a lot of her fears, he'd opened up her life with his warmth and love.

She sighed, maybe it wasn't fair, running away without giving him a chance to explain.

But what if he touched her? What if he overcame her with his lethal charm? A charm she found so utterly irresistible.

No, it was too dangerous to put herself in that position.

She remembered his face explaining about his fictitious fiancée, and the story he'd come up with about her trying to commit suicide. How sincere he'd seemed, how genuine and concerned.

What a bunch of *bullshit*! And she'd fallen for it. Taken in every lying word. How could she have?

She needed to talk to Nikki – get it all out. Nikki would help her be strong, and right now she could use all the support she could get.

Outside the wind was howling, and in the distance she could hear thunder. On the weather report this morning the weather man had said a September storm was blowing in. El Niño was warming the waters around Malibu, causing a series of storms and bad weather. This was supposed to be the first of many.

Why had she acted so hastily? One call to the realtor and she could've gotten the electricity turned on and a fridge stocked with food. Lights and a telephone would be very welcome right now.

Cassie had left her suitcase in the hall. She rummaged through it, finding a warm tracksuit, thick socks and running shoes. She put on the outfit and felt better – certainly warmer.

And then she heard a noise which chilled her.

'Lara?' A woman's voice – loud and clear. 'Lara? Are you there? Are you waiting for me, Lara dear?' A long ominous pause. 'In case you're wondering, this is your good friend, Alison Sewell. Are you ready for a reunion? Because *I* certainly am.'

70

They were arguing furiously in the truck as the rain pounded down and Aiden drove too fast.

'You're making a mistake,' Aiden said, scratching his chin. 'Why would you wanna piss Mick off? He told you – he doesn't *know* where Summer is.'

'How can we be sure?' Nikki replied, the set of her jaw saying she wasn't going to give up on this. 'He's some kind of sick paedophile anyway.'

'Hey – you've been working with him for the last two months,' Aiden said sharply. 'If he *was* after Summer, I've gotta think you would've suspected something before now.'

'I have to make certain,' she said stubbornly.

Aiden shrugged. 'OK, OK,' he muttered. 'Dunno how I got involved with you. Drugs were a lot easier.'

'Nobody's asking you to stay,' she snapped. '*You* were the one who forced this relationship.'

'Oh, I forced it, huh?' he said cynically. 'I didn't notice you racing out of my apartment after we hit the sheets.'

Without warning, she buried her head in her hands. 'I'm sorry, Aiden,' she said, too upset to fight. 'I keep on thinking of Summer out there by herself. She's only a kid, and I feel it's all my fault. I was never there when she needed me, now I realize I should've been.'

'Hey,' he said, reaching over and squeezing her hand, 'it'll work out. You'll see.'

Mick was renting a large ultra-modern house at the top of Benedict Canyon. Aiden turned his truck into the driveway and pulled up outside the front door.

By now Nikki had firmly convinced herself she was going to find Summer. She got out of the truck and rang the doorbell, nervously tapping her fingers together. Aiden stood behind her, smoking a cigarette in the rain. She rang three times before there was any response.

By the time Mick's voice drifted down from an upstairs window they were both soaked. 'Who's there?' Mick called out.

'Nikki and Aiden. Can we come in?'

'What're you *doin'* here?'

'Can we come in?' she repeated, determined to get inside his house so she could check the place out for herself.

'Hold on,' he said. 'I'll be down.'

They waited five minutes before he appeared at the front door. *Long enough for him to hide Summer*, Nikki thought.

'Why are you here?' he asked, blocking the door, dishevelled and barefoot in a black and yellow striped towelling robe with nothing underneath.

Nikki pushed past him into the house. 'Where is she?'

'Oh, Christ!' Mick groaned, his wild-man hair standing on end. 'Don't you *listen*? I told you on the phone, I do *not* have your freakin' daughter.'

'I don't believe you.'

'Who gives a shit if you do or not.' He turned to Aiden. 'This is insane.'

'I know,' Aiden said, his long, thin face expressionless.

'You don't understand, Mick,' Nikki's tone was even and calm. 'I won't be mad at you, I just need to know she's safe.'

'Mick?' a girlish voice drifted down from upstairs. 'Mick – what's going on?' And down the stairs came an exquisite Oriental girl in a short silk robe.

Mick grimaced. 'Say hello to Tin Lee,' he said. 'We're holding Summer captive under our bed. Whyn't you come up – take a look.'

Aiden pulled Nikki out of the house by her arm. 'Satisfied?' he said, bundling her into the truck.

'I . . . I had a feeling.'

'Go ahead – search the freakin' house,' Mick yelled after them. 'I make one freakin' mistake in life and I'm supposed to pay for it for ever.'

'I'm sorry,' Nikki said.

'So you should be,' Mick grumbled, slamming the front door.

☆

Cold, wet and frightened, with nowhere to go, and shocked because her father was in LA, Summer decided to head back to Tina's. The only problem was she didn't have any money to get there, although if she took a cab she could always pay the driver when they reached her destination, that's, of course, if Tina was home. Now all she had to do was find a cab, which was virtually impossible in the driving rain.

She ventured down the street, her skimpy dress clinging to her body like a second skin, her long blond hair plastered to her head, raindrops dripping off the tip of her nose.

Cars and trucks zoomed to a halt – a pretty girl on the street alone after midnight was fair game, even if she did resemble a drowned cat.

She kept walking until she reached the Sportman's Lodge, then she went inside and asked if they'd call her a cab.

She was tired, hungry and dispirited. Sometimes life didn't seem worth living.

☆

'Anyone phone?' Nikki asked, running into the house, shaking the rain out of her short hair.

'Two hang-ups,' Sheldon said. 'The police need Summer's picture. And someone named Jed phoned.'

'What did he say?'

'He wanted to speak to you.'

'Did you ask him if he'd heard from Summer?'

'No, I didn't,' Sheldon answered. 'If you hadn't rushed out of here with your tattooed boyfriend, maybe you would have been able to get more information.'

'Don't criticize Aiden. He's a better man than you any day.'

'You say the most ridiculous things.'

'Really?' She glared at him, how dare he talk down to her as if they were still married. 'Oh, by the way, Sheldon, how's your teenage wife? How old are you now? Fiftysomething? You must make *such* an adorable couple when you go out in public.'

'I'm not interested in petty fighting,' Sheldon said coldly. 'I'm only interested in finding my daughter and taking her back to Chicago.'

'I've been thinking,' Nikki said. 'Summer's obviously not happy with you – perhaps she should stay here with me.'

'No,' Sheldon said flatly. 'She's coming with me.'

'Don't tell me no,' Nikki answered heatedly. 'When we find her, we'll ask Summer what *she* wants to do, exactly like you did when she was a little girl.'

Aiden drew her to one side. 'I gotta get outta here,' he mumbled.

'What's the matter?'

'I can't take all this fighting crap – it's not good for my karma.'

'Is that all you're worried about?'

His burnt-out eyes were restless lasers. 'I gotta cut loose, Nik. Please understand.'

'What does *that* mean?'

'It means I'll call you later.'

'Thanks,' she said indignantly. 'Walk out just when I need you.'

'If I thought I could help, I'd stay. But this shit between you and your ex is getting to me, dredging up too many bad memories.'

She tried to focus on Aiden for a moment. He was right, there was nothing he could do. 'OK,' she said, 'I'll call you if there's any news.'

'It'll be all right,' he said, giving her a hug.

After Aiden left, she went into the bedroom and called Jed back. She told him who she was and that Summer was missing.

'Sorry to hear that, Mrs B.,' he said.

'Who were Summer's friends when she was here?'

'Guess I was closest to her,' he said. 'I introduced her to a lot of people.'

'Anyone in particular you can think of?'

'There was this one girl she kinda hung with – Tina.'

'Do you have her number?'

'Got it somewhere.'

'It's important, Jed. I know she could still be in Chicago, but my gut feeling tells me she's here.'

'When you find her, ask her to call me,' Jed said. 'It wasn't like I was her boyfriend, only she did introduce me to Mr Barry, said she'd talk to him about putting me in one of his movies. I'm an actor, y'know.'

Surprise, surprise. 'Now's not the time to discuss it, Jed,' she said impatiently. 'Just give me Tina's number.'

He did so, and Nikki immediately called.

'Ha! I knew you'd call!' Tina crowed, before Nikki had a chance to say a word. 'Get your cute little suburban ass back here, Summer. I got *big* news about Norman. Move it, girl!'

Nikki didn't need to hear any more, she quickly replaced the receiver without saying anything. Then she called Jed back. 'Sorry to bother you again, do you have Tina's address?'

'I got it written down somewhere, think she's in one of those high-rise buildings off Sunset. Oh, an' Mrs B., while I got your attention, can you talk to your husband about maybe like interviewing me?'

'If you give me Tina's address, I'll take care of it next week,' she promised.

He gave her the information and she ran back into the living room, where Sheldon was pouring himself yet another hefty brandy. 'Let's go,' she said urgently. 'I think I've found her.'

'Thank God!' Sheldon responded. 'And then I'm taking her straight back to Chicago where she belongs.'

We'll see about that, Nikki thought. *Because this time I'm not letting her go without a fight.*

71

Alison Sewell. The madwoman who'd stalked her for almost a year – sending letters, photos and gifts; turning up at her door; insulting anyone who got in her way.

Oh, God! This couldn't possibly be happening, this had to be some bizarre nightmare. Besides, Alison Sewell was in jail – locked up and out of her life. Lara had actually been in the court room when the judge had sentenced the crazy woman. She'd never forgotten the look of hatred that spread across Alison's face when their eyes had met for the briefest of moments.

The old house was filled with the noise of the relentless rain, howling wind, and the crashing of the surf as the big storm began whipping the sea down below into a frenzy.

Had she imagined the sound of Alison Sewell's voice? Maybe the storm was messing with her mind.

No. Impossible. She wasn't hearing things. The woman was actually in her house.

Get a grip, she told herself. *If she is here, you can deal with it. Ask her what she wants. Tell her she's trespassing and that she has to leave immediately or you'll call the police.*

Oh yes? With what? Your phone doesn't work. You're trapped here, alone with an obsessed maniac. And nobody except Cassie knows where you are.

'Alison?' she called out, trying to keep her voice firm and strong. 'Alison Sewell. Where are you? Can we talk?'

☆

Cassie left Granita feeling a lot better after stuffing down the whole smoked-salmon pizza and finishing off a full glass of red wine.

'Better get home before the storm hits,' Wolf warned her.

Rain was now pounding down. She'd borrowed an umbrella from the front desk, and balancing the carton of food in one hand she managed to get into her car and stay comparatively dry. Lara would be wondering what had happened to her, but Cassie was sure she'd be pleased when she came back with supplies, including plenty of candles, a couple of extra flashlights and the special chicken dish from Granita.

Maybe when she got back, Lara would reveal to her what dastardly deed Joey had committed to be suddenly cast out in the cold.

She attempted to start the engine on the Saab. It coughed a few times and wouldn't turn over. 'Damn!' she muttered, trying again. Fourth time lucky – the car started. She switched on her windshield wipers, the rain was so heavy she could scarcely see a thing.

She moved slowly out of the parking lot and headed toward the stop light on the corner. Her car phone rang, startling her.

'Cassie, my dear.'

She immediately recognized Richard's voice.

'Richard!' she exclaimed, wondering what he was doing calling her in her car at this time of night.

'Where are you?' he asked.

'In my car, obviously,' she replied.

'I was speaking to Lara and we got cut off. I thought she said something about being with you.'

Now it became clear. Lara was thinking of getting back with Richard, and *that's* why Joey was yesterday's news. Of course! This was excellent, Cassie had always favoured Richard over Joey.

'I'm on my way back to Lara now,' she said. 'I'm sure she told you the house has no power, no food, nothing. I went to the market to stock up. Looks like it's turning into a bad storm.'

Richard thought fast. *What house was she talking about?* 'I trust you got everything you need,' he said.

'I hope so,' Cassie said.

'I was thinking,' he added smoothly, 'that because of the storm, maybe I should drive out to be with you and Lara.'

'Then you'd better remind me how to get there.'

'Sounds like a great idea to me,' Cassie said cheerfully.

'You came out with Nikki one day, when Lara was renting. You complained about how long it took to get there.'

'That's right,' he said, with a self-deprecating chuckle. 'And I *still* can't remember the way.'

'Stay on the Pacific Coast Highway for about half an hour until you reach Point Dume Road. Then you make the first turning on the left past that, and it's way down. There are no other houses – so you can't miss it – just look for the big gloomy house at the end. I can't imagine *why* Lara bought it.'

'Nor can I,' he murmured.

'Please come soon. I know *I'll* be glad to have a man in the house tonight.'

'Uh . . . Cassie, since I got cut off from Lara, I didn't get a chance to tell her I was coming, so why don't you leave the door open and I'll surprise her.'

'Can I ask you something?' Cassie said. 'I know this is very forward of me, but are you and Lara getting back together? Is that what this is all about?'

'You guessed it,' he said.

'I *knew* something was going on when you spent all that time in her trailer this morning,' Cassie said, quite delighted. 'I'm *so* pleased. Of course,' she added, a touch guilty, 'I feel sorry for Nikki, she's a nice woman, but in my opinion you and Lara always belonged together.'

'You're very smart, Cassie.'

'Thanks, Richard. We'll see you soon.'

'Don't forget – it's a surprise, so not a word.'

'Got it,' Cassie said, grinning happily. Maybe, when Richard arrived, she could leave and go home to the comfort of her own bed. What a pleasure that would be.

The red light changed to green and Cassie proceeded across the intersection, making a left-hand turn onto the Pacific Coast Highway.

She did not see the Porsche careening out of control heading in her direction, she was too busy thinking about Richard and Lara and what would happen next.

The Porsche smashed into the side of the Saab with a

sickening crunch, sending both cars out of control. The Saab began spinning in circles before somersaulting across the slick surface of the wet road and turning over with Cassie trapped inside.

When the first rescuers reached the car, they couldn't tell whether she was dead or alive.

☆

When it rains in LA it doesn't take long before everything falls to pieces. Mudslides slither down the hills and cliffs; rivers overflow; gutters stop up; roofs leak; cars crash; in fact, everything goes out of control.

By the time Joey turned off San Vicente and headed down toward the ocean there were flood warnings in operation and the sea was crashing its way toward the well-kept decks of Malibu houses. Police and fire teams were already out on the roads, turning cars back and trying to direct the rest of the traffic, which was now moving at an extremely slow pace.

This gave Joey plenty of time to think. Exactly what was he going to tell Lara when he finally arrived? The truth, that's what. The truth about his fucked-up life, his efforts to break away from his background and become an actor, and how he'd gone back to see his mother and gotten caught in a trap, taking the rap for a murder he didn't commit.

And how had his mother repaid him? She'd run off with another loser, without even leaving a forwarding address.

But he wasn't perfect either. He'd used Madelaine, just as he'd used most women for sex or whatever he wanted from them. Then Lara had come into his life, and she'd made him aware that it was possible to care for another person and to have no ulterior motive.

Yes. He would tell her the truth. That she made everything special. She *was* his life, his true love, his soulmate. He'd throw himself on her mercy and hope she could forgive him.

It wasn't like he wanted anything from her. All he wanted was to be there for her, by her side, ready to support and protect her in every way.

Traffic had slowed to a crawl. He attracted the attention of a cop standing in the middle of the road. 'What's happening?' he asked.

'Big accident up ahead,' the cop said. 'I don't advise you continuing on this road unless you live here.'

'I do,' he lied.

'OK, take it easy.'

'I'll do that.' He switched on the radio. Billie Holiday was singing the blues. 'Good Morning Heartache'. Very suitable.

He couldn't wait to reach his destination. His love. His future.

☆

Alison could hear the bitch calling out to her. Yes, Lara Ivory remembered her name. And so she should. She'd been her loyal friend, but that wasn't enough. No. Lara Ivory had seen fit to betray her.

Of course Lara remembered her name. Soon *everybody* would know her name.

She started thinking about what photographs she had of herself. Which one would they put on the cover of *Time*? There was that snap Uncle Cyril had taken of her and her mother when she was nineteen. She hated it, but if they cut her mother out it wasn't so bad. And she was younger then, prettier.

You were never pretty, a voice in her head taunted her. *You were always the ugly girl. Always the slob. Nobody liked you. Nobody wanted to spend time with you. Sewer ... the Dump ... Big Boy* —the hateful nicknames came back to haunt her.

People would think she was pretty when she was on the cover of *Time*. People would look at her in admiration when her picture adorned the front of *Newsweek*. TV would get into the act, too. *Hard Copy* would run stories on her. *Inside Edition* would speak about her. *Prime Time. Dateline.* Even *Sixty Minutes*.

She'd be more famous than anyone in the world. The media would cover her case for months.

Alison Sewell would be right up there, along with Charles Manson, Mark Chapman, and the rest of them.

Alison Sewell. The first woman to gain such a distinguished honour.

'Alison. Why don't you come here, we can talk.'

She heard the bitch's voice again. 'Don't worry, Lara,' she called out. 'I'm coming right now. I'm coming to slit your pretty little throat.'

72

The cab driver couldn't seem to keep quiet. 'Damn American weather,' he kept mumbling. 'Damn California. Damn riots. Damn fires.'

Summer huddled on the back seat. She didn't want conversation, all she wanted was to shiver her way into oblivion.

'What's wrong with you?' the driver demanded, twisting his head. 'In my country – girls – they no run at night by themselves. This no right.'

'Where are you from?' she forced herself to ask. Maybe if she got him talking about his country, she could tune out while he blathered on.

'Beirut,' he said proudly. 'Beautiful place, till the bombing. Those bastards took everything, a man's pride, his home, those bastards took it all. Damn terrorists!'

'How long have you been in America?'

'Too long.'

'Aren't we going the wrong way?' she asked, peering out the window. 'Shouldn't you have taken Coldwater Canyon?'

'I go Sepulveda. Weather bad for canyon. Big flooding.' He gave a hacking cough before continuing his litany of complaints. 'Everything in LA too much. Flooding, fires, riots, car-jackings. They put gun to my head one day. Those bastards!'

'That's awful,' she said, not really caring at all.

There was a red light ahead. Her cab stopped just in time as the car in front of them smashed into the back of a Cadillac standing at the stop light.

'You see, you see,' her cab driver shouted excitedly. 'American maniacs!'

The driver of the Cadillac got out of his car, screamed at

the other driver, and ran up to the cab driver's window. 'You see that?' he yelled. 'You're my witness.'

'No see nothing,' her driver said, staring straight ahead. 'Nothing.' Then he manoeuvred his cab around the two cars and drove on.

'How long before we're at the address I gave you?' Summer asked.

'In this weather? With lousy American drivers? Don't know.'

'If you hate Americans so much, why'd you come here?' she asked, fed up with his complaining.

He let out a crafty laugh. 'Good thing about America – money – money – money!'

☆

'What's with the traffic?' Nikki said impatiently, stuck behind a line of cars on the Pacific Coast Highway.

'I don't know why you didn't let me drive,' Sheldon responded irritably.

'Because it's *my* car and I know where we're going.'

'You never *could* drive,' Sheldon said.

'According to *you*, I was incapable of doing anything,' Nikki replied. 'Maybe that's why you married me, so you could take a child and mould her. Is that why you married Rachel, too?'

'I refuse to listen to your garbage,' he said, staring straight ahead.

'I was such a baby, wasn't I? So malleable. *That's* why you were able to talk me into leaving Summer with you, when she should have come with me, and you know it.'

'Summer is a very well-adjusted girl. Or at least she was, until she stayed with you in LA. Examine the way you conduct your life. Richard seemed decent, now you're with someone who looks like he belongs in a rock 'n' roll band.'

'Aiden's a very fine actor.'

'I always said you were damaged. Now you've proved me right.'

'I'm not getting involved in a fight,' Nikki said with a weary sigh. 'I've achieved so much since you and I were together. If you'd had *your* way, I'd still be locked in the house while you systematically screwed your way through all your patients. God! I cannot believe you're a psychiatrist. It seems criminal.'

A policeman with a flashlight slowly moved down the line of cars, talking to the drivers. He reached Nikki's window. 'Big accident up ahead, ma'am,' he said. 'There'll be a delay.'

'How long?' she asked, impatiently.

'We're trying to move it along as fast as possible. But unless you have to make the journey, I suggest you turn around and go home.'

'Thanks,' she said. 'We have to get into town.'

At least she had an idea where Summer was now. If she was with her friend, Tina, it wouldn't be long before she found her.

And when she did, she was never letting her go again.

☆

The cab finally pulled up in front of Tina's apartment building.

'You'll have to wait a minute,' Summer said. 'I've got to get my money – it's inside.'

'Oh no, no no,' the driver said, his face turning purple. 'I no wait. You run out back door, I know American girls.'

'If you don't trust me, come in with me,' Summer said impatiently.

'I no leave cab,' he answered sternly. 'Somebody steal.'

She sneezed. 'I'm going inside. Either you come with me, or wait here for your money. I really don't like *care*.' With that she flung open the cab door and ran into the apartment building, almost slipping on the front steps.

God, she hoped Tina was home. What was she going to do if she wasn't? The wacko cab driver would probably have her arrested if she didn't pay him.

She rang the doorbell of Tina's apartment and waited.

Seconds later Tina flung open the door. 'About time,' she exclaimed. 'OhmiGod, look at you! What did you do, go for a swim in the ocean?'

'I've come to collect my things,' Summer said frostily. 'Then I'll get out of your way.'

'Don't be so lame,' Tina said. 'You look like you've had a crummy night. Come in. Anyway, I told you on the phone, there's a whole new development, so you'd better get spiffed up.'

'What new development?'

'Well . . . fifteen minutes after you left, Norman came out of the bedroom, dumps the two babes he's with, and says, "Where's Summer?" How'd you like *that*?'

'He did?' Summer said, perking up.

'He certainly did. So I told him you weren't pleased with the situation and had gone home. That excited him no end. Seems he likes a girl who's hard to get.'

Now Summer was really interested. 'What happened then?' she asked.

'He said, "I'll get rid of everybody – bring her back." And *I* said, "Show me the money!"'

'What're you talking about?'

'I told him you weren't coming back for nothing, and if I had to go find you, we wanted to get paid for our time.' Tina grinned. 'You know what? He gave me a thousand bucks and said, "Go find her." We're rich!'

'I've had the most horrible night,' Summer complained. 'I nearly got raped. Then I was lost, and couldn't get a cab. Now I'm hungry and tired.' Inexplicably she burst into tears. 'I think I made a big mistake coming back to LA.'

'No way,' Tina said, putting her arm around Summer's shoulders. 'I told you – we're gonna make a fortune. We got off to a bad start, that's all. Now go take a shower, and wash your hair. I'll fix you some hot soup, then I'll call Norman and see if he wants us back tonight or tomorrow.'

'I'm not going anywhere tonight,' Summer said, vigorously shaking her head. 'I have to sleep.'

'If he wants us to, we gotta go. If we *don't*, then I think he'll like lose interest. You don't want to miss out, do you?'

'Oh, wow!' Summer said, suddenly remembering. 'There's an angry cab driver downstairs waiting for me to pay him.'

'I'll take care of it. You go shower. And Summer—'

'Yes?'

'Sorry I acted like a major bitch before. Didn't mean to. Sometimes coke makes me crazy.'

'OK,' Summer nodded, relieved they were friends again. 'All is forgiven.'

The two girls hugged.

'I'll go pay your cab driver,' Tina said. 'Be right back.'

☆

Finally they crawled past the accident on the highway. Nikki could see two cars, both of them overturned and in bad shape. She looked quickly to see if one of the accident vehicles was Aiden's truck, he drove like a madman. Fortunately he wasn't involved.

Sheldon had slumped into silence, which was a good thing because she didn't have anything to say to him. She did not care to be in his presence. She should have left him at the beach house and come to find Summer by herself. But then again, maybe she'd need his support.

Why had Summer run away? That was the question.

She turned down Sunset. The twisting street was like a river, a slick of rain water rushing down toward the inadequate drains. Lightning flashed, accompanied by loud rumbles of thunder. Keeping to the inside lane, she drove as fast as she could without endangering both of them. When they drew closer to Beverly Hills she said, 'I have to make a right on San Vicente, so watch out, I can barely see a thing.'

Ten minutes later Sheldon said, 'Make your turn at the next stop light.'

She reached the light, veered to the right, and as they were turning into the apartment building on the left, Sheldon urgently said, 'Look – isn't that her?'

She glanced over. Summer was getting into a red sports car. Before she could cross in front of oncoming traffic, the sports car roared off in the opposite direction.

Sheldon sat up very straight. 'That *is* her,' he said. 'Follow that car.'

Nikki didn't need asking twice.

73

She'd faced danger before. Sitting in the next room while her father had shot her family to death. The endless hours in the motel room before he'd turned the gun on himself. It had been raining *that* night, too; and the night Morgan Creedo's car had smashed into the truck, decapitating him.

Oh, yes. Danger. Lara knew what that was about only too well. But all the same, her throat was dry, her hands shaking. She was trapped in a dark house in the middle of a storm with an obsessed stalker.

She backed across the living room, feeling her way around the furniture until she reached the glass doors that led outside to the terrace. Slipping the catch, she opened the door and eased herself outside into the driving rain. If she could reach the stairs and get down to the beach, then she'd make a run for it – hopefully get to another house for help.

But what if Cassie came back, and walked into the situation? What if Alison attacked *her*? Oh God! Now she was in a quandary. Did she run, or did she stay? She had no weapon, nothing to defend herself with. Plus she wouldn't be much help to Cassie if Alison Sewell carried out her threat and slit her throat. Then the two of them would be dead.

No, the best thing was to go for help and call the police. Get out, that was the smart thing to do.

Fortunately, Alison Sewell had no idea there were stairs leading down to the beach.

The ground was thick with mud and overgrown plants. Lara kept on tripping as she ran toward the gate at the top of the outside steps. Unfortunately, when she reached the gate and tried to open it, she realized it was padlocked.

Now what?

She glanced back at the house. A flash of lightning lit up the sky.

In the momentary glare she could see Alison Sewell standing by the glass doors she'd just escaped from. Alison was holding a knife. And on her face was an expression of pure hatred.

☆

Richard smiled to himself. Ever since he'd come back from Mexico, his nefarious past firmly behind him, there was nothing he couldn't do.

He wanted to direct successful movies. Done.

He wanted to marry Lara Ivory. Done.

Now he wanted her back, and nobody was going to stop him. And if they tried to . . .

Well, he'd killed once – there was nothing to stop him doing it again if it meant protecting Lara.

Who else would think of calling Cassie in her car? God, he was clever. He'd come a long way from the sixteen-year-old street-smart kid who'd run away from home. Not to mention the twenty-eight-year-old drugged-out loser who'd shot Hadley and thought that was it. Over. *Finito*.

Yes. He was a true survivor. He'd reinvented himself, become an upstanding member of the Hollywood community – admired and respected.

And yet . . . only Lara had made him truly happy, and look what he'd done to her.

He was determined to make up for his cheating ways. When he and Lara were back together he'd treat her like a queen. No more make-up girls or Kimberlys or actresses who begged him to fuck them so they'd get more than their share of close-ups. No. Once again he was reinventing himself just for her.

He called the front desk and told them to bring his car around. Then he put on his raincoat and set off.

Soon he would experience a reunion with the love of his life.

As far as he was concerned, it couldn't be soon enough.

☆

The bitch was attempting to run. But running was no good, because Alison Sewell could run faster than anyone. She'd chased more celebrities than she could remember. Tracked them down and caught them in her lens.

Outside the rain was coming down in fierce torrents. Lara Ivory couldn't get away from her, no sense in trying.

Alison pulled the hood of her parka over her head and resolutely headed for the spot where she'd last seen Lara standing.

Bitch! She wouldn't be the pretty girl when Alison got through with her. No – not Lara Ivory who'd represented all the pretty girls Alison had been forced to look at year after year. The actresses on film. The haughty supermodels strutting down the runways showing off their skinny bodies and fake tits, smiling at the camera as if *they* were the only pretty girls in the world. She hated them all!

Lara would be punished for every one of them. Michelle Pfeiffer's calm beauty; Naomi Campbell and her superior smile; Cindy Crawford with her cute little beauty mark; Winona Ryder's winsome charm.

Yes, Lara Ivory would pay the price. She'd pay the price for all of them.

☆

'Oh, fuck!' Joey exclaimed, as he approached the accident site and recognized the remains of Cassie's car. Abruptly he pulled the Mercedes over to the shoulder of the road and jumped out.

Oh Jesus, God. What if Lara was hurt? What if she was *dead*? He couldn't bear the thought.

He raced over to the wrecking crew who were busy untangling twisted metal. 'Where are the people who were in this car?' he asked urgently.

'They took 'em to the hospital,' one of the guys said.

'What hospital?'

'Dunno, it wasn't long ago.'

'Was anybody . . . killed?' he asked, barely able to get the words out.

'You'll have to ask that cop over there. He was here when the ambulance came.'

He ran over to the cop. 'That your car over there?' the cop said. 'Get it outta here. Can't you see what's going on?'

'I knew the people in the Saab. Are they OK?'

'Yeah, yeah – the woman's pretty cut up with some broken bones, but the ambulance guy said she'll be all right. The man in the Porsche bought it. Straight through the windshield – no seatbelt.'

'There were two women in the Saab. Are they *both* OK?'

'Only one in the car – the driver. Kind of a large lady. Got a feeling her bulk saved her.'

'Only one? You sure?'

'Yeah. They've taken her to St John's. Now do me a big one an' get your car outta here.'

'It wasn't Lara Ivory?'

The cop laughed. 'The movie star? Are you kiddin' me? If it'd been Lara Ivory, I'd've known about it.'

'Thanks,' Joey said.

'They're talking mudslides down the highway, and some flooding, so if you don't havta go there, I'd turn back.'

'I gotta get home.'

'You'd better hurry, 'cause we may be closin' the roads soon.'

'OK, thanks.'

He ran back to the Mercedes. Something didn't feel right. He was filled with the same kind of uneasiness he'd experienced when he'd visited his mother that fateful day, and she'd ended up shooting Danny.

A lot of cars were turning around and heading back to town, which meant the traffic ahead was easing up. But the road was becoming more hazardous. People were dashing across the highway lugging sandbags; small boulders were beginning to roll down from the sodden cliff.

He knew he'd better hurry and get there while he still could.

☆

One look at Alison's face was enough to convince Lara that she had to get away as quickly as possible. And how was she going to do that when she couldn't even reach the steps down to the beach?

She hid in the heavy shrubbery surrounding the terrace,

holding her breath, desperately thinking what she could use as a weapon if Alison came at her.

Then she remembered, there was a small garden shed at the side of the property. She began scrambling toward it.

☆

Once past the accident, Joey made good time. He tried calling the hospital on the car phone. They informed him Cassie hadn't been admitted yet. Next he phoned her sister, told her what had happened, and to get over to the hospital as fast as possible.

All he could think was thank God Lara hadn't been in the car.

The rain was blinding, the condition of the road getting more hazardous by the minute, but he managed to make good time, slowing down when he came to Point Dume Road, searching for the turning past it, finding it and making a sharp left.

Now he found himself on nothing more than a dirt road, dark and deserted. The wheels of his car were spinning and sliding in the mud, and as far as he could see there didn't seem to be anything down here. He slowed the Mercedes. Maggie must have made a mistake and given him the wrong directions.

He was ready to turn back when he almost ran into a car parked by the side of big open gates that led to an isolated house.

Two thoughts crossed his mind. Whose car was it? And why were there no lights on in the house?

Keeping the bright lights on the Mercedes, he drove through the gates, and drew up outside the house.

☆

Lara moved silently through the thick shrubbery, her arms getting scratched and torn by rose thorns and jagged palms. She kept going, sure that there must be something in the shed she could use as a weapon – something she could use to fight back.

She refused to be a victim. She'd been a victim too many times in her life, and it was not going to happen again. She was Lara Ivory – survivor. She wasn't an actress playing a part – this was real life, and she was in a situation she was going to have to get out of herself.

Watching her father shoot himself, she'd had no control. Now she was in control, and nobody was going to destroy her.

She stumbled up to the shed, and was about to open the door, when a huge body leaped on her from behind.

'Got you!' Alison Sewell yelled, wrestling her to the ground, rolling in the thick mud. 'Got you, you pretty little bitch,' Alison crowed triumphantly.

'What do you want from me?' Lara shouted. 'What have I ever done to you?'

Alison put her hefty arms around her, holding her in a tight bear hug. 'All I wanted was to be your friend,' she yelled above the noise of the howling wind. 'But you didn't want a friend like me, did you? I wasn't good enough for the likes of you. I was too ugly, wasn't I?'

'What are you talking about?' Lara shouted, desperately struggling to escape.

'As if you don't know,' Alison yelled, straddling her, pinning her to the ground with her weight.

Then she raised the knife.

Lightning lit up the sky. Lara looked up, saw the knife, and let out a long anguished scream.

'Now we'll see who's the famous one,' Alison yelled, cackling wildly. 'Now we'll *really* see!'

74

Summer took a shower, washed her hair and touched up her make-up. Tina was more than solicitous. She made her a hot cup of celery soup, apologized repeatedly, then told her that she'd spoken to Norman, and he'd insisted they come back that night, because he was leaving on location the next day. 'We gotta close the deal,' Tina said excitedly. 'If you play it right, maybe he'll invite you to visit the location. How cool would that be?'

Summer was tempted. The soup and the shower had made her feel better, and to tempt her further, Tina lent her a very hot Dolce & Gabana pants suit.

It was past one in the morning, and she decided that maybe Tina was right – she'd be wise to close the deal while she had the opportunity. Although deep down she wished she could just go to sleep.

'OK,' she said at last. 'If you think so, we'll go.'

'Excellent!' Tina exclaimed, and they set off.

☆

'For God's sake,' Sheldon said. 'You're losing them.'

'No, I'm not,' Nikki retorted. 'I can see the car ahead of me.'

'They only have to make one green light, and you're fucked.'

'Oh, Sheldon,' she mocked. 'Using four-letter words. What happened to *you*?'

'I don't like you, Nikki,' he said, staring straight ahead.

'You liked me when I was young.'

'Well, I certainly don't like the woman you've grown into.'

'Then shut up and leave me alone,' she snapped. 'The only reason we're together is to find our daughter.'

☆

As they drew closer to the hotel, Tina said, 'Listen, there's something I forgot to tell you.'

'What?' Summer asked.

'Cluny might still be there,' Tina said. 'But that's cool, 'cause she's so famous.'

'Why might she still be there?' Summer asked suspiciously.

'I think he kind of like, you *know*, hangs out with her. Nothing romantic, but um . . . she's sort of like his friend.'

'I don't get it,' Summer said.

'Look,' Tina said reassuringly. 'I'm sure it'll be you and him alone together. If she's there, I'll keep her busy in the other room.'

Summer shook her head. Somehow she felt as if she was being sucked into something she didn't want to do. And yet – Norman Barton and his puppy dog smile. If she could be Mrs Norman Barton, *nobody* could touch her. And now that her father was in LA, she had to find someone to protect her.

'OK,' she said, with a little sigh. 'I guess if you keep Cluny in the other room, it'll be all right.'

'*And*,' Tina said, lowering her voice, 'Norman has primo grass. I told him that's what you were into.'

'You did?' Summer said, thinking that the last thing she felt like doing was smoking a joint.

'Hey – we're here,' Tina said. 'You want me to report that scuzzbucket who tried to rape you?'

'No, no,' Summer said quickly. 'Absolutely not. It was my own fault. I shouldn't have gone to his house. It was a dumb move.'

'You can say that again,' Tina said. 'C'mon, let's go.'

She jumped out of the car, gave the keys to the parking valet and they entered the hotel.

☆

'Make the turn,' Sheldon ordered.

'I can't, there's traffic,' Nikki replied.

'Do it!' he commanded, pissing her off.

'Don't panic, Sheldon,' she said coolly. 'They went into the hotel. We're five minutes away from being with her.'

The traffic eased up and she crossed into the hotel driveway.

'Are you a guest?' the parking valet asked, as he opened her door.

'No, we'll be out shortly,' she said. 'Please keep my car somewhere close.'

They entered the lobby. No sign of Tina or Summer.

Nikki went up to the desk, closely followed by Sheldon. 'Excuse me,' she said. 'Two young girls just came in here. Can you tell me where they went?'

The woman behind the desk said, 'I'm sorry, we cannot divulge that kind of information.'

Sheldon hammered his fist on the desk. 'One of those girls is my daughter,' he said. 'She is fifteen years old. I suggest you tell me where they went, otherwise I'll summon the police, and you can tell *them.*'

'Just a moment, sir,' the woman said, startled. 'I'll get the manager.'

'Do what you want, but I'm not leaving this lobby until I have my daughter back.'

☆

'Hey.' It was Norman Barton himself.

Summer gazed into his puppy dog eyes and thought, *No, I haven't made a mistake. It's really him. And he's really cute.*

'What *happened* to you?' he said, grinning. 'Saw you for a second, then you were gone.'

'It seemed to me you were pretty busy,' she said.

'Never too busy for a honey rabbit like you,' he said, taking her hand and drawing her into the suite.

Cluny was stretched out on the couch, looking quite out of it. She waved vaguely in their direction. Summer noticed that there was still a small mound of white powder on the glass-topped table and her stomach dropped.

'Want a snort?' Norman said, indicating the supply.

'I don't do coke,' she replied disapprovingly. 'Nor does Tina,' she added, shooting Tina a warning look.

'But if you've got any grass . . .' Tina said quickly. 'Then we're talking!'

'Hey, cutie,' Norman said, pulling Summer into the bedroom, 'let's go see what I got for you.'

'Just me?' she said, staring straight at him.

'Just you,' he replied, chicklet teeth flashing in her direction.

☆

The manager of the hotel was Beverly Hills perfect, with crimped silver hair and a nut-brown suntan. 'What seems to be the problem?' he said, ignoring Nikki and giving Sheldon an *all guys together* look.

'There's no problem at the moment,' Sheldon replied stiffly, taking charge. 'I'm Dr Sheldon Weston. My underage daughter is in this hotel, and I would like to know where she is.'

The manager didn't want any trouble. He glanced at the desk clerk. 'Do you know where this gentleman's daughter might be?'

'Uh . . . yes, Mr Bell. She and another young lady went up to Mr Barton's suite.'

'That would be the penthouse suite,' the manager said. 'I can escort you up there and we'll see if your daughter is there. I usually wouldn't dream of disturbing my guests at this late hour, but since you seem so certain—'

'Oh, I'm certain,' Sheldon said ominously.

'Yes, he's certain,' Nikki added. 'And she's my daughter, too, so let's go.'

☆

Norman handed Summer a joint and told her to sit on the bed. 'I'm watching this great Mel Gibson movie,' he said. 'But you know what? You're so cute and pretty, I thought it'd be nice to have you hang with me.'

It was exactly what she wanted to hear. Hang with him. Become Mrs Norman Barton. Escape from Chicago for ever.

'I . . . I thought about you a lot while I was at home,' she ventured shyly.

'Where's home?' he asked, jumping on the bed beside her.

'Chicago.'

'Yeah? Did a promo tour there once. Kind of a happening city.'

'Maybe if you take me with you next time,' she said boldly. 'I could show you around.'

'Honey, all they do is move me from limo to limo. I never get a chance to see the sights.'

'That's a shame.'

'They pay me good.'

'Sometimes,' she said wisely, 'money isn't everything.'

He looked at her like he couldn't quite believe she was so naive. 'You really don't know what this is all about, do you?' he said.

She summoned all the sophistication she could muster. 'I've been around.'

'Hey,' he said, his attention suddenly taken by the action on the screen. 'Take a look at Mel Gibson with that insane long hair. He's really a cool dude, huh?'

'I love Mel Gibson,' she said.

'Yeah.' Norman grinned. 'He make you cream your panties?'

'Excuse me?'

He laughed. 'Jeez! They sure make them innocent in Chicago.'

☆

The manager knocked on the door of Norman Barton's suite. Cluny strolled over to answer it. Everybody recognized her.

'Hi, guys,' she said, totally sanguine. 'What's going on?'

'I'm so sorry to disturb you,' the manager said, trying not to stare at her smooth brown breasts almost escaping from a skimpy little wrap dress. 'I was told two young ladies were visiting Mr Barton's suite. One of them has to go home with her father, he's here to collect her.'

'Are you kidding me?' Cluny said, hands on narrow hips.

'I want my daughter,' Sheldon thundered, pushing forward. 'And I want her *now*.'

'Hold it,' Cluny said, shutting the door on them.

Tina was in the john. Cluny called out her name. 'Some old dude who says he's your father is here.'

'*What?*' Tina said, emerging.

'He's outside with the manager. We'd better get the coke off the table in case they start barging in.'

'I . . . I don't *have* a father,' Tina said. 'My old man's long gone.'

'Then it must be the other kid's.'

Sheldon began hammering on the door.

'Shit!' Tina said. 'You're right. It must be Summer's dad. What're we gonna do?'

'Quick, get rid of the coke, then we'll tell 'em nobody's here,' Cluny said, quickly sweeping the coke into a plastic bag and shoving it in her purse. When that was done she went back to the door and opened it.

'Where's my daughter?' Sheldon demanded.

'Um . . . Tina's the only person here,' Cluny said.

'Tina?' Nikki questioned. 'Where is she?'

'I don't think Mr Barton would appreciate you coming up here to disturb us in the middle of the night,' Cluny said, suddenly getting very haughty in her best supermodel way.

The manager was embarrassed. He began to apologize, but he hadn't reckoned on Nikki, who suddenly shoved past him into the suite.

Tina stared at her, startled.

'Are you Tina?' Nikki asked.

'Uh . . . yes. Why?'

'Where's Summer?'

'Uh . . . she's not here,' Tina started to say.

'Bullshit!' Nikki replied. 'I saw her come in with you.' And before anyone could stop her, she marched over to the bedroom door and flung it open.

Summer dropped her joint and jumped off the bed. 'OhmiGod! What are you doing here, Mom?'

'*Mom?*' Norman Barton said.

'We're going home, Summer,' Nikki said, attempting to remain calm, although she was completely unthrilled to discover her daughter sitting on a bed in a hotel room with some half-assed actor. 'And we're going now.'

Reluctantly, Summer slouched to the door. She could see that her mother wasn't in the mood to argue. 'I . . . I . . . dunno know what to say . . .' she mumbled.

'I'm sure you'll find something,' Nikki said. 'Your father's here, too.'

Summer stopped in her tracks. 'Oh no!' she shrieked. 'I'm not going anywhere with him. It's over, Mom, *over*. I'm *never* going back to him.'

'Why not?'

'Make him go away or I'm staying here.'

Nikki frowned. 'What are you talking about?'

'Please, Mom,' Summer said frantically. 'I can't tell you now. Not in front of all these people.'

Sheldon appeared behind her at the door. 'Summer,' he said sternly. 'What do you call this behaviour?'

'What the *fuck* is going on?' Norman Barton exploded. 'Cluny,' he yelled. 'Get rid of all these people.'

The manager swept in and ushered them all out into the corridor, Tina too. By this time Summer was sobbing uncontrollably.

'What's the matter with her?' Sheldon said. 'Is she on drugs?'

Tina turned on him. 'No, she's not on drugs, you filthy old perv. She's freaked at seeing you.'

Sheldon went very pale. 'I suggest you hold your tongue, young lady.'

'And I suggest you keep your pants zipped up,' Tina retorted.

'Will someone explain to me what exactly is going on?' Nikki interrupted.

'I guess Summer hasn't told you,' Tina said, heatedly. 'And if she hasn't – it's about time somebody did.'

'Told me what?'

'Your ex-old man has been creeping into Summer's room ever since she was ten, doing all kinds of dirty things to her. Why do you think she's so screwed up? And how come *you* didn't do anything about it?'

Nikki felt the bottom drop out of her world. She looked at Sheldon. He stared at the ground, white-faced. 'Is it true, Sheldon?' she asked, her voice rising.

'This . . . this crazy girl doesn't know what she's talking about,' he blustered.

Nikki turned to Summer. 'Is it?'

Summer nodded, her cheeks streaked with tears. 'I . . . I wanted to tell you, Mom, but I couldn't. You were never there, and I didn't want to upset you, and . . . please, Mom, let me come home with you. *Please!* I never want to see him again.'

Nikki held open her arms. 'And you never have to. That's a promise.'

75

Richard reached Sunset just as they were closing the road. Police barricades were already in place.

He leaned out of his window. 'What's going on?' he asked a cop.

'Sorry, we're closing the highway. There's flooding and a threatening mudslide.'

'I have to get through,' Richard said.

'It's for your own safety,' the cop said.

'It might be for my own safety, but what about my pregnant wife alone in the house?'

'I don't know about that.'

'Look, I can't leave her there, she's already panicked.'

'I have my orders.'

'And I have my wife. I'm Richard Barry, the film director. My wife is Lara Ivory.'

The cop was immediately interested. 'I didn't know Miss Ivory was pregnant,' he said. 'I'm a big fan.'

'She is, and she's alone. So if you'll lift the barricade, I'll take my chances.'

'Well,' the cop looked around. 'As long as you're careful out there.'

'Of course,' Richard said, and waited while the man summoned another cop to help him raise the barricade.

☆

Lara could hardly breathe, she knew if she didn't do something quickly, she'd suffocate.

Alison was sitting astride her, grinding handfuls of mud into her face. The mud was in her mouth, her eyes, her nose.

While she was doing it, Alison kept taunting her. 'Bitch!' she yelled. 'Pretty ... little ... *bitch*! Where shall I cut you first? Where would you like it, *Miz* Ivory?' Then she'd grind another handful of mud onto Lara's face.

'What did I ever do to you?' Lara managed to gasp.

'You wouldn't be my friend,' Alison screamed, wild-eyed. 'You had me thrown in jail. And for that you're going to die. Do you hear me, bitch? YOU'RE GOING TO DIE!'

☆

Grabbing a flashlight from the Mercedes, Joey entered the dark house. He was sure Lara wasn't there, because what would she be doing alone in the pitch black? Cassie must have taken her somewhere and dropped her off. Maybe to Richard's. The thought filled him with rage.

He almost tripped over Lara's open suitcase in the front hall. At least that proved she'd been here.

With the flashlight guiding him, he made his way into what he presumed was the living room. Across the room a glass door banged back and forth in the wind. He moved over to close it. A jagged streak of lightning lit up the sky, and outside on the terrace, he saw Lara – his Lara – with someone on top of her, the two of them struggling on the ground.

He ran outside, frantically screaming her name. As he drew closer he could see she was being attacked by a large woman. Jesus! What the fuck was going on?

He reached them, and was about to drag the woman off Lara, when she turned and struck out with a lethal hunting knife, slashing him across the cheek. Blood began pouring from his wound. The pain was intense, but he hardly felt it. All he knew was that Lara was in danger and he had to save her.

He went for the woman once more, grabbing her shoulders, trying to haul her off Lara.

She roared with anger and slashed out with the knife again, this time cutting him across the left hand.

He smashed into her face with his elbow and she loosened her grip on Lara, who managed to roll out from under her.

'Run!' Joey yelled. 'Get the hell outta here!'

☆

Richard drove through the heavy storm. Once he reached the house, Lara would realize he was her saviour. She'd finally know for sure how much he loved her.

It had taken him a long time to understand what true happiness was, and now that he did, he had no intention of losing it again.

Up ahead he heard an ominous rumbling. It wasn't thunder, it was a different kind of noise, reminiscent of the big Northridge 1994 earthquake.

For a moment he almost pulled the car to the side of the road to see what it was, but the rain was so strong, and sea water was beginning to creep across the highway, so he figured the safest thing was to keep going.

He did so. And as the rocks came tumbling down, enveloping his car, his last thought was of Lara.

☆

Now Joey was fighting with the woman who'd cut him. She was as big as any man, and strong, but at least he'd gotten her off Lara.

'You ignorant scum – get out of here!' Alison screamed. 'Or I'll cut you like a stuffed pig. Out of my way, you fucker!'

He attempted to prise the knife out of her hands as they struggled. Grabbing the wrist of her knife hand, he bent it back until she yelped with pain. But still she held on.

They were on their feet now, rocking toward the side of the terrace.

He made a concentrated lunge to get the knife. They fell against the fence, and with that, the flimsy fence – badly in need of repair – gave way, and they both began falling down the side of the cliff toward the roaring ocean below.

Joey's life flashed before him. Somewhere Lara was screaming. Desperately he tried to hold on to something, somehow or other managing to grab the branch of a tree.

Alison Sewell wasn't so lucky. He could hear her blood-curdling screams as she smashed into the sea below.

In excruciating pain, he tried to haul himself up the side of the cliff. Below him he could hear the raging surf, waves beating against the bottom, hungry for another victim.

'Joey, Joey!' Somewhere Lara was desperately calling his name.

'Down here!' he yelled. 'Get a rope, a sheet, anything. Dunno if I can make it on my own.'

'Joey, you've got to make it. You have to. For me!' She was screaming over the noise of the wind. The sound of her voice gave him hope.

Then he felt the branch start to give. Was this how it ended?

Oh, sweet Jesus. Was this it?

ONE YEAR LATER

☆

The best of Hollywood turned out for Richard Barry's memorial service. The two women he'd been married to arranged it, making sure every detail was exactly as he would have wanted. Both of them were dressed in black – a sign of respect for the man they missed. For when he was good he had been very very good. And when he was bad, he'd been a total asshole.

In April, Richard had won a posthumous Oscar for *French Summer*. Lara Ivory, the star of the film, had made the presentation. Nikki Barry, his widow, had accepted on his behalf. The added bonus was that Nikki also won for best costume designer. A double celebration.

Now they were honouring the man who at one time had meant so much to them. An Oscar-winning director killed in an unavoidable act of nature.

☆

Linden arrived with Cassie. Since her unfortunate car accident she'd lost forty pounds, and somehow or other an improbable romance had blossomed between her and Lara's publicist. She'd left Lara's employ, and now worked as a partner in Linden's firm. They were very happy together.

☆

Mick Stefan wandered in next. He'd handed over his new white Rolls Royce to a parking valet, and was now worried that the guy might scratch it. *Revenge* had opened to critical acclaim and excellent box office, and Mick was currently directing a sixty-million-dollar-budget action adventure movie starring Johnny Romano and Norman Barton as two mismatched cops.

He had a seventeen-year-old French movie star girlfriend, and a new mansion in Bel Air.

Mick Stefan was on a roll.

☆

Summer came with Reggie Coleman, a boy she'd met in high school. He was a year older than she, handsome and nice with no secondary agenda. He made her feel good about herself. In fact, he made her feel sixteen, and it was a nice feeling.

She lived at home with Nikki and planned to attend USC Film School when the time came.

Summer was finally enjoying being a teenager.

☆

Aiden Sean made it to the ceremony late. He'd spent the last year in and out of drug rehab. He tried his best, but it wasn't easy.

Nikki remained his good friend, always there for him.

Their romance was dead – a mutual decision.

☆

Tina didn't make it at all. She'd been 'discovered' by Cluny, and whisked off to New York to be a model. So far she'd appeared on three magazine covers, and was currently shooting a spread for the *Sports Illustrated* swimsuit edition.

She and Cluny had become more than friends.

☆

Nikki watched her gorgeous daughter walk into the ceremony. It was amazing what a little love, attention and caring could do. She was so proud of Summer – what a transformation!

Sheldon had returned to Chicago a much chastened man. Summer had refused to take action against him, and in return for her silence, he'd promised never to see or contact her again. Nikki considered this far too lenient a punishment.

Since working with Mick on the post-production of *Revenge*, Nikki had the producing bug in a big way. She'd read countless scripts and books, but had not discovered anything that fired her imagination, until one day, while sorting through Richard's personal papers, she'd come upon a fascinating manuscript written in the first person. She'd started to read, and become totally hooked. It was the story of a young man who runs away from home at sixteen and then lives a wild and interesting life – becoming everything from a thief to a male hustler to a movie star in Asia. The opening lines of the manuscript had really grabbed her attention: *Here's the truth of it – I can fuck any woman I want any time I want – no problem.*

The manuscript ended with a brutal murder, after which the protagonist takes off for Mexico.

Had Richard written it? Since there was no author's name attached, she assumed that he had – which was really something, because the material was so raunchy and un-Richard-like. Still . . . it was a powerful read, and she was sure it would make a fantastic movie. She'd hired a writer, and was now busy developing the script. She even had an actor in mind for the lead. Joey Lorenzo. He would certainly do the role justice.

☆

And as for Lara and Joey, true love, soulmates – call it what you like – they'd recognized a certain sadness and need in each other, and although the sex was just as great as ever, it was the mutual need and understanding that had drawn them together. They were inseparable. Fate ruled.

Lara shuddered whenever she remembered the night of the storm. How she'd summoned the strength to drag Joey up from the side of the cliff she'd never know. God must have put his hand on her shoulder and helped her.

Nobody could help Alison Sewell. Her body washed up three miles down the coast, five days later. There was a brief investigation. Nobody cared. Only Lara, who paid for a proper burial.

Joey confessed everything about his past. He bared his soul with searing honesty and Lara believed him. In return, she'd told him about *her* demons, the nightmare stories she'd never revealed to anyone.

They were married quietly a month later in Santa Barbara. Six weeks after that Joey landed a key role in a movie starring Charlie Dollar, following that with the lead in a low-budget thriller. He was good. He was very good.

☆

The memorial service was a fitting tribute to Richard Barry. Many people he'd worked with got up and spoke. There were tears and there was laughter. Summer made a particularly moving speech – calling Richard the father she'd never had.

As Lara and Joey walked away from the service, she reached out for his hand. 'Joey,' she murmured, thinking how handsome he was, and how much she loved him, 'there's something I've been meaning to remind you about.'

'What?' he asked, thinking she was just as beautiful inside as she was out, and that he was possibly the luckiest man in the world.

'You owe me a honeymoon,' she said softly.

He lifted her hand to his lips. 'I know. We leave for Tahiti tomorrow.'

'Joey!'

'Don't fight it. Look what happened last time we didn't go to Tahiti!'

She smiled, basking in the glow of his love. 'That's true.'

'Have I ever let you down?'

'No. Never.'

And as they reached their limo, the paparazzi pressed forward, multiple flashbulbs blinding them.

And Lara knew she would never be frightened of anything again because she had Joey beside her, and he was her world.

Visit **www.panmacmillan.com** to read more about all our books and to buy them. You will also find features, author interviews and news of any author events, and you can sign up for e-newsletters so that you're always first to hear about our new releases.